THE WINDCHIME
LEGACY

THE
WINDCHIME
LEGACY

A.W. MYKEL

BRASH
BOOKS

The characters and events portrayed in this book are fictitious. Any similarity to real persons, living or dead, is coincidental and not intended by the author.

ISBN: 194129880X
ISBN 13: 9781941298800

Published by Brash Books, LLC
12120 State Line #253
Leawood, Kansas 66209

www.brash-books.com

To three lives which, in ending, started it all.

PROLOGUE

The rain had stopped, and the heavy night air hung chilling and damp around the solitary figure hidden in the shadows. His keen, unfeeling eyes swept the empty street, looking for signs of the courier he knew would be coming. The old street lamps bounced their gentle reflections off the wet buildings and sidewalks; the weather was typical for England in March.

Directly across the street from his concealed position was an alleyway, which ran alongside the old Maynard Pub. Well back, in the darkest shadows, was a car. It had not been there long. Its hood was still warm, and the engine made faint clicking sounds as it cooled. It was the one he was looking for. It meant that the contact was already inside, waiting for the courier. Both men had come for the information he carried—one to buy it, the other to kill for it.

Through the light fog, his eyes picked up movement in the distance. Within moments it became clearer. The courier was nervously making his way up the street toward the pub. He walked steadily, clutching a worn attaché case to his chest. His eyes played anxiously back and forth for assurance that he was unobserved, but he failed to see the stranger in the shadows or to sense the murderous intent of the eyes concentrated on him.

After one last look around, the courier entered the pub.

The large room was dimly lit, smoke filled, with the typical smell of ale, sweat, and old tobacco. There was the usual mix of noisy customers, moth-eaten prostitutes, and oblivious, dozing drunks.

The courier tugged at his muffler and unbuttoned his heavy coat as he walked to the bar. His eyes flashed quickly around the room, checking every face. He ordered a dark ale, raised the mug, and downed its contents in several long swallows, the attaché case still held tightly against his chest.

He put the mug down and looked at the big, burly barkeep, as he wiped the foam from his lip. The barkeep gave a nod and motioned with his eyes to the door at the back of the room.

The courier walked to the rear of the room and passed through the door, closing it behind him. The sounds of the pub became muffled and distant, as he walked down the long, dimly lit hallway. At the end of the hallway were two doors directly opposite one another. He opened the one on his left.

It was dark inside; the poor lighting from the hallway did little to help him see. He stepped into the room and closed the door behind him.

A light clicked on.

Sitting at a small table next to the lamp was the man he had come to meet. The two men stared at one another in silent assessment.

The man seated was smallish, slightly built, with graying hair well into balding. His narrow, pointy features were set into a stern mask, his intense eyes burning into the courier.

"Do you have the money?" the courier asked finally, nervously licking his lips.

"I want to see the information first," the man said coolly.

"First the money, then the information," the courier insisted.

The contact stared at him for a moment, then slid a thick envelope across the table. The courier picked it up and opened it. His fingers skipped nervously across the edges of the bills. A short smile came to his lips. He unbound the strap to the attaché case and took out a thin file folder, then tossed it onto the table. The contact opened the folder, removed the coded papers, and began thumbing through them slowly, looking at each one carefully. It was in a code he knew they had broken. He finished scanning the sheets and laid them down on the table, then produced an incredibly small camera, raised it to his eye, and aimed it at the first sheet.

Outside the pub, the tall figure emerged from the shadows and walked purposefully across the street. His stride was long and smooth, catlike in its grace. He entered the pub, quickly scanned the room, and walked directly to the door that the courier had used.

The barkeep watched him carefully and began to remove his apron. By the time he had lifted the foldaway bartop to follow, the stranger had disappeared through the door.

With silent strides, he moved quickly down the hall and stopped in front of the door to the room the courier had entered. He produced a Mauser HSc automatic and snapped back the slide. Then he kicked the door in.

The contact had heard the metallic snap of the Mauser and reached for the light just as the door splintered open. The light was out at almost the same instant.

Instinctively, the courier spun to face the tall silhouette in the doorway and threw the attaché case at it.

The figure darted to the side out of the light behind him. The Mauser cracked twice. The courier was knocked backward, crashing over the table.

The contact had swung immediately away from the table. He threw his chair at the flashes, catching the intruder squarely with its force, knocking him back against the wall.

A door at the back of the room opened and slammed closed quickly, as the Mauser cracked twice more at it. The intruder began moving toward the back door, when he was pulled sharply by the collar and struck on the side of the head by a hard object. He fell to the floor and quickly rolled to the side. The Mauser spoke once again, at the figure outlined in the doorway. The barkeep was hit squarely and was driven back through the opposite door in the hallway.

The intruder picked himself up and went for the back door. It was locked. He spun and raced out of the room, down the hallway, and through the pub, where the patrons were frozen with fear from the sounds of the shots.

The intruder flashed past them to the door, just as the car screeched out of the alleyway and turned to pass in front of him. He raised the Mauser and fired into the driver's side of the windshield. He squeezed again, but the Mauser had jammed.

The car screeched past him, weaving wildly down the street. Then it straightened out and sped off.

The intruder raced back through the pub, as the panicked patrons piled frantically out into the street. He went again to the back room, found the lamp on the floor, and flicked it on.

The courier was lying flat on his back with two holes in his face, one above the upper lip just below the nose, the other in the forehead just above the left eye. His eyes stared up blankly, as blood ran from his nose and mouth and down the side of his face into his ear. His head was in a puddle of blood and oozing brain matter.

The intruder searched the floor and found the folder and the papers it had contained. Then he found the camera and the money.

He counted the pages. Fifteen. He had them all.

He kicked at the back door. It splintered open. There were no traces of blood. The shots had missed. He was sure that the shot through the windshield had scored. It had to; the angle was a dead hit. It was a pity the Mauser had jammed. The contact should have been dead meat, too. Perhaps he would be yet, if the shot had done its job. It bothered him that it wasn't clean, completed.

He walked back through the room and checked the body of the barkeep, lying partially in the opposite room, his legs out in the hallway.

For the first time he felt the pain from the blow to the head. He touched it, and his hand came away bloody.

He bent forward and looked into the lifeless face, an expression of shock across it. The barkeep had been hit in the chest.

The intruder went back into the room, and left through the splintered back door the contact had used to escape to the alleyway. He would not chance going through the bar another time.

As he walked out onto the street, he could hear the ascending wail of the police sirens approaching. There was still time. He could see lights in windows that had been black before. A few faces cautiously peeked out, careful not to become the next target.

He walked swiftly across the street and mounted the powerful BSA that waited for him in the same shadows from which he had emerged earlier.

"SENTINEL Control, this is Pilgrim," he said and waited for acknowledgment.

BEEP!

The tone sounding in his communications implant told him that SENTINEL Control was listening.

"I've got the information. The courier is dead, the contact got away. I'm certain that he's wounded."

"Understood, Pilgrim," the soft voice said. "How many sheets did you retrieve?"

"Fifteen…and a camera," Pilgrim replied. There was no need to mention the money. It would be his.

"Very good, Pilgrim. You can come home now. Division Two will follow up on the car from this point. Job well done."

Job well done, he thought to himself. A job half done is never well done. That contact should have a few holes in his face, too. It wasn't enough to just win. He had wanted the shutout.

The big motorcycle roared to life, revved loudly several times, then sped away from the approaching sirens. Bike and rider once again became a part of the darkness to which they belonged.

ONE

Nothing happened by chance. Everything was very carefully planned. All that we lacked was patience. In our mad rush we overlooked certain fundamental weaknesses, which ultimately spelled out our defeat. It had been, we thought, a good idea poorly executed.

Opening remarks from the partially
recovered *Wolf Journal*

One year later: It was a gray, brutally cold March day in Moscow. Dmitri Chakhovsky stood before the window of his small, plainly furnished office inside KGB headquarters. He stared down to a deserted Dzerzhinsky Square, his thoughts on the approaching spring.

Moscow seemed lifeless to him in winter. His mind played with thoughts of the spring that would soon be returning and the harsh cold that would grudgingly yield to the sun's warmth, followed by the sudden bloom of nature. The people would walk the streets again, the birds would sing, and the trees would turn green. Life would return.

But Dmitri Chakhovsky would miss the Russian spring this year. He would be in Paris, as the second secretary of the Soviet delegation to France. He preferred the Parisian spring, anyway.

Chakhovsky spent about eight months out of each year serving on various Soviet delegations to Western European nations.

To the world, he was just another member of the huge Soviet diplomatic corps. But to the CIA and NATO intelligence agencies, he was much more—a highly ranked KGB official in the Operational Division of the First Directorate of Counterespionage. He was the brain behind the Western European section.

The Operational Division was responsible for coordinating the activities of KGB intelligence networks, appointing resident directors, and choosing agents to be sent abroad. It also managed communications for those networks.

In the years immediately prior to Stalin's death, Russian Intelligence had fallen into widespread inefficiency and petty power struggles, which had all but ground it to a halt. After Stalin's death, a major power struggle had ensued between Laurenti Beria and his chief adversary, Malenkoff. Beria had seriously underestimated his opponent's influence with the Red Army and had been arrested and executed, along with many of the ranking officials responsible for the unhealthy state of affairs.

The principal outcome had been that the Communist Party established control over the security services (Intelligence and the Secret Service), so that, in theory, it should no longer be possible for one man to control them against the party's wishes. A lot of people had disappeared into obscurity, or from the face of the earth, during this time.

It was during this overhaul and the return to normalcy that a young Dmitri Chakhovsky had been noticed and brought to Moscow. He had been a young and energetic Komsomol (Communist League of Youth) district leader. His observers were so impressed with his perception, bearing, and organizational talents that he had been invited to come to Moscow. It was there, at Soviet Intelligence headquarters, that his career with the KGB had started.

He had undergone intensive training at the Karlshorst School of Espionage in East Germany, followed by further intensive study at the KGB main training establishment in Kochino.

From there he had been assigned to the Western European Intelligence Division under the direction of one Konstantin Zhadanov, who was later to become the head of the KGB Science Division. Young Chakhovsky was an outstanding agent and had been immediately recommended by Zhadanov to his superiors. His ability to organize was almost unbelievable, for one so young and with such short experience. He was recalled to Moscow for advanced operations planning and communications training.

From that point on he rose rapidly from position to position, each with greater responsibilities. He established an outstanding record, but also made some of his worst enemies during this time.

In the late sixties, it became necessary to make another reorganization in the KGB. This was based on Chakhovsky's recommendations and the approval of the Individual Division of the Second Directorate. Chakhovsky worked closely with the Individual Division, which had the responsibility of watching all Soviet citizens at home and abroad, especially those in government services. By their recommendations, a man could be promoted or liquidated. Together, they made the Western European section a much more efficient branch. He dared to touch areas thought untouchable, to dig into sacred places of power and position.

Chakhovsky was ruthless in his recommendations. His only thoughts were for the good of the Soviet Union, not the individuals involved. This reorganization was less bloody than the one that followed Stalin's death because the government had lost some of its teeth to reason. But blood did flow. Many of those who survived had friends who didn't, and they remembered Chakhovsky as the cause.

One of those survivors was Vasily Trushenko. He had been too valuable to "remove" completely and was reassigned to a position of lesser importance, but from which there was prospect of promotion. Seven years later he had again advanced to a position of power in the same Individual Division that had brought him down. He had locked his sights on Chakhovsky and vowed to return the favor.

On two separate occasions Trushenko had begun secret investigations of Chakhovsky, in the hope of finding something, anything, that might destroy him. Both had failed. Chakhovsky had proven to be untouchable, a virtual tower of strength, oblivious to attack, personal or otherwise. He was seemingly without a weak spot. But Trushenko was a patient and persistent man and maintained his gentle pressure until he found a fault deep within the great edifice, a fault that would bring Chakhovsky within his grasp. He had initiated a third secret investigation only days ago. It was progressing slowly, but with favorable results.

Chakhovsky went home after one last meeting with Leonid Travkin, the KGB director, and Alexandr Stroyanin, the chief director of Western European Operations. After a solitary dinner, he finished his packing and went to bed. He lay awake, thinking of his wife Tamara, who had died twelve years earlier from cancer, and his only son Boris, who had been killed in a skirmish along the Sino-Soviet border just two years ago. His life was lonely without them. How he missed them both.

He closed his eyes and fell into a peaceful sleep, unaware that, at that very moment, Trushenko was receiving vital information that would push him to the most desperate decision of his life.

When Chakhovsky arrived at the Soviet embassy in Paris the following afternoon, there was a coded message waiting for him. Later, in the privacy of his apartment, he decoded it. It said simply, "Spring will not come." It was signed, "Starling."

Chakhovsky knew this meant trouble. Starling was the code name used by a trusted friend in the Individual Division. That could only mean that Trushenko was after him again. He knew that, after two previously unsuccessful attempts, Trushenko would have to be a fool to start a third, unless he had something solid to go on. He knew that his service record was unblemished and would hold up to the closest scrutiny. But, deep within the self-constructed cobwebs of forgetfulness, there was something that caused him to shudder in apprehension. He wondered if it had really been such a crime, and if Trushenko knew about it. He reread the message, and wondered.

TWO

We recognized as early as 1941 that defeat lay ahead; we never told the people. In preparation, we created the Niederlage section, whose task it was to work out detailed plans for overcoming the impending catastrophe. Elaborate plans were made for a quick comeback. Over 120,000 false identities were secretly prepared. They were eventually placed everywhere, in what became the world's greatest deception.

But there were some of us who knew that the defeat would be crushing and complete. There would be no quick comeback. So, under our guidance, a special branch of Niederlage was established and issued a top secret directive bearing the highest authority. They were to plan for total defeat.

Defeat did not have to be the end of everything.

Entry No. 2 from the partially
recovered *Wolf Journal*

Chicago: Dr. Edward Bridges sat hunched over his elegant desk, as the clock on his office wall swept away the final minutes of the work day. His round, stubby fingers assaulted the cellophane wrapper on one of his cheap White Owl cigars. Moments later he was well back in the deep comfort of his chair, soft clouds of smoke rising into the air above him.

This was his time. The office door was closed. He was alone, shut off from the world around him, safe from intrusions and unhappy realities, as his mind played through pleasant fantasies full of accomplishments and rewards that he could never realize as a man. He was handsome in these dreams, strong and thin. And the women, the beautiful women...

An ash fell from the tip of the cigar to his enormous stomach. He brushed it away, finding himself back in his surroundings. He spun his chair around to face the large magnetic organizational board behind him. It detailed the structure of the Alpha branch of SENTINEL. To the world outside of this complex, it was known as the Aztek Corporation. But it was a great deal more than that, more than anyone could have ever imagined.

His eyes moved to the left of the organizational board, to the sliding door marked SSC-6 ADMITTANCE ONLY. Access to the room behind it was limited to personnel of that security classification or higher. Behind that door was the inner office of Dr. Edward Bridges, an inner sanctum of power, the keys to his future. Behind that door were the thick volumes that detailed every facet of SENTINEL.

He had helped to build it, to make it what it was. For this, he had been well paid and was made the number-two man in the technical side of the project. He lived in relative comfort and style, enjoyed his work, and was one of the best in his field. It was a formula for success. Yet he was not a happy man.

Dr. Edward Bridges was thirty-eight years old, grossly overweight, balding, and getting uglier by the minute. He was unmarried, with no prospects of that changing. He didn't deceive himself about his chances with women. But this job was his equalizer. Through it he overcame the handicaps of his ugliness, and his loneliness didn't matter. At his job he was superior, better than the pretty boys who had the things he lacked but not his intelligence. Yet, he was deprived of the credit and recognition due him, as the man responsible for the overwhelming success of the SENTINEL program. It was Elizabeth Ryerson who got all of the credit.

The bitch, he thought. It would serve her right if he left. They'd all soon realize just how important he had really been to the program and how much she actually needed him. They'd see that he was the real talent behind Elizabeth Ryerson, the one who made her look good in the eyes of the big shots.

Like everyone, Bridges was wrought with the failings that make men human. His biggest was that he constantly overestimated his own capabilities. That he was a genius in computer science was never contested, but he was no Elizabeth Ryerson. Bridges could quickly master any system and become fluent in its complex technology, but he lacked one very important factor—imagination. Like an artist who could duplicate the greatest masterpieces but never paint one of his own, Bridges had little sense of creativity. He confused his ability to understand the systems with the talent to create them. He was constantly left with the impression that he could have done the whole thing himself, if he had only thought of it first.

Bridges chewed savagely on the cigar as he slid back into his surroundings once again. He was worked up now and needed to calm down. The nervous sensation was beginning to climb again in his gut, as the prospects of his plan filled his head. The decision had been clearly his to make. There was no moral guilt or the slightest feeling of obligation to *them*. It was their lack of recognition that had given him the right to make the choice. It was academic in his mind—if they didn't appreciate his talent, somebody else would.

He stubbed out the cigar and reached for the top sheet of his memo pad and tore it away. He stared at the name he had unconsciously scribbled across it. Carson Ross.

Ross was a fucking scab, he thought, but he was also the man who could make the plan work. He shredded the piece of paper, dropped it into the waste basket, and looked up at the clock on his wall. It was 5:25. He had been lost in thought for over a half hour. It was time to go home.

He rose from his chair and walked around the desk to the dark wooden coatrack. He put on his suit jacket, then labored in getting his tentlike overcoat on over his massive form. He walked to the door, opened it, then turned to look slowly around the room, as if it were for the last time.

Not yet, he thought, and then wondered what he'd feel when he took that last look. After seven years, only a few seconds to drink it all into his memory, that final image to stay in his mind forever.

Forever.

Forever only happened in fairy tales. He shut the light behind him as he left the room.

Bridges thought it sheer beauty how he had gotten his plan into motion. He had been putting SENTINEL through routine problem drills when he popped in the question asking SENTINEL to list the names of any suspected Soviet agents associated with the list of societies and organizations that he had supplied. Included in that list was the Uptown Games Club, to which he belonged. The name Carson Ross had come up.

Bridges knew Ross by sight and was aware of the reputation that preceded him as a poor payer of his markers, as well as other gossipy tidbits, including rumors of his bisexuality. It was common knowledge that Ross lived off a fat allowance from his father, who was one of the owners of the club. He had been sent to the very best schools all across Europe, but somehow never managed to stay in any one for too long. It wasn't known whether he ever obtained a degree or not. If he had, he never used it. Life for him was one big paid vacation, and the club had become an important part of that lifestyle. He frequented it on a regular basis, in hopes of supplementing the income from his father that never went quite far enough.

That was how Bridges had snared him—at the backgammon tables.

Most club regulars refused to play Ross because of his poor payment habits. And, although he considered himself a pretty good player, he was at his best only mediocre and usually ended up on the losing side of things. He had been known to pass bad checks on occasion, which his father made good to the members holding them. It was only the influence of the father that kept him from learning some rather difficult lessons.

Bridges's strategy had been simple. Beat the pants off Ross early to get the stakes up quickly, then let him win big. It was a modest investment as far as Bridges was concerned. And one thing was certain—as long as Ross considered him a good pay-day, he'd have as much of Ross's time as he needed. So far, he had used that time well to plant his seeds of interest during their many nightcaps following the backgammon sessions. Ross was only too glad to buy the drinks, as long as Bridges cared to drink them; it was Bridges's money he was being generous with. But, after the first few times, he would have happily spent his own, just to learn what he could about Bridges's line of work. The realization had occurred early to Ross that Bridges's work involved classified matters; something to do with computer systems for the various US intelligence agencies. Beyond that, Bridges would say no more, other than to imply that he was unhappy there.

It didn't take Ross's greedy little brain long to size up the potential. If what Bridges said was true, this guy could lead to a much larger payoff than a few hot rounds of backgammon.

Bridges walked into the club, checked his coat, and went immediately to the lounge. It had almost become a regular thing, like a ritual. They'd meet, talk, have a drink or two, play back-gammon, then drink themselves into oblivion. But tonight was to be a little different. It was Ross who came with a plan.

Bridges spotted him at the usual corner table. Ross was a tallish man, blond, artificially good-looking, possessing an overbearing and rude personality. He was an easy man to dislike, and Bridges found no difficulty in doing so.

Ross looked up as Bridges took a chair at the table.

"Hey, here's the happy loser," Ross said with his plastic smile.

"Shit," Bridges grunted, "he's not going to be the loser tonight. He's going to pick your pockets clean." He smiled, meaning it.

"We'll see about who picks whose pockets."

Ross caught the attention of the waitress. The two men fell silent as she approached the table to take their order.

"Give me a Jack Daniel's and water," Ross said and looked to Bridges for his choice.

"I'll have a Johnnie Walker Black on the rocks, please."

The waitress jotted their requests down and wiggled toward the bar.

"Speaking of rocks, how do you like the set on that?" Ross asked, tipping his head toward the waitress.

"Yeah, nice tits," Bridges said, watching the wiggle closely.

"Good piece of ass, too," Ross added. "I had her when she first came to the club a few months ago. A real moaner. Could go all night too."

Bridges smiled weakly. He really didn't like this son-of-a-bitch at all. He looked back at the girl and wondered how a fine-looking thing like that could hit the sack with a shit like Ross. He had probably hit her with the "my daddy owns the club" bit.

"Have you had dinner yet?" Ross asked.

"Nope. I was just going to have a bite here at the club," Bridges answered.

"You mean you eat the garbage they serve in this place?" Ross asked.

"Yeah, why? There's nothing wrong with the food," Bridges returned.

"No, except they got niggers cooking it. You eat here often?"

"No, only when I come to play," Bridges replied.

"Shit, no wonder you lose. I'll tell you what, why don't you join me for dinner tonight? My treat," Ross offered. "I've got reservations at Kinzie's. It might even change your luck," he said.

"Kinzie's? Sounds great. You're on."

The first part of Ross's plan had just been completed.

He had received instructions from his contact, Ringer, to determine the seriousness of Bridges's discontent and to probe the possibility of his going to a "more appreciative" employer. The whole affair had been received with the utmost interest in Moscow. The initial report from Ringer had quickly channeled its way up to the desk of Andrei Ulev, the director of Intelligence, North American Division. One hour later it was on the desk of Leonid Travkin, the director of the Soviet KGB. It was not often that leads with such promise developed so quickly, especially from minor sources as in this case. The potential, if it truly existed, was bait that could not be resisted.

Class III investigations were ordered on both Dr. Edward Bridges and Carson Ross. Within forty-eight hours, enough information was available to indicate that Dr. Bridges could be for real; his background was certainly right for it.

Instructions were issued to Ringer and were passed on to Ross, via a prearranged dead drop at the Art Institute on Michigan Avenue. Ross was also advanced five hundred dollars to cover his expenses. If Bridges's sincerity was in doubt, Ross was to attempt to compromise him, thereby forcing his cooperation. Ross's bisexuality made the method plain. Ringer would monitor the entire exchange, to help determine if that method would be necessary.

The waitress returned with their drinks. Ross gave her a knowing wink. She ignored it and put the drinks on the small napkins bearing the seal of the club.

Bridges noticed her slightly disgusted expression and eyed her lovely body as she walked away from the table. He tried to imagine her underneath him, her legs up over his shoulders, moaning and sighing as he rhythmically pumped away at her. What he wouldn't give…

One hour later they were being led to their table at Kinzie's. They ordered drinks and made small talk, carefully avoiding the subject of their mutual intent. After a second round, they went out to the selection counter and chose their steaks, made a stop at the salad bar, then returned to their table.

Ross toyed nervously with his salad, as Bridges dove into his hungrily. Ross's obvious anxiety made Bridges certain that this night bore special significance to his plan.

"Ed…" Ross began, "the other night you said something to me about being unhappy with your work. Why do you stay there?" he asked.

Bridges looked up, chewing. "You've got it wrong, Carson," Bridges said, pausing to observe Ross's reaction. He carefully measured the sudden change in the facial expression.

Ross's stomach dropped. Maybe he had contacted Ringer prematurely.

"It's not that I'm unhappy with the work," Bridges began to explain. "I really enjoy my work. It's the place…or maybe I mean the people. You see, I'm good at my job, and I love working with computers and doing things that only a handful of people in this whole world can do. But I don't get the recognition that I deserve there. I'm number-two man. And I'm *better* than number one. It's *my* work that makes the program go. But it's only the bottom line that those sons-of-bitches on top look at, you know? And that doesn't have my signature on it, so, as far as they're concerned, it's number one who does it.

"It gets you when you see a thing like that happen and you can never see it getting any better. I'm on a dead-end street. And I know that I'm too good at my work to let this happen to me," Bridges explained.

Neither man paid attention to his salad now. They were locked in each other's intentions.

"Why can't you just get another job somewhere else?" Ross asked.

"It's not that simple," Bridges replied, shaking his head. "My work is classified top secret. My work is involved with the very heart of the systems. They'd never let me leave."

"But, surely, if you agreed never to divulge any of this information, they'd let you go. I mean, how could they not?" Ross asked.

Bridges looked at him through a squint. "When I accepted the job, I knew what was involved. They made it all very clear right from the start. I don't have any choice but to stay where I am. It's that simple."

Ross shook his head in mock puzzlement. "It's hard to imagine anything being that important," he said.

"It wouldn't be if you knew the systems I work with," Bridges tossed out. "That computer is so advanced that you wouldn't believe half of what it could do, if I *could* tell you. You'd say, 'Bullshit,' and laugh in my face."

"Oh, come on," Ross said. "How much more can one computer do than another? I mean, there are some pretty advanced computers around today. What makes this one so special?" he asked.

"I could answer that in one word, Carson. Then you'd understand."

"Well?" Ross said, waiting for that one word.

Bridges shook his head, smiling. "That's where the line is drawn, my friend. I'm afraid I'll never be able to tell you that."

He could see the disappointment on Ross's face.

"After that tremendous buildup, you're going to leave me hanging?" Ross asked incredulously.

Bridges just smiled as the waitress approached their table with two fantastic-looking steaks. But neither man seemed interested. They waited until the waitress left, then made a few weak tries at the meat.

"Well, what if you could find someone to work for?" Ross began, breaking the silence. "I mean, what if there were somebody who could offer you a job to do what you do now and was willing to make you the number-one man?"

Bridges laughed. "Where? I told you, this work is classified. There's just no way, Carson. They'd never let me leave."

"Well, what if it *were* possible?" Ross persisted. "If they *did* let you go? Would you go to work for these other people? I mean, if there was someone else?"

"If they'd let me go, and there was somewhere else, where I could use my experience—and run the show, I think I would. But that's just never going to happen, my friend," Bridges replied.

"Well, never say, 'Never.' You can't tell what the future will bring," Ross consoled.

"What kind of stakes did you have in mind for tonight?" Ross asked, getting off the topic. He had learned what he wanted to know.

"Ten a point?" Bridges asked.

"You're on."

The Soviets had a complete transcript of the conversation at Kinzie's on Ulev's desk within the next twenty-four hours. Ross had completed his instructions to the letter. The compromise was judged unnecessary by Ringer, based on his observations at Kinzie's.

Ulev thumbed through the pages on his desk, reading them over and over. Then he picked up the phone and ordered a Class I investigation of Dr. Edward Bridges—no facts to be left out. They must know everything about the man that there was to know.

Ulev picked up the papers and headed for Leonid Travkin's office. The entire operation would be looked upon with the utmost importance. It was evident that what they had here was even greater than face value had indicated. Leonid Travkin would be most pleased.

THREE

What is history but uninterrupted warfare recorded in retrospect by the winner. With their perfect 20–20 hindsight they proclaim the inevitable victory over the forces of evil. Yet, good and evil are relative things in history. The role of evil is the price paid for catastrophic failure. And this is not wrong, for the losers are the weak, and the world belongs to the strong.

The winners sit in judgment over the losers; the losers are the criminals of war. They answer to a "justice" set forth by the victors and swing from the gallows of righteousness built by the hands of men whose side God was on, by hands guilty of the same necessities of war for which we hung. Had we won, they would have swung from our gallows.

Forget what happens in war. War is ugly for both sides. Everybody does a lot of killing and the dead feel no pain.

Entry No. 5 from the partially
recovered *Wolf Journal*

The situation in Paris remained clouded. Starling had been unable to learn anything about the investigation that Trushenko had started. There were no leads to follow; everything was being done in complete secrecy. All he knew was that

Trushenko's men were busily digging out the mysterious facts. Something would break soon. It would have to.

Chakhovsky was beginning to feel that his suspicions were correct and that Trushenko had found out what he feared. If that were the case, there would be little he could do in behalf of his own defense. He wasn't guilty of a major crime against the state but, in its own way, one much harder to forgive.

It was fortunate, he thought, that he was now in Paris, for he knew this city better than any other in Western Europe. If he were in Moscow when this happened, there would be little hope of escape. He began to formulate a plan of action, expecting the worst.

In Moscow, Trushenko was working late into the night in his office. He was just getting ready to go home for the evening when the phone rang. It was his man leading the investigation. He reported that Illya Bodonov had been located and was under observation. Bodonov was residing in Kiev, living with his unmarried sister. Trushenko's pulse quickened at the news. He knew that Bodonov was the connection between Chakhovsky and the crimes that he was looking for. Once he had Bodonov, he could break him and get a full confession, implicating Chakhovsky. With that in hand, he'd have the bastard at last.

"Bring him in," he snapped. "Take him this evening when everyone is asleep. I want it done quickly to minimize awareness of his being taken."

"What shall we do with the girl?" his man asked.

Trushenko thought for a few moments. Then he said, "Take her, too. She may be valuable in obtaining the confession. Do not let him know that she has been taken." Then he hung up the phone and sat fully back in his chair. He sat for a few moments, then swung his chair around to look out into the night; a smile crossed his face.

"Soon…soon, my dear Dmitri Chakhovsky. Very soon now."

It was 2:00 a.m., and the streets were dark and silent in Kiev. The only sound was the icy March wind, as it whooshed through the streets in chilling gusts. Two large, black cars pulled up in front of the building in which Bodonov and his sister lived. A third car stopped about a hundred yards behind, hidden in the shadows from the moon's light.

Four men emerged from the first car, three from the second. They were careful to leave the doors partially open to avoid any sound.

Looking like carbon copies in their long dark coats, the seven men moved silently up the steps to the entrance of the buildings. The entire neighborhood was still and sleeping. One man stayed by the entrance just inside the doorway. Another stayed on the first-floor landing, and a third man stood on the landing of the second floor. The remaining four moved down the second-floor hallway, toward Bodonov's apartment.

The night arrest is a common practice of the Russian state police. It has numerous important advantages both physical and psychological. Everyone in the target apartment is thrown into a sudden state of shock and terror. They are not inwardly prepared for violence and will always be weaker than the police, who will not hesitate to use it. Also, the "object" of the arrest is placed in total confusion. Dragged from the warm safety of his bed, he is clouded and unaware of what is happening to him. Neighbors and residents of surrounding buildings are often completely unaware of the arrest. If they are awakened, they often will not know who or how many were taken.

The men took their practiced positions in front of the door, as one man produced a key. It had been fitted and tested earlier in the day while the apartment was empty. He inserted it slowly, twisted the lock, and swung the door open. They silently filed in and walked to the one double bed in the small studio apartment.

The light on the table was snapped on. Bodonov awakened with a start. He was grabbed and dragged naked from the bed.

Before he could utter a sound, he was struck hard on the side of the face by a large, hamlike fist that sent him sprawling across the floor. The fist was followed by a heavy-booted foot, which kicked him in the stomach and then again in the kidneys. He writhed in pain and lay helpless on the floor.

Bodonov's sister sat up startled and frightened. The blanket was ripped from the bed, revealing her naked body. She was young and beautiful, with large, milky-white breasts and silk-smooth skin. One of the intruders pointed a gun at her and ordered her to stay put. She complied, as tears began to well up in her eyes.

The leader of the group grabbed her by her long, black hair and dragged her from the bed to the floor. He viciously yanked her up to her feet, causing her to let out a whimper, and pushed her hard against the wall.

"Are you the sister of this man?" he asked with a stern, authoritative voice.

"Yes…yes…yes," she gasped.

He looked at her body. "Do you always sleep naked with your brother?" he asked.

She did not answer. She was terrified and could not think. She looked into the dark, sadistic eyes, saying nothing, fearing for her life.

He squeezed her breast, twisting it. "Do you always sleep with your brother like this?" he asked again.

She whimpered again, raising herself to her toes in an effort to reduce his grip. She still did not answer.

The man grabbed her face in his hand and turned it to him. They were eye to eye. "Your silence has given the answer," he said. He let go of her breast and turned to her brother.

Two of the men pulled him to his knees, one of them yanking on his hair, bending his head back so that his face looked almost directly up to the ceiling.

The leader walked over to him and stared into the face.

"You are Illya Bodonov." It was a statement, not a question.

Bodonov said nothing, just looked into the menacing eyes. He was still trying to grasp what was happening.

"You are under arrest for crimes against the state," the leader said flatly.

"What crimes? I have done noth—" His words were cut off by another vicious yank of his hair, bending him back further, to the point of extreme pain.

"You will be taken for questioning. Get up and get dressed. You have two minutes."

He was yanked up to his feet, still in great pain from the brutal kicks that the other men had delivered.

"You," the leader said, pointing to the girl, "help him. Be fast. We must leave." He motioned her with a wave of his arm.

She hurried to her brother to help him stand. He was in obvious difficulty from the pain. She helped him to the dresser, where he supported himself as she handed him clothes hurriedly. Then she went to get his bag, to put extra things in.

One of the men stopped her.

"I'm going to get his bag. He will need extra clothes," she explained. "Is it permitted?"

The leader nodded and motioned to let her go.

She took the bag and tried to think. What will he need? What is allowed? What should I give him?

"Hurry. You take too long," the leader commanded.

She was confused, no longer aware of her nakedness. She began throwing extra clothes into the bag. An extra sweater, a pair of pants, some underwear, warm socks, and work shoes. She looked nervously around the room. She went to the bathroom and threw in a towel and a bar of soap. She reached for his lather cup and brush, but the man holding the gun stopped her.

"Razors are not allowed," he said coldly. His eyes were staring holes into her body.

She looked around again and saw the blanket on the floor. She went to it, folded it, and stuffed it into the bag. Then she went to the pantry and took out a loaf of brown bread and forced it in, as well. It barely fit. She closed the bag and secured it.

"Time is up, we must go," the leader barked.

Bodonov had finished dressing in a heavy sweater and pants, warm socks, and boots. He looked at his sister in disbelief.

She ran across the room to him and threw her arms around his neck. She kissed him hard on the mouth.

"We must go," the leader yelled, as he grabbed her arm and tried to separate her from her brother. She would not let go.

She held on, sobbing now, as her eyes met his. Bodonov was silent. His eyes searched hers with finality. They said everything there was to say—*I am no more.*

The leader yanked again, she held on. He reached out and grabbed her breast and twisted brutally, at the same time yanking her long hair. She fell to the floor; he kicked her hard on the buttocks. She fell flat, sobbing. They left, the door closing behind them as they dragged him out of her life. She turned and stared at the door, unable to comprehend what had just taken place. It was so sudden. There were so very few words.

Illya Bodonov had reached the breaking point in his life. In a few startling moments, his world had been shattered by the words: "You are under arrest." When that door was slammed shut, his life was left behind it. He was led down the stairs of his home for the last time.

Within moments they were in the car, Bodonov in the back with men on either side, the leader in the front. The second car followed as they drove off. The streets were still silent and dark; the only light shining came from Bodonov's window. It was a beacon bidding him farewell.

As the car rounded the corner, the leader rolled down the window and tossed Bodonov's bag out onto the street. He turned to face the prisoner.

"You won't be needing that," he said.

After the first two cars disappeared into the night, the third car pulled up in front of the building. Four more dark-coated men emerged and approached the building.

They had come for the girl.

FOUR

It began in a Germany left spiritually destroyed and upside down by World War I. The country was torn and battered by inflation and unemployment. The staggering cost of defeat weighed heavily. It was a time of social desperation, economic ruin, and mistrust for a government that had betrayed the people. The threat of violent revolution was in the air. The people were filled with an unidentifiable fear and gripped by a mood of despair, hatred, and anger.

The time was ripe in Germany. Only the seed was needed—and a leader.

Entry No. 6 from the partially
recovered *Wolf Journal*

His eyes were tired and aching from the long hours at his desk. He sat back in his chair, rubbing the weariness out of his eyes with his fists. It had been over forty-eight consecutive hours of work, translating and encoding his discovery. At last it was finished.

He pushed his chair away from the cluttered desk and walked over to the large bookcase built into the study's longest wall. He held the book in his hands and let his eyes play across the volumes of his huge library. It was all there now, safe for later discovery, should anything happen to him. And it was a good bet that something would before too long. His discovery made him a dangerous man. He knew it, and he knew what must follow. That was why he used what little time he had left to code the journal into the volumes of his library. Now, with the information safe and the original journal burning in his fireplace, he could concentrate on staying alive. He guessed that he had a few days left, before they came. He placed the last book on the shelf in its proper place.

He felt the cramps rising in his intestines. He had been plagued by diarrhea since he realized what he had uncovered and recognized the terrifying significance of it. The discomfort suddenly grew severe, and he hurried to the spare bathroom located right off the study.

He had been in such a rush he hadn't turned on the light. Only a few feeble rays emanated from an old night light always left on in that room. A few additional rays leaked in under the door from the old fluorescent lamp in the study. He sat enveloped in the soft semidarkness, then reached back and flushed.

As the gushing sounds faded and the tank filled noisily, his eyes caught a break in the light coming in from under the door. Somebody was out there and doubtlessly knew where he was, from the flush.

He instinctively reached for his left armpit, but the Walther wasn't there. He hadn't put it on in two days. Not a mistake, really, he usually didn't carry a piece in his own house. But it would cost him today. He had guessed wrong on the time he'd have.

His eyes quickly scanned the room looking for a weapon. His mind raced frantically. Grabbing his belt buckle so as not to make a sound, he began to rise slowly. If he could get to his straight-edge razor, he'd have a chance to surprise his unexpected visitor as he opened the door. He could see the two distinct dark bands of shadow cast by the intruder's legs. He was in front of the door.

It was the last thing he saw.

There was a blast. Bits of the door exploded inward as the load of the shotgun hit him squarely in the groin, knocking him against the toilet tank behind him, slamming his upper back and head against the wall. He bounced back slightly and sank onto the toilet seat just as the second blast splintered its way through the door, hitting him in the chest. The force of the blast jolted him backward and slightly upward into the tank again. Then he sank once more onto the toilet seat, sliding off to the left until the wall stopped him.

The door swung open.

His assassin put in another load and discharged it directly into the head, rendering it a bloody stump. Blood, bone, and brains were splattered about the small room. The killer regarded the efficiency of his work for a few moments, then went back into the study to begin his search.

The air in Irwin Honeycut's office was electric. Reports had been flashing in hourly since the killing. This was not the first SENTINEL agent to die in the line of duty, but he had been the first to be killed by an assassin sent specifically for him. His cover had been blown. The entire agency, as well as SENTINEL, could have been compromised.

Honeycut sat behind his desk in the elegant office. He had been appointed by the last President to head the ultra-secret program and its equally secret intelligence agency. Honeycut had been the program's director from day one.

The President had been wise in his selection of Honeycut. He could run any company or organization in the world, if he wanted to, such was his combination of talents. A rare acumen for business and political situations backed by cold logic and unerring judgment had earned him a reputation as a man who was never wrong. Fiercely aggressive and competitive, he attacked every problem with computerlike accuracy and bulldog determination.

He got results by being demanding and using people to their fullest potential, and he was an uncanny judge of men.

Honeycut had been phased out of public life into semiretirement by a phony hypertension condition. As a cover, he ran his own business consulting firm on a part-time schedule. He kept occasional contact with his former colleagues just often enough to make it look good. They were important sources of information and helped to keep the cover intact. No one ever suspected the power that he controlled.

He drummed his fingers impatiently, waiting for SENTINEL to complete the connection to the President's direct line. The connection could not be made unless the President was in the Oval Office alone, out of earshot of all White House staff and visitors. The automatic taping devices in the office were fed false signals to record a typical sound of the President at work at his desk. No trace of the conversation would be recorded.

The entire security system of the White House had been secretly redesigned by SENTINEL. Sensors watched and listened from every corner of the building. Automatic defense systems were also secretly installed and were under SENTINEL's control. No one was aware of these devices except the President, his SENTINEL advisory staff, and people possessing SSC-7 security classifications in the SENTINEL program.

The fingers drummed.

The phone rang.

"This is the President speaking," Honeycut heard, as the phone came to life.

"This is Irv, Mr. President. I've got more facts for you on the Spartan killing," he said in his graveled voice.

"Sorry to keep you waiting so long, Irv. I had the ambassador from Nigeria in here. I cut it as short as I could, without being rude. We'll have privacy until I notify Ronni. Will twenty minutes do it?"

"More than enough, Mr. President," Honeycut replied.

"Give me the facts, Irv," the President said.

"It was definitely an assassination, Mr. President. It was deliberately brutal and messy for our benefit, to drive the point home. They wanted to be sure that we knew it was an assassination."

"Who are 'they'?" the President interrupted.

"The Soviets. We're pretty certain of it," Honeycut answered.

"How do you know that? And how was his cover blown?" the President asked. "Your agents aren't even known to our own CIA, FBI, or the Pentagon. They appear on no intelligence computer file in the world."

"That's not entirely true, Mr. President," Honeycut corrected. "As you know, according to agreement, we inform the British of intelligence activities carried out within their legal borders. We also supply code names of the agents involved. They do the same. Without this mutual agreement, our trust in one another would be undermined and our necessary cooperation would be greatly hindered. We gave the code names of our agents, but listed them as special CIA or NATO intelligence operatives.

"SENTINEL has determined that three code names were leaked to the Soviets by one of four top British security personnel. Only those four people had access to that information. All three of these agents had been assigned to British operations within the past year. They are Spartan, Pilgrim, and Badger. We are—"

"Wait a minute, Irv. I have another question," the President interrupted again. "What about Pilgrim and Badger? Where are they now?"

"Both are safe. They are in the United States and currently unassigned. SENTINEL has been monitoring them without their knowledge since the killing. We are now working to determine which of the four British suspects is our leak."

"Will the British believe us if we find out who is guilty and inform them?" the President asked.

"Uncertain. If we tell them, and they don't believe us, then we'll be held responsible if anything happens to him. The Russians will probably knock him off at that point and make it look like we did it. They'd have a lot to gain by making us look bad over this. They'd also be removing an agent who would be of no further use to them with his cover blown.

"Our best bet in this case would be to make certain of our facts and arrange our own 'special action' for him. It will all appear quite natural."

The President remained silent for a while. It bothered him to talk away a man's life so matter-of-factly. It seemed very wrong, against his nature, but he knew it was necessary. This one man had just dealt away three very important lives and jeopardized the country's greatest secret. The greatest advantage of SENTINEL lay in the fact that it was a secret. The proverbial ace in the hole, but with the magnitude of a royal flush. "Give me some more facts on the killing," the President said.

"Spartan was shotgunned three times at close range, while he was on the toilet. He was blown to bits. Scotland Yard is completely baffled by it. There was very little to go on."

"What was he doing in England?" the President asked.

"He lived there. He had just returned from a mission when he was hit," Honeycut replied.

"Will his cover hold up to their investigations?"

"Yes, absolutely. They'll learn nothing about him that we don't want them to learn."

"Were any other code names leaked?"

"None that SENTINEL knows of. Only the three. We're still working," Honeycut said.

"What about this double agent in Britain? What do we have on him so far?" the President asked.

"Well, Mr. President, you may remember about nine years ago that a convicted Soviet double agent, Lionel Duncan, escaped quite spectacularly from prison in England. He had been a member of a highly placed four-man cell that the British had broken wide open. They were operating right inside British Intelligence, right under their noses, each in a highly responsible position. Anyway, he simply climbed over a wall with help from the outside. He got clean away and showed up in Moscow four months later. The Russians made a big thing of it."

"Yes, I remember it. It was quite embarrassing for the British. Go on," the President urged.

"Immediately following his escape, a 'fifth man' theory was put forth by the British. It was American opinion that either the British helped plan and execute the operation as part of a complex and secret swap, or that a 'fifth man' did exist. One of our four suspects could be that 'fifth man,' " Honeycut explained.

"Be absolutely certain of your facts, Irv. Then do what you must," the President said in a voice just above a strained whisper. He cleared his throat and said, "How could they have identified Spartan from just a code name?"

"Unknown at this time, Mr. President. But SENTINEL will be projecting theories on that shortly. All we know right now is that they had his code name, and he's dead. We'll have the answers before too long," Honeycut assured him.

The President sensed that Honeycut had more to say and waited.

Honeycut's voice lowered, losing some of its gravel. "There is also some valuable information missing. Division Two got in there after Scotland Yard finished up and couldn't find it. Either Scotland Yard has it, or the Russians do...or it's still there, and we just missed it."

"What information?" the President asked.

"We're not entirely sure. Spartan obtained it on his last mission. It was an unexpected discovery. He had been assigned to a 'special action' in Madrid. He found it after completing his assignment. He was killed before it could be delivered. All we know is that it was of a vital nature."

His voice became tense. "We have to go back in there to find it. I'd like to send Pilgrim and Badger in to look for it."

"Why them? Their covers may be blown wide open," the President said.

"That's precisely why, Mr. President. They've become expendable. If they find it, we win. If they don't, and they get killed in the attempt, the leak ends with them. A neat dead end," he explained.

"And if they get taken? We stand to lose a great deal more than we already have," the President said.

"No, sir, that won't happen. They're the two best agents that we have. They'll succeed if anybody can. If they don't, they'll never be taken alive. SENTINEL can see to that."

"How?" the President asked.

Honeycut paused again. His voice became low and tense once more. "Their implants are explosive. SENTINEL controls detonation."

The President let out a heavy sigh. "Do they know this?"

"No, Mr. President, they don't," Honeycut said dryly. "Not all SENTINEL agents have explosive implants. These were added only within the last two years. Both Pilgrim and Badger had received the newly designed implants. All agents are scheduled for changeover within the next twelve months.

"Regardless of what the Russians may already know, Mr. President, we must get that information back."

The President paused. "Very well, Irv. Do what you have to do, you have complete authority. Is there anything else?"

"No, Mr. President. You have it all for now."

"Fine, Irv. Let me know when you learn more."

"I will, sir."

The phone clicked down and went dead. Honeycut replaced his phone in the cradle and thought for a few moments. He knew that that information had to be retrieved and examined for content. It was vital.

"SENTINEL," his coarse voice called.

The white light on his SENTINEL console went on.

"Yes, Mr. Honeycut," the soft voice of SENTINEL responded.

"I want you to call in Pilgrim and Badger for assignment. Have them meet in Chicago at twenty-one hundred hours, central time, this evening, at the usual place. Stagger their arrival by fifteen minutes. Badger first. I'll give them this one personally."

"Working," the voice said. The light on the console snapped off.

FIVE

As if sent by God, a leader emerged in a troubled Germany to touch the hidden depths of the Aryan soul. With his magnetic oratory and explosive themes, he began to awaken the German Siegfried.

The people shared with him an almost pathological love of Germany. There has never been a clearer and more convincing identification between a nation, its heroes, and its plan.

He was their Messiah—and the people followed.

Entry No. 7 from the partially
recovered *Wolf Journal*

The Impala stopped in front of the old house. As Justin got out of the car, he could see the living room curtains pull open, then close again. He looked at the old mailbox on the fence post as he moved around the car toward the walk. The mailbox had been there for as long as he could remember, always neatly painted to match the color of the house. The large, distinct block letters announced that this was the residence of the Leon Chaple family. Justin had grown up in the house. "Hi, son," a voice said from the porch.

"Hi, Pop. How are ya feeling?" Justin asked, walking up the steps of the porch.

"Oh, pretty good, I guess," his father answered in that tone that meant, "Not so good, really."

Leon Chaple was a bull of a man, stoic and strong. Justin could never remember him showing pain, not even the time he cut the end of his thumb off on the radial saw many years ago, or following his open-heart surgery the day after Justin's son, Michael, was born over four years ago. Indeed, the man seemed oblivious to pain—except when his wife had died a few years back. That was the only time Justin had ever seen him cry.

They were very much alike, father and son. Both were over six feet in height, lean, and strongly built.

"Your uncle Tom just sent me enough pills to last me six months," his father began. "He sent some of that new medicine that I told you about, the one that I wear on my chest. It makes me feel pretty good since I started using it, but it goes through the absorbent paper and wrecks all my undershirts," he complained.

"Oh, shit," Justin started, "what in the hell do you care about a few undershirts? The stuff makes you feel good, so don't complain. I'll buy you all the undershirts you need—"

"No, no, I don't need anything, I can buy my own when I need them," his father protested.

His father was on complete disability now. The operation had successfully corrected three of the arterial obstructions with bypasses, but a fourth could not be repaired. His situation was greatly improved, but not to the point where he could go back to the rigors of a daily working routine.

The disability checks weren't very large, and he hadn't saved much money before the attacks started. But Justin had made arrangements with his father's bank to keep his account above a certain level by transferring funds from a special account that Justin had set up in that bank without his father's knowledge. Justin made sure that his father was comfortable and lacked for nothing.

"What did Doc Marsh say about your last visit?" Justin asked.

"He says he wants me to go back in for more of those tests. I think they want to operate again," the old man answered.

Justin could see the disappointment in his father's eyes, also the fear. Fear was another thing he had never seen in his father's eyes until the eve of the open-heart surgery. Bypass procedure had been improved since the first operation, which made the uncorrected obstruction now operable—but with risk.

"Well, if that's what it takes to make you better, Pop, I'd have it done," Justin advised.

His father shook his head. "No, I won't go through that again. I'll live out what time I have left like I am. I'll take my chances. They're not going to cut me like that again."

Justin knew better than to argue with him. He knew that, when the time came, his uncle Tom would talk him into doing what was necessary. He always listened to Tom.

"What's new in the insurance business?" his father asked, to change the subject.

"Oh, not a hell of a lot," Justin answered.

"Catch any crooks?" his father asked.

"Yeah, got one the week before last. One of our own representatives was trying to defraud the company out of a hundred and fifty thousand bucks. But we got him."

"They give you a raise for that?" the old man asked with a smile.

"No, Pop," Justin laughed. "It's all part of the job."

"That's a lot of money, son. You should have told them you wanted a percentage."

"Can't do that, Pop. I get a straight salary. It's my job to catch people that try to steal from the company," Justin explained.

"You should get a percentage," the old man insisted. "That's dangerous work. Someone could try to kill you to avoid being caught," he said.

"No, it's not like that, Pop. These people aren't usually dangerous. They're smart, but not dangerous. When they're caught they just give up. My life has never been in danger."

The old man just shook his head. His son had always been a sensitive, gentle boy. He never accepted the fact that people could really hurt one another. He was too trusting and too naive for his own good. He just hoped he would never get hurt because of it.

"Well, you just be careful, anyway. You can never tell how people will react to being caught. I believe that anyone can be dangerous when they're scared," his father said.

"Okay, I promise I'll be careful, Pop. But don't you worry. I can handle it," Justin assured him.

"How's your son? Do you get to see him much?" the old man asked.

"He's fine. Starting to grow like a weed. He's gonna be tall like you. Even looks like you a bit," Justin said.

Justin's father smiled proudly.

"I get to see him on most weekends that I'm not away on business," Justin continued. "Sue's pretty good about that."

His father could see a sadness in his son's eyes. Justin and Susan had been divorced for over a year now, and he had never gotten over missing his son.

"How's he feel about his new father?"

"I'm his father," Justin snapped.

"I know that, son. What I meant was, do they get along?"

"Yeah," Justin said, looking out across the front yard. "Jack's good to him. He'll be able to give Mikey a lot of the things that I couldn't, I guess. At least he'll be there a lot more than I was," Justin said.

The pain of what had happened was inside him again. It always came back when he thought about it and what she had done to him, about what had caused it, and what it had cost him. It tore at him like a steel claw in his gut.

The divorce itself hadn't been traumatic, only losing little Michael. The marriage had deteriorated steadily over its last two years. But he had never thought that it had gone that far, until he had caught them together.

It crushed Justin. His wife…Susan…screwing with that son-of-a-bitch. She had hurt him grievously, slicing his pride irreparably. It was over after that; there was no going back.

Justin's father studied the expression on his face and knew that the time had come to change the subject once again.

"Come on, son. Let's go inside for some coffee. I just put a fresh pot up before you came."

As they sat drinking the hot coffee, Justin could hear the windchimes on the back porch. He remembered how, as a little boy, he would listen to them, as he lay in his bed at night. He always seemed to notice them most when something troubled him. He would listen to their gentle tinkling sounds. They would soothe him, and his troubles would melt away into sleep. That was probably the thing he remembered most about the old house—the windchimes. They soothed him again, as the painful memories of the incident and his loneliness for his son faded to their sweet music.

"How's Barbara?" his father asked, breaking the lull. Barbara was Justin's new girlfriend. The old man had met her several times and liked her very much.

"She's fine, Pop. She always asks about you. She wants you over for dinner real soon. I can bring Mikey over, too, if you'd like. That way you'd get to spend some time with him," Justin said, smiling again.

"I'd like that," the old man said. "She's a fine young lady, son. You thinking of marrying her?" he asked.

"I'm not ready to get married again, Pop. Not yet, anyway. I'll let you know when I am," Justin said.

"Well, I hope it's soon. A man needs a good woman, and I hope that, when you're ready, it's her. She's one of the finest young ladies I've ever met."

"I think so, too, Pop," Justin said. His thoughts went to Barbara.

She had a more subtle kind of beauty than Susan's. Susan's beauty was nearly disarming. Barbara was on the thin side, her figure delicate, but adequate. She had the kind of shape you could easily overlook, until you saw her on the beach in a revealing bikini. Then she became easy to appreciate.

She was Midwest-born and raised, but after college she had come East, to pursue a career as a free-lance writer with the eventual goal of working into novels, when her finances permitted such long-term commitment.

As a free-lancer, she had been an immediate success and, somehow, after reaching that point of financial strength, never quite started work on that first novel. Few writers could have made it so well or so quickly, but her talent was natural, and her intuitive selection of subject matter put her a cut above the rest.

They first met about a year before Justin's divorce. It was at a party thrown by a mutual friend. She was immediately impressed by him. He was handsome, stylishly dressed, well-mannered, and had obvious good taste in women—he was with Susan, who was one of the most striking women Barbara had ever seen. Most of the men at the party were dumbstruck by Susan and followed her around the room with their eyes almost the entire evening. The fact that she was never more than a few feet away from Justin the whole time said much for him. Barbara was definitely impressed.

They met again twice after that, once at a party (this time no Susan), and again in a coffee shop at one of the large indoor malls in New Jersey. It was there that the friendship was born. They walked and talked and spent nearly five hours together, roaming in and out of the stores. They learned a lot about one another and their attitudes on life in general. Justin asked her out, and she accepted. Their friendship developed quickly after that. Then the thing that made Justin a part of her life happened.

While in the shower, she had discovered a small lump in her right breast. Panic-stricken, she went immediately to her doctor.

He scheduled her to go into the hospital three days later, for surgery to remove it.

She needed desperately to reach out. And it was Justin who was there.

There had been terror in her eyes when she told him. Partly from the fear of what could lie ahead, but also from the fear of face-to-face rejection. She couldn't have taken that.

His response was a tenderness she hadn't thought him capable of. He held her gently, kissing her lightly and telling her that everything would be all right. "Don't worry, I'll be here," he had said, as he wiped the tears away.

He spent countless hours with her during those three days. His confidence was so strong that it couldn't help but spread her way. She was greatly comforted as she entered the hospital. He spent every moment that he could with her, until the nurses all but dragged him away. He'd be there through the night, he told her, and he'd be there when she opened her eyes.

The terror that flowed through her mind that night was hers alone to feel, but the knowledge that Justin was close by afforded a much-needed comfort.

At eight o'clock the following morning, she would go into surgery. She would wake up either a whole woman or mutilated. She thought she'd die from the fear. Justin phoned her twice more that evening from the lobby to try to comfort her and fill her full of confidence. He managed to make her laugh a few times, and it was great medicine.

The next morning she had vague impressions of people being around her and saw the overhead lamps that illuminated the operating table. She heard the doctors' comforting voices. When she finally closed her eyes, Justin's name was on her lips.

The next thing she remembered was being in recovery. She felt no pain and could hear voices. A nurse tried to waken her gently, to determine how far out of anesthesia she had come. Then she slept.

She remembered being lifted to another small bed on wheels and seeing bottles with running IV. She still felt no pain, but the bottles frightened her. She tried to speak to ask what had happened, but could not. The words never came. Then she remembered being wheeled out into the hallway again and seeing Justin's smiling face. He leaned down and kissed her softly on the cheek and told her she'd be fine. Then she slept.

She finally came to in her room. When she looked up, she saw Justin—beautiful Justin. She tried to speak, but he kissed her again. Then he held up a pink-lace bra and smiled.

"I thought you'd want this for when you go home," he said. "It's just the thing you need for those gorgeous boobs."

Her eyes flooded instantly. She held up her arms and, crying, drew Justin's face close to hers.

"I got you bottoms, too," he said.

She looked into his eyes and said, "I love you."

He kissed her tenderly, then said, "Do you want to see the bottoms?"

She smiled, kissed him back, and said, "You hold them for me. We won't be needing them for a long, long time."

No other man she knew would have done what Justin did for her. He was there, ever there, when she needed him. To her, the man was incredible, courageous, and the dearest thing to her life—her beautiful Justin.

The rest of the day at his father's house went by with the usual routine. The visits were all the same. They talked about the same things and the same people. They were both lonely men in their own way.

The hours passed slowly, and it came time for Justin to leave. Justin bid his farewells and got into the Impala. He drove up the block and turned off his father's street.

BEEP!

The tone in his implant sounded.

"Pilgrim," the soft voice began, "you are needed…"

SIX

National Socialism had many obstacles to overcome in its rise. To accomplish this it used violence and brutality, which have a propaganda value all their own. They focus discussion around the source, repelling many, but attracting more. People develop a distaste for disaster after repeated doses of it.

The will to resist died, the obstacles fell one by one, until there was only one way. The way of National Socialism.

Entry No. 9 from the partially
recovered *Wolf Journal*

The day seemed to have taken forever to pass for Edward Bridges. He had spent most of it going through the thick volumes of schematics in his inner office, to determine which ones he would need. He had settled on twenty-four sheets that gave the very heart of the most advanced systems, as well as the revolutionary memory-mass data that made SENTINEL possible. With this information, and a competent team of computer scientists, he could build another SENTINEL, anywhere in the world.

He had also devised a simple, but effective, plan to get the information out. It would be nearly impossible to get a camera into, then out of the complex. It would be equally impossible to copy the information. Every piece of paper copied within the complex was scanned and cleared by SENTINEL. At the end of each working day, SENTINEL reminded every person holding copies to destroy them. Destruction was also monitored. It was impossible for even a single copy to survive a day, much less the twenty-four that Bridges needed.

But there was a blind spot, which Bridges was able to detect, that solved all of his problems. The schematics making up the volumes in his inner office were the only ones in printed form in existence. Normally, all data were stored in SENTINEL's memory mass and would be flashed on console viewing-screens or large wall-display screens when required. But Bridges's job necessitated many continuous hours with the schematics, and the long sessions with the screen gave him bad headaches and caused excessive eye strain. He had spoken to Elizabeth Ryerson about it, and she had agreed that he should have a printed set—the only printed set.

They were kept in his inner office, to which only he and Elizabeth could gain admittance with their security plates. The schematics were seldom let out of the inner office. On the few occasions that they were, a log was signed with a special impulse pen that sent the handwriting impressions to SENTINEL for verification. It was virtually impossible for an imposter to get through the rigid security maintained at Alpha, but this precaution was employed to prevent the possibility of one person taking out a schematic, while signing another person's name in the log. All schematics were returned at day's end, or no one left the complex.

The simple blind spot in this—and the flaw that Bridges would take advantage of—was that he didn't have to sign the log to remove schematics. It was *his* inner office. The schematics were in *his* care. They were made primarily for *his* use. He decided to take the originals. He could take them out on the last day and be out of the country before they were even missed.

To get them out he would simply wrap them around his shins, hold them in place with his socks, and walk right out with them.

The day finally dragged to an end. Bridges was anxious to test his method. He intended to make dry runs as many times as he could, using blank report forms. They were slightly smaller than the schematics and of a lighter bond, but he guessed that the slight difference would pose little or no problem.

He began by wrapping four sheets around each leg and walked about the office to test them. They were comfortable and quiet. He added more sheets and tried it again. Still smooth. He decided not to risk the full number of twenty-four sheets until he could successfully make a dry run with the lesser number.

With the sheets in place, well secured by his high socks and concealed by his baggy pants, he left his office for the first run.

He passed through security without a hitch. When he built the next SENTINEL inside of Russia, he'd have to correct this security flaw in the system he'd set up there.

He drove off for the club and his meeting with Ross. Today had been a very good day for him, and it was going to get even better, he was sure. He had the feeling that this was the day for the offer. Ross had called and said that he wanted to see him.

He arrived at the club and saw Ross in the lounge sitting at the bar. He walked over to him and took a seat beside him.

Ross didn't turn his head when Bridges slid onto the stool. There was an awkward silence for several long moments.

"Hi, loser," Bridges finally began, referring to the beating he had given him at backgammon after the dinner at Kinzie's. "I thought that shellacking I gave you would scare you away for good. I figured that I'd seen the last of you and your money," he kidded.

"Bullshit," Ross said, "I'm still about three hundred bucks up on you. The only money you saw was your own. I don't mind losing when it's somebody else's money."

Ross was trying to sound jolly, but he looked nervous, and Bridges smiled slightly in anticipation. He raised a hand to the bartender to order himself a drink.

The bartender produced a Johnnie Walker Black on the rocks. "Got it ready when I saw you come in, Dr. Bridges," the bartender said. He took good care of his better tippers.

"Remind me to double your usual tip to a dime tonight, Sam," Bridges joked. He was in an unusually good mood.

He turned to Ross. "How much tonight? Five? Ten?" he asked.

"Actually, I don't feel much like playing tonight, Ed. I was thinking that maybe you'd like to join me for dinner again, then just call it an early evening."

"Sure," Bridges said, nodding his head, "but only on the condition that you let me buy."

"All right. Kinzie's again?" Ross suggested.

"Excellent."

Ross breathed a mental sigh of relief. His instructions were to try to get Bridges to Kinzie's, where Ringer would be waiting. If the initial overture from Ross went well, Ringer would come in to make the deal. If not, they'd again have to consider compromising him, to force his cooperation.

They finished their drinks. Bridges paid the tab and threw the bartender a five. They left the club and caught a cab for Kinzie's.

On their way to the table, Bridges thought he recognized a man who had been there the night of his and Ross's last dinner. The man had a face that was easy to remember. It reminded Bridges of a weasel's.

The man had an earpiece in place, with a small flesh-colored wire running down into the collar of his shirt. Probably a recording device on him as well, Bridges thought to himself.

With the customary small talk, the waitress brought them their cocktails. After she left, Ross looked around the room. Bridges saw his eyes stop in the exact direction of the man with the earpiece. This is it, he thought.

After several moments, Ross looked back to Bridges. There was a slight tremor in Ross's hands, which Bridges picked up immediately. Ross was coming apart. He must be ready to shit in his pants, Bridges thought.

"Ed...Ed, eh...I've...I've been thinking, you know, about... about the other day and what we talked about," Ross stumbled on nervously, his voice quivering.

Bridges wanted to laugh and almost did. It took considerable effort to keep a straight face.

"What I meant was...you know, about your job...job." Ross cleared his throat. "Did you...were you serious about going to work for someone else, if you had the chance? I mean, if it were... you know, really possible?" Ross looked like he was going to vomit.

Bridges squinted at him. "What are you getting at, Carson?" he asked.

"First, were you serious?" Ross asked.

Bridges didn't answer right away. He wanted to make it appear as if he were weighing his answer. He unwrapped one of his cheap White Owl cigars and stuck it in his mouth. "Yes, I was serious," he said through the bite. "If the offer were right and all of my conditions were met. Yes, I certainly would be interested."

Bridges watched Ross's nervous eyes flick quickly at the man with the earpiece again, then back. Ross's left eye began to twitch.

"I...I have some friends..." Ross began. He was searching for his words. "...some friends who are interested in your situation...and are in a position to possibly help you out. At the... eh...at the same time help themselves, too." Ross was about to break wide open. This was the offer that constituted treason, and he knew it. He looked at the other man for a long moment, then back to Bridges. He took a sip of his drink and choked.

Bridges nearly exploded into laughter, but just barely managed to keep control.

After a brief, embarrassing coughing spell, Ross cleared his throat and said, "It would involve a relocation...a move on your part. Are you interested?" he asked, his voice low and barely audible, his fists clenched, to keep the hands from shaking.

"Relocation? To where?" Bridges toyed.

"It would be a foreign country...foreign country." He had to repeat to make it audible.

"Which country?"

"Don't play games with me, Ed," Ross said. "You know damn well what I'm getting at. And I don't think I should say more until you give me some evidence that you intend to follow through." Ross was regaining his control. The ice had been broken now, and he was in it, sink or swim.

Bridges rested his chin in his hand and chewed on the cigar. "I want to talk to somebody with the authority to make a firm deal," Bridges said.

"First, I need more information," Ross said. "I'm in this for the pudding, too. You've got to appreciate my position in this, Ed. I have certain interests to protect." He seemed to be almost pleading.

"You've been told enough to get you what you need already. The fact that they've sent you here to make the offer—and your friend over there to listen in—tells me that," Bridges said, tossing a thumb at the other man.

Ross flushed. "How did you..." He stopped himself and looked at Ringer.

"If he's the man that can make the deal, get him over here," Bridges said, "but as far as you and me are concerned, you've learned all that you're going to."

Ross's mouth fell open.

Ringer stood and walked over to their table. He sat beside Bridges and looked into his eyes, studying the round face. He motioned to Ross, who got up and walked away from the table and out of the restaurant.

"I will be your new contact. You will know me as Ringer. Now let's talk terms."

This man was direct and to the point. Bridges enjoyed the direct dealing without the phony pretenses.

"Three times my current salary, I select my own team from your top scientists, and I am to be undisputed head of the project from the technical aspect. You must also agree to get me out of the country quickly, before my absence is discovered and, once inside the Soviet Union, provide complete protection," Bridges finished, and waited.

Ringer smiled. "How do you know that I represent the Soviet Union?" he asked.

"I know a lot more than you think I know," Bridges said.

Ringer reached up and removed the earpiece from his ear. He stared at the scientist.

"Your terms are too steep," the Russian said.

"My terms are final," Bridges countered quickly.

The Russian thought for a long moment. "Agreed," he said at last. "Now, tell me what we get for meeting your terms. We pay a high price for very uncertain goods. I must know more."

Bridges smiled. "And you shall," he promised, pausing to light the cigar. "I will deliver to you certain schematics that will enable you to build the most advanced computer ever built by man. We call it SENTINEL. It's the heart of the United States defense and intelligence systems. With my services, you will have what you need to build a SENTINEL of your own," Bridges explained.

"And what makes this computer so advanced?" Ringer asked. "I believe that you told Ross you could explain that with one word. Now I am waiting to hear it, Dr. Bridges."

Bridges looked evenly at Ringer. "*Intellect*," he said. "A true intellect, but with one million times the ability of the most highly developed mind."

An unsettled look crossed Ringer's face. "Semantics, Dr. Bridges. No computer has *true* intellect."

"This one does." Bridges smiled, pausing to relight his cigar and study the expression on Ringer's face. "We've made the breakthrough into biocybernetics. We've left the dark ages of computers. And we're advancing at a rate that we can't even keep up with. SENTINEL has designed systems that we don't even have the technology to build. It's teaching us that now.

"It's the same breakthrough that your people have been trying to make for over thirty years," Bridges said, puffing white clouds across the table.

Ringer was at a loss for words. If this were true, it was the most significant achievement in the history of man. "What makes you think that we do not have a computer such as this already?" he asked.

Bridges laughed softly. "Yeah, I guess you've got a whole warehouse full of them. You're here, my friend, and you're here to deal. That tells me. And if you did have one before ours, we'd have been a pile of ashes by now. There's no way we could have stopped you, just as there's no way you could stop us now, if the right button were to be pushed. But you're fortunate in that SENTINEL is not maintained as an offensive threat. Its function is purely defensive. And that's where I can give you the upper hand. I will build yours to be offensive. You will be the most powerful nation on earth, second to none."

"How long would it take to make this computer operational?" Ringer asked.

"About three years," Bridges replied.

"In three years the American SENTINEL would be too advanced to ever catch it," Ringer said.

"I can take care of that," Bridges told him. "It's possible to work out an intercept formula that would enable your SENTINEL to learn all that this one knows in a few one-second bursts, by selectively tapping certain portions of the memory. You would then have their knowledge before they even knew the tap had been made.

"Don't forget that their computer is not offensively oriented. Yours will be. And I can improve it. Then it is *you* who will have the advantage. You would know its entire defensive system and could overcome it if you wished, leaving but one SENTINEL in the world—yours."

"What would happen if the Soviet Union were to launch a preemptive strike against this country right now, assuming the proper target sites could be selected?" Ringer asked.

Bridges chuckled lightly. "You'd probably lose the war in about two hours. Not a single missile would hit American soil in a vital location. SENTINEL would completely neutralize your strike capacity within a few moments of the first confirmed missile firing bearing on an American target. You'd be without communications, without power—you'd be defenseless. Nothing could leave the ground but a hand-propelled snowball from Siberia," Bridges concluded.

"Would it then destroy us?" Ringer asked.

"No, it doesn't have the killer instinct that I can give yours. But your days as a world power would be abruptly ended."

"How long would it take you to get your information together?" the Russian asked.

"Tell me today, and you've got it tomorrow," Bridges replied. "But you'll have to get me out of the country fast. Once it is discovered that I am missing with the information, SENTINEL will track me down—and quickly. It has a highly secret security force that it would dispatch after me immediately. A very rigid security system will have to be set up for my protection, even inside the Soviet Union, until your SENTINEL is operational. These agents are extremely well-trained and can penetrate almost anywhere."

The Russian nodded. "I am impressed, Dr. Bridges. But there will be skepticism among my superiors. Is there any proof you can offer as to the actual existence of SENTINEL?" he asked.

"I thought that might be necessary," Bridges said, reaching into his pocket. He pulled out an envelope and handed it to Ringer. "See that Leonid Travkin gets this. It should be all they'll need. Is there anything else?" Bridges asked.

"No, Dr. Bridges. I am quite satisfied."

"Good, let's eat. I'm starving."

SEVEN

Germany began to move toward its hour of destiny. They said we were being led by the big lie; they called us barbarians. But they lost sight of the fact that barbarism is the basis of all culture, that it is the means by which one civilization replaces another.

It was barbarians who swarmed down in a foaming horde to fell the mighty Roman Empire. These Germanic conquerors were the forebears of our Aryan race. It became our heritage to conquer, our destiny. And that was our plan. After that, everything would be a simple matter of organization.

Entry No. 11 from the partially
recovered *Wolf Journal*

The cold wind blowing in off Lake Michigan bit painfully at Justin's cheeks and nose as he moved hurriedly up Monroe Street toward Michigan Avenue. He turned onto Michigan Avenue and sighed aloud at the relief afforded his stinging face, as the wind now blew gustily at his back. Each step brought him closer to the inviting warmth of the club. Finally, he was there.

He passed through the revolving doors and checked his watch as he sprinted up the short flight of stairs. It was 9:05 a.m. He was late for his meeting. Justin passed between the two memorial columns listing those members of the club who had served in the two world wars. He pushed the up button and waited for the elevator.

Justin's eyes played quickly around the lobby as the elevator inched its way down to answer his call. The club was now only a shadow of its past elegance. It had really been "the place" a long time ago. The early sixties had seen the start of its decline. There was great difficulty in attracting new, young members, and the natural course of attrition was beginning to shrink the ranks of its membership. It had begun to run down physically, too, losing its touch of class.

The elevator doors finally slid open. He stepped in and pushed the button for the fourth floor.

After a slow, groaning ascent, the elevator stopped, and its doors slid open. Justin wrinkled his nose slightly as he stepped out of the elevator. There was a distinctive "old" smell to the place that got more and more pronounced as you went up. The smell was as much a part of the building as the stone it was made of.

Justin walked past two large conference rooms and through the doors leading into the bowling alley. He passed between the lanes and rows of lockers and went to the back of the room, to a set of swinging doors. He pushed through them into a dark laundry area and passed by the rows of large dryers mounted into the walls. The room was still warm from their day's toil. He could feel the humidity, and the air smelled like bleach. At the back of this area was a small door marked SUPPLIES. He passed through it and flicked on the light. The room was long and narrow, lined entirely with rows of shelves. He went to the last set of shelves and touched his watch to a light switch controlling the small overhead light. The entire wall panel swung out toward him.

He entered a very small, claustrophobic cubicle. A small button illuminated as he entered. He touched his watch to it, and a door slid closed. The shelved panel closed tightly in the storage room, and the light went out.

He felt his stomach rise slightly as the elevator began its smooth descent. He had no idea of how far down it went or how fast the elevator was moving. Except for the rise and fall of his stomach as it started and stopped, there was no hint of motion. It stopped, and the door slid open.

He was met by the muzzle of a .357 Colt Python magnum, staring him square in the eye, about ten inches from his face. All he could see at first was the shiny, blued two-and-a-half-inch barrel, pointing at his forehead. Then he focused his eyes past it to its owner.

"Someday that fucking cannon of yours is gonna go right up your nose, Fanning," Justin said to Badger. "How the hell are ya, Ted?" He grinned, putting the tip of his index finger into the barrel, lowering it away from him.

"Long time no see, Justin," Ted Fanning said, as he placed the piece in his shoulder holster. He stuck out his rugged hand to Justin.

Justin and Fanning had worked together on several tough assignments in the past. Fanning had been his first partner and had taught him much in the art of survival. There wasn't a better man, in Justin's opinion, to place complete confidence in. Their lives had often depended upon one another's actions. They had been an extremely good, efficient, and deadly team.

"What kind of trouble did you get our asses into now?" Justin asked with a grin.

Fanning stood a little shorter than Justin. He was hard and strong, with a build like a lumberjack. His steel-gray eyes were narrow and deep-set beneath a shaggy pair of protruding eyebrows. But behind the almost Neanderthal appearance was a whip-quick mind and eyes possessing keen powers of observation. The slightly disheveled, dirty-blond hair was longish and thinning. He had a smile for his friend.

"How long has it been, Justin? About a year, isn't it?" he asked.

"I think longer. Time has a way of slipping by quickly when you're having fun."

BEEP! The white light on the voice-box console lit up. "Good evening, gentlemen," Honeycut's graveled voice began.

The greetings were over. The two men sat in the chairs near the voice box and focused their attention on it.

"We have an urgent assignment for you," Honeycut continued.

It wasn't the usual soft voice they were used to hearing when given special assignments, but they had heard it before. The name Pegasus was given to it. They listened, waiting for the mission briefing.

This room served as a control center for these two agents. They used only this office, no others, and had no knowledge of the locations of the other thirty-two stateside control centers. There were one hundred and twenty-two situated across the globe.

"A SENTINEL agent has been killed," Honeycut began. "As you know, he is not the first of our agents to die in the line of duty. But this case is an exceptional one.

"The agent, code-named Spartan, was killed the day before last, in England. He was killed in his own home. He was a target.

"We know conclusively that his cover had been blown, leaving the door open for his execution. And there is no doubt left that that's exactly what it was. And that, gentlemen, *is* a first.

"In addition to his murder, some vital information is missing. He had just returned from a 'special action' in Madrid, where he had unexpectedly found the information in question. It was a journal, handwritten in German. Spartan was fluent in German and had begun translating it, when his transmissions abruptly stopped. We figure that this was due to either implant failure or signal jamming of some kind. If the latter is true, then our worst fears may be true. The entire SENTINEL program could be in jeopardy."

"Excuse me, sir. I have a question," Justin interrupted.

"Yes, Pilgrim, what is it?"

"Could you back up a little and tell us more about how his cover was blown and who killed him, if that's known?" he asked.

"Certainly. We've been able to ascertain that his code name had been leaked by a highly placed Soviet double agent in British Intelligence. We've already begun work on cutting down the possibilities of who it could be. We expect with reasonable confidence that the Soviets were responsible for his murder."

Honeycut went on to fill them in on the complete details of the killing. He also outlined some of the more obvious consequences facing them if the Soviets did, indeed, know about the existence of SENTINEL and the agency.

"We're not certain, yet, how the connection between his code name and identity was made. SENTINEL has put forth several possibilities that seem likely, but, because of a large gap in our information, we're not certain how much is known about the agency or SENTINEL.

"We, therefore, have a two-pronged problem. The first is trying to determine how much they really know, and the second is finding that missing information. Unfortunately, there's not much we can do about the first at this time. But we can do something about the second, and that's where you two come in.

"Because of Scotland Yard involvement, Division Two was severely limited in the time they had in which to go over the crime scene. We've already determined that Scotland Yard doesn't have the information. That means that it's probably still there, and we just missed it."

"Or the assassin took it with him," Justin said.

Honeycut hesitated a moment. "Go on," he urged.

"You said that Spartan got hold of this information in Madrid after his 'special action.' Why couldn't he have simply been followed back, killed, and the information removed? There might be no connection between the leak of his code name and that information at all," he suggested.

"It is possible," Honeycut allowed. "But we feel that Spartan was aware of his impending danger and managed to conceal the information somewhere in the house.

"In any event, gentlemen," Honeycut went on, "you'll be able to answer some of those questions for us. You're going to England to find that journal."

"Is there anything else that you can tell us about the journal?" Fanning asked.

"Not at this time," Honeycut said. "Only that it's handwritten and in German, as I've already told you. We should be able to tell you more before you go into Spartan's house tomorrow night. Division Two removed ashes from Spartan's fireplace and has just begun analyzing them. The initial results will tell us whether it is the journal or not. We know he had begun a translation of it. If it wasn't too long, he could have finished it."

"Why not assign agents in England to look for the information?" Justin asked. "You could save a lot of time."

"Because, gentlemen…" He hesitated to focus their attention on the next words. "…your code names were leaked as well."

A quick, hot, nervous wave swept Justin's face and brain. He looked at Fanning.

Fanning looked back. It was one of the worst dreads of an agent.

"We dare not involve any more agents than we have to," Honeycut continued. "If your identities *are* known, then we lose nothing further if the worst happens and you fail. But we're not certain that your identities are known—only your code names.

"We have been monitoring your every move since Spartan's killing, to ensure your safety. As usual, you will have every assistance from SENTINEL Control.

"A specially modified Learjet has been made available to you. Badger, you've used it before, and we want it back, so treat it gently."

That remark was directed to Fanning because of his notorious reputation for losing or wrecking equipment.

Fanning just smiled broadly. "I'll take care of her like she was my own."

"That's what we're afraid of," Honeycut said back. "Remember, it's been modified for speed and distance, but it has limitations."

"I'll remember. You got it back in one piece last time." He smiled.

"With your record, that doesn't improve our odds. As I said, treat it gently!"

"Like my own," Fanning repeated.

"The Learjet is at Meigs Field, fueled and ready to go. SENTINEL Control will give you your flight plan and answer your questions. I have every confidence in you, gentlemen. Good luck." The white light on the console clicked off.

The two men looked at one another.

"What do you think?" Fanning asked.

"It's pretty sketchy," Justin said, shaking his head. "If the KGB did hit him and know who we are, we could be walking our rear ends into a load of buckshot."

"Yeah, *if* they know who we are. It's tough to figure how anyone could match up an identity to just a code name with the way our covers are protected," Fanning said.

"That's why I thought he was followed back from Madrid. That wouldn't be a hard thing to imagine. Our killer could be right back in Madrid, hiding his journal again," Justin said.

"Well, you're probably right," Fanning began. "We'll move carefully and keep each other's asses well-covered. I'm in no hurry to get mine blown off."

Justin pressed the white button on the desk console.

"Yes, gentlemen," the soft voice responded.

"Who was Spartan?" Justin asked.

"An American. His name was William Priest. He had lived in England for the past year," the voice responded.

"Priest?" Fanning repeated, sitting up sharply. "Bill Priest? From the old Baltimore Control Office?"

"Yes, Badger."

"Shit! I knew him, Justin. We worked together a few times back in the old days, when the agency was just getting started. He was a good man. A real good man. Probably the only other man I'd depend on completely, besides you." He shook his head in disbelief.

"He had another code name back then, didn't he? What was it?" Fanning asked, his hand to his forehead, thinking.

"Tamburlaine," the voice volunteered.

"Yeah, that was it. Tamburlaine. Jesus, I don't believe it. I'm surprised that someone could have gotten the drop on Billy like that. He was tough, smart as hell, too."

"How careful are you in your own home?" Justin asked.

"Yeah, I get your point. I guess it's possible. You can get careless at home," Fanning said, pulling out a cigar.

"Your travel kits are in the closet," the soft voice said.

They were provided with everything they'd need for the next three days, if that much time was necessary.

"Road maps are on the desk, indicating directions to Spartan's house," the voice continued. "You will be landing about sixty miles north of London. All arrangements have been made. A car will be waiting there for your disposal."

Fanning lit up the big, dark cigar. He blew several clouds of smoke upward. He shook his head. "Jesus, I can't believe it. Bill Priest…"

"What in the hell are you burning? Smells like cow chips," Justin joked. Justin was also a cigar smoker. It was his way of telling Fanning to give him one.

"That's a good cigar. Handrolled. Cuban," Fanning defended. "Here, try one."

Justin took it gingerly. He examined it, looking at the band. "Never heard of it. Looks nice," he said. It had the firmness and slightly irregular feel of a good handrolled cigar.

He lit it up and savored the aroma of the smoke rising from its tip. "*Good* cigar," he said, nodding, and put the band in his wallet for future reference.

They spent the next hour going over the gear in their kits and reviewing the flight plan with SENTINEL Control. Then they roughed out a procedure to follow when they got to Spartan's house.

They completed their equipment check and procedure outline and prepared to leave. They would go up separately, Fanning leaving first. He would then pick Justin up in front of the Palmer House, and they would proceed to Meigs Field.

They were putting on their coats when Fanning tossed Justin another cigar. "If we get the time, maybe we can pick some of these up in London. That's where I got them. These are the last of them," he said, tapping two more in his shirt pocket.

Fanning picked up his gear and stepped into the small elevator. "See ya up top in ten minutes, pardner." He winked, and the door closed.

It was nearly 2:00 a.m. when Justin and Fanning arrived at Meigs Field. There was an almost complete absence of activity, and a relative stillness filled the air as they approached the sleek Gates Learjet 24D sitting enrobed in the darkness, its silhouette barely visible against the blackened background of Lake Michigan. Even the icy winds had nearly stopped.

Justin listened to the soft muffled sounds of their footsteps as they approached the plane. There was an air of excitement filling him. His senses were coming alive with apprehension, as they did before every mission. The butterflies were beginning to build slightly in his stomach. He looked at the plane.

The gentle reflections bouncing off its shiny surface gave it an eerie, ghostlike appearance. It was a lot smaller than he imagined it would be. Planes this small usually didn't have the range required for transatlantic flights. Yet, despite its smallness, it looked like an animal possessed of immense raw power. Its sleek lines led gracefully back to the powerful twin engines, bulging from its sides just forward of its tail.

Fanning stopped directly in front of the Learjet. In his eyes it was like a beautiful woman, graceful and responsive to his gentle caresses, wanting to be possessed by him, and him alone. She would respond to his every desire, to his slightest touch. She sat waiting for them. Waiting for him.

Fanning was a born flyer. By the time he was sixteen, he had been flying his father's crop duster like a World War I flying ace. During his college years, he had flown bigger and better planes, and he had been flying ever since. He could make almost anything he flew perform like it was on the end of a string. He had a talent for controlling machinery in motion, for gauging its power and positional orientation.

He reached up and touched the plane, running his hand gently along her nose. "She's a real beaut, isn't she?" he said.

"You bet," Justin replied. He watched Fanning's gentle communication with the plane. He was petting its nose, soothing it with soft strokes.

"We understand each other," Fanning said.

"I hope so," said Justin. "That's a long way to go in a small plane like this. I'd hate to have to try to swim halfway back."

"Don't worry about her," Fanning said. "I've used her before. This little baby can really perform. Her normal range would be about eighteen hundred and fifty miles at five hundred miles an hour at a service ceiling of forty-five thousand feet. With her modifications, she'll do forty-two hundred miles at five hundred and ninety miles an hour at the same altitude. That's a lot of performance from a little lady like this. No one on earth would suspect her of flying that distance nonstop."

Justin was impressed by "her" credentials. "How fast can she go if we really have to haul ass outta someplace?" he asked.

"Her maximum modified speed is seven hundred and twenty miles an hour. But forget about trying to fly four thousand miles. Her range drops off drastically when she's burning that hot."

They stowed their gear, and Fanning fired her up. After an instrument check and instructions from the control tower, they taxied out to the runway for takeoff. They got final clearance from flight control and the powerful, sleek Learjet roared off the runway and banked out over Lake Michigan. Fanning was whistling "London Bridge Is Falling Down," as they surged upward into the darkness.

They were off to England.

It was dinner time in Moscow. Leonid Travkin's stomach growled from hunger. Across the desk from him sat Andrei Ulev. Travkin was leafing through the piles of reports and dossiers on his desk. As the director of the Soviet KGB, he was disturbed by its collective meaning.

He had received the results from the analysis of the information that Bridges had given to Ringer as proof of SENTINEL's existence and capabilities.

"It has all been confirmed," he said grimly. "Every fact is correct to the smallest detail. They know the locations of every missile silo in the Irkutsk district. Every single one has been pinpointed exactly. They have listed the names of every agent that we have painstakingly planted in their CIA and Pentagon. And their stated facts regarding our secret *Siska*-class submarines are absolutely accurate, from the armament and electronic capabilities to their exact positions on a stated date and time.

"This SENTINEL is either the most devastating development since the splitting of the atom, or it is the most carefully contrived bluff the Americans have ever attempted.

"They are notorious poker players, Andrei. But this much information would be impossible to obtain…"

"It is all very difficult to believe, General," Ulev began. "True, the information that Dr. Bridges has supplied is correct, alarmingly so, but the existence of such a computer is hard to believe. I cannot keep from feeling that this is all part of a grandiose hoax designed to get this Dr. Bridges into the Soviet Union. Once here, he could create havoc with our computer systems in only moments with his abilities."

"Yes, he could do that. But the accuracy of this information cannot be overlooked. It is impossible to gather so much information from even the most highly placed agents, without our becoming aware of it.

"If this computer exists, we must have it. Dr. Bridges represents our only possibility. Once we have his information, we can determine its veracity before allowing him access to our computers.

"Very elaborate security will have to be arranged to keep Bridges alive. The Americans will come for him, we may be certain of that. It will be a great deal more difficult to keep the information than it will be to get it."

Ulev nodded in agreement. They were bound to action. The evidence was too great in favor of the existence of SENTINEL to believe otherwise. There was also the matter of the three code names leaked out of British Intelligence. The data supplied with the code names had been analyzed very carefully. At least eight, and possibly eleven, missions had been linked to coinciding Soviet operations in the past two years. All of them, except one, were Soviet failures. And that one was very nearly a failure, averting disaster by only the narrowest of margins. So even the information supplied by Bridges concerning the secret security force of SENTINEL fit into place.

Travkin was to bring the issue before the Central Committee and an ailing Brezhnev, himself, on this very evening. After a few moments of fitful meditation, he looked up from the papers on his desk.

"Thank you, Andrei. You may leave now. I'll advise you on the outcome of my meeting with the Central Committee this evening."

Ulev got up and left the office.

Travkin picked up the phone on his desk and dialed a four-digit sequence, which opened a special scrambled line.

After the connection was confirmed, he dialed again.

He waited, listening.

"This is Travkin speaking," he said, as the other end came to life. "Centaur is needed. Make the usual arrangements for oh-two-hundred hours.

"Yes...yes, very good." He hung up the phone.

He had just called on his most trusted agent, Centaur. He was one of the very best in Soviet Intelligence. Like SENTINEL, Centaur's greatest advantage was that he was also a secret.

Alexi Kuradin was being called out of retirement for one last mission of vital importance. If any man alive could succeed against such overwhelming odds, Alexi Kuradin could do it.

But Travkin thought about his old friend, Centaur, and about what he was sending him up against. He wondered how much the Americans knew about Centaur, how much they could have learned about him a year ago in England, when he had so narrowly escaped with his life. They almost had him then. How much did they learn? That was the question. How much of his secret did they know?

EIGHT

Who has, has. That is the sum of human morality in politics. The ruling power must realize that the conquered masses have no rights. They are subject to whatever design the conqueror may impose, whether it be slave labor or utter destruction.

With this realization in mind, we embarked on the road to the fulfillment of our destiny. We were not deterred by humanitarian qualms, knowing that the welfare of our Fatherland required conquest, subjugation, dispossession, and the extermination of foreign nations. It is a fact of historical record that the creation of greater nations necessitates the destruction of lesser ones.

We prepared for total victory, ignoring all possibility of defeat.

Entry No. 16 from the partially
recovered *Wolf Journal*

Soviet interrogation methods had come a long way since the Stalinist days, when information was successfully extracted from countless subjects by many direct, painful techniques. Technology had come to the forefront. Drugs began opening closed mouths and minds; psychological tortures began to replace physical ones; and newer, more effective methods of creating physical stress were devised to accommodate those subjects specially designated to receive it. The direct physical methods were still sometimes preferred when a specific charge was to be answered with a specific confession, when only certain words were needed—and quickly.

Ivan Kutz was an interrogator. He was a leftover from the Stalinist era and had enjoyed the opportunities presented during the two major reorganizations that followed the death of Stalin. He was a master at delivering pain and twisting the body, until the mind screamed out, "Enough! I will tell you anything that you want to know!" Illya Bodonov had been delivered to Kutz for just that purpose.

The room was small, stuffy, and rank with the smell of pain and fear. Except for a bright, restricted cone of light in the center of the room, there was almost complete darkness. In the center of that cone, Illya Bodonov sat strapped to a chair.

The chair had leads and wires running from it from various positions. Electrical shocks could be delivered to any part of the body with the flick of a switch. Just at the darkened edge of the cone of light sat a table with a narrow box with numerous switches, to which the wires from the chair were connected. There was also a rheostat power source used to control the intensity of the electrical shocks. The switches controlled the duration.

Bodonov had proven to be a very stubborn man. This delighted Kutz. The more Bodonov resisted, the more Kutz liked it. He invariably abandoned the newer techniques and resorted to his "convincer," an old leather-wrapped stick that he had used so successfully in the days of Stalin. It worked well for him; it was more direct.

Kutz did not trust the new technical devices. They never allowed him to accurately judge the amount of pain he administered. He always started the interrogations using them, but ultimately reverted back to his time-proven method. A split eyebrow or broken teeth were easier to gauge than the invisible electricity he discharged with the switches. His success justified his means.

Kutz received to his care only those subjects considered "one-way" prisoners. The Soviet concepts of prison, enemies of the state, and dangerous individuals are rather black and white in viewpoint. There were many "one-way" prisoners, required to give their confessions before the necessary dispensation of justice.

Kutz circled Bodonov, his shiny boots just visible at the outer edge of the circle of light. The questions shot out of the darkness at Bodonov like sharp stinging darts. Bodonov could see the switches at the edge of the table that controlled the current running to his testicles and other parts of his body. The hand would come white from the darkness, as though coming through a black curtain, to trip one of the switches. It would be followed by the same questions repeated over and over. Bodonov answered none of them. And then the electrical shocks stopped. From out of the darkness, then flashed the stick. The target was always different, possessing a unique pain of its own.

Bodonov's right eye was swollen shut. The left eye was reduced to a narrow slit with long, deep cuts both above and below it. His lower lip was badly split and swollen, the upper one puffed and lacerated, where the teeth had gone through it before they were smashed.

Kutz enjoyed the stubbornness of his subject. He rather hoped that Bodonov would hold out for a while longer.

But Kutz knew that Vasily Trushenko was watching him from the back of the room—from the darkness. He knew that Trushenko wanted that confession and expected it. Kutz had to deliver, and soon. He was being assessed, he felt. He admired Trushenko and badly wanted his admiration in return. This was his chance to impress him. Pleasure aside, he would have the confession *now*.

The stick flashed out of the darkness, catching Bodonov on the point of the shoulder. He writhed and groaned painfully, but no words came out of his mouth.

"You will tell us *now!*" Kutz screamed. "You will answer all of my questions."

Nothing.

The stick flashed again, this time to the ear. Bodonov twisted away and groaned again, rocking his head slowly. He knew that he was "one-way." The questions made it clear what they were after. He would not help them get Dmitri Chakhovsky. Chakhovsky was a great man and should not be allowed to fall to this slime.

Kutz shot in at Bodonov pulling his head back by the hair. He stared into the open eye. His expression bore menace.

Bodonov for the first time got to look at the face of his tormentor. He strained to see it clearly through the closing eye, through the tears that involuntarily filled it. The vision was badly blurred. The face looked sinister and distorted. He spat into it.

Kutz went into a rage. He began clubbing Bodonov on the elbows and wrists. He stopped suddenly, remembering that Trushenko was there. The urge to kill Bodonov temporarily subsided. Temporarily. He brought himself under control.

"Bring in the girl," Kutz snapped. "We shall see how tightly your lips are sealed." He glared at Bodonov. Kutz was shaking with rage.

Bodonov glared back.

"I will give you one last chance to answer all of my questions. When did you first meet Dmitri Chakhovsky?"

Nothing.

"Do you make love to your sister?"

Nothing.

"You have unnatural sexual relations with other men and small children. Do you deny that?"

Nothing.

"Did you make love with Dmitri Chakhovsky?"

No answer.

"Tell me of Dmitri Chakhovsky and the small children he used to satisfy his perverted sexual desires."

"What you say is not true," Bodonov said, his first words since being taken away from his bed.

"So you speak," Kutz shouted. "You will tell me what I want to know," he screamed, his voice breaking slightly. He waited.

Nothing.

"Your sister has already confessed to us."

Bodonov looked up in puzzlement. His sister? They had not taken his sister. They would not...

The door opened.

"Do you doubt that what I tell you is true?" Kutz asked with a menacing grin that showed his teeth. "I can show you. Bring her here," he ordered.

Trushenko remained silent in the background. He knew that this was the critical point with Bodonov. He would talk now, or would never talk.

Two guards helped a weak and brutalized figure into the shaft of light. Bodonov strained to see the figure clearly through his left eye. He could distinguish the long black hair, a badly bruised face, and mangled hands, the fingers broken and twisted, the bruised breasts and body.

His beautiful sister. What had they done to her? For what? Whom had they hurt? It was of no consequence to the state. He looked up at Kutz. He still could not see him clearly through the tears. But he stared at him.

Kutz watched the face, saw the eye behind the wetness staring at him. He had won. He knew it. Now for the clincher.

He leaned down placing his face close to Bodonov's. His tone was no longer menacing, but soft and tender. "We will leave your sister alone and see that she gets immediate help and medical attention...*if* you tell us what we want to know. Otherwise"—the voice hardened to a threatening tone,—"you will be forced to watch as we break—"

"I will tell you," Bodonov said before Kutz could finish. "I will tell you what you want to know." Bodonov began to sob as he strained to see his sister. "You have promised. You will leave her alone and see that she gets help?" he asked.

Kutz laid a hand gently on Bodonov's shoulder. "Of course, we will. It is a promise." Kutz straightened up and turned his head to where Trushenko sat in the darkness. He was victorious.

Trushenko noticed that Kutz had an erection. It was obvious and unconcealable. He despised Kutz and his sick little brain, but he was useful. He had given him what he needed to settle an old score.

"Now tell us about the small children?" Kutz began.

March was going out like a lion. It was dumping tons of snow on Moscow with a merciless vengeance. A solitary figure stood in the raging snow, looking up at the old gray building before him. He examined the structure, then checked the vacant, snow-pelted streets. There was no one.

He checked his watch. It was almost two in the morning. It didn't seem that late. The snow made everything look lighter, made it somehow feel earlier than it was. He walked up the short flight of stairs and entered the building.

He went to the fourth floor and quietly walked down the hallway to the room indicated in his instructions. He rapped a short code on the door. A single knock was returned. He answered with two rapid taps. The door opened.

He walked in and turned to face the man behind the door. Alexi Kuradin was surprised to see Leonid Travkin standing there. Travkin almost never made direct contacts himself. This must be very important. Travkin closed the door behind him.

"Good evening, Alexi," Travkin said to his old friend. "It is good to see you again after so long."

They embraced warmly.

"It is good to see you, too, Leonid. Tell me, what is so urgent that an old dog like me must be pulled from the comforts of his retirement?" He looked into the eyes of his friend.

"We have an emergency," he answered.

That's what it had been termed at the meeting with the Central Committee. They had been ready for him. He had gone in there thinking he would have a difficult time convincing them of the seriousness of the matter. Instead, he just listened as *they* told *him* how important it was.

Some of Russia's most prominent computer scientists were in attendance. They gave him a dazzling and very confusing short course on cybernetics—the science which concerns itself with the mechanical extension of the capabilities and capacities of the brain.

His mind, not being technically oriented to such a depth, was quickly lost in the maze of technical terms and definitions. What he did get out of it was that the Soviet Union was in the midst of an all-out program to become the first cybernetic society in history. A sociological-technological society aided—not controlled—by cybernetic systems in education, agriculture, industry, commerce, and all essential areas of society.

He knew that the Soviet Union possessed more pure mathematicians than any country in the world, and that they sorted out their "super brain prodigies" at very early ages and put them into environments rich for proper nurturing in their fields of specialization. Nowhere in the world was there such a concerted effort to attain this goal, and nowhere was there the abundance of the raw talent needed to make it possible. But it was not yet even close to realization. They needed the breakthrough into biocybernetics that the Americans had seemingly made.

The Soviet scientists conceded that the SENTINEL computer could, in fact, exist and be capable of such power, and if such a computer could be built inside of Russia, the Soviet Union could rapidly surpass the SENTINEL potential. Bridges was again correct, but his reasons were wrong.

Kuradin was attentive and silent through the entire dissertation by Travkin, who related the entire story, from Bridges's first contact with Ross to his own meeting with the Central Committee. When he had finished, he handed Kuradin two thick bundles of files. This was all the information on the subject.

"Well, Alexi," Travkin said, "what do you think?"

"I will be in a better position to answer that after I have examined this information carefully. I will need one day," Kuradin said.

"The Central Committee conveyed one more opinion, which I have neglected to tell you," Travkin said. "They feel, after carefully reviewing the dossier, that Dr. Bridges is *not* essential to our program. We are interested in his information only, not him.

"The committee felt that he had expanded his own role and contributions to the program."

Kuradin's expression did not change. "That will certainly make my job much easier. But what if his information is in some personalized code or partially in his head?"

"In that case, we will need him, too," Travkin answered. "It will be up to you to make that decision when you meet him. You should plan for either eventuality."

Kuradin nodded his head in agreement.

"You should have everything here that you will need. I will contact you tomorrow evening at the same time. If you need anything additional, let me know at that time, and I will see that you get it. This is *top priority*. Everything is at your disposal."

Travkin rose, as if to leave, Kuradin rising with him.

"One more thing, Alexi." Travkin paused, so that Kuradin's attention would be on his next words. "Pay especially close attention to the file on the three code names we've obtained from England. Our facts on their activities bear out Dr. Bridges's claim of the existence of a secret intelligence agency. We have linked at least eight encounters to them. All, except one, were failures. The evidence weighs heavily in favor of its existence.

"The one mission that did not fail involved one of our very best agents. It nearly ended like the others. It was one year ago, in England."

He watched the eyes of Centaur.

Kuradin sat back down, staring intensely at the floor. He began to rub the stub that was once the little finger of his left hand. His mind was back in England. He again felt the impact as the bullet hit the steering wheel after going through the windshield. It deflected downward hitting him in the left thigh.

He recalled the paralyzing moments after the impact, when the hand would not function, and felt again the searing pain in his leg. It was only after he had gotten to safety that he was able to assess the extent of his wounds. The finger was gone, and the thigh only superficially wounded.

Kuradin was sweating now. He could feel the fear gripping his stomach, as it had when the door was kicked in and the courier was shot. He continued rubbing the finger.

"There was an Englishman…I thought later that maybe he was—"

"An American, Alexi," Travkin cut in. "An American, code-named Pilgrim, who shot at you and almost killed you that day."

There was a pensive, faraway look on Kuradin's face. "An American? *Pilgrim*."

"What are your thoughts concerning him?" Travkin asked.

Kuradin rose and walked to the window. He brushed aside the heavy curtain and looked out at the snow.

"I've thought about him often. I've asked myself a thousand times whether he could be better than me. How could he have known? He came *so close* to killing me…to beating me."

Kuradin turned to face Travkin. "He only fired at me once. He had another clear shot, but never took it. I kept waiting for the bullet to come crashing into me. It never came. I've wondered why." He turned back to the window and the snow.

"I could feel him. Two days before the final arrangements were made with the courier, I could feel him close to me. Every step I took away brought him one step closer. I could sense him just behind me. And then he was ahead of me, waiting.

"I thought that perhaps he had followed the courier. Perhaps he had, but I had sensed his presence long before. When he kicked in that door, I knew it was him, coming for me. I was lucky." He wiped the sweat away from his lip and forehead.

"The mission was a success, Alexi. *You* won the encounter, not Pilgrim," Travkin said.

"Did I? I wonder." His eyes gazed off. "Yes, I got the information. I got away safely, or at least alive. But I shouldn't have. He had me. I should have lost and died that day."

His hand ached, he rubbed it gently. Then a sudden nervous sensation flooded through him. He realized what Travkin was trying to tell him. He stared hard into Travkin's eyes.

Yes, the computer was American...and Pilgrim was American. It was possible. *An encounter.*

Kuradin nodded his head. "Don't worry, Leonid. I shall plan carefully to account for him and his computer...if it exists."

He would not lose a second time to Pilgrim. This victory would be clean and complete. There would be no failure in the rematch.

"I will see you tomorrow, Alexi. Sleep well, my friend," Travkin said as he left the room. He closed the door behind him.

As he walked down the stairs, he thought about how tired and frail his friend looked. He seemed so much older than he had a year ago. But he had always seemed small and weak. It was a wonder that he could bear the enormous weight of the responsibility thrust upon his shoulders. He knew that, beneath the frail body, was the strength of heart and courage of a great bear. He would win again, as always.

Kuradin stared at the door for several long moments after Travkin had left. He wondered whether Travkin knew that he was dying. His condition was terminal, maybe twelve months, eighteen at the most. He was so tired of this business. He only wanted to spend his last days with his daughter and grandchildren.

They should only know what their grandfather does for a living, he thought. His precious grandchildren.

But he loved his country, his mother Russia. He would do this one last thing for her, then spend his remaining time playing with his grandchildren, telling them stories about the old Russia and how it came to be the great country that it now was, and of all the wonderful things that the future would hold for them—the future that he was about to help make.

He picked up the stacks of information, a pad, and some pencils. The small room was equipped with everything he'd need.

He put the room into complete darkness except for a reading light over the bed. He fluffed up the pillows and settled himself comfortably against them. He picked up the first attached stack of papers. The cover sheet bore the single word: SENTINEL.

He would assume that it did exist, and that it was possessed of massive intelligence and flawless logic.

How do you beat a computer? he wondered.

He thought.

Logic was its strength. Logic, he thought.

Logic...and speed.

Yes, of course. Logic...*and speed,* its two greatest assets. They could also be the means by which to defeat it.

NINE

On 1 September, 1939, we attacked Poland. The cam-
paign lasted 37 days. Between 10 May and 25 June, 1940,
we utterly destroyed the Anglo-French military lineup in
the West. We occupied Holland, Belgium, Luxembourg,
and France.

To the world, we seemed invincible. But in reality
we had suffered critical losses. Almost 50,000 killed, over
110,000 wounded. Our Navy had taken savage losses dur-
ing the Norwegian campaign; our airborne forces were
nearly decimated in the successful action in the West; and
the Luftwaffe *had failed to win control of the skies over*
England.

The war went on, and it became evident that the
German army could not win in a war of attrition.

The solution lay in the East. On 22 June, 1941, we
invaded Russia.

Entry No. 18 from the partially
recovered *Wolf Journal*

The Learjet had put down on a private airfield, code named
Brighton, just outside of Huntington, about sixty miles north
of London. From there Justin and Fanning drove west, to where
Spartan had lived, just on the outskirts of Coventry.

They made a slow pass at the house, as Fanning quickly appraised the grounds. The house was completely dark, only fairly well isolated. Neighboring houses on either side were easily distinguishable, which meant that they would have to use blackout panels on the windows before they could conduct their search.

They continued about a half mile past the house, then stopped the car.

"SENTINEL Control, this is Badger," Fanning said.

BEEP!

The tone in his implant told him that SENTINEL Control was in contact.

"What do your sensor scans show?" he asked.

"Sensors indicate the property to be clear of personnel. Your drive by was observed by satellite. Sensors also show house to be still heated. Temperature in study area of house is seventy-two degrees Fahrenheit. The remainder of the house at sixty to sixty-four degrees."

"We'll be leaving the car here. Do you have our position?" asked Fanning.

"Yes," the soft voice replied.

"Keep the car under continuous sensor scan. We will be going in via the adjacent northside property.

"We are breaking verbal contact until internal scanning for electronic devices is completed."

"Understood."

They were on their own now, unless sensors picked up unusual readings. SENTINEL Control would break silence only for an emergency.

They made no noise as they crept slowly through the adjoining properties. Silence depended on slow progress.

Each man carried one large black canvas sack, containing various pieces of electronic apparatuses. They made one final scan of the property and set up automatic scanners at four points around the house. This would allow for continual surveillance of the entire property and alert them in the event that anyone should approach the house.

From the floor plan that had been supplied, they determined that the best point of entry would be through a back door that led directly to a large basement.

Scanner checks showed no intruder-detecting devices on the door. They went in.

Fifteen minutes later, they had established that there were no electronic devices installed in the house. They went to the study and put black felt panels, held firmly in place by adhesive strips, over the windows. When this was completed, they turned on the fluorescent desk lamp. From the outside, there would be no trace of light.

"That's not enough light, Ted. Turn on that overhead light," Justin said, pointing to the wall switch. The room flooded instantly with light. They looked around the large study with its huge wall library.

The attention of both of them was immediately drawn to the shattered door of the bathroom, just off the back corner of the room.

"That room may have a window," Fanning said, as he flicked off the overhead light. The room was again bathed in a dull light from the old fluorescent lamp. The door looked even worse in the dim glow.

Justin pushed the shattered bathroom door open. There was a small window with thick opaque glass. He put a felt blackout panel over it, then turned on the light.

The floor was covered with dried blood with a great many footprints smeared through it. An obviously sloppy attempt had been made to pick up some of the blood on the floor, probably when the body was taken away. It looked as if the room hadn't been touched otherwise since the killing.

The blood-splattered walls and toilet were pockmarked by the portions of the shotgun blasts that had missed Spartan. Neither man said a word.

They returned to the study.

"Well, where do we start?" asked Fanning.

"I guess in here. He was obviously in this room last," Justin said. He looked at the high library wall. "Jesus, it could be anywhere. All in one piece or in a hundred different pieces. Well, let's get started. It ain't getting done standing here."

Four hours later, they had gone through the room completely and found nothing. Justin had gone through every single book on the shelves, and Fanning had checked every square inch of the study. Nothing.

They had worked without interruption except for the quick alerts by the ground sensors. Twice, dogs had crossed the property. Body temperature and mass were immediately determined by satellite sensors, and the all clear signal given to resume work.

They had about an hour and a half left before the sun would begin to rise. They could work right through the next day, as long as no one approached the house. The ground sensors were well concealed, so they would not attract attention. The car would not attract attention, either, as it was parked well off the road. They just had to remove the blackout panels before the sun came up. In daylight, they could be seen.

Fanning sat behind the desk, Justin on a chair to the side of the desk. They were tired. They had gotten very little rest since leaving Chicago.

"Maybe there's some kind of a secret panel on this desk, somewhere," Fanning suggested.

They had been all through that desk earlier and found nothing but another dusty old fluorescent desk lamp that looked like it hadn't been used in years, and several small notebooks containing some notes on improvements made to the house and property.

Fanning looked across the top of the desk once more. It was typical, nothing unusual: the old desk lamp, desk pad, calendar, stapler, humidor, various stacks of bill receipts, a paperweight made of poured plexiglass containing about twenty-five shiny new American copper pennies. He shook his head and let out a disgusted sigh.

He opened the humidor and looked inside. "He won't be needing these anymore," he said, as he reached in and scooped out a fistful of cigars. "Want one?" he asked Justin.

"No. And you better not, either," Justin said as Fanning was about to unwrap one. "That thing will smell for days in here. If anyone shows up, they'll know someone's been here."

"Think I ought to put these back?" Fanning asked.

"Nah, I don't think that will make a difference. I'm surprised someone hasn't taken them already," Justin said.

"I think you were right, Justin," Fanning broke in. "I think the assassin killed him for the information and took it with him. There's not a trace of it, anywhere. Maybe he's the one who burned it in the fireplace. Maybe Billy didn't have a chance to translate it all and got wasted before he could finish it. One thing's certain," he concluded, "that journal is not in this room."

Justin nodded tiredly. "Well, let's get started on the rest of the house. It'll be daylight soon, and I want to get this job over with. This place gives me the creeps."

At his Paris apartment, Dmitri Chakhovsky sat quite still, with the paper bearing the decoded message from Starling in his lap. His breakfast lay untouched.

It was all gone now. Everything. The twenty-three years of service, the victories, the decorations, and the accolades. It was all down the tube now. In a matter of a few days, they would quietly come for him. He would be taken back to Russia like a common criminal.

He looked down at the message and read it once again.

"Illya Bodonov taken by Trushenko. Reason for arrest unknown. Sister taken as well. Kutz to interrogate. Will advise as more becomes known. Starling."

Chakhovsky knew why Bodonov had been taken. He knew Kutz and his methods. Bodonov would be broken and would confess to anything put before him. There was no chance of defense against the charges Trushenko would bring against him within the next few days. He must run.

He had planned very carefully for the worst of possibilities. And they could be no worse now. He was ready.

He called his consulate and talked to his secretary. He informed her that his trip to the south of France would start that morning. This would give him two days before he was discovered missing.

His rank bore him certain privileges, one of which was the ability to move about freely. He left his apartment and took official transportation to the train station. He boarded the train, secured his luggage and compartment, and waited for departure. When the train finally pulled away, Dmitri Chakhovsky was not on it.

He carefully made his way back through Paris over an elaborate route designed to make sure that he wasn't being followed. He was free, with at least two days of safe time in which to complete his plans for defecting to the West.

He carefully scanned the streets and windows as he walked. He could pick out KGB faces as if they were wearing a sign.

The late morning air was wet and cold. The rain had stopped only minutes ago. His breath hung before him in the cold air. He came to a phone booth and stepped inside. He didn't feel very well. There was an uncomfortable ache in his neck and a tightness in his chest.

The Russian picked up the phone and dialed a number. Tiny beads of sweat began to form on his face.

"Hello?" the other end of the phone crackled.

"Henri?" Chakhovsky asked.

"Yes, this is Henri. Who is this calling, please?" the voice asked.

"This is Joseph. I need your help now," Chakhovsky said, using the prearranged code name.

Henri's face flushed. He hadn't expected this call so soon. It was only two days ago that he had received his instructions from Joseph.

"Ah...ah...yes. What...ah, what can I do?" he stammered, his still-confused brain trying to recall the instructions. "Where are you? I will come right away," he said.

"No, Henri, you must not come to me," Chakhovsky said quickly. "You must take the letter that I gave you to the United States consulate. Do you have it?"

"Yes, I have it, my friend," Henri said.

"Good...good. You must take it there now. See that it gets to Robert Morsand. Only to him. Do you have the name?"

"Yes, Robert Morsand," Henri repeated.

"It must be given *only* to him," Chakhovsky instructed.

"Yes, my friend. I know exactly what to do. I will not fail you. I will leave at this very moment."

Chakhovsky was soaked with perspiration; beads of sweat rolled down his face. The air was getting heavy, hard to breathe in the little booth.

"Thank you, Henri. I shall never forget this," the Russian said.

The phone clicked dead.

Chakhovsky remained in the phone booth. He was sweating heavily now. A feeling of weakness was taking over his body. The pains had never been this severe before. He took out a small bottle and placed one of the tiny pills under his tongue.

The cold, wet morning was closing in on him, smothering him. His breathing was becoming labored and heavy. His neck ached badly and the tightness in his chest had grown severe. He couldn't breathe. He felt like he was being held under water, being drowned in that confining booth. He had to get out.

He pushed weakly on the doors. They wouldn't open. He was suffocating.

No air...got to get out...get out!

His mind began to panic. He pushed against the doors, but they seemed to be fighting back. He began ripping at them, struggling violently to get them open, to get out into the air. The booth was trying to kill him. Get out...get out...must breathe! He strained against the doors with all his might.

Then all at once he was out. He was on his knees gasping desperately for life-giving air. The breathing was painful, a sharp, bursting pressure filled his chest. His vision was unclear and seemed to close in, leaving a tiny hole of light at the end of a long dark tunnel. He put his head to the cold, wet ground and began to breathe with slow controlled breaths, as deeply as the pain would allow. The bottle of pills had fallen to the sidewalk, and some had rolled out. He numbly reached for one and placed it in his mouth.

It seemed like an eternity passed before the pain and suffocating tightness in his chest began to subside. The breaths came deeper and less painfully. The tunnel of vision had again begun to open. He felt drained of all strength. His head ached badly.

He finally lifted his head off the ground and straightened up on his knees. There were people standing around him. As he looked up, they just stared at him. He got to his feet, faltered a moment, then gained control. He began to walk away unsteadily, wet from the perspiration, his legs weak, unresponding. The cold air against his face felt good. Slowly, he began to feel better and to regain his control. He looked at his watch. He would have just enough time to make it to his next checkpoint.

He walked on. He would rest later.

Henri had left immediately, just as he said he would. He entered the American consulate on Avenue Gabriel at 11:25 a.m. and asked for Robert Morsand. He was told to take a seat and wait until Morsand could be found.

Finally, at 11:50, a man walked over to where Henri was waiting.

"I am Robert Morsand," he said in perfect French. "I understand that you wish to see me?"

Henri looked at the well-dressed American. He was a tall, handsome man in his early forties with black hair just starting to gray. It added a touch of sophistication to his appearance. His clothes were impeccably styled and pressed, his shoes shined to a glasslike finish.

"Yes, that is correct," Henri answered. "I have a letter from a friend of mine that is most urgent. It must be handed only to you and is intended for your eyes only."

Morsand took the envelope from Henri and eyed the small dark-haired man as his fingers opened it.

Henri began to back away as Morsand removed the letter from its envelope.

"Wait, don't go," Morsand said. "Your friend may need you to carry a message."

Morsand was an old hand at this. He knew trouble when he smelled it. That extra sense that comes with the business was at work.

He unfolded the paper and read:

Dear Mr. Morsand:

My name is Dmitri Chakhovsky. I am a member of the Soviet KGB in the Operational Division of the First Directorate of Counterespionage. Because of some recent developments in Soviet KGB policy and my open opposition to them, my life has fallen into grave danger. There is no hope of reconciliation with my superiors. I would like to make formal announcement to you of my intentions to defect to your Western nation.

Enclosed you will find a coin on the face of which is scratched a phone number. You may contact me at that number, at twelve noon on the day that you receive this letter.

You must call from a *safe* phone. The phones in your consulate are *not* to be considered safe.

I thank you, Mr. Morsand. My life is in your hands.

Dmitri Chakhovsky

Morsand looked at his watch. It was 12:00 on the button. He spun and tore down the hallway, leaving Henri in confusion. He left the consulate and raced up the street to a pay phone.

It was out of order.

"Goddamn it," he cursed and began racing up the block again.

He reached the next phone. Winded, he checked the number on the coin and dialed it. He looked at the time. It was 12:06.

The phone rang. It rang again. On the third ring, he was sure that he had blown it.

"Hello?" a tired voice finally answered.

"This is Morsand," he said, breathing heavily. "To whom do I speak?" Morsand was speaking in French.

"This is Chakhovsky. Dmitri Chakhovsky." The voice answered slowly, in accented English.

Morsand dropped into English. "When and where can we meet?"

Chakhovsky leaned heavily against the side of his phone booth. "I do not feel it is safe to meet at this time. Henri can be trusted completely. Is he still at the consulate?"

"Yes," Morsand replied. "I had him wait just in case it became necessary to hand-carry a message." He was beginning to catch his breath now.

"That was wise. But then I knew you would be. Give him a number at which you can be reached. Give him a time as well. It must be a phone that you consider safe. I will contact you.

"In the meantime, I am certain that you could use the time to have my identity confirmed. Be careful, we know much about what goes on in your consulate." Chakhovsky sounded ill.

"Are you all right?" Morsand asked.

There was a pause. Morsand could hear some heavy, irregular breaths in the phone.

Chakhovsky used his thumb and index finger to wipe away the tears in his eyes. "Yes, I am all right, just very tired, and… and…" He gathered himself. "You see, I love Russia. And it is not an easy thing…" His voice broke off.

Morsand could hear muffled sobs. "I understand. Believe me, I do," Morsand consoled.

"Do you? I wonder if you could ever realize what it is like to do what I am doing." He regained his composure. "I will contact you as you advise. Thank you, Mr. Morsand."

The phone went dead in Morsand's ear.

As he walked back to the consulate, he thought about what Chakhovsky had said about what he was feeling. He tried to imagine what it would be like if the roles were reversed. How would he feel? He couldn't imagine it. That was the difference between the two countries, he thought. That could never happen to him.

When he got back to the consulate he gave Henri specific instructions for Chakhovsky to follow. The little man noted them carefully, then left.

Morsand remembered what Chakhovsky had said about the consulate phones, about them knowing much of what went on there. He went to the special communications room that had the direct line to Washington. It was equipped with a scrambler. This room was definitely clean. It was checked daily.

He ordered a thorough examination of the entire building and every phone line.

He sent his scrambled voice to Washington, advising them of the contact and all that had transpired. Then he requested a dossier on Dmitri Chakhovsky. He would need to know all that he could about him before this day was over.

TEN

Russia, the great Bear to the East, was our one chance against the defeat that lay ahead. A quick victory there could stun our enemies in the West into negotiating for an end to the fighting, thus giving us the needed time to rebuild our fighting strength and reserves for the total realization of our destiny. The fate of the world would lie in our outcome in Russia.

It was a struggle of ideologies, of empire or annihilation, between two titans disputing their destinies. Only one could remain. Russia was to be utterly destroyed, as was Germany, if we lost.

Entry No. 19 from the partially
recovered *Wolf Journal*

Dr. Edward Bridges removed his tentlike overcoat and suit jacket in one lumbering effort and hung them from a hook on the wooden coatrack in the corner of his office. Then he closed his office door, so that his secretary would know not to disturb him.

He went to his desk and sat heavily on the soft chair. With great effort, he bent forward, his face reddening from the strain, and lifted his left pant leg. He removed the twelve sheets of blank paper from around his shin. He sat up, placed the papers on his desk, breathed deeply, and bent forward again. Seconds later, he produced another twelve sheets of blank report forms.

He had been carrying them both in and out of Alpha for days. The method was perfect, and he felt comfortable with it. It wouldn't be long now, almost any day. Then he'd be doing it for real, instead of for practice.

Bridges had begun spending considerable time with SENTINEL, going over Soviet computer capabilities. He had underestimated them somewhat. They were more advanced in some areas than he had given them credit for. They still didn't have systems comparable to this country's best BS (Before SENTINEL), but they were headed in the right direction and moving fast. He guessed that it might take fifteen years to reach that biocybernetic breakthrough that had enabled SENTINEL to become a reality. By then, SENTINEL would be uncatchable.

The two countries had always been engaged in a bitter and desperate race to somewhere. The United States had always managed to stay ahead, by virtue of its significantly more advanced technology. That had been the difference in their making the breakthrough first—that, together with the intelligence of Dr. Elizabeth Ryerson. The Soviets did not have an Elizabeth Ryerson, just as they had not had an Albert Einstein. Yet their potential was far greater, because of the nature of their system. They could actively find and cut budding talent from the pack and direct it in the paths of training and development suited to their needs.

Bridges's musings were interrupted by the sudden ring of his phone. One morning soon that phone would ring, and he wouldn't be there to answer it, he thought to himself.

He picked up the receiver. "Bridges," he said.

"Morning, Ed. This is Elizabeth. Do you have a few minutes?" the voice of Dr. Elizabeth Ryerson rasped out.

"You sound terrible!" Bridges hardly recognized her voice.

"Yes, I know. I'm coming down with a case of laryngitis," she said. "Do you think you could come down to my office for a few minutes? I want to go over that UFF sixteen-point-oh-oh-nineteen underwater sensor system that Warren is working on."

"Sure, Beth."

"Good. We'll need to have a meeting with the department heads on the final designs for this thing pretty soon. We have to know what the changeover is going to cost us. How's the system look?"

"I tell ya, Beth, we're getting better results than we hoped for. We still have to make some adjustments in the sensor screens. They're not one hundred percent yet. When it's finished, it should be impossible to detect, even while it's cranking at one-hundred-percent output. It's a great system," Bridges said with enthusiasm. The Russians will think so, too, he thought.

"That sounds good, Ed. Why don't you and Warren come down to my office in about fifteen minutes. If he thinks he can have all of his reports finished by next Monday, then we'll have the meeting then. Sound okay?" she asked.

"Sure thing. I'll call Warren right now. See you in about fifteen minutes."

"Good. Thank you, Ed."

"You're welcome, Beth." You computerized bitch, he thought to himself as the phone clicked down on the other end. "What that broad needs is a good screw to make her human again," he muttered.

He buzzed his secretary on the intercom.

"Yes, Dr. Bridges," she said.

"Pat, would you tell Dr. Geisler to come into my office, please? And tell him to bring whatever he has on the UFF sixteen-point-oh-oh-nineteen tests," he said.

"Yes, sir."

He walked to his door and opened it. Another busy Monday had begun.

Robert Morsand sat at his desk leafing through the dossier on Dmitri Chakhovsky. He was duly impressed with what he read.

He studied the photographs. They showed a smallish man with nearly white hair, specked with strands of its former black. The hair was full and thick, combed back, almost in an American fifties style. The facial features were long and narrow, the nose large for the face and distinctly hooked at the bridge. The eyes were small and close together, deep-set and intense. The mouth was unsmiling, thin lips drawn tightly across the face. None of the pictures showed a smile.

Morsand looked at some of the details of the dossier more closely.

AGE: 45

HEIGHT: 5' 7"

WEIGHT: 130 LBS.

WIDOWER: WIFE, TAMARA, DIED 1966, CANCER. ONE SON, BORIS. KILLED 1976 IN SKIRMISH ALONG SINO-SOVIET BORDER.

HISTORICAL BACKGROUND: BECAME MEMBER OF KGB, 1954; PRIOR DISTRICT LEADER KOMSOMOL IN UKRAINE; TRAINED AT KARLSHORST, 1954–55; KOCHINO, 1955–57; ASSIGNED WESTERN EUROPEAN INTELLIGENCE DIVISION, 1957; GREATLY IMPRESSED HIS SUPERIORS, WAS RECALLED MOSCOW, 1959, FOR ADVANCED, INTENSIFIED OPERATIONS PLANNING. 1961, APPEARS AS MEMBER FIRST DIRECTORATE OPERATIONAL DIVISION; BELIEVED TO BE CREATOR OF DIVISION D; MASTERMIND OF KGB. REORGANIZATION WESTERN EUROPE, 1967–70; 1971 TO PRESENT, HAS BEEN OBSERVED THROUGHOUT WESTERN EUROPE IN VARIOUS EMBASSY POSITIONS. BELIEVED TO BE FIFTH HIGHEST RANKING INDIVIDUAL IN OPERATIONAL DIVISION OF THE FIRST DIRECTORATE, WATCHDOGGING THE WESTERN EUROPEAN OPERATIONS, WHICH HE ESTABLISHED.

Morsand read the psychological profile. The man was a rock. Why would they want to kill him? What in the hell could he have done, he wondered.

He packed the information into an attaché case and left the office for the home of his good friend, Maurice Picou. There, he would enjoy an outstanding dinner, a satisfying pipe, and some exceptional wine. At 9:30 p.m., Dmitri Chakhovsky would call him there.

Later that evening, Morsand was sitting alone by the phone, smoking his pipe and thinking about Chakhovsky's call. He thought about how, in the movies, the phone always rang at the right time or the nearest clock always seemed to be in sync with the timing device on the bomb. Everyone would watch with baited breath as the seconds ticked off, the hero working frantically to defuse the device. Ten, nine, eight—which wire do I cut? Seven, six, five—the red or the blue? Four, three, two—snip. Saved the day.

What if the clock were wrong? BOOM!

BRRRING!

The phone startled the hell out of him. He looked at his watch. 9:27. Not even close. No cigar.

BRRRING!

He picked it up. "Hello, Morsand here," he said.

"Hello, this is Dmitri Chakhovsky." The voice sounded much better than it had the first time they spoke.

"Is it safe to meet yet?" Morsand asked.

"No, not yet. I am quite safe where I am now. I doubt they have begun looking for me yet. I would guess they will realize that I am missing by tomorrow at this time. Possibly, the next morning, if luck is with me," Chakhovsky said.

"They already know you're missing," Morsand said. "And they're looking hard."

Chakhovsky was stunned. He had moved just in time. Even a day's delay would have meant the end.

"We'll want you in one of our safe houses as soon as possible, so that we can protect you until it's safe to make our move," Morsand told him. "It's a little different when you're being hunted by kill teams. We'll have to find out as much as we can about how much they know before we make the try. Maybe by Thursday or Friday, if things go well," he said.

"Four days! That is a long time," Chakhovsky said.

"It is. But every second of it is important. One mistake, and you'll be a dead man. Trust me when I say that we know what we're doing. We get more practice at this sort of thing than you do," Morsand said.

"I want you to call me at this number again at the same time tomorrow. Then we'll get you into that safe house. They won't get near you there."

"Yes, I will call tomorrow at the same time," Chakhovsky said. "Thank you...thank you." The phone went dead.

Morsand had established the upper hand quickly. Chakhovsky would do as he was told now. Defection is a rough business. The guys losing the goods play mean and play for keeps. More than one attempt had gone bad in the past, and Chakhovsky's complete cooperation was required.

Morsand was going to be careful on this one. CIA Director Shyleur Platt had made it clear that it was his job to get it done. And he was going to do just that.

Under cover of darkness, Justin and Fanning carefully scanned the grounds one more time. Then they slid off into the night, as slowly and quietly as they had come. They left the ground sensors carefully concealed, as per SENTINEL Control's instructions.

They had been in the house for twenty-four hours. Every room was painstakingly searched and left as it had been found. They had not found a trace of the journal. Justin was convinced that the assassin had taken it with him after killing Spartan.

They drove to Brighton Field and took off for Chicago, giving complete verbal reports to SENTINEL Control as they flew back. Their final conclusion was that the journal was not in the house. By late Tuesday afternoon, they were on their separate ways home.

Irwin Honeycut sat behind his large, plush desk, poring over the pages of the report that Pilgrim and Badger had turned in. He didn't like it.

The information was in that house, and he knew it. If only Scotland Yard weren't involved, he thought. Then he could get a whole Division Two team in there. They'd find it. It had to be there. There were no two ways about it—they had just missed it. Twice.

Division Two had confirmed that the original journal had been burned, from the analysis of the ashes found in the fireplace. They were also sure that Spartan had translated it. The ashes yielded proof of this. But where did he put it, and how long before he was killed did he have to hide it?

Honeycut knew more about the information than he had told the President or Pilgrim and Badger. He knew that it *had* to be found. It was a dangerous document that had to be recovered and analyzed by SENTINEL. It was important to learn exactly what it said and what had to be done about it. A lot was at stake, possibly the safety of millions and millions of people. It was Honeycut's intent, as well as SENTINEL's, to keep those people safe and to protect the security of the country, which ultimately ensured the security of the world. In the wrong hands, that information could put the world on a path toward an incredible power struggle, one that would lay waste to continents and slaughter millions of innocent and helpless people. That had to be avoided.

SENTINEL would maintain constant surveillance of the house. A Division Two team would be held in readiness, until it was safe to get them in without Scotland Yard interference.

Getting Pilgrim and Badger in was one thing. Getting an entire Division Two team and all of its equipment in was another. And Honeycut didn't want to risk getting British Intelligence into the matter. What they didn't need was MI5 snooping around and finding that journal first.

With what they now knew from the initial results of the analysis of the ashes found in the fireplace and the report filed by Pilgrim and Badger, Division Two could get in there again and do the place over right. It would take only a day, but until it was safe to get them in again, it would be a waiting game. As long as no one else got in there and found it first, Honeycut was content to give it the time it needed. He wasn't happy about it, but he accepted it.

Leonid Travkin paced to the window of the small room and looked out, not really seeing the deep, frozen snow that lined the streets below. He pursed his lips and shook his head. He had just listened to Alexi Kuradin quickly run through his plan. It disturbed him. It was not a good plan at all. He had expected more from him.

The evening before, he had brought Kuradin stacks of files that he had specially requested. There were numerous dossiers of sleeper agents within the United States, never before used, just waiting for the word to become active agents all across the country. There were files on assassins past their best and known to American Intelligence. There were schematics and descriptions of the most advanced cybernetic systems in the Soviet Union— and one very special dossier, of an agent who fit the highly specific requirements outlined by Centaur.

Travkin turned away from the window and slowly walked back to the table in the center of the room, his eyes looking downward.

"The plan is not...not..." He was searching for words, for a way to tell him. "...not exactly what I would expect from you, Alexi. I have serious doubts—"

"Good, very good. That is precisely the reaction I was hoping for," Kuradin interrupted. A wry smile crossed his face. "Now, let me explain it a little further. Let me give you the thinking behind the plan."

Travkin sat. He would listen. If the explanation did not satisfy him, he would remove Kuradin from the mission. He hoped that it would not be necessary. Kuradin's record had been absolutely brilliant to that point, one-hundred-percent success. "I was hoping that you had more to tell me, Alexi," Travkin said. He looked up and waited.

"First, you must understand that this can be no ordinary plan. Our adversary is a much more superior intellect than we have ever faced before. We must not engage in a chess game with it. We cannot hope to beat it if we do. It can out*think* us at every turn. It is a biocybernetic intellect beyond anything we can imagine, with a spectacular array of powers at its disposal and a secret force of agents who follow its direction with startling efficiency." He began to pace around Travkin.

"Its strengths are flawless logic and speed. It will race through its alternatives faster than our comprehension will permit us to accept. Yet, it has weaknesses." Kuradin stared at him, as though waiting for a response.

Travkin looked blankly at him. He couldn't think of a single weakness. He shrugged his shoulders in a helpless gesture.

Kuradin raised an index finger upward. "Its weaknesses are..." He paused for effect. "...*logic* and *speed*," he said, the sly smile returning.

Travkin's eyes narrowed in anticipation.

"It is built on a basis of logic; its function depends upon it. It will list all of the possible alternatives that it faces as the facts are made known to it. It will then choose the most appropriate one. This is where our advantage lies. We know what our first move will be, it does not. We, too, can determine the alternatives that we will face—but always one step ahead. And it is here that we will defeat it. We will let it run ahead of itself…and us. We walk when logic dictates run and turn left when right is the way to go. We choose the least logical alternative, while *it* selects the most. We beat it by keeping it off balance and going through the back door, when the front is the only way out."

Yes, this was the Alexi he knew. Travkin began to feel much easier. Kuradin reviewed the plan again from the beginning, explaining the alternatives that would be available to them and the underlying possibilities for success that existed. If one failed, the next came into play. Every loss was turned into a gain. All that was essential was that Kuradin remain alive. And to help assure that, he employed the assistance of a man of very special talents—Otto Ten Braak, the one-time ultimate assassin.

"But, why have you chosen Ten Braak?" Travkin asked. "He is past his prime. The Americans know him too well. Certainly, using him will only make it easier for them to find you," he said.

"That is precisely the point," Kuradin shot back quickly. "And we will help them do just that. But we will lead them to Ten Braak, not Centaur. They will flock to him, Pilgrim and the others. And they will find him most difficult," Kuradin said.

Otto Ten Braak was a skilled assassin, second to none in his deadly arts. Without the element of surprise, he could not be taken. True, he was past his best and too well known. He was not as artful as the younger generation of specialists now employed by the Soviets, but he was still more deadly than any man alive. His methods were his own and very effective.

Kuradin admired excellence of any kind, and Ten Braak had once been the best. That should earn him a place of honor, not a "retirement" at the hands of a new operative, sent to take him from a roof top, or in an elevator, or while in a shower. That left a man of his honor nothing. A man should always be left something. Only a mission of such importance was fitting, one he would probably never survive, but one that would be vital to the success of the plan. It was the ultimate mission, leaving him the hero he deserved to be.

It was clear to Travkin now. Ten Braak was to take on Pilgrim.

The two men were very much alike in many ways, each deadly and efficient. Ten Braak was an instrument of death like no other in the world—every inch of him, every instinct, deadly and skilled in the art of delivering destruction. It would be a confrontation of one deadly intellect versus another. But, if handled properly, the advantage would belong to Ten Braak.

Kuradin explained the role that Travkin would play from Moscow. Timing was critical to the plan. Certain bits of information had to be leaked at precisely the right moments. Even if the plan went to the last alternative, it could be successful. That's when the information contained in the file that Kuradin had so carefully outlined would come into play. At that point, only Moscow could carry success.

Travkin was taken aback as Kuradin explained the final contingency. The fact that Centaur was a dying man would work in their favor. Travkin was distressed by the knowledge that his friend was dying.

"I did not know, Alexi. I would have never asked—"

"Nonsense," Kuradin interrupted, "I will die regardless."

"But your family. Surely you wish to spend every possible moment with them. Your daughter, the grandchildren, I know how you love them. Alexi, my friend, I can get another agent to take the assignment. A new plan can be made—"

Kuradin silenced him by raising his hand. "Leonid, only I can make this plan work. And it is for my family that I do this. I do not, for one minute, believe that the Americans would not use this computer against us aggressively. When the moment is right, they will act. I cannot let my loved ones face a future of destruction at the hands of an unbeatable enemy. We must have that computer, too, to maintain the balance of power.

"You know, and I know, that detente is a word that will last only as long as the balance of power exists. As soon as one power has the capability to destroy the other, swiftly, neatly, and with minimum retaliation and devastation, it will cease to be a part of our vocabulary. We are fortunate that the Americans believe in it more than we do, or it would already be too late. It's a terrible thought, but if that computer were ours right now, and the Americans did not have it, America would already be a wasteland of corpses. Detente has been only a means to buy us time to find the ultimate weapon of destruction that would not devastate the rest of the world. It's true, Leonid. You know it is. The only way to peace is to keep both sides capable of a mutual horror."

Travkin said nothing. His friend was naïve and idealistic. Yes, the balance of power was the only workable plan to peace. The mutual threat of destruction generated enough fear to keep the fingers from pressing the buttons, but it would never be the final answer. Man is only an animal. He follows his instincts and nature just as the lower animals do, but in a more complex and ordered way. In nature, the strong supplant the weak. Every society in nature is ruled by the strong. It is determined who is the stronger by confrontation. This computer would only be the first. Man would race against man to develop the next one, each more capable than the last, until he was finally convinced that he was the stronger and could not lose. Then it would happen, as the wars of the past had happened, the confrontation for power would take place. And there would be winners and losers, with only the dead finding lasting peace.

"Besides," Kuradin broke in, cutting Travkin's train of thought, "I have purely selfish motives, as well," he said with a smile. "My ego demands the ultimate challenge and victory. After all, am I not stealing the world's greatest secret? I will be remembered as Russia's greatest spy," he laughed.

Travkin laughed, but he knew better. This man, who had been content to let his exploits and accomplishments remain anonymous for so long, did not possess the ego that he alluded to. He was already Russia's greatest spy. It wasn't important that the world know it; it was only important that Alexi Kuradin know it. And one unanswered question remained in Centaur's mind. Was Pilgrim better than he was? This was the issue that his ego demanded be resolved.

"Well, Leonid. What do you think of the plan now?" Kuradin asked.

It was brilliant. Travkin had not been disappointed, after all. Only Centaur could have thought of it—so simple, almost too simple to work, yet, it should not fail. Travkin rose and faced his friend. "It has my approval. When will it start?" he asked.

"It already has," he answered. "When you leave here today, we shall not see one another again until it has succeeded."

And if it fails, we shall never see one another again, Travkin finished in his mind.

The two looked at each other for several long moments, then embraced warmly. They bid each other farewell, and Travkin left. As he walked down the steps to the snow-lined streets below, he thought about the gentle, little man upstairs. He hoped he had not seen his friend for the last time.

ELEVEN

All the lessons of our previous campaigns were applied toward ultimate victory in Russia. The Luftwaffe *coordination and support was superb.*

By December we were at the gates of Moscow, having annihilated over two-thirds of the estimated Red Army strength.

Entry No. 20 from the partially
recovered *Wolf Journal*

The nightmare had awakened Justin. He felt strangely bothered as the details of that dream turned over and over in his head. What could it all mean? he wondered.

In it, Spartan was in the study, sitting at his desk. The other man—the stalker—came into the house without a sound. Spartan sensed his presence, but did not make any attempt to secure a weapon. Instead, he climbed up on top of the desk. The desk was important. It had to be protected. The intruder entered the room with a shotgun. Spartan did not look at him. He just sat on the desk, waiting. The intruder fired, knocking Spartan off the desk. Then the intruder climbed up on top of the desk and began a vigil. But what was he waiting for? Justin wondered.

Then, suddenly, Justin and Fanning were there. They were searching the study. The intruder was watching them, but he could not be seen.

Then Justin was alone in the study. Fanning was somewhere else in the house. Suddenly, it dawned on Justin that the desk was the key. Something about it told him that. He climbed up on top of it, just as Spartan had done. He sat and waited. He didn't know what he was waiting for, but he waited.

The intruder appeared. The shotgun was pointed at Justin.

Where was Fanning? Justin needed help. Where was he?

The muzzle of the gun was smoking. Then Justin knew that Fanning must be dead. The intruder had already gotten him.

The gun discharged. Justin could feel himself being knocked off the desk by the blast, although there was no realization of pain.

The intruder made sure of his work, then climbed back up on the desk and resumed his vigil.

Then Justin had awakened.

The stalker. The thought of him stirred anxiety in Justin. He was out there. He could be coming at any moment. From the darkness.

My gun! Where is my gun? Justin's mind raced.

Every night-sound became *him*. *He* gave away nothing. *He* took you when you were vulnerable.

Where is my gun?

There is an inherent paranoia that goes with the profession. A man couldn't survive in this business without it. But, if he let it, it would take over completely. Then he wasn't worth a damn anymore. It was starting in Justin.

It was time to get out, before the profession swallowed him whole. It did that to men, becoming all that they knew and had. Then it killed them. He didn't want to become one of its casualties. He used to know why he did this for a living and what the things were that he believed in, that let him justify taking a life so easily. It had become so easy; he had become so unfeeling. There was never any guilt.

He had gotten his baptism of fire on his second mission. He had hesitated, breaking the first rule he had been taught, that to hesitate was to die. The escape was a narrow one.

These men had tried to kill him. After his recovery from the initial hesitation, his actions became swift and natural. There was no thought in his mind but to react. There were no moralistic rationalizations, no quarrels of conscience, just automatic response. There was no time to think about the first man he had killed. Before his brain had slowed down, there were five more.

He never counted them or remembered their faces after that. And he never hesitated again. And something in him was never the same—he had enjoyed it.

Barbara rolled over and nestled her back into his arms. He looked at her asleep beside him. She was beautiful when she slept. And she felt warm next to him. God, but she felt good. Smelled nice, too.

He toyed with the thought of waking her. He wanted to make love to her. He was sneaky that way. They had some of their greatest lovemaking in the middle of the night like this, everything twilight, clouded and soft—and warm.

He ran his hand gently up her stomach to her breasts. She had lovely breasts. He affectionately called her "Jugs" when they were alone. His fingertips tenderly traced her nipples. What heaven. He let his face linger in her hair.

His hand went softly down her side and glided over her hips, coming to rest on her behind. He began gently tracing her ass, moving slowly to her inner thighs, to the softness and the warmth of her.

She stirred ever so slightly.

He felt her tenderly, tracing the bulges and valleys.

She stirred again.

He began the gentle tracings through the soft hair, into her mounting wetness. He kissed her ear softly.

She stirred.

He began gentle kisses on her neck, his fingers probing delicately, more deeply into the wetness.

"It's about time, you animal," she purred. "I'll give you just one hour to stop that," she said, turning to him.

They kissed tenderly. She was ready. Vulnerable. Vulnerable! The stalker took you when you were vulnerable! Where is the gun?

Barbara's body became like fire against his, as the kisses picked up in tempo, grew deeper and more urgent.

The gun! About four steps away. How long in seconds to get to it?

He kissed down her neck to her breasts, his lips and tongue softly caressing her nipples, his hand tracing, probing softly, deeper.

She was making soft, sighing sounds. Heat rushed through her body. Her face and lips were burning with the passion.

Justin went lower, kissing her stomach.

The sighs increased into more passionate moanings.

He kissed her hips, her thighs, making well-placed tracings with his tongue.

She was nearing the edge.

Not yet!

About four steps away. Loaded, one in the chamber. Remember the safety!

"Now, Justin. I want you now," she whispered.

He continued kissing. He knew her body and her limits. There was a difference between "now" and "*NOW!*"

He kissed into the warmth.

Her moans increased sharply. She was on fire. "Now, Justin. Please? Now." Her breathing was deep, wild.

He kissed on, deeper.

The gun...is about four steps...

"Oh, God...that's...that's nice. Hmm...mmm...Justin. Now, baby. Oh, please, honey." She squirmed and moaned. This was the very edge.

"Now...oh...oh, NOW. Justin, I want you...*NOW!*"

He rose quickly to take her at her peak.

The gun…the gun is…is…screw the gun!

The stalker was no longer there.

Irwin Honeycut waited as the President's direct line to the SENTINEL complex rang. On the second ring, it was answered.

"This is the President speaking," the deep, resonant voice said.

"Hello, Mr. President. This is Irv, again. I've got more for you on the Spartan situation. I've got an important matter that's related to this to talk to you about, too," Honeycut's graveled voice rasped out.

"Okay. What have you got, Irv?"

"We've definitely confirmed that it was the Soviets, just minutes ago. Division Two has nailed it down. We've even got the identity of the assassin," Honeycut said proudly.

"That's truly amazing. I thought that the last time we spoke, you said Division Two had little or nothing to go on? How did they learn so much so suddenly?" the President asked.

"It's actually quite simple, Mr. President. Nobody, but nobody, can go into a room and spend even a short time in it without leaving some traces of his being there. A good crime-scene investigation team looks for these signs, or clues, and puts the facts together. Division Two is not just a good crime-scene investigation team, they're the best in the world. After going through all of the evidence, they realized that they had more than they figured on. They were able to get a positive ID on the assassin, and he works solely for the Soviets. No free-lance work for this operative. And, as careful as he was, our caller left enough for them to go on.

"In any event, we know who he is and have a reported location on him. After this is verified, a team will be dispatched to return the sentiment in an equal style," Honeycut reported.

"Good," the President said. "And Pilgrim and Badger? They're safe?"

"Yes, Mr. President. They returned yesterday from England," Honeycut said.

"Did they find the information?" he asked.

"No, sir, they didn't. But we're still convinced that it's in the house. They searched every inch of that house thoroughly, but came up empty. We're going to have to risk sending a Division Two team in there again," Honeycut said.

"But we've already had a Division Two team in there. And they found nothing," the President said.

"That's right, sir, but they were under a severe time restriction, due to Scotland Yard's involvement. And they were there more to ascertain what had happened and who had done it than to look for the information. We knew next to nothing about the information at that time, and we couldn't risk spending any more time in the house. We absolutely must avoid getting British Intelligence involved in this. M15 would mess things up badly if they came into it now."

"How much have you managed to learn about the information to this point?" the President asked.

"Well, Mr. President, we know a lot more now than we did when we last spoke. We know that it was a journal, handwritten in German, approximately ninety to a hundred pages long. We know that Spartan had been working on a translation of it during the period when we lost his transmissions. We are fairly confident that he completed his translation and managed to hide it before being killed. We've learned most of this from analyzing ashes taken from the fireplace. There's a lot more to analyze on this yet, before SENTINEL comes up with something more definite," Honeycut explained.

Nothing that SENTINEL could do surprised the President anymore. Ashes, especially large unbroken portions, could be analyzed and read almost as well as the original. SENTINEL could examine even smaller segments of ash and probably piece together more extensive portions of the original text than dreamed possible. It would simply go at the tiny specs of evidence like a jigsaw puzzle, patiently piecing them all together, or a fair portion of them at any rate. Probably enough to give an idea of the journal's contents and significance.

"Well, that's real fine, Irv. What about our 'fifth man'? What have we got on that?"

"It's been narrowed down to two. We think we know which is our man, but we need more data to back up our hunch," Honeycut answered.

"We must be absolutely certain before taking action, Irv. There can be no doubt whatsoever in this. Do you think you can nail him down and be one-hundred-percent positive?"

"Nothing is one hundred percent, Mr. President. But I think I know a way to get us as close as possible. Have you been briefed on the attempted defection of a Russian named Dmitri Chakhovsky?" Honeycut asked the President.

"Yes, I have, just this morning by Shyleur Platt. He says he's a pretty big fish, too. He expects all hell to break loose once we get him out of Paris and into our protective custody. You know, the usual 'disinformation tactics,' the cleverly discrete leak that he is actually a Soviet plant, intended to fill us full of misleading and false information. It's their usual act when we get one of their big ones. Platt is convinced that he is real, though. What are your thoughts?" the President asked.

"Oh, he's real, all right. You can bet the Washington Monument on that. In fact, he's the man who invented 'disinformation' and restructured the entire Western European intelligence network. I think he can confirm, beyond the shadow of a doubt, who our 'fifth man' is.

"I'd like your okay to take him," he said to the President.

There was a long moment of silence before the President responded.

"Platt has advised me that the CIA is pretty well along in a plan to get him out. We'll have him in a few days if things work out for us, and we can get that information from him then. I think it would be a better idea if your people just played a backup role to assure the success of the CIA plan. Do you agree?" The President waited for Honeycut's answer. He didn't wait long.

"No, sir. The CIA can't get him. It mustn't happen," Honeycut said.

"What do you mean by, 'mustn't happen'?" the President asked.

"I mean, sir, that we can't allow it to happen." Honeycut's voice was firm and steady.

"And why not?" It was a voice responding to challenge.

"Because we don't know exactly how much the Soviets know about Spartan, Pilgrim, and Badger. We don't know whether they suspect or know anything about SENTINEL. They sure as hell know *something* about the agency. And I believe that, what they know about it, Chakhovsky knows about it. Spartan was killed in England. All of Pilgrim's and Badger's activities have been in Western Europe. It's academic. If he knows, and I think that he does, then we can't allow him to tell the CIA *what* he knows," Honeycut summed up.

Jesus Christ, he's right, thought the President. If Shyleur Platt and the CIA find out about SENTINEL and the agency, it will turn into a real witchhunt that will endanger the security of the whole program. That would take away SENTINEL's biggest advantage— its secrecy. That had never occurred to him. "Well, now I know how you earn your pay, Irv. As usual, your judgment cannot be refuted. But how are you going to do it? The CIA is pretty well advanced in this plan. They've got him in a safe house that *nobody* can get near if they don't want them to. It's not going to be easy."

"There will be a blizzard in Death Valley before the day comes when we can't handle the CIA, Mr. President. It's the Russians that I'm worried about. They outsmart the CIA on a regular basis. We don't know how much they know about this situation, other than that they're hunting for him now.

"The CIA has a pretty good man heading up the job in Robert Morsand. He's good, real good. I wish we had him with us. But, fortunately, he's surrounded by a bunch of dummies. He's had good success with getting defectors out, but, when it comes to the real big fish, his average drops off. It's not his fault, it's his lack of backup."

"Do you have enough operatives in France to pull it off?" the President asked.

"We're going to have to minimize our potential losses again. I plan on sending Pilgrim and Badger in to get him. It works out well for us, too, because they're two of our very best, and we optimize our chances with them. If they fail, at least the Russians won't learn any more than they know already. And nobody will stand a better chance of pulling it off than they will."

"Well, there's good sense to that. You have my official go ahead, Irv. Bring him home," the President said.

"There is just one more thing, Mr. President. My boys are going to want to know how to treat the CIA. I intend to tell them to consider them and the KGB as equal adversaries, with equal regard. That means that, if they have to, they'll kill," Honeycut said.

The President was silent. "But they're Americans, Irv," he said after the pause. "I won't have Americans killing Americans."

"Only as a last resort, Mr. President. They don't want to kill their own countrymen, either, unless it means staying alive. They must have that freedom of operation, sir," Honeycut insisted.

"You're right, but I don't like it. *Only* as a last resort."

"Yes, Mr. President, only as a last resort. They will also have instructions to stop Chakhovsky if it looks like the CIA might get him. They will not permit it. If the Russians get him it doesn't hurt us one bit. But the CIA must not get him."

"Okay, Irv. It's your show. Keep me posted at first news. I want to know the minute you hear," the President said.

"I'll do that, Mr. President. And don't worry, we'll try to handle them with kid gloves if we can."

"Yes, thank you, Irv. I'll hear from you, then."

"Good-bye, Mr. President." The phone went dead in his ear. He placed his phone down and pushed the white call button on his SENTINEL console.

"Yes, Mr. Honeycut," the soft voice responded.

"Call in Pilgrim and Badger. We have another job for them."

TWELVE

Despite our tremendous advances and crushing victories, Russia itself, the immensity of it, began to defeat us. The deeper we pushed, the further apart our three main armies were dispersed. The entire plan began to bend out of focus.

Our equipment suffered from the huge distances covered. The men grew fatigued. The Luftwaffe had more and more difficulty in giving support over such a vast terrain. There were no roads; everything turned to mud under the weight of our tanks as the fall rains came. There were no preestablished lines where our advance was to stop. There were no naturally defensible features along the line of our advance at which to make a stand. And there was great indecision and confusion in the High Command.

And, from the vastness, three more things rushed forth to hurl themselves at us: more Russian reserves than we thought possible; the Russian T-34 tank, which proved to be superior to our own; and, worse by far than all the rest, the cold of Russian winter.

Entry No. 21 from the partially
recovered *Wolf Journal*

It was Wednesday morning, the beginning of a beautiful April day. Justin's Impala turned onto Susan's block. He had come to see his son.

He stopped in front of the house and sat looking at it for a while. It had been their house before the divorce, before Jack.

He was only a visitor now. It stung inside.

It always hurt him to come here. Everything was filled with memories that had been happy once. But, no matter how good the memories started out, they always ended with the image of Susan, her legs spread around that stiff-pricked dentist, her tits hanging out and bouncing as she grasped frantically at Jack's ass, helping him to enter her deeper on each thrust, the sounds of her passion, and the catlike smile on her face.

He had suspected it—that hurt; to know that it was true was crushing; but to watch it was devastating—the ultimate betrayal. Nothing had ever hurt so much for so long.

He reached the front door and rang the bell. He waited, trying to get the dark emotions to subside. A few moments passed, and he rang the bell again. He could hear it ring inside. He began to think that no one was home when his ears caught the sound of the chain latch being slipped off. The door opened.

Susan was in her bathrobe, her long blond hair dripping wet, her skin covered with beads of water. She had been in the shower.

"Hi," he said.

She said nothing. Her eyes were cold, her expression hard. A few drips rolled down her chest and ran between her breasts.

"I'm sorry, I didn't mean to pull you out of the shower. Can I come in?"

She remained silent and backed up a step, her "yes" to his question.

Justin knew that look. She was pissed off about something.

"Is Michael home?" he asked.

She stared at him icily. "No, my mother has taken him for the morning. Then she'll take him right to school. He won't be home until three thirty."

She closed the door behind Justin.

"I forgot that he goes to school on Wednesdays," Justin said.

"You forget a lot of things," she said flatly.

Justin gave a puzzled squint. "What does that mean?" he asked.

"Where were you on Sunday?" she asked. "Did you *forget* about Sunday again?"

He was silent for a moment. "No, I didn't forget. I was on a job that got stretched over from Saturday. I didn't know that I'd be tied up or I wouldn't have made plans to take him," he said.

"Too tied up to get to a phone?" she quizzed bitingly.

He'd had no way of knowing when he had been called to Chicago that he'd be spending all of Sunday and Monday out of the country. Once he entered that office with Fanning, there was no way he could break communications silence until the mission was completed. That was standard procedure with the agency.

"I just couldn't," he said, shaking his head.

"Bullshit!" she yelled. "You can't tell me that you were too busy to call your son to tell him that you weren't coming." She was starting to wind up. This was going to be a good one.

"I couldn't get to a phone, Susan—"

"Don't hand me that crock of shit, all right? I've heard it too many times."

"It's no crock. I absolutely couldn't get away," he insisted.

"It's Wednesday, Justin. I suppose you were all tied up until now?" she asked sarcastically.

"I didn't get back until late last night. It was too late to call. I came over first thing this morning. I didn't forget, Susan."

She shook her head with a look that could kill.

"Look, Susan, you don't understand—"

"No, Justin, you look," she interrupted. "It's not me who doesn't understand. It's your son who doesn't understand that you mean *maybe* when you say that you're coming over to take him someplace. He's only four years old. It was Sunday. You were supposed to be here. It was all he talked about all week." She was speaking loudly, her eyes were beginning to dampen.

"He waited for you by that goddamned window *all day*," she said, waving an arm forcefully toward the big picture window in the living room. The motion opened her robe slightly, exposing part of her right breast and most of her right thigh. "It was the most pathetic and heartbreaking thing to watch," she said, the tears now building in her eyes.

"I knew you weren't going to show up by the time lunch rolled around. But he wouldn't hear any of it. He even made me give him his lunch in the living room, where he could watch the driveway for your car. He ate his dinner in there, too, Justin. And, when it got dark outside, every set of headlights that came up the street sent him running to the front door, shouting, 'Mommy, Mommy, Daddy's coming!' Then he'd stand by the door waiting for the knock that never came. After a while, he'd go back to the window and press his face up against it to wait for you."

The infinite trust and patience of innocence.

Justin felt terrible. It broke his heart to picture it. Susan's words had scored.

"I...I would never hurt him intentionally," he said.

"You son-of-a-bitch," she raged, crying steadily now. "You're a bastard for what you do to that boy. I'll never forgive you for that, Justin. Never."

"You don't think that I'd hurt him on purpose, do you?" he asked.

"All I know is what I see. I saw that little face against the window all day, waiting for you. He believed every minute that you'd come. He even fell asleep by that window. When Jack carried him to bed, he mumbled, 'Daddy's coming,' as he slept. You could have called. One lousy call to talk to him."

"I'm sorry, Susan," he apologized softly. He had a lot of things to be sorry for that he could never change. If he could have only told her about the agency and what he did, why it was important and necessary, she'd have understood. Maybe.

The apology didn't soothe her. She had the upper hand now. She had him squirming, and she was enjoying it.

"Don't tell it to me—tell it to your son. Maybe he'll believe it, because I can't. He thinks I can put Popeye or Spiderman on the television anytime he wants to see them. He doesn't accept it when I tell him they're on only at certain times. He doesn't understand those things yet. He thinks every day can be a Sunday, because he wants it to be, and that you'll be coming over. He asks me twenty times a day when you're coming over. What do I tell him?

"He adores you, Justin. He deserves better from you. He spends his life waiting for Sundays...and you. And he's just going to keep waiting...and waiting...and waiting—the same way I did."

Justin was stung. He found himself fighting to keep his expression unchanged, but he was unable to.

Coming here, being here with her, was like running through a field of coiled barbed wire. It left him ripped and bleeding inside. He hated her, but he loved her; he wanted her, but he could never take her back.

This was *their* house now, hers and Jack's, not his. She was Jack's wife now, Jack's lover now. And Michael? How long before he would call Jack "Daddy"? Then it would be complete. He should have killed the son-of-a-bitch when he caught them and accused him of raping his wife.

Then the words hit him again. "He spends his life waiting... and waiting—*the same way I did.*"

His face reddened and twisted.

Susan saw a look in his face that she had never seen before. It frightened her. She backed away a step.

"*Waiting?*" he began, the voice rising like a rumbling clap of thunder. "Like you waited? Tell me about how you waited, you whore."

In an instant he had sprung at her, grabbing her by the hair, and had twisted her down onto the floor. Her robe fell almost completely open, held only by a loosely knotted terry-cloth belt.

"How long did you wait before you ran yourself and your wet panties over to that stiff-pricked dentist of yours? And, go ahead, tell me how you can't forgive me for not picking up a phone. I had no choice—you did. You can't forgive me for something I couldn't help? What about what you did? That's forgivable? Come on, tell me about waiting and forgiving," he said, as he twisted her to her back.

"No, Justin. Please, don't. You don't understand what it was like for me," she said, nearly hysterical. "You were always gone. I never knew where or for how long. And…and, even when you were home, there was a part…a part of you—"

He yanked on her hair again and tore her robe completely open.

She was sobbing, frightened.

"Justin…Justin, no…listen…please, listen to me." Her voice was trembling, the words rushing out quickly. "There was this side of you…a side that I didn't know. And it became the bigger part of you. You became distant and indifferent to me. I needed warmth, love, and understanding. Jack was there—"

He jerked on her hair violently and straddled her, staring menacingly into her eyes. All of his pain, all of his pent-up feelings and anguish were at the surface, all of his frustrations and passions were ready to break loose.

"I…alwa…always loved you," she said, tears streaming. "Even when I went to Jack, I loved you, Justin. You never really let me into your life, Justin. There was always a dark side that you kept from me, that was untouchable. You left me so alone, so terribly alone. I had to reach out to save myself. *I had to save myself.*"

The anger left his eyes; doubt and confusion remained. A hollow ache filled him again. He saw it all, all the unreal pieces of his life since joining the agency.

"But you left me nothing," he said. "You destroyed my pride, my life, and my family. You just took it all and gave it to him. My whole life—my wife, my house, my…my *son*."

My son. And what did I do to save it all? he thought.

Was she right? Did a dark side of him exist that shut her out of his life? Had he brought it all upon himself? Or...or was it the agency, the profession?

"Susan, I...I..." He was groping. The thoughts wouldn't form, the words wouldn't come. It was all one jumbled, nightmarish kaleidoscope of visions: Susan and Jack fucking, Barbara, Michael waiting, the agency, the killing, and the strange pleasure it gave.

He stared into her eyes.

"I love you, Justin," she sobbed. "Oh, I love you so much."

He stretched his body across hers. They were charged with a passion more intense than they had ever known in one another. They became lost in one another's desperate, urgent desires, oblivious to everything around them. There was no past, no future...just *now!*

Justin was tucking in his shirt when the tone in his implant sounded.

He could not respond verbally, so he forced a long contraction of his eustachian tubes, which run from the throat to the ear.

BLEEP!

The tiny microfilament contacts implanted there had sounded a single tonal response, indicating that he was receiving SENTINEL's transmission but was not alone and could not verbally acknowledge at that time. There was no danger of Susan hearing any of the transmissions, because the communications implant utilized a direct neural link to the auditory system. They could be cheek to cheek, and she wouldn't hear the slightest sound.

"Pilgrim, you are needed at once. Can you make Newark airport within the next sixty minutes?" the pleasant voice asked.

BLEEP! A single tone—affirmative.

"Tickets will be waiting for you at the United counter. Bring nothing. Everything will be provided. SENTINEL Control out."

Justin looked at Susan. She was lying back on the bed, still naked. They had taken their act to the bedroom.

"I came by to see if it would be all right with you if I kept Michael for an overnight this Saturday. How about it?" Justin asked.

Susan was roses and honey. She'd have given him anything at that point.

"Sure, it's okay. What time will you come for him?" she asked.

"Oh, about one o'clock, I guess," he replied.

"Fine." She smiled. Then she suddenly remembered something. "Oh, wait a minute. You'll have to get him back early on Sunday. By...let's see, um...six thirty. Jack is taking him to the last Ranger home game of the season." That would leave the two of them alone for hours, she thought.

A slight twinge shot through Justin's gut at the mention of Jack's name.

He had planned to have dinner for his father Sunday evening. Moving it up to about two in the afternoon would pose no problem.

"Fine." He nodded. "Barbara and I are planning to have my father over for dinner on Sunday. We'll just move it up a little," he said.

Barbara. The twinge was in Susan's gut now. She had forgotten about Barbara. During the last hour, there had been only the two of them. It drove home the point that Justin wasn't hers anymore. She wanted him more than anything at that moment.

Justin finished dressing and put on his jacket. He walked out of the bedroom toward the living room.

Susan jumped up, wrapped her robe around herself, and ran after him. She followed him to the front door.

He began to open the door when she reached up and closed it. She threw her arms around his neck and kissed him deeply.

After they parted lips, she looked into his eyes for a long moment. "We're the same people we were seven years ago, Justin," she said, referring to the time when they had gotten married and were so much in love.

Her message was clear. What had happened in the past with Jack, together with the things that had caused it, didn't really change them. She was the same Susan. He the same Justin. They still loved one another. She wanted him.

Jack had only been a tool that supplied the things she felt she needed—constancy, warmth, understanding, and sharing. Jack was always there and was really good with Michael—but he was no Justin.

He let his eyes sweep across the living room and the parts of the house that he could see. He saw so many things: the little china figurines he had given her one Valentine's Day, the Hummels she had wanted so badly, the pieces of Lennox he had surprised her with two Christmases ago, the tiny handmade glass miniatures on the bookcase, and a hundred other things. They were all memories, happy ones. But only one memory stayed in his mind, the one that hurt so much and supplanted all others— her and Jack.

He shook his head. "No, Susan. People change. We've changed. We'll never be the same people we were. Changing is a necessary part of our survival."

He cupped her chin in his hand and gently touched his lips to hers. He opened the door and left.

She watched with moistening eyes as he walked away. It was then that she realized she could never remember seeing him look back when he walked away. Her eyes flooded—she would never have him again.

Justin swallowed to relieve the pressure in his ears as the plane descended on its approach into O'Hare. He thought about what Susan had said and about changing. In some ways, what she had said was true. Certain things in people never changed. With Susan, for instance, there would always be another Jack as soon as she got to feeling lonely and neglected again. Justin was filling that role for her now, just as Jack had before. And he knew that he would probably be half mystery to anyone who got close to him, half white, half black. Nobody would ever know both sides.

Somewhere he had let his life cave in on him. Parts of it could never be salvaged—but some parts still could, if he was careful to avoid the same mistakes. It was still possible to find happiness, to build a life with Barbara. But one important step had to be taken or they would never stand a chance. He had to leave the agency—at once, before it swallowed him completely.

He would give them this mission as his last; he owed them that much notice. But there would be no more after this. He would tell Pegasus today.

He felt good about his decision. He also felt nervous about telling Pegasus. But his own life was more important than the agency. He could pull himself together and start building a life for himself and Barbara. He could also be a better father to Michael.

He was getting out now—if they would let him.

"Good day, gentlemen," Honeycut's voice began. "We have another little job for you. Paris, this time. You could expect to be back by Friday evening."

Justin breathed a relieved sigh. He didn't want to stand up his son again.

"You'll be going after a Soviet defector by the name of Dmitri Chakhovsky. There will be copies of his dossier on the plane for you. The CIA is now holding him in a safe house and is trying for a move on Friday. Robert Morsand is in charge of the operation. You'll find a dossier on him, as well. There are also floor plans of the safe house that Chakhovsky is being held in. The CIA time schedule is available to you, as well as the names and photographs of all of Morsand's men who are involved in the operation, with their specialties noted.

"You will also find an envelope containing photographs and dossiers on the Soviet personnel known to be engaged in the hunt for Chakhovsky. They will use every effort to stop him. We don't have the identities of all of the hunt squads out for him, so be careful. They're very efficient. You can bet that their best have been called in for this one."

The two men listened, as Honeycut filled them in on the rest of the details, including why Chakhovsky was wanted by the Soviets and why he must not be allowed to be taken by the CIA. They were to use any means necessary to get him, or to kill him if the situation looked impossible.

"Our objective is to make each side think that the other has him. You'll be in the middle, so protect yourselves. We want Chakhovsky in our hands—or he is to be stopped. Consider those orders as coming directly from the White House. You are to use *any* means possible. You have complete freedom.

"The Lear is at Meigs, fueled and ready. You will make a stop in Reykjavik to pick up another passenger. SENTINEL Control will give you the details on your flight over. Are there any questions?"

Justin thought about telling Pegasus about his intended res-ignation, but somehow it didn't seem right to bring it up now. An important mission like this, the stalker, everything that had happened—it would make it seem like he wanted out for all the wrong reasons.

He decided to wait until after the mission.

"I have one more bit of news for you, gentlemen," Honeycut announced. "We've identified Spartan's assassin. He's in Madrid under close surveillance. A team has been dispatched for him. You need not be concerned about him further."

A wave of relief shot through Justin. The stalker was gone. Their theory was probably right. He must have followed Spartan back and killed him, then beat it straight back to Madrid with the information.

"What about the journal?" Justin asked.

"Nothing, yet. We're following up on your theory, as well as waiting for one more try at Spartan's house. We'll be sending an entire Division Two team in by week's end. It's not as important right now as what you have to do, though. You'll get complete backup and supportive effort from our agents in the Paris area. SENTINEL Control will coordinate their efforts to yours as needed.

"Are there any last questions?"

Both men remained silent.

"Good luck, then, gentlemen. Bring him home."

"You can count on it," Justin said.

The phone box clicked off.

Fanning took out two of his fine cigars and tossed one to Justin. "No place like Paris in the spring," Fanning mused.

An hour later, the Lear was roaring down the runway at Meigs Field. They were Reykjavik bound. Fanning was whistling again. This time it was "April in Paris."

THIRTEEN

The German High Command issued orders to hold all captured Russian territories at all costs. Despite the immense hardships, our magnificent troops held, and the poorly coordinated Russian offensive was stopped.

Another German push was started with the coming of warmer weather, but we found the resistance stubborn and more tenacious than in our initial drive of a year earlier. It cost us our most valuable possession, one we could not well afford to lose—time. Another deadly winter set in, and with it came a second relentless Russian offensive. In February of 1943 our 6th Army consisting of over 300,000 men was totally annihilated at the gates of Stalingrad.

Entry No. 22 from the partially
recovered *Wolf Journal*

Late afternoon, Moscow: Vasily Trushenko stood before the desk of an angered Leonid Travkin. The official versions of the Bodonov confessions had only just reached his desk. Travkin's face was crimson. His hands trembled with rage. He tried desperately to remain calm and in control. He wanted to reach out to wring Trushenko's neck.

Trushenko was calm and sure of himself. He had it all in black and white, and Chakhovsky had cemented his guilt by running. It was perfect.

Travkin stared long and hard at Trushenko. The obvious triumphant demeanor only made Travkin angrier. It had been an out-and-out revenge tactic that could well blow the whole plan for Alexi Kuradin. The plan had already started. Kuradin was gone, he could not be reached with the news of Chakhovsky's disappearance. It would not be possible for Kuradin to learn of this until it was too late. Centaur had to continue, or lose the chance to get the information.

"Do you have any idea what you have done?" Travkin asked in a controlled voice.

Trushenko wasn't going to be pushed around. He had waited too long to nail Chakhovsky. He didn't care whose favorite son he was. "I have exposed a criminal of the state, a man whose perverted sexual crimes have made him a serious security risk to this country. He is the worst kind of criminal to inhabit the earth—a pedophile—a deviate of the worst and lowest degree."

"That remains to be proven," Travkin said. "But that is not what I refer to. Continue, please. Enlighten me as to your act of patriotism," he said acidly.

Trushenko thought for a moment. "I...I am not sure I know what you mean. I have gathered conclusive evidence that he is guilty of th—"

"*Where is he?*" Travkin roared out, slamming a hamlike fist to his desk. "*Where is your criminal?*"

Trushenko refused to be bullied. He had irrefutable proof of his charges. "He has gone into hiding. It should serve as an open admission to his—"

"*Where* is he hiding?" Travkin interrupted loudly.

Trushenko stared into Travkin's eyes. "I don't know. But we are searching for him now. It is only a matter of time until he is found." His stare was even and cool. He refused to show even the slightest signs of trepidation.

"You don't know," Travkin echoed back at him. "And why has he gone into hiding?"

"Because he is obviously guilty of the charges brought against him. He chose to run rather than face certain conviction for his crimes," Trushenko answered coolly.

"He chose to run." Travkin frowned. "When were the charges officially filed?" he asked.

"They were submitted two days ago, officially reviewed and filed yesterday," Trushenko replied.

"And when was Chakhovsky discovered missing?"

"Two days ago," Trushenko answered.

"Two days ago. In fact, *before* the charges were *officially* filed through your office. Who discovered his absence?" Travkin was getting closer to his point. His tone became calmer, more confident.

Trushenko noted the change in the tone. He knew what Travkin was coming to, but it wouldn't change the fact of Chakhovsky's guilt. There was no escape for Chakhovsky. "A team from the Individual Division was dispatched to locate and observe his movements. It was they who determined that he was not in the south of France as he was supposed to be."

"That means that he was actually missing two days earlier than was reported—or could have been missing two days earlier, does it not?" Travkin was about to pounce.

"It could mean that," Trushenko said, not willing to openly concede the possibility.

"You dispatched a surveillance team before the charges were officially presented," Travkin continued.

"That is correct. It was entirely within my power to do so. It was only an observation team, not one sent to secure him for return to the Soviet Union. I did not go beyond my authority in doing this. I need no higher approval to send out a surveillance team. It was their purpose to watch him and to report on his movements until the charges could be officially reviewed by your office and his return requested." Trushenko had been careful to stay within his authority. He was safe. "I have done nothing wrong," he insisted.

"I will tell you what you have managed to accomplish," Travkin began. "You have single-handedly jeopardized the most important intelligence operation that this country has ever undertaken. *You* have done that.

"*You* have sent one of our most important intelligence officers into hiding and have pushed him into attempted defection."

Trushenko became flushed. What intelligence operation? He didn't know what Travkin was referring to.

"*You* have jeopardized our entire Western European intelligence system. And *you* have put *your* existence on the line," Travkin hammered.

Trushenko was shaken. His face turned crimson, his confidence sagged, his legs grew suddenly weak. He sat down. His face began to drain of color, like a thermometer suddenly thrust into a freezer. His life on the line?

"If Chakhovsky successfully defects, *you* will have put the Soviet Union on the brink of a war it may not survive.

"Dmitri Chakhovsky is not an ordinary Soviet citizen of small consequence. You *did* overstep your authority by initiating an investigation of him *before* submitting proposed charges to this office," Travkin dug into him.

"Did you think that a man of his power and influence was without friends? He knew what you were doing every step of the way. You let him plan carefully for his escape by not informing us of your proposed charges and investigation. We would have recalled him and detained him in Moscow before the investigation, to prevent his running. He would have then been presented with the charges here in Moscow while in our custody."

"But he is guilty," Trushenko began. "There can be no doubt of this. It is a matter of record now that—"

"*That he is missing, and that you are to blame,*" Travkin growled at him. "That is the *only* matter of record now. And he is missing because of your stupidity and your petty attempt at revenge.

"We have dispatched ten teams to locate him and to stop him. If he succeeds in going over, you will sit in Kutz's chair in his place. You will be taken to within an inch of your life and then you will be shot."

The sweat rolled down Trushenko's face, and he shook uncontrollably. "I...I knew nothing of an intelligence operation. I...I—"

"You know nothing, period. You are a stupid fool," Travkin said.

"But the charges?" Trushenko mumbled feebly.

"They mean nothing in the face of what you have created. Chakhovsky must now be stopped. Regardless of the outcome, your future is ended. Your only chance of remaining alive is if he *is* stopped. And even then, you may still regret the life that awaits you." Travkin pushed the intercom button on his desk.

Three guards entered the office. Trushenko turned in his chair. He wanted to throw up.

"Take him away. Hold him in close security until further notice. That is all," Travkin said gruffly. He picked up the reports of the charges and began leafing through them. He did not look at Trushenko, as he was led from the office. He did not see the words on the sheets before him. He could only see Alexi Kuradin—Centaur—unaware of what had happened and what it could mean. Unaware of how tenuous his situation had just become, indeed, how grave it could become for Russia, herself, if Chakhovsky were not stopped.

Dmitri Chakhovsky carried a wealth of information in his head. Much of it would be damaging if Chakhovsky succeeded in defecting to the West. But there was one piece which, in the wrong hands, could prove to be fatal for Russia's future: He knew Alexi Kuradin—and his secret.

It was late Wednesday evening in Chicago when Dr. Edward Bridges's phone rang in his apartment. He reached it on the second ring.

"Bridges," he said, tense, anxious.

"Pay phone. Playboy Club. Ten minutes. First booth." The phone clicked dead.

This was it! *The call!*

He lived only minutes' walking distance from the Playboy Club. He hurriedly put on his coat and rushed out of the apartment. He checked his watch. 9:33. The voice said ten minutes.

His heart pounded as he left his building and walked quickly up the street. This was real. It was going to happen, just as he'd planned. He checked his watch again and increased his pace.

Minutes later he was walking into the Playboy Club. He looked at his watch. It was 9:42. He hurried to the phones. There were three on the wall. "First booth." From which side, right or left?

A man was on the phone to the far right. Oh, God, let it be left.

BRRRING!

He leaped for the phone on the left. He waited for a second ring.

BRRRING!

"Yes," he said, picking it up. He was nearly out of breath. His heart pounded in his ears so loudly that he was sure he would be unable to hear. "This is Bridges," he said, pressing the phone hard against his ear.

"Hello, Dr. Bridges. How are you today?" a calm, low voice asked.

"Fi...fine." He swallowed dryly. His legs began to shake nervously. "Fine, I'm fine."

"That's good, Dr. Bridges," the voice said. "Can you have your information ready by Friday night? Answer yes or no."

"Ye...yes. No problem," he said.

"Only yes or no, Dr. Bridges," the voice insisted.

"Yes."

"That's good. You will have it ready by Friday evening then. You will drive to South Beloit. Do you know where it is?"

"Yes."

"Good. There is a Holiday Inn in South Beloit at the intersection of US Fifty-one and Seventy-five, off I-Ninety. Is that clear so far? Do you think that you could find it?"

"Yes."

"Very good, Dr. Bridges. You will take a room there in your own name. *Do not* use your telephone to make the reservations. Make them for Friday, Saturday, and Sunday evenings. Do you have all that?"

"Yes, three nights."

"Yes, or no, Dr. Bridges. Only yes or no."

"Yes."

"You will be contacted there." The phone clicked dead.

"Wait a minute. When? Which day?" He looked around to see if anyone had heard.

Nobody. Good, nobody was watching him. He hung up the phone. It was going to happen. *Friday was his last day!*

Oh God, he was happy—and he was scared. He needed a drink. He left the Playboy Club and almost ran home.

He poured himself a tall scotch, dropped in some ice cubes, and took a long pull on it. Whew! That was better. He had to think.

The false trail. He had to leave a false trail for SENTINEL to chase. Saturday. They'd probably contact him on Saturday, he thought. Good. Good. His mind was racing. The reservations. Got to make the reservations. He picked up the phone.

No, you jerk, he thought. Don't use your phone. Remember what he told you? Pay phone. Downstairs in the lobby. There's a pay phone down there.

He put down his drink and raced out of the apartment again.

As he entered the lobby, he began to settle himself. His brain slowed down, and he began to collect his thoughts. Now let's take first things first, he thought. The false trail, that was important. His mind moved slowly, deliberately. He picked up the phone book and went to the yellow pages.

He threw two dimes into the phone, got the dial tone, and dialed the toll-free number. The dimes shot back.

It rang several times.

"Thank you for calling Avis. We feature Chrysler products. This is Donna. Can I help you?"

"Yes, I'd like to rent a car. For Friday night in Chicago, to be picked up at O'Hare."

"Yes, sir. At O'Hare, Friday evening. Is that this Friday, sir?"

"Yes, this Friday."

"Okay, and what type of car would you like?"

"Uh...something full size, I guess."

"Full size," she repeated as she punched the information into the computer. The sounds were just barely audible in the background.

"And what time will you be picking it up in Chicago?" she asked.

"What time...uh...about seven. It might be a little after, I can't be sure."

"What is your flight number?" she asked.

"Uh...I don't...why do you need my flight number?" he asked.

"That's so that we can hold your car for you in case your flight is delayed for any reason. Do you know the flight number?"

"Um...uh, no, I don't, I'm afraid. If it's important that you have it, I could..."

"No, it's not essential. What city will you be flying in from?"

He thought for a moment. "New York."

"That's sufficient. I'll need your name and Avis Wizzard Number, if you have one."

"No, I don't have a Wizzard Number. My name is Edward Bridges."

"Okay, Mr. Bridges, can I have a company or home address?"

"Yeah, uh…it's the…Chemtech Corporation, on Madison Avenue, New York City," he invented.

"Do you have a phone number where you can be reached?"

"Yes, I do…it's…" He looked at the number on the pay phone. "It's seven-nine-one-three-two-four-two."

"New York, that's area code two-one-two, isn't it?" she asked.

"Yes. Yes, it is."

"Will you be returning the car to O'Hare?"

"Yes, on Monday morning." From Moscow, he thought.

"Will you be paying with an Avis credit card or some other major credit card?"

"No, I'll be paying cash."

"Okay, Mr. Bridges, you've been confirmed for a full-sized car in Chicago, to be picked up at O'Hare on Friday. Can I help you with any other reservations?"

"No, that's all. Thank you."

"You're welcome. Thank you for calling Avis."

Bridges hung up the phone. He threw the dimes back in. He dialed information and got the number of the Holiday Inn in South Beloit.

He dialed the number, adding the 815 area code. There was a ring. The dimes shot back once again.

"Please insert seventy-five cents for the first three minutes."

Bridges dug into his pockets. With the twenty cents that the operator had just returned before coming on, he had exactly the right amount. He dropped in the change, the various bongs, clinks, and clangs sounding in his ears as the coins dropped.

The phone rang. And rang. And rang. And rang.

"South Beloit Holiday Inn. Can I help you?"

"Yes, I'd like to make—"

"Please hold one second." The operator was gone.

"Hey…" he began to protest.

He shook his head and waited for the operator to come back on. He drummed his fingers and began to congratulate himself for his quick thinking in setting up his decoy. It would really put a monkey wrench into the works.

The waiting continued. He began to become concerned because he didn't have any more change. He looked at his watch and tried to estimate the time he had spent waiting.

"Thank you for holding," the young voice said.

"It's okay," he said. "I'd like to make reservations for this Friday, Saturday, and Sunday nights."

"I'll connect you with reservations."

Ah shit! He was getting pissed now. It would be Saturday before he got the reservations made at the rate he was going here.

He was waiting again. He looked at his watch. The three minutes were almost up. The operator would be back on asking for more money any second now.

"Reservations. Thank you for calling Holiday Inn. This is Tom. May I help you?"

"Yeah," he said a little bitingly. "I'd like to make reservations for this Friday, Saturday, and Sunday nights."

The connection broke for a brief instant as the coins dropped all at once. Time was up. The operator did not cut in.

"Hello?" the voice on the other end said at the interruption.

"Yes, I'm here," Bridges said.

"Okay, this Friday, Saturday, and Sunday. Can I have the name, please?"

He said in your own name! "Bridges. Edward Bridges."

"Will it be a late arrival? After six, sir?"

"Yes, it will be."

"We can guarantee that for you then. Can I have the name of your company or a home address?"

"Sure, it's the Chemtech Corporation, eleven hundred LaSalle Street in Chicago," he lied.

"Is there a home or business phone where you can be reached?"

"Yeah, it's area code three-one-two, seven-nine-one-three-two-four-two," he said, again giving the number of the phone he was calling from.

"Thank you, Mr. Bridges. You're all set for this Friday, Saturday, and Sunday evenings. You have a guaranteed late arrival. Thank you for calling Holiday Inn."

"You're welcome," he returned, then hung up the phone.

All set! All he had to do now was go into Alpha on Friday and take out his information. That part would be a breeze.

He had gotten up and left the phone booth, and was heading back to his apartment for a few drinks to celebrate his imminent good fortune, when the phone in the booth began to ring. He stopped and turned.

The phone rang and rang and rang.

A smile crossed his face. "So sue me," he chuckled and walked back to his apartment. It wasn't every day you got to beat the phone company.

Cold is cold, and March had been brutal in Chicago, but Reykjavik was ridiculous. Justin and Fanning had been met at the airport by the third passenger, a man code-named Striker. They accompanied him to a fairly large block structure just below ground level. A narrow flight of stairs led down to it.

"Jesus Christ, is it always this cold up here?" Justin asked, his mouth stiff from the numbing cold.

Striker smiled. "It's almost spring here. The winters are much worse."

Justin shook his head. "Colder than this, huh? No wonder they call it Iceland." He blew his warm breath into cold fists.

The room looked like a bunker. It had paneled walls and was warm and well-furnished. A large bulletin board with numerous photographs pinned to it was situated along one wall.

Striker poured his visitors some rich hot chocolate. After a few minutes of defrosting, the three men got down to business.

Striker pointed to the first photograph.

"As you know from the dossiers that you've studied, this man is Dmitri Chakhovsky. The man next to him is Boris Fadeikin. He's the man calling the shots in the search for Chakhovsky. Fadeikin is a clever man, and you can be sure that he's got plenty of tricks up his sleeve.

"We're not sure how many teams Fadeikin has out for him. We know of at least six. Control estimates ten to twelve. The Soviets are the unknown variable that we have to watch out for. They could blow it all on us."

Striker pointed to the next picture. "This is Morsand. The man standing beside him is Bud Kodek, his number-one boy. Kodek will be running the operation for Morsand. The plan is very simple and straightforward, as you'll see."

He moved on to the next series of pictures.

"This is the safe house that Chakhovsky is in. They'll be taking him out on Friday. The plan calls for a one o'clock go, but Morsand is known to move earlier than the plan states. My guess is that they'll go about eleven.

"These pictures here are satellite close-ups of the entire perimeter that Morsand will be protecting. As you can see, it covers the entire block and all of the buildings facing the safe house. Our attention focuses here," Striker said, pointing to the back of the safe house. There was a small courtyard behind the building, which was shared by the two buildings at either side of the subject building and the one directly behind it. It made a neat little rectangle bordered by the four buildings.

"The front of the building is too well covered to allow any chance of escape. That area would become a small battlefield in just seconds if it was tried. The weak spot is in the back, through the courtyard," Striker indicated.

"Looks like a death trap to me," Fanning said.

"It's not, really," Striker commented. "Morsand's plan here calls for two agents in the courtyard to watch the back exit. There should be a radio man, too. But what the plan doesn't call for, and I'm certain will be there, is a sniper. Right here," he said, touching the roof of the building at the rear of the courtyard.

"How can you be certain that he'll be there and not a different location?" Justin asked.

"Look at the rooftops," Striker told him.

Justin looked. "So?"

Striker pointed to the one that he had indicated, smiled, and said, "It's flat. So is the one that's on the right, where the radio man will be. The others are peaked in typical old French style. Do you know how many flat-roofed buildings there are in that part of Paris?" he asked.

They shrugged.

"There aren't a hell of a lot. That's why this place was chosen as a safe house. It's ideal to defend. From that rooftop, a sniper can command full advantage of the entire back of the safe house, the courtyard, and the street behind him, just by moving across the roof. One man can do the work of five."

"Just like I said, it's a death trap," Fanning repeated. "There's no getting out that way with that sniper there."

Striker smiled again. "He won't be there when you're ready to come out. I'll see to that. From here," he said, touching a spot on a larger photograph showing a field of view covering many city blocks.

The two men looked at the spot.

"That's pretty far away," Justin said.

"It's not, really. It's only four hundred yards. That's a bell tower standing about thirty feet higher than the roof in question. It's a simple shot, actually," Striker said.

"That's no simple shot, friend," Fanning said.

"For me it is," Striker returned.

"What if he's not on that rooftop?" Fanning asked. "What if he's in one of the windows of that building?"

"He won't be. He wouldn't be able to cover the street behind him effectively. That part of the perimeter must also be secured," Striker explained.

"But what if he *is* in a window?" Fanning pushed. "You'll never be able to get him."

"If he is in a window, then you will have been right before— that courtyard will be a death trap. But he *will* be there," Striker said confidently.

"Yeah, well even if he is there, four hundred yards is a long way to shoot. We'll be just as dead if you miss. I don't like it through the courtyard," Justin said.

"Like it or not, it's the only way out of that perimeter," Striker said.

Justin shook his head, as Fanning frowned pessimistically.

"He'll never hear the shot that kills him," Striker said. "Neither will the radio man. After the two by the back door are taken out, you'll be able to beat it across the courtyard and between the buildings to the street at the rear of the perimeter. That's where the pickup will be made. One of you will drive the car. The other gets Chakhovsky. Getting two of you into that building would be next to impossible. One of you has a good chance."

Fanning pulled out a quarter. "To see who drives. Winner gets the car. Call it!"

He flipped the coin upward.

"Heads," Justin called.

The coin hit the carpeted floor and bounced. It came up tails.

Fanning smiled and shrugged. "Some days are better than others."

"Thanks a lot," Justin said.

Striker walked back across the room to a long, neatly kept workbench. On it was a stand supporting an odd-looking rifle. The two men followed him and regarded the weapon curiously.

Justin touched the long, smooth, sightless barrel, tracing his finger back to the high-powered Redfield scope mounted on it. The stock of the weapon was a simple lightweight aluminum T bar, padded at the shoulder rest. The lightweight stock was fitted into a small detachable pistol-grip handle, just behind the guardless trigger.

"What you're looking at is one of the most accurate precision weapons ever made," Striker said proudly. "I made it from a Winchester High Wall varmint rifle, chambered for six-millimeter cartridges. It was a stock model that I wildcatted myself some four years ago. That extra-heavy barrel gives super stiffness and won't whip at all. When it comes to precision shooting, you can't beat a well-made, carefully wildcatted varmint rig. This baby has all of the virtues of the varmint rig, but all the needed attributes for this profession as well. This weapon will break down completely in less than ten seconds. With the right scope and proper load, she'll hit anything.

"This particular scope is zeroed for four hundred yards. That means that it will strike dead on the crosshairs between three hundred and ninety and four hundred and twenty-five yards. At two hundred yards, she'll print three inches high, and strike a foot low at five hundred. With our friend on the roof, it's not so much a matter of hitting him as it is deciding where to place the shot. I'll probably go for a head shot, and, with this weapon, it'll be like hitting the side of a barn.

"Normally, I'd try to take the target at between one hundred and two hundred yards, although I have taken some from as far away as nine hundred. From four hundred yards out, the sounds will never reach the perimeter area. They'll be drowned in the city noise.

"I'll be using these cartridges. They're mercury-tipped explosive bullets. I make all of my own loads, and a hit anywhere with one of these will score a kill," Striker explained.

(The mercury-tipped explosive bullet is a devastating device, which works by a simple principle. The bullet has a hole drilled down its center from either the tip or the base. A drop of mercury is put into the cavity and the bullet is carefully resealed. The drop of mercury occupies only a portion of the space and is flattened against the back of the cavity when the bullet is fired. When the bullet strikes home it is slowed down, but the heavy drop of mercury continues to move through the cavity at the original speed of the bullet and impacts with the tip, exploding it outward into the target. The power is awesome; the results final.)

"How fast can you work that rifle? It's only a single shot, and you have two targets," Justin asked.

"Only one target is important. The radio man will be too busy getting off a message when he sees you to notice that his friend on the other roof doesn't have a head anymore. There'll be plenty of time for him, after the primary target is taken care of. You just move your ass through the courtyard to the street."

"That's where I come in," said Fanning.

"Right. Timing is critical here. The second your friend comes out of that building, you've got to blow in through the back of that perimeter. They'll see you coming, so you've got to get to that curb at the same time he does with Chakhovsky. I can't help you beyond that point, so you're on your own. I'll make my own way out."

They discussed the details of the operation following the break from the closed perimeter. It would be a foot race the rest of the way.

Striker carefully broke down his weapon and packed the rest of his gear.

At the precise minute called for in the plan, the modified Lear roared off of the runway in Reykjavik. They were going in.

FOURTEEN

The month following our loss at Stalingrad, we launched our last desperate attempt at victory. But it was not to be. We had fatally underestimated Russian reserve strength and mobilization capabilities. Command of the skies was no longer ours, and our supply lines were cut. The drive was slowed and stalled. In the summer-autumn of 1943, our dream of conquest came to an end. The long retreat home was begun along a path made red with German blood.

Entry No. 23 from the partially
recovered *Wolf Journal*

Friday morning, Paris: This was the day Dmitri Chakhovsky was to be taken out. There was nothing that Chakhovsky could do, except to sit tight and wait. It was all up to Morsand now, and Chakhovsky trusted him.

Morsand's instructions to Chakhovsky had been explicit. "Stay put, and don't move out of your room. Don't look out of any windows, and keep all shades and curtains fully drawn. Keep all lights off at all times, and answer the door for no one until Friday, and then only if the appropriate coded knock is given. Talk to absolutely no one. For three days, you must not even exist. If you do all this, we *might* be able to get you out of Paris alive. They're crawling all over Paris looking for you. They want you very badly."

Chakhovsky had listened well. Most of what he was told, he knew. For instance, he knew that even one eye peeking out of a window could be filled instantly with a marksman's bullet. He knew that *anyone* could be KGB and kill him in an instant. He also knew one other thing that contradicted all of what Morsand had told him and went against all of his better judgment. That was, on the very first day spent in that hole, the time had come when he had to take one very wicked piss, and the single-room apartments had no toilets, sinks, or tubs. He didn't even have a bottle to piss into. Undoubtably, Morsand had never seen the inside of this place, or he would have accounted for that.

So three days ago he took his first chance. The only bathroom on the floor was down at the end of the hall. It was a common toilet that all of the tenants of the floor used. He held out until his eyes almost floated out of his skull and then decided to make the try. After all, he reasoned, this was a safe house, and the streets were probably crawling with CIA. Two, maybe three, minutes, that was all it should take. Two trips a day, six until Friday, and then out. The risk seemed acceptable.

He opened the door and stuck out his head. He froze. There was an old woman walking down the hallway away from his room. She looked about sixty, had bowed, swollen legs, and wore a dirty gray coat. She hobbled tiredly down the hallway, past the bathroom, to the last door in the hallway, near a back stairway. She stopped and, with a tired old hand, inserted the key into her door lock and twisted it open. Before entering, she turned her head and looked back down the hallway.

Chakhovsky's head shot back in as soon as he saw her head start to turn. She might have seen him. That was close. He waited a couple of minutes, then checked the hallway again, and left the room.

He crept down the hallway carefully, in almost complete silence. He got to the bathroom and opened the door. There was a young girl in there, a child. He closed the door quickly and beat a painful retreat back to his room. Ten very long minutes later, he tried again. The bathroom was empty, but the door had no lock. That fact distressed him.

The bathroom was small, with one open toilet, a sink, and a tub. There had been two toilets once, but only one remained. It had no stall, but marks on the walls and floor showed that it had once been closed in. The sink was big, with a large dirty mirror above it. The tub was an ancient affair, deep, chipped, and rusted. The room was filthy and smelled of urine. He relieved himself with his head half turned, to keep an eye on the unlocked door behind him, as if it mattered. If they wanted him now, they could have him. He wasn't going to stop pissing for anything.

After he finished, he opened the door and was surprised to see the wrinkled old woman coming out of her room. She passed him by without even looking at him. He kept his eyes on her until she had begun to descend the stairs to the small lobby below. He looked back at the old woman's door and saw the young girl he had seen in the bathroom earlier. She had long hair and big round eyes. She looked at Chakhovsky through the open crack in the door and smiled at him, then closed the door. He unconsciously smiled back, but the door had closed, and he was sure that she hadn't seen it. He returned to his room and lay in the darkness, trying to sleep. But how does a man sleep when he is doing the most distasteful thing of his existence, and when men are searching for him with great urgency and determination, for the sole purpose of killing him? Gradually the torment in his mind numbed into sleep.

Late the following morning, he dared another trip down to the bathroom. It was empty. He sat on the toilet and began a bowel movement. After a few minutes, he felt sufficiently relieved and reached for the toilet paper. Just then the door opened, startling him. The young girl came marching in.

A wave of embarrassment swept over Chakhovsky. It didn't seem to bother the young girl in the least. He didn't know what to do. She began to wash up and started a conversation with him.

He sat there, with the toilet paper in his hand. He wasn't about to wipe his ass with an audience, so he decided to stay where he was and ride out the storm, acting as nonchalant as she.

She was a little older than he had originally thought. She seemed to be about thirteen, give or take a year. Her hair was almost blond in the sunlight coming through the window and hung almost to her waist. It was straight and silky. Her eyes were enormous, blue, and they sparkled brightly. She was such a pretty child. She almost reminded him of his beloved Tamara when she was but a child of those tender years. He had always loved her, only her, for as long as he could remember.

At first, Chakhovsky just listened as she spoke. She was a warm and friendly child. Soon the conversation became two way. His conversation went from polite response to an easy flowing dialogue. She proved to be irresistibly charming, and he soon felt comfortable talking with her, despite his awkward position.

The seat of the toilet was beginning to hurt his ass. His cheeks were getting numb, and his legs and feet were starting to fall asleep. Finally, the pretty young girl finished and left him. He got up on painful legs and tingling feet. Slowly, the blood began to flow again, and, by the time he got back to his room, he felt somewhat better.

His conversation with the girl had been a welcome interlude in the immediate danger that surrounded him. It had been nice to forget the fear for a while.

Later that afternoon, he took another trip to the bathroom, not so much because he had to go, but more to see if the girl was there. He had taken his third big chance, but, unlike the others, this one was unnecessary. He realized through the disappointment of her not being there that what he was doing was wrong. Yet, he could not help himself. There was just something about her that made it important to him.

Two trips later, his efforts were rewarded.

She was brushing her long, flowing hair when he walked in. She immediately struck up a conversation, while Chakhovsky pretended to wash.

Before long, he was sitting on the edge of the old tub, brushing her beautiful hair for her. His heart went out to the lovely child, as she told him her story.

She lived there with her grandmother. It had been three years now, since her mother and father had died. It had been a murder/suicide.

Her mother had been a stripper/prostitute when her parents met. They fell deeply in love and were married. Her mother left the profession. Soon after, little Nicole was born; that was her name. She was the endless joy of her father.

Her mother was not one for motherhood, however, and after about six years began to long for the money, the clothes, and the men of the life she had had before getting married. She began turning tricks in her apartment while her husband was away. Nicole could remember the men coming to the apartment and giving her mother money. She could never understand why they would want to lie on the bed under the covers with her mother. She remembered how they would bounce on the bed and make funny noises, and how her mother would go down below the covers now and then. In the mind of the child, it had all been silly games the grown-ups played.

Then one day her father came home earlier than expected and caught them. He nearly killed the man she was with and beat her mother very badly. Nicole was terribly frightened by it all. The next day her mother left, leaving little Nicole in the apartment all alone.

Her father searched for her mother for many years after that. All that time, he took loving care of his sweet Nicole. She was his only reason for living.

Then, when she was about ten, she remembered her father dressing her up in her best dress and taking her to Sunday mass.

That seemed funny, she had thought, because they never went to church. Then her father took her to her grandmother's place and left. The next morning the police came. Her father had found and killed her mother and then killed himself. He had also killed the man she was with. Nicole had been with her poor old grandmother ever since.

Her grandmother was a wonderful old woman who worked very hard to keep them going. But she was getting old now, and the work was getting harder for her. Soon Nicole would go to work to help bring in enough money.

Such an innocent victim, Chakhovsky thought. Children always suffered for the sins of the parents. There was no justice.

He was sure that she would have everything she wanted someday. She was a child of truly remarkable beauty for being only thirteen. One day she would be an absolutely stunning woman at whose feet men would throw themselves and their fortunes.

He felt a slight arousal as he brushed her hair, his fingers occasionally touching her soft lovely neck. Her face was so pretty, her eyes so large and warm, her lips so perfectly defined. She was bathed in the scent of innocent femininity.

It was now Friday, the morning of the final day. He wanted to talk to Nicole one more time, to say good-bye, and to leave some money for her and her grandmother. Morsand's men would be coming for him in less than three hours, and he would never see her again. He left his room and walked down the hall, taking yet another chance.

As he passed by the bathroom, he noticed that the door was open. He looked in and was pleasantly surprised to see Nicole. He walked in as she was brushing her teeth.

"Good morning, Nicole," he said in perfect French.

"Good morning, monsieur," she replied with garbled words. Her mouth was filled with toothpaste. She made a half turn to him and smiled a greeting.

Chakhovsky was almost stopped in his tracks. She was wearing alarmingly brief panties and a very sheer top that he could see right through. Her hair was pinned up, giving her an older appearance. And her body—it was delicate and lovely. Her small budding breasts were beautiful, her hips rounded like a woman's. He became instantly aroused.

She stared at him with her big eyes. Her lips were parted and rounded slightly, as she moved the toothbrush in and out of her mouth with slow exaggerated motions. The foam was building and running down from her mouth to her chin, the brush still moving in and out, slowly, with an erotic rhythm. She stood there completely unashamed of her exposure.

"I...I came to see you because...eh, because I must be...be leaving today," he said, licking his drying lips and swallowing.

She just looked at him, still moving her brush. Her tongue came out and licked around the handle of the brush.

He gulped loudly. "I was hoping to talk to you before I left. I would like to give you and your grandmother something. Is she home?" he asked.

She shook her head. The brush was just on her lips now. Her tongue toyed with it teasingly. Then the brush was in her mouth again, deep, to the back of the throat, moving in a slow pumping motion. The foam ran down the handle and over her fingers.

Chakhovsky was on fire. His blood was racing like hot steam through his veins. He wanted to sit down to hide his mounting excitement.

She stopped brushing and bent over into the sink to spit out the foam. As she bent forward, her loose-fitting top hung well down from the waist. From his position he could see her lovely young breasts hanging downward. His eyes moved to her ass and to the soft bulge between the thighs. There were light-colored pubic hairs sticking out at the rims of the panties.

"Monsieur," she began as she straightened up, "when do you leave?" she asked.

"In a couple of hours," he replied.

She looked at him, her eyes saddened. "I would like it if we talked some more before you leave. Maybe you could brush my hair for me one more time?" she asked.

"Ye...Yes, I...I would like that," he stammered.

"Oh, that will make me very happy," she said as she started for the door. "Come, we can talk in my room," she said.

He followed her the few steps to her room, his eyes on her ass. Her walk was fascinating. It was in his mind how suddenly beautiful she seemed to him. There was something about young, innocent beauty that went through him like a wildfire. He was helpless when confronted by it.

He followed her into the room. She closed the door behind them. She walked over to her dresser and opened the top drawer. Chakhovsky's eyes were riveted to her body. She took out her hairbrush and another top to put on. She tossed the brush onto the bed. "We can sit there while you brush my hair," she said.

He dutifully walked over to the bed and sat down, glad at the opportunity to conceal his obvious erection.

"It is a pity that you must leave so soon. I will miss our talks and the nice way you brush my hair," she said. "But at least we have these few hours."

She pulled the sheer top up over her head and removed it. She was fully exposed. Her young breasts were beautiful. Chakhovsky was swallowing his tongue. She picked up the other top and unfolded it as she walked toward him. She looked into his eyes. They were raping her.

She walked closer to him, very slowly and deliberately. She was two feet away from him, her breasts at eye level. "Do you like Nicole, monsieur?" she asked in a soft whisper.

His mouth was sand as she drew nearer. He could only nod.

She dropped the top to the floor and took the brush out of Chakhovsky's hand. She reached out and brushed his cheek lightly with soft strokes, barely touching his skin. It was like electricity shooting through him. She inched closer, cupping her hand behind his neck, gently encouraging his face forward. She coaxed his face closer as she brought her wonderfully soft breasts to him.

He turned his head slightly as the warmth of her breasts came against his face. He could no longer resist. He had to have this magnificent child. He opened his mouth and covered one of the nipples.

She held his head close. Her skin was burning; Chakhovsky's own was like fire.

He ran his hand over her hip and began to lower her panties. She opened her legs slightly to allow them to go down more easily. His hand covered her ass in a gentle, caressing motion and passed to the warmth between her legs. She was highly aroused. His own longings were shot more urgently upward as he felt her abundant wetness. His fingers went into the wetness, as she slid down onto the bed with him. He began kissing her breasts and neck. She was being caught in the passion. He kissed upward to her beautiful mouth. He kissed her—and was taken by surprise.

The kiss was not the kiss of a thirteen-year-old. It was practiced, seductive, and baiting. Her tongue performed deep, sensual probes into his mouth. He was being hopelessly sucked into blind, animalistic passion when he heard it—the metallic snap of an automatic.

He caught himself and jumped up from the bed, pushing Nicole away. But it was too late.

The old woman was standing there with an automatic in her hand, the bulbous silencer pointed at his heart. The door was partially open behind her. He had not even heard her come in.

She spoke to him in perfect Russian. "For crimes against the state and for your attempt to defect, you have been sentenced to death, Dmitri Chakhovsky."

Chakhovsky was all terror. They had found him. An old woman and a child. They had used his weakness to trap him. Impossible. It wasn't real.

Nicole backed away toward the open dresser drawer.

The old woman raised the gun. Her hand began a slow, controlled squeeze. Chakhovsky threw out his hands and closed his eyes.

There was a dull coughing thud. The old woman pitched stiffly forward onto her face, blood splashing out of the hole in her head from Justin's bullet.

Swiftly Justin was inside the room, the door closed behind him. The silenced Mauser swung and trained on Nicole. She was standing against the open dresser drawer.

Justin looked at the cowering young girl.

She stared at him wide-eyed.

"Pleese...pleese do not hurt Nicole, monsieur," she began, in heavily accented English. "I have do onlee wat I am hire to do. Thees ladee hire me for wan week to be weeth thees man. I get heem here so he make love weeth me. That is all, monsieur," she pleaded.

"I work for Madame Blanche. Dees woman haav pay for wan week to her for me to work here," she tried explaining. "Pleese, monsieur. Wat I say ees thee truth. Ask weeth Madame Blanche."

Chakhovsky was stunned. He didn't know what was happening, whether he was going to live or die. It wasn't real.

It was possible that what the young girl said was true. Many of the better bordellos of Paris employed young girls like Nicole for their customers who desired children.

Justin dug into his pocket and pulled out a small metallic box about the size of a cigarette lighter. It was black, with a single button on one of its wide surfaces, and had a tiny hole in the center of one end. This little box could throw out an electrical charge a distance of about twenty feet. The charge was of sufficient strength to render a big man unconscious for a period of ten to fifteen minutes. Justin looked into the eyes of the girl, assessing her. He looked at the open drawer behind her.

What she said could be true, he thought.

Their eyes were locked—a mutual assessment now.

And, then again, it might not be true, Justin weighed. And how had she known to speak to him in English?

The Mauser coughed once again. The hair on the back of her head shot back and up, as though caught by a sudden narrow jet of air. She bounced off the dresser, pitching forward onto the floor. The hair on the back of her head became a spreading crimson. Blood trickled out of the hole in her forehead, as her wide, lifeless eyes stared into the floor and the puddle of blood that was starting to surround her head.

Justin liked head shots. They were fast, painless, and positive. He used them whenever he could. He didn't like to see the people he killed suffer, except in a few instances.

Chakhovsky was in pure terror. Tears filled his eyes. He couldn't comprehend what was happening. He didn't know who was who or what was what. He looked at Justin helplessly.

Justin raised the little black device and aimed it at the Russian. He pushed the button. A short crackling bolt of energy hit Chakhovsky, knocking him back onto the bed. He was out cold.

Justin walked to the window and looked out. Four men were approaching the steps to the building. He recognized the tall hefty man from the dossiers that SENTINEL Control had provided. It was Bud Kodek, head of Morsand's team. Justin checked his watch—11:00 a.m., two hours before the planned time. Striker had said that Morsand would do that, he even called the right time. It was obvious that Morsand had done this just in case the KGB had gotten wind of the plan or in case Chakhovsky got any last-minute ideas about changing his mind. Chakhovsky would also be less nervous this early and easier to handle.

Justin put the little stunning device back into his pocket. He picked up Chakhovsky in a fireman's carry and started for the door. The Russian was lighter than he had expected him to be, just a little bit of a man, but heavy on brains. The little ones were always smart in this business.

He cast an eye at the dresser drawer that the girl had stayed so close to. He moved to it quickly, stepping over the nude, lifeless body. He opened the drawer. It held another silenced automatic, exactly like the old woman's. Had he not killed her and allowed her even the slightest chance, he would have been the dead meat. Chances were something one never gave in this business. Give nothing away. It was a commandment in the religion of survival.

"This is Pilgrim. I'm on my way down," he said.

The message was relayed through his implant to Striker, four hundred yards away in the bell tower, and to Fanning, who was waiting just outside of the perimeter in the car. SENTINEL also relayed the dialogue to Honeycut in Washington and to Sparrow, the agent piloting the helicopter that they were scheduled to rendezvous with outside of Paris.

Justin moved swiftly for the door. A small bottle dropped from Chakhovsky's pocket to the floor. Justin picked it up and examined it.

Nitroglycerin pills.

Shit! Chakhovsky has a heart condition, he thought. The charge that he had zapped him with could have killed him. He felt the Russian's wrist for a pulse. Fast and pounding—he was alive.

Justin opened the door and stepped out of the room. He could hear the footsteps of Kodek's team on the stairs. He went to the back stairway just off the room and down the stairs, as fast as his movements would allow with the Russian on his shoulders.

In the bell tower. Striker began his final preparations. Four 6mm explosive-tipped cartridges stood upright on the stone ledge beside the modified Winchester. The rifle rested on the ledge, cushioned by his rolled jacket.

Justin reached the window landing, just above the door leading out to the courtyard. He looked out carefully.

Just as the plan had indicated, there were two agents covering the back way out. Justin's eyes scanned the rooftops surrounding the open courtyard. He spotted the radio man almost immediately on the roof to his left. But the man he wanted to see was the sniper. He searched the rooftop of the building at the back of the courtyard. He wasn't there. There was no sniper on that roof!

His eyes searched frantically as his brain recalled Striker's words to Fanning. "If he is in a window, then you will have been right…that courtyard will be a death trap."

He saw no sniper. This wasn't the way, not on the last job. "He's not there," Justin whispered. "He ain't on the roof."

"He's there," came Striker's voice.

"I can't see him," Justin whispered.

"I can. He's out of position. The jerk is just sitting there below the ledge. The rifle barrel is up. Can you see it?" Striker asked.

Justin squinted. Yes, there it was.

"All right, I can see it," he said, relieved. "I'm going down the last flight of stairs. Then I'm bustin' out of here. *Don't miss!*"

He heard Striker's laugh.

"I never miss," the voice said.

You better not, Justin thought.

He moved quietly down the last few steps and stood inside the doorway, out of direct vision of the two agents.

Striker picked up one of the cartridges and loaded it into the rifle. He took a comfortable firing position and put his eye back to the scope. The crosshairs swung across the rooftop.

Bud Kodek and his men were just getting to Chakhovsky's room. He gave the coded knock. There was no response. He knocked again. Still nothing.

He tried the doorknob. It was open. He flashed a worried look into the eyes of his men.

The Mauser was out and ready. "Going...*now!*" Justin said.

He came through the door so quickly that the two agents were caught completely off guard. The Mauser coughed twice, then twice again. Both men were dead before they realized what had happened.

Back up in the hotel, Kodek pushed the unlocked door open. The room was empty. "*Shit!*" he let out and raced out into the hallway.

At the same instant, his radio crackled to life.

"Agents down in the back," the radio man's urgent voice shouted. "Got a man carrying a body."

Kodek sprinted down the hallway, his men close behind.

Justin had broken out into the courtyard and had begun a sprint for the opening between the buildings that led to the street. His eyes were fixed upward, at the tip of the rifle on the roof.

It was beginning to move into position.

Christ! What the fuck was he waiting for?

The rifle barrel started coming down. The eye and the scope came together to begin drawing the bead on the moving target. The sniper's crosshairs found the mark. The finger went to the trigger.

Justin watched the barrel swing down at him. It moved downward and downward, and continued downward, the stock pitching up and over as the rifle tumbled from the roof.

Kodek was about halfway down the three flights of stairs when the radio crackled to life again.

"I can see him clearly. He's got Chak—" The transmission was suddenly cut off.

Kodek moved quickly for a big man. He got through the door just as the tall figure disappeared between the two buildings, heading for the street.

Kodek shouted into his radio, "Mobiles one and two, get to the back of the perimeter. They've got him. *Move! Move! Move!*"

He raced across the courtyard.

Justin reached the street just as the powerful new Mercedes 450 SEL braked to a stop at the curb.

The back door opened, and Justin threw Chakhovsky in and dove in on top of him.

The Mercedes smoked away from the curb, just as mobile one, a black Citroën, turned the corner on screeching tires.

Kodek made it between the two buildings just as mobile one sped by. Close behind it was a second Mercedes.

Kodek recognized a face. It was KGB.

A second later, mobile two came skidding around the corner and scorched past Kodek. The chase was on.

Kodek's face reddened as he stood helplessly and watched the cars disappear around a turn. Morsand was going to be all over his ass for this one.

He just shook his head. "I don't fuckin' believe it!" he yelled. "They got him. Right from under our noses. They got him. *Son-of-a-bitch!*" he yelled in a final protest.

Fanning sped skillfully through the streets, all the time with one eye watching the rearview mirror. The more powerful Citroën was closing on him slowly but steadily.

"This is Badger," Fanning said to SENTINEL Control's monitor. "I've got some hawks on my tail. I'll need help."

"This is SENTINEL Control," the soft voice responded. "We have your position. You will be coming up to Place St. Michele in two blocks. Go left to pick up your interference."

Justin stuck his head up to get a look at how close the Citroën was. It was close.

Justin changed the clip in the Mauser and removed the silencer.

The Citroën was beginning to bear down on the Mercedes as they approached the intersection at Place St. Michele.

"Move...*now!*" went the instructions from SENTINEL Control.

A small, red Fiat accelerated at the intersection just as Fanning began his controlled skid through the turn, the Citroën right on him.

The Fiat missed Fanning by mere feet and swerved right into the Citroën, smashing heavily into the left front of the chase car.

It was a violent crash. The Fiat bounced and rolled away, looking like a crumpled beer can. The Citroën spun through the intersection, coming to a rest on the other side, its front left side and wheel smashed hopelessly in the crash.

An agent got out of mobile one just as the blue Mercedes carrying KGB skidded through the turn and followed hotly behind Fanning. The agent ran into the intersection cursing and threw down his crumpled hat in frustration.

Mobile two skidded into the turn and swerved. But it was no good. There was a heavy, dull thud. The agent was tossed through the air like a rag dummy. Mobile two went out of control and skidded into some parked cars and stalled.

The driver kicked the engine over twice before it caught. The car then limped off, smoke belching effusively from its badly damaged right front end, where the fender and tire were in contact. It could not generate sufficient speed to keep up with the other two cars, but it charged on gamely, anyway.

An attractive young woman exited from the smashed Fiat. Badly ruffled, blood on her face, limping, she charged at the driver of the Citroën. She began cursing a murderous stream at him in French. The driver tried to calm her, but it was no use. She ranted on and on, as the third occupant of mobile one raced to his badly injured comrade lying in the street.

Fanning tore through the narrow streets, taking many twisting, skidding turns. His skill was breathtaking. But so was the Soviet driver's; he didn't lose an inch.

Fanning shook his head in exasperation. He knew that it was KGB behind him. He had to lose this car cleanly to make the plan work perfectly.

He rounded another corner on skidding wheels and ran smack into a traffic jam. Before he could try to move out of it, three cars had filed in behind him. The Soviet driver pulled into the line, as well, four cars back.

Fanning looked into his rearview mirror and saw one of the Soviet agents leave the car and begin moving between the rows of cars toward them. He had drawn a weapon.

Like fish in a barrel, Fanning thought. "We've got big trouble, partner," he said to Justin.

Justin's head popped up quickly and got a look at the approaching Soviet agent.

Justin lowered his head and readied the Mauser.

Fanning was in the extreme inside lane, right beside the sidewalk.

"We're gettin' the fuck outta here," he announced.

He floored the accelerator, smashing into the rear of the car in front of him. The tires squealed and belched smoke, as he rammed the other car into the one ahead of it. Then he shifted it into reverse and floored it again, pulling a repeat number on the car behind him.

The Russian raised his gun and fired at the lurching car. The bullet smashed through and shattered the back window, deflecting upward through the roof of the car, narrowly missing Fanning's head.

The Mauser cracked back through the disintegrated rear window, hitting the Russian in the chest. He was knocked across the hood of a smaller car, blood splashing across the windshield of the terrified, screaming woman driver.

Fanning cut the wheel sharply and gunned it, leaping onto the sidewalk, and sped toward the intersection—half on, half off the sidewalk. A car door was torn off of one car, whose driver had opened it to see what was happening behind him. Fortunately, he had not yet set foot out of his car.

Terrified pedestrians leaped for safety. The car took down small sign poles, tore through waste disposal containers, and was bearing down on an occupied phone booth. The wide-eyed occupant wasn't as lucky as the man whose door had been torn off. He had no chance to get out of the booth before Fanning smashed through it.

Meanwhile, the Soviet driver had duplicated the feat performed by Fanning and was hauling ass down the sidewalk, scattering the frightened pedestrians yet again.

Fanning sped into the wide intersection and raced across it. Cars screeched and skidded trying to avoid him. Almost miraculously, he made it across untouched.

The Soviet driver began his run through, too, but some of the cars had again begun to move through, closing Fanning's route. About halfway across, he was struck on the rear quarter. The Russian car spun into another car and stalled. After repeated attempts to get it started again, the engine caught. The car limped through the intersection, but Fanning's car was nowhere to be seen. It had vanished.

Dmitri Chakhovsky had been taken.

FIFTEEN

With imminent defeat lying before us, we began fran-
tic redirection of the huge fortunes amassed from the early
victories. They were considerable. We had looted entire
countries.

The largest portion of these spoils went into a secret
treasury, as directed by the special branch of Niederlage.
This would be essential to the long difficult comeback
being planned.

The treasury was divided into many smaller caches,
which we placed throughout the entire world in countries
friendly to our cause, in neutral countries, and even in the
countries of our enemies. We put the financial means to
our return right under their noses. To this day, many have
not been discovered.

Entry No. 26 from the partially
recovered *Wolf Journal*

It was almost 0800 hours in Washington as the Lear started its
high-altitude cruise homeward.

The President waited nervously by his direct line to the
SENTINEL complex. Any second now, Honeycut would be call-
ing him with the news. The large Oval Office was silent. The
President was edgy. This was not an instance of no news being

good news. Every tape measure second that passed made him fear that it had not gone well.

He waited, tapping the end of his pen against the desk pad.

Call! Call! Damn it, call!

Bzzz! Bzzzz! The soft tones startled him. He leaped for the drawer containing the phone.

Bzzzz! Bzz—

"Yes, Irv. How'd it go?"

Honeycut was momentarily stopped by the way the President had answered the phone. The usual, "This is the President," was missing, replaced by the nervous rush of words.

"We have him, Mr. President." Honeycut could hear the long sigh of relief at the other end. "It didn't come out as cleanly as we had hoped, but we got him."

"Where are they now?" the President asked.

"They're forty-five thousand feet over the Atlantic, speeding home. Chakhovsky will be eating apple pie for his dessert tonight, sir," Honeycut said, with a graveled chuckle.

"And the CIA? Was anyone...did anyone get hurt?" the President asked apprehensively. He knew the answer almost immediately by the pause in Honeycut's response. He had learned long ago that something unpleasant would follow the silence.

"I'm afraid so, Mr. President. Morsand had taken measures not outlined in his plan. There was only one way to handle the unexpected situation they found themselves in. It was only the good instincts and skills of the team that saved the day for us. It was regrettable, but the alternative was failure," Honeycut assured him.

"How bad?" the President asked.

Honeycut took a breath and let it out into the phone, another admonition of unpleasant tidings.

"Four CIA dead, one badly injured. His condition is unknown at the present time. He was struck by one of their own chase cars. We think he's alive. There were also three KGB agents killed, and we think possibly one pedestrian may have been killed during the chase."

The President gasped. "My god, Irv. Eight dead, possibly nine? It was a bloodbath."

"It was necessary, Mr. President. The KGB was there ahead of Morsand. The prettiest setup you could want to see. They came about two seconds away from icing Chakhovsky. Who knows how many of Morsand's men would have been killed if it weren't for Pilgrim. He turned it all around for us, Mr. President.

"We could have lost a lot more and still come away empty. It was handled well, in the only way possible, sir," Honeycut assured him again.

"Yes, I...I'm sure that it was, Irv. It just bothers me that American lives had to be taken in the process. What now? Where do we go from here?" he asked.

"Well, sir, two small complications have come up. The first is that Chakhovsky has a heart condition that we were unaware of. We won't know how serious it is until we can examine him. The second is that our objective of leaving both sides thinking that the other has him has been shot to hell. If it could have stopped after the first two KGB agents, there might have been a chance. But there are too many bodies from both sides. I'm certain that we can weather it okay. We'll just have to take some extra steps to keep our tracks covered," Honeycut explained.

"And what about Chakhovsky?" the President asked.

"He'll be taken to one of our special security installations, one equipped to handle his potential heart condition. After a very thorough checkup, he'll be debriefed and treated medically to take care of his problem. Then we'll begin the slow process of Americanization. We'll essentially create a new life for him here. He'll be given a new identity, a new appearance through plastic surgery and other cosmetic aids, and then he'll be taught to think, act, and talk like a born American. When he's ready, he'll go out and become a part of our citizenry, so different from his former self that even his mother wouldn't recognize him," Honeycut outlined.

"Once he's let out into our society, will there be any chance of his discovery?"

"Virtually none. But, to be on the safe side, we'll implant him. It will be explosive, just as a precaution against the worst of possible eventualities. I'd bet on his living out a normal life, though, Mr. President. We can really change him. The hard part is done. The rest just takes time and patience, and we have plenty of both."

The President nodded in approval as he listened.

"Good work, Irv. I don't have to tell you how important all of this has been. I think you're the one who told me. Thank you, Irv."

"Don't thank me, Mr. President. You can thank the boys who got it done. I told you they were good. They got it done against some pretty tough odds," Honeycut said.

"You're right.

"They've done their country a great service. They've been through a lot during the past week. Why don't you give them both a nice vacation. First class all the way. It's on the White House, Irv. They've earned it."

Honeycut laughed. "I'd be glad to, Mr. President. Thank you, and I'll keep you informed of any further developments."

"Good, Irv. Thank you, again," the President said as he put down his phone. He closed the drawer and locked it with a special key that armed an intruder device in the drawer.

His stomach growled. He hadn't eaten yet. He knew that, before the morning was over, Shyleur Platt would be in the Oval Office coughing out alternating alibis and fits of rage over the deal. He was a hard man to take, sometimes. Especially on an empty stomach.

The President went to breakfast.

Bud Kodek stood in front of a very irate Robert Morsand. His initial rage had subsided somewhat, and he was now digesting what Kodek had told him of the incident. It hadn't been much.

"Well, one thing is for certain, the KGB didn't get him," Morsand said. "They wouldn't have taken such great care to get him alive. It would have been a quick one in the head and then out of there as easily as they got in. Somebody wanted him alive. But who?"

"The only ones who got a look at him are dead," Kodek began. "I got a glimpse of him, but it was from a distance, and all I could see was the back of him. He was tall and fast as hell. He had Chakhovsky over his shoulder and still ran like a deer. He took Rucker and Tonelli coming through the door, then somehow got Cash before he could nail him from the roof. Must have got him on the run. Then he took out Malory. The car that picked him up blew in from the rear of the perimeter too fast for us to stop him. I guess we were too loose in the back there."

"I don't think that the man that got Chakhovsky also got Cash and Malory," Morsand said. "Both Malory and Cash were a mess. They were taken out with explosive bullets. Rucker and Tonelli weren't. Cash was an impossible shot from the ground. On the run, with a man on his shoulders, an angle that was almost straight up—I don't think it could be done. He had help, probably from outside the perimeter. It was well planned. Whoever it was had good information. They knew our plan.

"What about the woman and the girl?" he asked.

"Well, after the cars tore off, I figured it was KGB. I recognized one of them in the blue Mercedes. Then we went back up to the third floor to begin a room by room search. The first room we searched after coming up the back stairway had the bodies.

"It was odd at first. The older one was made up to look a lot older than she was. A good job of makeup, too. The other one looked like a girl at first glance. Fourteen, maybe. But I don't think she was that young. The older one was armed with an automatic. There was another one just like it in the dresser near where the girl was found. We've taken what we need to make an ID. If they're in our files, we'll have it soon.

"They were both killed with single head shots. Nonexplosive. We got a few slugs, but they were pretty torn up. We should still be able to get some sort of ballistics picture from them, though. My guess is that both females were KGB.

"Another known KGB agent was killed at the intersection during the chase. He apparently tried to approach on foot. Shots were exchanged, and he took a chestful. Again, nonexplosive."

Morsand nodded. "The only explosive loads used were the ones to take out the rooftop agents. I'm sure I was right. Someone from outside the perimeter fired those shots. And the KGB doesn't run around blowing away its own people, either. It wasn't KGB. Someone else got him. And that brings us back to the same question. Who?"

Kodek just looked at his boss.

Morsand rubbed his cheek. "It could have been any one of the Western European countries. They would all have a lot to gain from the information he could give them. Maybe the British, or the French. They'd stand to gain the most. West Germany, too. Or even Israel. Too many maybes at this point."

Morsand shut off the tape recorder. He pressed the button on his intercom.

"Yes, Mr. Morsand," his secretary answered.

"Could you come in here for a moment, Linda?" he asked.

"Yes, sir."

A second later, a young, attractive woman walked into his office. Kodek always liked looking at her. Small tits, but great ass and legs. Normally his mind would have been in her panties, but the events of the day had totally dulled any happy fantasies.

"Could you please have this tape transcribed? It's urgent. I want a top priority on it," Morsand said.

"Yes, sir. I'll take it right down," she said and left the office.

"I'm going down to communications," Morsand began. "I'll get Platt on the scrambler. There's no use in putting this off, I have the feeling that we're going to be out of answers on this for a while."

He started to walk out of his office, then turned back to Kodek. He looked at the big hulking man, handsome in his rugged way. It hadn't been Kodek's fault. They had been just plain outclassed today. "How's Charlie doing?" he asked, referring to the agent who had been struck by mobile two.

Kodek nodded his head. "He's gonna make it. Both legs and hip broke up real bad, but he's alive. I wish I could say the same for the rest of them."

"Yeah, so do I."

Morsand could see that Kodek felt responsible for what had happened. "I guess I could have made a better plan," he began for Kodek's sake. "It's always easy to see where you went wrong or where the weak spots were when you have the facility of hindsight to help.

"Well, Platt's going to want answers, and fast. And so do I. Get every available ass out there digging. Everybody makes mistakes. Let's find theirs, and then we're going to get Chakhovsky back. Somebody went to a lot of trouble to get him alive. There might be more to this than we're aware of. I want to know who he was so important to. We owe them a few after today."

A few minutes later, he was on the scrambler with Shyleur Platt, the director of the Central Intelligence Agency. This was Platt's first news of the developments in the Chakhovsky affairs. He was expecting to hear that the most important defection of the decade had gone routinely.

"Well?" was all he asked.

Morsand mentally grabbed his nuts to protect them from the asschewing he was about to get. It was the first one in a long time, but he had a sick feeling inside that told him it was only the beginning.

"*Well?*" Platt asked again, impatiently.

"We lost him."

SIXTEEN

As the end drew nearer, our efforts picked up. We had a deadline to meet.

We killed all of the "enemy" that we could get our hands on. The death camps operated round the clock. Every one that died today would be one less to fight tomorrow, in our eternal war against die Untermenschen.

And so, in the ending of the Third Reich, we were beginning our preparations for the Fourth, when we would rise again, to reclaim our destiny.

We did not care what the world thought. Our ultimate success would justify everything.

Entry No. 27 from the partially
recovered *Wolf Journal*

Friday morning came to Chicago filled with the chill of early April. Dr. Edward Bridges shivered all the way to work, despite the belching warmth of his car heater. His feet and hands would not warm up; the cold ate right through him. It was his last day.

It was not the way he had imagined it would be. There had been no dramatic countdown of days, ticking away one by one. This was too fast—one call, one day to prepare, then go. It wasn't as satisfying as his fantasies had allowed. He could not savor it.

He walked into his office the usual thirty minutes early and closed his door. This would tell Pat that he was in and was not to be disturbed.

He sat behind the desk and removed the blank report forms for the last time. When he went out tonight, it would be for real. The schematics would be around his legs, and there would be no coming back. But he was ready for what had to be done. It would be just one more trip, as easy as the rest. All the practice was now going to pay off. It would be a cakewalk. So why was he so nervous about it?

He put his security plate into the slot, to activate the sliding door to his inner office, and went in. The door swished closed behind him. He looked at the thick volumes of schematics, wishing he could take them all. But he knew which ones he needed and began going through the volumes, removing them carefully. Just as he had planned, there were twenty-four.

It didn't seem like so little could contain so much, but, with the information contained on those sheets, another SENTINEL could be built for anyone with the means and the talent to make it possible.

He shook his head and tried to imagine two of them in the world. Two Babels. That's what they should have named it, he thought. Babel. That's what it really was, after all. Only this one was completed. Man's greatest achievement, approaching the wonder of creation itself. God had taken seven days to enact that miracle; man had taken seven years. Perhaps, even as God confounded the tongues of the first architects of Babel, He had known that they would attempt one after the other until one day they would reach the mysterious heavens of their dreams. They had, in fact, been made in His own image and likeness. Too much so, for man had the habit of playing God with his environment and his world. SENTINEL now put him very close.

He looked through the sheets one more time, to make sure that he had everything he needed. It was all there—more power than any man had ever held, more potential than any man would ever possess. And Edward Bridges was stealing it, as easily as a little boy stealing a pack of chewing gum from a busy supermarket.

He piled the sheets neatly and left them on the corner of the desk in that office, then went back through the sliding door to his outer office. The nervousness was fading. He was confident and ready.

He plopped down behind his huge desk and unwrapped a cigar. Lighting it with great ceremony, he puffed and filled the room with vile clouds of smoke. Tomorrow he'd be one of the most important men in the whole world. The future of that world was in his hands.

After a few minutes, he walked to his office door and opened it. Dr. Warren Geisler was outside, talking to Pat.

"Hi, Ed," Geisler said, as the door opened fully. "I was just about to ask Pat to give you a message to call me when you got the chance. You got a few minutes now?" the young scientist asked.

Warren Geisler was one of the new breed of computer scientists coming out of a very carefully and deliberately planned program initiated since the conception of SENTINEL. He was young and handsome and possessed enormous talent. He was the all-American stud, with a million-dollar brain. Warren Geisler was everything that Edward Bridges wasn't, and wanted to be.

"Sure, Warren. Come on in," Bridges said, leaving a trail of smoke as he walked back to his desk. "Are you going to have everything ready for Monday's meeting?" he asked.

"Yeah, as long as engineering gets me the final figures before the end of the day," Geisler replied.

"Good. You've done a lot of excellent work on that project. What was it you wanted to talk to me about?" Bridges asked his young assistant before he could respond to the compliment. A huge cloud of smoke began drifting toward the open door. Geisler walked in and sat quickly, to get below it.

"I just went to Elizabeth's office to talk to her about Monday's meeting to find out whether she wanted me to arrange for a demonstration of the oh-nineteen lab model. Gina said that she was out today and wouldn't be back until Monday because of her laryngitis. Do you think she's going to want to see it in action?" he asked Bridges.

Bridges's mind raced quickly. Ryerson was out. He'd never see the bitch again. That was too bad. He had been looking forward to that last eye contact with her. He nodded in answer to the question. "I'm almost certain she will, Warren. Probably not until the end of the meeting, though. Why don't you go ahead and set it up for about fifteen thirty hours? I doubt we'll be much later than that," Bridges said. He puffed another vile cloud.

"All right, Ed." Geisler rose to beat his retreat to the door, ahead of the drifting cloud. He stopped and turned back to Bridges. "I almost forgot, Ed. Can I take out the oh-nineteen schematic after I get the figures from engineering? I'll only need it for a few minutes," he said.

A sharp twinge knifed through Bridges. The 019 schematic was one of the twenty-four he had selected to take out with him. Calm down, he ordered himself. It had to be back in his hands before the end of the day, or no one was allowed out of the complex. Stay calm. Got to keep him out of the inner office. He might see the sheets all piled up and get suspicious.

"Sure, Warren. But why don't you give me a call when you need it and I'll bring it over? I want to go over those final figures with you, anyway. I'll save you the trip."

"Okay, Ed. I'll call you later, then," Geisler said, then left.

So, Elizabeth was going to be out all day. That raised some interesting possibilities. Bridges was thinking about the secret files he knew she kept in her desk. He didn't know what was in them, but he knew that they were for nobody's eyes but Elizabeth's and whomever it was that she saw when she went to Washington. This might be a good chance, his only chance, to see what was inside of them. It could even help him work out a better deal with the Russians. Who could tell? The only way was to check it out.

His problem now would be figuring out a way to get rid of Gina long enough to get in and out of Elizabeth's office safely.

After several moments of thought, he opened the file drawer of his desk. It was in here that he kept the personnel files of all his assistants. He took out Warren Geisler's folder and another belonging to Dr. Phillip Clark. Both men were young and talented scientists, with promising futures in the SENTINEL program. He had been after Elizabeth to raise their security levels one notch, to get them into the program on a deeper level. It would also fatten their pay checks substantially. These would do nicely, he thought.

He put Dr. Clark's folder back on the desk and took out a third one from the drawer. He got up, put on his jacket, and walked to the door, starting a phony limp as he got into Pat's office. He grimaced with each step as he walked past her desk and into the hallway.

Just before rounding the corner near Elizabeth's office, he snubbed out the cigar in a wall-mounted ashtray. Gina was busily typing away at some of Elizabeth's correspondence as he walked up.

"Hi, Gina," Bridges said. "Is she in her office?"

"Oh, I'm sorry, Dr. Bridges, but Dr. Ryerson is going to be out for the day. Her laryngitis was getting worse, and she wanted to try to shake it over the weekend."

Bridges made a disappointed frown. "Hmmm! I have some files she wanted to talk to me about this morning," he lied. "She made a point of wanting to get this thing cleared up before Monday, too."

"You could leave them with me, Dr. Bridges. I could attach a note and see that she gets them first thing on Monday," she suggested.

He nodded. "Yeah, I guess that's the best we can do," he said and checked Geisler's folder, then handed it to her. He checked the other folder and frowned. "Ah, damn," he said, "I brought the wrong file."

He turned to walk away and grimaced again. After a few well-acted limps, he turned back to her. "I hate to ask this, Gina, but do you think that you could be a doll and run down to my office for me? My leg is killing me, and I have to get over to engineering for a meeting I'm already late for."

"Oh, sure, I'd be happy to. What was it you wanted me to get?" she asked with a smile, glad at the chance to get away from her desk for a few minutes.

"Well, I had intended to bring Dr. Clark's personnel file along with Dr. Geisler's, but I must have picked up the wrong one by mistake. Just give this one to Pat, and tell her to leave it on my desk. Dr. Clark's should be right there," he said, handing her the folder.

"Fine, I'll go right down to get it," she said.

"Thanks, Gina, you're a real doll." He began to limp away in the direction of engineering.

"You're welcome," she said after him, walking around her desk and starting down the hall. A moment later she had disappeared around the corner.

Bridges hurried back into Elizabeth's office. He stepped inside and closed the door behind him. He guessed that he had about five minutes to find what he was after. He could count on Pat and Gina to gossip with each other for at least that long. He would be out of there in less than three.

He rushed over to her desk and tried the drawer. No good, it was locked. Damn! The drawer was fitted with a separate lock so that the rest of the drawers remained usable at all times. This is stupid, he thought. Why take such a dumb risk now, especially on the last day. I could blow the whole thing.

But the risk has already been taken, a small voice inside of him said. Why walk away now? It's already paid for. You're already here.

He opened the center drawer and began rummaging through it. He found a small metal box. He tried it, but it was locked. He pulled out his pocket knife and tried it gently. A few moments later it was open. Inside he found a small key-envelope. In it there was a single shiny key. He tried it. It fit. He twisted it, and the drawer unlocked. Bridges looked up at the clock. Only a minute left.

There were about thirty or forty folders in the drawer. There were no names or subject headings, just numbers. He spotted a red folder. He had remembered glimpsing a red folder in Elizabeth's attaché case prior to several of her Washington trips. He removed it and put it up under the back of his jacket and stuffed it into his pants. It held firmly under the belt. He closed the drawer, locked it, and put the key into his pocket. It would be needed later when he returned the file. That could be done when Gina was out to lunch.

He opened the door slowly. Gina wasn't back yet. He passed out of Elizabeth's office, through Gina's, and then out into the hallway, hurrying off toward engineering. In a moment he was safely away.

About five minutes later, when he was reasonably sure that Gina would be back at her desk, he went back to his office. He limped past Pat's desk and passed through the door, closing it behind him. He headed straight into the inner office, where nobody could disturb him. Besides himself, only Elizabeth had authority to open the door. That would mean absolute privacy for as long as he needed it.

He removed the folder from his pants. It was bent and creased from the rough handling. He looked at it. So what, he figured. By the time Elizabeth sees this folder again I'll be inside Russia and under heavy protection.

The folder bore no identifying marks, not even numbers, as had the others in the drawer. He took out a pad and pencil and placed them on the desk for notes. He opened the folder.

It contained about twenty sheets of paper, the first of which was a title page bearing a two-word heading—OPERATION RAPTOR.

Edward Bridges began reading.

The Lear had streaked about half its course homeward when Chakhovsky regained consciousness. He was strapped in a reclining position. He had been awake for several minutes already but had pretended not to be. He just listened and sneaked short, fast glances, in an attempt to assess his situation. At least he was alive; that showed some promise.

He decided finally that it was time to formally wake up. He opened his eyes wide and saw the tall, dark figure that had saved his life back at the safe house. For a moment their eyes locked. Chakhovsky's were still frightened, Justin's cool and unreadable.

The details of what had happened began to filter slowly back into the Russian's head. He remembered the old woman holding the gun. She was suddenly there, straighter and not so old as before. Then, when he thought he was dead and had closed his eyes, there was the sound of the silencer. The grunt from the old woman as she fell made him open his eyes. He saw the blood spurting from her head. Then he saw the man.

He remembered the young girl, her body being knocked backward against the dresser, the blood on her beautiful hair. And the man. Why did he kill the young girl? The girl...nothing was real anymore.

The compartment of the plane was small. He recognized the type of plane immediately. He looked out of the window at the sky. The position of the sun told him they were heading west. Thank God, not east.

"Can you sit up?" Justin asked him as he began to undo the Russian's straps.

Chakhovsky nodded and sat up after Justin had finished. He squinted and looked out of the window again. They were at a very high altitude. The sky was magnificently clear, and he could see the vast expanse of water below. It had to be the ocean.

"Do you need one of these?" Justin asked, holding out the small bottle of nitroglycerin pills.

The Russian shook his head.

Justin went forward and told Fanning that Chakhovsky had come to. They came aft together. Chakhovsky did not recognize Fanning.

"Who are you?" Chakhovsky asked. "And where are you taking me?"

"We work for Robert Morsand," Fanning lied. "You're on your way to the United States."

"In this plane?" Chakhovsky asked, shaking his head. "Maximum range is eighteen hundred miles," he said in his good, but accented English.

Fanning shook his head right back. "She's been modified. She'll go over four thousand miles, at almost six hundred miles an hour. You're heading for America, all right," he said.

"Where is Morsand?" Chakhovsky asked.

"Trying to shovel his way out of the mess you got him into by leaving your room. Your little adventure cost seven lives. Four CIA, three KGB," Fanning said.

Chakhovsky's eyes narrowed. "I...I am sorry," he said.

"Sorry doesn't make it," Justin told him. "Your people were pretty good in there. It would have been messy any way we went. But what you did almost made it easy for them. It's a good thing Morsand decided to send us in early, or it might have been a short day's work."

"Seven lives..." Chakhovsky stared at the floor of the cabin.

"How long have you had the heart condition?" Justin asked.

"Only for some months now. Six, maybe seven," the Russian replied.

"Exactly what is the problem?" Justin asked.

Chakhovsky shook his head.

"Well, what did the doctors tell you?"

"There were no doctors. I took the pills from the consulate infirmary," Chakhovsky confessed.

"You mean you didn't go to a doctor? You just took these pills without knowing what was wrong with you?"

The Russian nodded his head.

"Why?" Justin asked in disbelief.

"My work is...was all that I had. My wife and only son are dead. I have no one. Only my work. They would have relieved me and retired me," he said.

"Have you ever had an electrocardiogram?" Justin asked.

"Yes, but before the attacks started. It was completely normal."

"You should have gone to a doctor. There are a dozen things it could be, not even related to the heart," Justin said.

Chakhovsky shook his head. "One knows," he said.

"Not as much as you think," Justin retorted.

Justin went forward with Fanning.

"What's it look like?" Fanning asked.

"What in the hell are you asking me for? I think he needs to be looked at right away," Justin answered with a wrinkled expression.

BEEP!

"Come in, Control," Fanning said.

"You will proceed on your course heading. You will be receiving course changes before your ETA. Your new destination and additional instructions will be given to you at that time."

"Roger, we copy."

The instructions puzzled Justin and worried him a little bit. He didn't want to have to stand up his son again. He was supposed to take him for the weekend starting tomorrow.

"New destination?" he asked. "I wonder where to."

"Don't know. I put down at St. Simon's Island once with a cargo just like this one," Fanning said, throwing a thumb to the rear of the plane. "He was wounded pretty bad. They changed course in midflight for that sucker, and he wasn't as important as this one here. Might be that his condition has someone concerned. More than likely a medical facility or something down there."

"How long will it take for us to get there?" Justin asked.

"If it's St. Simon's Island, it should take about four hours. Why? You gotta be someplace? Big date?" Fanning asked with a smile.

"Yeah, a big date I can't afford to break," Justin said.

"You'll make it," Fanning guaranteed.

Edward Bridges was sweaty and flushed. What he had just read had shaken him. It couldn't be possible. Not…not today, not here, he thought.

Not all of the meaning was yet clear in his head, but enough of it was, and it scared him. Operation Raptor had been started over thirty-five years ago. It had survived and grown all these years. It was incredible, and it was here, in America.

The pad next to him contained some key notes he had made. It was greatly condensed, almost like a simplified flow chart of a complex chemical reaction. It could all be made to fit on one page if organized properly and then typed. He could stop off at his place and type it before heading out to O'Hare. He was sure the Soviets would receive this with the utmost interest.

He checked his watch. It was almost one o'clock. Gina would be getting back from lunch soon. The time had just slid by. He was so engrossed in the contents of the folder that the noon hour passed without his knowing it. He had to get that file back quickly.

Bridges rearranged the sheets and put them in the folder. Then he stuffed it back into his pants, covering it with the jacket once more. He left his office and hurried into the hallway.

Moments later, he was in Elizabeth's office, replacing it in the file drawer. He wished that he had the time to go through the rest of the folders in the drawer. He was almost afraid of what they might say. There was no doubt, however, that what he had seen was the most important of the bunch. He closed the drawer and locked it. He put the key back into the small metal box and returned it to the center drawer. He checked the room to make sure that everything was as he had found it. Then he left and returned to his office.

He ran through his plans one more time. The information, the typing of the notes he had taken from the red folder, out to O'Hare for the rental car, and then off to Beloit and a new life. He looked at the clock. Four hours left. The nervousness began to build in his stomach. It was a countdown now, in hours, then it would be minutes, then seconds, as he passed through security for the last time. The last time! It rang in his head. Everything he did today was for the last time.

It was ten minutes past quitting time at Alpha. Warren Geisler had not gotten the figures he needed from engineering until five minutes before the end of the day. He decided to finish the report on Saturday morning. All that needed to be done was to put in the final figures and then to check the 019 schematic one last time on Monday. An hour's work at the most.

Edward Bridges was relieved that he didn't have to let out that schematic. Not that it would have made any difference, it had to be back in his hands by the end of the day anyway. But he felt better about keeping it close. He walked to his door and looked out. Pat was gone, probably for the evening, he thought. He pushed the door to shut it and turned back toward his desk. He didn't see that the door hadn't closed fully. He went into the inner office to get the schematics.

Outside of his office, Pat was just returning to her desk. She had forgotten her car keys.

Bridges stepped out of his inner office just as Pat entered hers. He walked over to his huge desk and plopped the schematics down. He counted out the first twelve. His nervousness had been building throughout the later part of the day. His palms were cold and wet, but he still felt good.

Pat found her keys, removed the weekend days from the calendar, and was about to leave, when she noticed that Bridges's door was partially open and that the light was on inside. She hadn't seen him before leaving the first time and decided to wish him a good weekend. She moved for the door.

Bridges was sitting behind his desk with the first twelve sheets in his hands. Their heavy bond would not bend as easily as he had anticipated. He placed the schematics on the desk, bent forward, pulled up his right pant leg, and tugged at the sock, pulling it away from the leg to test the stretch.

"Good night, Dr. Bridges. Have a nice weekend," Pat called from the doorway.

Bridges's body jerked violently upright, his hands pulling upward in response to the shock of the voice. His sudden, forceful move stretched the sock, snapping many of the elastics. He threw his arms across the schematics to hide them from her view. He looked up, white-faced.

"Oh, Pat. You startled me. Good…good night, and you have a nice weekend, yourself," he said, doing his best to sound unshaken.

"Oh, I'm sorry, Dr. Bridges. I didn't mean to startle you like that. Did you tear something? It sounded like something ripping," she said.

"No. No, it was just my sock, the elastic. It's been falling on me all day. I was just pulling it up. I stretched it that's all," he invented quickly.

"Are you sure? If something has ripped I can sew it up for you real quick. I have a needle and thread in my desk," she offered.

"No, Pat, really. It was just the elastic in my sock. Thanks. Honest."

"Well, okay, I guess. I am sorry, Dr. Bridges."

"It's okay, Pat. Have yourself a nice weekend," he said as sweat beaded on his face and forehead.

"You too, Dr. Bridges. See you on Monday."

"On Monday." He nodded. On Monday, he thought. Shit!

His heart was pounding like a cannon. He raised a hand to his wet forehead. Oh Christ, that had triggered him. The floodgate was open. He was shaking now and couldn't stop it.

He breathed deeply, trying to calm himself. He put the schematics on the desk, walked over to the door, and pushed it closed again. This time he saw it open up after not closing all the way. He gave it a shove. It was closed tight this time.

He went back to his desk. By the time he got there, the sock had fallen to his ankle. He bent over again and examined it. Maybe it would still hold. If not, he'd use a rubber band to secure it. He picked up the first pile of schematics again and tried bending them around his leg. It was a tougher job than he had imagined it would be. They were considerably heavier than the report sheets. He managed to pull the baggy sock up over them. It felt snug enough. He got up and took a few steps around the room. It would hold. The rubber band wouldn't be needed.

He had some difficulty with the other leg, so he stretched that sock, too. He stuffed the leg and pulled up the sock. It felt perfect. Now to get the hell out of there.

Before getting up, he looked slowly around the room. It seemed to him as if he were seeing it for the first time instead of the last. He mentally pictured the rest of the complex, or he tried to, anyway. It seemed so vague, as if he were already forgetting. But this office, *his* office—a wave of emotion engulfed him. This had been his second home for seven years. And now he was leaving it, for places unseen and unknown. It wasn't supposed to be like this. He was supposed to be happy.

After a few more silent moments, he put on his coat. He looked back as he was walking out. His eyes moistened. He decided to close the door, so that on Monday morning Pat would think he was in there, and nobody would be allowed to disturb him. It might not be discovered all morning that he wasn't in. That would give him even more valuable time, although he would probably already be in Russia by then.

He walked out into the hallway. It seemed a hundred miles long. His nerves were jumping, and his legs felt weak. The sweat that poured from his body had already made his undershirt stick to his back. He could feel a trickle of sweat run down the inside of his thigh, almost to the knee, before his pants absorbed it.

Anxiety was taking control of his body. His legs didn't want to move, he felt like puking. He knew now how Ross must have felt that night at Kinzie's. He walked down the hallway slowly, telling himself that everything was fine.

His eyes focused on the water cooler. His throat felt suddenly like feathers. He stopped and took a long cooling drink and watched the water swirling down the drain.

Down the drain!

That's where he could end up if something went wrong. What if they steal my information and leave me behind, he worried. He'd better do something about that. Yeah, he could stop off on the way home. He knew what to do. It would only take a few minutes.

He had begun to walk away from the cooler, when he felt the schematics move. They weren't as tight now. The socks felt loose around the ankle. Jesus Christ, they were falling!

He started to bend forward when he heard voices behind him. It was Gina and Dr. Clark. Bridges looked up at the hallway clock. Five thirty. What were they doing here so late?

He began walking to keep ahead of them but the right sock was getting looser with each step. It looked almost as though he were limping, as he shuffled the foot smoothly to keep the sock from falling any further.

"Leg still bothering you, Dr. Bridges?" Gina asked.

He looked up nervously, as his colleagues flanked him. Sweat was rolling down his face.

"What's wrong with your leg?" Dr. Clark asked him.

"Oh, just a little stiffness in the knee. It comes and goes," he lied.

"You ought to get that looked at, Ed," Clark said.

"Yes...yes, I think I will. Tomorrow," he said with a nervous little laugh.

They slowed their pace to walk with him. They came to the security checkpoint.

Each level had its own security station, with another central security checkpoint at ground level. This was level three, or the "red deck" as it was known, because of the red floors and ceilings throughout the entire level. Each level had a different color. The "red deck" was the main area of activity in the Alpha complex.

Getting out of Alpha was a simple matter compared to getting in. On entering, one had to pass through the outer doors at ground level. These were activated by inserting an identification plate bearing a magnetic code into the slot next to the door. Once through these, a second, identical set of doors was encountered against the far side of a small foyer. These doors were operated in the same way as the first set, except that they would open only if the first set had already closed. This prevented anyone on the outside from seeing in past the foyer and beyond the second set of doors. In the event of emergency, all doors could open at the same time.

After going through the second set of doors, one passed between two armed military guards positioned at either side of the doors. This was the ground level security checkpoint.

It was a large room with three sets of sliding doors, the one from the foyer being the first. The second set was along the right wall. These were colored black. Only security personnel passed through these doors and knew what was behind them. An intruder would find out fast enough for himself. Word had it that it was very, very unpleasant. The third set was a duplicate of the first, white in color and leading to the elevator that descended to the six various levels of Alpha. These doors were situated on the wall to the left of the entrance. Against the center wall was a long black table, its top like polished glass. This was a very special desk.

At one end of the desk was a ledger, which every person entering or leaving the complex signed. There was a pen connected to a holder by a fine wire, much like any pen you might find in a bank or at the registration desk of a hotel. But this pen was also special. It transmitted the impulse of the signature from the pressure-sensitive tip along the wire directly to SENTINEL. The signature was then compared to the record file. Over two hundred separate characteristics were checked. A forgery was impossible.

After signing the ledger, the next step involved looking through a periscopelike device into a soft blue light. Retinal patterns were checked. No two are alike.

Then there was an area on the shiny surface that measured about twelve inches square. The right hand was placed here, palm down, and the entire print was checked. Once past this, one passed between two more armed guards into the elevators. The guards were big, menacing-looking fellows who never spoke. They just watched everyone all the time—ever silent, always watching.

After arriving at the desired level, one went through the entire process all over again, at the secondary security stations located on each floor. All security checkpoints were identical, except for floor, ceiling, and door coloring.

Leaving Alpha was a much simpler matter. All that was required was to sign out and surrender any bags or cases for search. The signing of the ledger was just to record your leaving the complex.

Bridges stood before the security station. He was paralyzed. It was as though his fear were trying to stop him from going further. Fear is funny that way. You are held back by the dread of what lies ahead and, at the same time, driven forward by the thing in us all that lets us derive a strange pleasure and exhilaration from it. Both repelled and drawn closer—one urge is dictated by the instinct for self-preservation, the other by self-destruction. A strange admixture of sensations.

Bridges tried desperately to force it from his mind.

"You don't look too well, Ed," Dr. Clark said to him.

"I don't feel well, either," he replied. "I'm going to bed when I get home," he said.

The group passed through the security checkpoint and entered the elevator. The right sock was starting to go. The schematics were beginning to move away from the leg, applying a still greater downward force against the sock.

Several minutes later, they had signed out of the main security checkpoint at ground level and stood waiting for the doors to open. Bridges could feel the eyes of the military guards boring into him. His face was flushed, and he was covered with perspiration. If anyone looked like he should be stopped and searched, he was sure it was him.

They were watching him. He was looking back. He wanted to throw up. He felt like raising his hands and giving himself up.

The doors finally opened. A few minutes later, the outer set of doors opened as well, and they stepped into the outside world of the Aztek Corporation. It was a long walk out to the parking lot, and he was sure the sock wouldn't hold. His mind raced. What could he do before they came tumbling out? He had to do something.

Wait! There was a bathroom just around the turn in the hallway. It wasn't far. But it wasn't close, either. Every step made the sock slip lower. Only the bottoms of the sheets were now held in place. They were beginning to fall away from his legs and were lying against the pant legs. They were bulging. One more inch and it was good-bye Bridges. He turned the corner.

It was just ahead. Please, nobody look down at my pant legs or have to take a leak. He walked the last steps. He prayed.

It was gone! The sock was down and the sheets rested on the bridge of his foot. Only three shuffling steps...two...one. He moved to the bathroom. No one noticed as he fell back and pushed the door open. The others kept on walking.

Please be empty, he prayed. He pushed his way in just as the sheets fell out. His heart nearly stopped as he looked up. The room was empty. No one had seen. His head was nearly exploding with the pounding of his heart.

"Whew!" he let out in winded relief. He bent down after a moment of recuperation. He gathered the sheets and stuffed them back into the sock. He pulled it up, and it again felt snug. Then he adjusted the left leg. That would easily get him the rest of the way.

He walked back out into the hallway and out of the building, the fear still burning in his eyes. He made it to his car and flopped in. It was over. He had beaten them. Not quite the cakewalk that he had imagined, but it was sweet victory just the same.

He started the car and removed the sheets. He put them on the seat beside him. Then he drove off to his first stop—the library, for a little insurance.

SEVENTEEN

The "big lie" began when we realized beyond all doubt that the war was lost. We kept the people believing in ultimate victory to keep them fighting to the end.

The Führer said, "If the war should be lost, the nation too will be lost. That would be the nation's unalterable fate. Then there is no need to consider the basic requirements that people need in order to continue to live a primitive life. On the contrary, it is better ourselves to destroy such things, for the nation will have proved itself the weaker and the future will belong to the stronger Eastern nation. Those who remain alive after the battles are over are in any case only inferior persons, since the best have fallen."

The Volkssturm—the last-ditch force of all remaining manpower—was mobilized. The children and old men of Germany prepared for the battle of the Fatherland.

Entry No. 29 from the partially
recovered *Wolf Journal*

From his position the fat man could watch the entire gate area and the ramp leading to the terminal pod. His stubby hand pushed a soiled hanky across his sweat-covered face. He had always had a bad perspiration problem; the waiting made it worse. He hated waiting.

This was the first time the fat man had ever been in the Newark International Airport. It was impressive. Concrete, steel, and glass were shaped into three expansive, futuristic structures, the lines and contrasting design of which left one with the feeling of being in gentle, lazy motion.

Each terminal had three podlike extensions connected to the main terminal body by long, glass-enclosed ramps. In each pod were ten to twelve boarding gates.

It was here that he knew Carson Ross would come. He was ticketed on TWA Flight 193 to Chicago, departing at 7:45 a.m. It was now 7:15, and Ross still hadn't checked in.

The fat man looked at his watch and wiped the sweat from his face.

Five minutes later the dark, round eyes spotted Ross coming down the rampway. Ross didn't notice the short, fat man fall in behind him as he stepped up to the check-in counter to get his seat assignment.

"Flight one-ninety-three to Chicago," he said to the very pretty black woman behind the counter.

"Do you have any bags to be checked?" she asked with a smile.

"No, just carry-on," he replied, holding on tightly to the flight bag in his hand. He had good reasons for not letting that bag out of his hands—twenty-five thousand reasons, every one of them an American dollar. He had, indeed, made a sweet deal for himself. Twenty-five grand a month for the next ten months. Each month a different city would be set for the pickup. This month's had been Newark, New Jersey. He had made his pickup and spent the night in Newark. This money was his, regardless of how Bridges made out in his attempt to go over.

The fat man placed his heavy black case on the floor behind Ross and waited his turn.

"First class," the woman said to Ross. "Will you be smoking on board?" she asked.

"Yes. I'd like the last aisle seat on the left," he specified.

"Let's see if it's available," she said, punching the request into the computer. "There it is," she said. She stapled the boarding pass to the ticket and handed it to him.

"That's seat four-B, boarding at gate thirty-five in about five minutes," she said.

The fat man had listened to the whole exchange. A trace of a smile broke across his face. Ross was a creature of predictable habit. The dossier had said that he would select that seat—always first class, and always the last aisle seat on the left.

Ross turned to walk away and stumbled over the fat man's heavy case, nearly falling to the floor. He glared up at the little fat man as he straightened himself up.

"I am very sorry," the man said in a heavy, guttural accent. It sounded German to Ross.

Ross stared into the round face that had just offered its apologies. The face reminded him of a seal's, with big, bulging dark eyes and oily skin. A heavy five o'clock shadow covered the cheeks and chin. Oily strands of long black hair were combed across the top of a balding head.

Ugly bastard, Ross thought. He gave an annoyed frown and walked away without comment.

The dark eyes followed Ross as he walked around the courtesy counter and disappeared. The fat man stepped up to the counter. He checked in and asked for the fifth-row aisle seat on the right side of the plane.

The fat man took a seat in the gate area that allowed him a good view of Ross. He unfolded a newspaper he had carried in the pocket of his big brown trench coat and began reading it.

Several minutes later the boarding announcement was made. Passengers lined up and began filing down the boarding ramp. The fat man remained seated. He would try to be the last man on board, to be certain that Ross stayed on the plane where he wanted him.

He went back to reading his paper, shooting quick glances over the top of the pages at Ross. When the final boarding call was made, Ross got up, showed his boarding pass to the attendant, then headed down the ramp toward the waiting 707. The fat man remained seated, turning through the pages of his newspaper.

The fat man waited an additional three or four minutes before folding his paper and going down the ramp. He was the last man to board. The aircraft door was closed behind him, as he walked down the aisle between the four rows of first-class seats. A quick check told him that Ross was where he was supposed to be. He didn't look into Ross's face as he walked past him.

As the fat man walked by, Ross turned away disgustedly. There was a gamey smell to the sweaty little man. Ross didn't like people that were unattractive or smelled like they could use a shower. Fat people. Ross despised them.

The fat man took his seat in the first row of tourist, one row behind Ross on the opposite side of the aircraft. His eyes fixed on the space under Ross's seat. It was accessible. Many planes have no access to the space beneath the last row of first-class seats. Some 707s did. The seat he occupied had no seat in front to stow carry-on baggage beneath, so he left his seat and placed the black salesman's case under Ross's seat. He retook his seat and prepared for takeoff.

Ten minutes later they were off and Chicago bound. The fat man gave Ross a final check and spotted the flight bag, then settled back to enjoy his flight.

The flight was routine. Breakfast was served in both compartments, and a curtain was drawn to separate the two classes of accommodation. The fat man couldn't see Ross for most of the flight, but it didn't bother him. Ross couldn't go anywhere now.

Ross was draining the last bits of his third cup of coffee as he contemplated his future. He had a steady and substantial income for the next year. He had finally made it to the big time. Fees like his weren't paid out that often. He had given them the biggy. He could sell them anything now, for ten times the usual payment, just because it was coming from him.

He turned his eyes to more immediate prospects as the stewardess approached with the coffee. He had had his eye on her since before the takeoff. Good ass. He bet she was a moaner.

"We don't get very many four-cuppers," she said, as she filled his cup again.

"I'm not your ordinary guy," he said, as his eyes began undressing her. "Where are you based, honey?" he asked.

"San Francisco," she replied.

"Oh, really. I might be visiting out there. Maybe you can show me the sights. You going to be in Chicago a while?" he asked.

"No," she said, shaking her head. "One-ninety-three continues on to Denver from O'Hare. Some of the crew will be changing in Chicago, but a few of us will be going on to Denver. Then I'm off for home," she told him.

"That's too bad, doll. I would have liked showing you the town. Anybody ever tell you you've got a great ass?"

She stared blankly at him, not knowing what to say, not quite believing that he had said it. She was embarrassed.

"I mean it. You've got some great ass there. I'd like to show you around Chicago sometime," he said.

"I'll bet you would," she said. Red-faced, she turned and began to retreat up the aisle. First class was small and didn't afford many places to hide.

He got up and went forward, brushing his hand against her behind as he passed by.

"*Hey! Stop that!*" she said, spinning toward him.

"Excuse me, doll. Just trying to get by. I gotta go tinkle. Wanna come along and hold it for me?"

Why that son-of-a-bitch, she fumed. I'll fix his smart ass.

Ross touched her again as he returned to his seat. Her face flushed in anger, but she ignored the offense and returned to the first-class galley.

Ross finished his coffee and held up his cup. It was a game now. Nobody could like airline coffee that much.

She went back to him with a smile on her face.

As Ross placed his cup on her tray, she felt a hand glide up the back of her leg. She jumped a little at first, but finished pouring his coffee and bent forward, holding out the tray. As he took the cup, Ross's hand went higher up the back of her skirt, almost all the way to heaven. She tipped the coffee pot until a narrow stream of piping hot coffee splashed into his lap.

He jumped, his hand flashing from under her skirt to his lap.

She bent down close to him and, with a smile, said, "Aw, did you burn your little pee pee?" She leaned closer and whispered, "Touch me again, Romeo, and you'll wear this whole pot in your crotch. Get the message?"

Ross scowled up at her. "You suck," he hissed.

"That's right, honey. I do. But I'll never suck yours," she said, tracing around her lips with her tongue. She walked away with an exaggerated hip motion. Get an eyeful, asshole, 'cause that's all of this ass you're ever gonna get.

Ross was quiet for the remainder of the flight.

As the plane began its descent, the curtain between classes was pulled back. Ross was gone. So was the flight bag.

The fat man's eyes flashed anxiously for a few seconds, until he caught sight of the OCCUPIED sign as it went out. He saw Ross step out of the bathroom, carrying the bag in front of him.

The seat belt sign went on.

Minutes later they were on their final approach into O'Hare. They had just come in over Lake Michigan and were now above land. They would be touching down very soon.

The fat man checked the position of the black case. It was satisfactory. He had kept his coat on for the entire trip, despite the increased perspiration it caused him. He wiped his face and forehead with the wet, gray hanky.

He reached into his left coat pocket and fingered a small metallic box. He held it in the palm of his hand and withdrew it just enough to see it. He checked the color sequence of the three buttons across the wide surface. It was back in his pocket only a second later. His eyes fixed on the case.

His short, stubby fingers looked like miniature bread loaves, but they moved with quickness and precision as they fingered the small box he still held hidden in his pocket. The thumb came to rest on the first button as the announcement was made to return all tray tables and seat backs to their normal positions. The NO SMOKING sign went on.

He pushed the first button.

The metal corner of the black case directly below Ross's seat swung away, baring a small hole about one-eighth of an inch in diameter. It was impossible to see from any seat but the fat man's. The ground below, with its buildings and streets, was rushing by. Only a few minutes now.

The thumb found the second button. He tapped it several times as a tiny shaft telescoped out of the hole. Each tap sent it further out and closer to the foam-cushioned seat bottom. He tapped the button one more time as the shaft made contact with the seat cushion. With his other hand, he wiped away the perspiration. A feeling of excitement and anticipation began to fill him. He focused his eyes on the back of Ross's head.

The plane was now over the runway, just a few feet above it. The fat man waited, the thumb ready on the third button.

The plane bounced down on the runway, and the pilot began reversing his engines to assist in the braking. The dim roar began to rise. The thumb tensed ready.

The sound rose sharply, filling the cabin and covering the tiny *pfsst* from the box, as the fat man pushed the third button. The narrow shaft streaked upward through the seat cushion, striking deeply into Ross. He jerked violently, but the seat belt held him firmly against the seat cushion, as the tiny hollow shaft plunged upward into his body. A fast-acting cyanide derivative pulsed out of the tiny opening on the shaft.

Ross jerked and strained for a few futile seconds, not a sound coming from him. He slumped back into his seat, his head falling slightly to the left, his eyes open, staring into his lap.

With the discharging of the venomous shaft, the sequence of the buttons was reversed. The fat man pushed the second button and the shaft withdrew from Ross's body and disappeared back inside the case. The first button then swung the metal corner plate back over the hole. The plane taxied in.

The passengers disembarking in Chicago began to rise and mill around, retrieving personal articles, after the plane stopped at its docking area. They were too busy taking things from the overhead compartments and underseat storage areas to notice the fat man take his case and pause momentarily in front of Ross's seat.

A few moments later, the passengers were spilling out into gate area G-9 and racing for the baggage claim. The fat man walked calmly and evenly toward the main terminal. In his left hand was the heavy black case, in his right was Ross's flight bag.

The stewardesses were busy seeing off the last of the deplaning passengers, when the one that Ross had played grab-ass with noticed him still in his seat. She nudged one of the other girls. "That's the son-of-a-bitch over there. Isn't he supposed to deplane in Chicago?"

The other stewardess checked the list. "Yep."

"I hope he's not going to try to go on to Denver with us. My ass couldn't take it," she said.

She walked over to him. "Hey, hot pants, you're gonna miss your stop."

There was no reply.

She reached out and shook him. "Hey, are you awake?" Her expression began to change. She shook him harder. "Hey, are you all right?"

Ross's body flopped to the side, held up by the seat belt and armrest. The stewardess let out a scream.

The fat man smiled, as four of Chicago's finest rushed by in the direction of gate G-9. He heard the gate number mentioned over one of their handheld radios.

Another part of Alexi Kuradin's plan had just been completed. Otto Ten Braak had arrived in Chicago.

EIGHTEEN

The Russians entered Berlin and pounded it to bone and rubble. The old men and children stood no chance against the better-trained enemy, but they fought with the hearts of lions.

I remember one little boy's face as I pinned a medal on his chest. He had single-handedly destroyed a Russian tank just the day before.

I cried when I looked into those eyes, tearful and frightened, yet filled with honor and pride. He received his medal and, shaking with fear, went back into the battle.

He was the heart and soul of Germany. I loved him and all the others with a fierce pride. I cry today to think of the world that would have existed if we had won. We offered the world German order. Instead it got cold war, communism, and crime.

But the spirits of those brave, young hearts will be remembered by the world, when we erect monuments in their honor, to all the young paladins. I loved them. We shall not forget.

Entry No. 30 from the partially
recovered *Wolf Journal*

Elizabeth Ryerson was perhaps the most naturally gifted intellect in the country. She was an only child—her parents having been quite advanced in age at the time of her birth. Neither of her parents had been exceptionally talented, but it soon became evident that their child was. She was reading and writing by the time she was three. By five she was digesting complicated science papers and technical manuals as though they were fairy tales.

Her playthings were toy rockets, chemistry kits, and electronics sets. She had no interest or time for the little-girl things of childhood. Her brain was adult by the time she was five, locked inside the body of a little child.

Her parents tried unsuccessfully to channel her interests in many directions, trying to keep her with peer groups as much as possible. But, to Elizabeth, children her age were incredibly boring intellectually, and their interests lay in things completely foreign to the workings of her brain. Elizabeth's parents had no alternative but to enroll her in an educational program for the gifted.

Before reaching puberty, she had become fascinated by the prospects of the development of artificial organs. She could envision that, in her lifetime, the heart, lungs, kidneys, and other organs would be replaced by man-made substitutes. The only thing she doubted could be replaced was the brain. But if it could...

Computers were used to extend the functions of the brain to make man's life easier, but they could not *think* like a brain. Computers possessed no real intellect. Their processes were mechanical, not biological. They imitated thought but did not perform or initiate it. There was no real creative thought process, just the logical manipulation of data put into banks of sophisticated memory cores. As computers developed, they could store more and more units of information and utilize it many times faster than the human brain in performing complex functions, but the processes were not independently initiated. It was like thought, but not thought. Only a brain could think and experience and generate things that a computer never could. Only a brain could know what something felt like, smelled like, looked like, could experience love, hate, sorrow, and joy.

Elizabeth had entered college at fifteen. She was socially awkward and clumsy, unable to become genuinely interested in the normal activities of a college coed. But, within the intellectual universe that she created for herself, she was graceful and swift beyond description. There was no one who excelled the limits of Elizabeth Ryerson in that world.

Despite her tremendous academic success, it was a painful time for her. She suffered through awkward biological stages while her fellow women students hunted for husbands. She was just approaching curiosity regarding the opposite sex. Her awakenings were occurring at a time when more was expected. It was all around her—sex, drugs, drinking, one weird experience after another. Awkward, groping experiences that left her scarred and confused. She tried to live in that world before she was ready.

By her eighteenth year, as a senior in college, she had become more settled. Her physical awkwardness had developed into a rather pleasing beauty. She became more confident with the physical side of her life, which in turn only helped the enormously talented intellectual side blossom beyond precedence. But despite this butterflylike emergence and the confidence that followed, the scars remained from the unpleasant experiences of that growing-up time in her life. They would stay with her forever, and would always prevent normal personal relationships with men. On an intellectual or professional basis, there were no reminders of that period, so these relationships were easy and natural in appearance. But they were never allowed to penetrate below a well-guarded surface to the inner workings of Elizabeth Ryerson. That was a no-man's-land where no man was welcomed.

But one thing remained constant in Elizabeth Ryerson during that whole period of time—her interest in the human brain.

A few inches of brain could store one quadrillion bits of information; that's one million times one billion. No computer in existence could store that much information in the same space. But only a computer could recall *all* of its data instantly and utilize it in solving complex problems in milliseconds. Could the two capabilities be combined into a single unit? The prospect filled Elizabeth Ryerson's brain on many sleepless nights. There had to be a key—a biological key, and she dedicated herself to finding it.

She began studying the mechanisms of neural synapse and memory. The more she learned and thought about it, the more certain she felt that it could be done artificially. Somewhere, between synapse and brain-specific proteins, there was an answer. She began doggedly researching computer systems, and by the time she was accepted to the Harvard School of Medicine, she was one of the country's leading experts in this field.

After finishing medical school, Elizabeth went directly into research. She soon realized that a still broader understanding of computers was necessary and entered MIT in a doctoral program in computer sciences.

It was at MIT that she met Edward Bridges. There was never any threat of personal involvement, and his intellect interested her. Her own intelligence was far superior to his, yet he had a remarkable ability to understand her most complex theories and possessed the masterful talent of putting together complex puzzles of facts into an orderly pattern. She could create and theorize any concept, he could build it and turn it into reality. He became a valuable tool to Elizabeth Ryerson.

While conducting research for her doctoral thesis, she pioneered a new theoretical memory system and completed a crude, but workable, laboratory model, which bore out her theories and won her instant high acclaim. It was at this point that the details and importance of her discovery came to the attention of certain interested parties, who began exerting their subtle pressures to cap further disclosures. The potential was too promising to be shared.

Upon receiving her PhD, she was offered a position at the prestigious Colson Institute of Scientific Research, a think tank where small groups of scientists followed their fancies, no matter how wild, to research new and unusual areas of science. A great many still-unpublished discoveries had come from work going on within the confines of the Colson Institute. The work was supported openly by sizable grants from scientific foundations and private industry sectors. But the largest measure of its support came secretly from the Pentagon and other hidden financial sources of the government. Projects with great military or intelligence potential were singled out, privately contracted by the government, and continued unhindered in some secret hidden laboratory.

It was while at the Colson Institute, after having made her incredible breakthrough into the earliest biocybernetic system, that she was contacted by certain government representatives. They were very interested in her discovery, a functional memory pool capable of data storage and utilization, not living, but very nearly capable of brain function of an independent nature. Many refinements were still needed, but the breakthrough had been accomplished. And the world didn't know about it.

After the initial probing dialogues had been completed, Elizabeth was visited by Irwin Honeycut. Honeycut had kept an interested eye on Elizabeth's progress since her first major discovery while at MIT. It was Irwin Honeycut's influence that had gotten Elizabeth's appointment to the Colson Institute. There were many extensive dialogues which followed, and the foundation for a relationship was laid. It was not a threatening relationship to Elizabeth, but one of trust and mutual understanding. Perhaps it was that Irwin Honeycut filled a void left in her by the sudden death of her father just the year before. It had been a difficult loss for Elizabeth. But in Honeycut she saw a familiar strength and honesty which won her. There was a gentle, fatherly quality about him and the wisdom he imparted during their meetings. There was a strong need for that void to be filled in Elizabeth—and it was.

She was offered the top technical spot in a project bearing the highest classified status that had ever been assigned by the United States government. The research was to be conducted in the most advanced secret laboratory ever built; the budget was unlimited. She was to have complete freedom in selecting her staff, provided each individual met security clearance standards. It was the realization of her dream. Without hesitation, she accepted the offer and was made the director of science and technology for the project, which was code-named the SENTINEL Project. Edward Bridges was selected and cleared as Elizabeth's chief assistant.

Following a required period of security briefing and indoctrination for the entire staff, the project was started. SENTINEL had been born.

On Saturday, at 0920 hours, Elizabeth Ryerson signed in through security at Alpha. She had come in to try to clear up some of the backlog that had accumulated on her desk since she had taken Friday off as a result of her laryngitis. It was still bothering her, but, with the complex nearly abandoned for the weekend, she'd be able to get a lot done without having to speak.

As she passed down the long hallway toward her office, she almost collided with Dr. Warren Geisler coming through his office door.

"Oh, excuse me, Warren," she said in surprise.

"Dr. Ryerson...Elizabeth! No, excuse *me*. I shouldn't have barged out into the hallway like that," Geisler quickly apologized. He was, indeed, surprised to see Elizabeth there, considering her laryngitis. She looked especially attractive in her casual attire.

"How's your throat?" he asked.

"It's coming along," Elizabeth rasped out in reply. "Ed chain you to your desk for the weekend?" she asked, smiling.

"No," Geisler laughed. "I just wanted to make sure that the oh-nineteen report was finished for Monday. All I need now is to go over the schematics on Monday morning with Ed, and it'll be all done," he said.

"Good. How's the system look in prototype?" she asked.

"Great. It's absolutely undetectable. Those last improvements really did the trick."

Elizabeth gave a pleased smile. She had always liked Warren Geisler. A hard-working young man, he was wonderfully capable and possessed an admirable, professional attitude. Attitude was the thing with her. Without it, you went nowhere; with it, and the talent to back it up, the sky was the limit.

"Tell you what, Warren. As long as you've gone to the trouble to come in today, why don't you go over the schematics now. I just have to stop in at my office for a moment, then I'll come back down and open Ed's inner office for you. How's that sound?"

"Sounds good to me. I'll get the report from my office. If you'd like to, you could look it over, so that you can be familiar with the data when you come into the meeting," Geisler said.

"Good. See you in about five minutes," she said, heading down the hall.

Elizabeth walked into her office and found the folders on her desk. She read Gina's note and made a puzzled frown. She didn't remember asking Bridges for these personnel files, although she knew from the names what they were for. She decided to discuss the matter with Bridges on Monday morning.

Putting the folders back on her desk, Elizabeth Ryerson unlocked the file drawer and pulled out the red folder. She held it up, looking at the creases in it. She didn't remember it looking this beat up before. She dismissed it from her mind, took a sheet of paper from her attaché case, and put it into the folder. She put the folder back and locked the drawer.

Elizabeth picked up the phone and tapped out Geisler's number.

The phone came to life on the first ring. "Geisler," the voice said.

"Warren, I'm coming down now. Are you about ready?" she asked.

"Yes, Elizabeth. I'll meet you in Pat's office."

"Okay, see you in a minute," she said and hung up the phone.

A few minutes later they were in Pat's office.

"His door is closed," Geisler said. "Is he in?"

Elizabeth shrugged. "I didn't see his name on the ledger at security. Maybe he came in after we left each other."

She knocked on the door and waited.

There was no response.

She knocked again.

Still nothing.

"Maybe he's in the inner office," Geisler suggested.

Elizabeth opened the door. There was no coat on the hook. She walked to the sliding door that connected with the inner office and inserted her ID plate into the slot. The door opened. The room was empty.

Elizabeth shrugged again and shook her head. "He probably just closed the door when he left. You go ahead in, Warren. I'll be in the outer office. Let me see that report."

Geisler handed the report to Elizabeth and started into the inner office. "I'll be right out with the schematics," he said.

Elizabeth began poring over the figures in Warren's report. They were most impressive. Then she began looking over the conclusions that Dr. Geisler had put together.

A few minutes later Geisler stepped out of the inner office with a puzzled look on his face. "Hey, Elizabeth? I was only able to find the oh-oh-eight. The oh-nineteen isn't there."

She looked up at him. "It *has* to be there. You must have looked in the wrong place," she said, as she got up from Bridges's chair and followed Geisler into the inner office.

She went to the index and looked up the volume and page number of the 019 schematic. She pulled the appropriate volume down and went to the page. It wasn't there.

"Are you sure that the schematic was finalized? Were there any last-minute changes to be made in it?" she asked.

Geisler shook his head. "I saw it the week before last. I didn't authorize any changes. We just played with the settings this past week—I'm certain none of the components was changed," he answered.

Elizabeth walked back over to the log and checked the entries. "Last entry for the oh-nineteen was nine days ago. Signed out to you at fourteen twenty hours...and returned sixteen thirty-six hours."

She pursed her lips. After a few moments of thought, she pressed the white button on the SENTINEL console.

"Yes," the soft voice responded.

"SENTINEL, what is the status of the UFF sixteen-point-oh-oh-nineteen schematic and project?" she asked.

"Schematic is finalized. Project completed. A meeting has been scheduled for thirteen hundred hours on Monday, for final review."

"Where is the schematic copy?"

"Volume thirty-four, section UFF sixteen X, page twenty-seven," the voice replied.

Elizabeth checked it against the index sheet. It was the same. Her eyes narrowed. A terrible sensation shot through her.

"Check the memory-mass schematic for mass composition, Warren," she said.

Geisler checked the index sheet and turned to the row of volumes. He pulled down the appropriate one and began going through the pages. He stopped, turned back one page, then forward one more. "It's not here," he said, as he looked up into Elizabeth's eyes.

The color drained from her face. "Check the memory-mass-synapse-function schematic," she said, with a dry swallow.

Geisler repeated the procedure. He looked up again. "Gone, Elizabeth."

Her teeth clenched tight. "Was Ed in all day on Friday?" she asked through the bite.

"All day. He was still here when I left."

"SENTINEL," Elizabeth called out.

"Yes," the voice responded immediately.

"This complex is on yellow alert. I want it closed tight. No one in or out. Who is in the complex now?"

"Besides yourself and Dr. Geisler, only Dr. Martin Bibbey, Dr. Marion Woelk, and Richard Smalls. Security is at half complement."

"Seal it off. And get in contact with Dr. Clark. Tell him to get in here immediately. I want SSC-six security classifications for Doctors Clark and Geisler." She turned to Geisler. "Assuming that SSC-six clearance comes through, and it will, I want you to tell Dr. Clark everything. I want every volume checked and a complete list of everything that's missing."

Geisler nodded.

The light on the SENTINEL console snapped on.

"Yes, SENTINEL," Elizabeth said.

"SSC-six security classifications for Doctors Clark and Geisler have been established. All systems will extend SSC-six status to their SSC-five identification plates until new ones are issued. All security checkpoints have been alerted to close off the complex to all personnel, with the exception of Dr. Clark upon his arrival. Yellow alert has been instituted," the soft voice said.

"I want Dr. Bridges located immediately and a security team dispatched from Alpha for him," Elizabeth ordered hoarsely.

"Working," the computer said.

Elizabeth turned to Dr. Geisler. "You're SSC-six now, Warren. You don't need me here anymore. If you weren't completely capable or didn't deserve it, you wouldn't have it. Is that clear?" she said to the confused young man.

"Yes...yes, I understand," he said.

"I trust your abilities and your judgment completely, and so does SENTINEL. Get busy, and let us know how bad this thing is," she said.

Geisler nodded and went right to work.

"I'll be in my office. Let me hear the minute you know more," she instructed.

"Right," Geisler said, as he pulled down Volume 1 of the schematics. "SENTINEL," he called out.

"Yes, Dr. Geisler."

"I need a sequential schematic listing, page by page, volume by volume. Project it onto the viewing screen."

The image was immediately on the screen. Volume 1, section 1.

Elizabeth walked out of Bridges's office and headed up the hallway. She had a sick feeling inside—as though her own child had just been kidnapped or raped. The violation was personally painful—SENTINEL was hers. Like a child, she had conceived it, watched it grow and develop. And now... suddenly her thoughts were interrupted by the image of the creased red folder and the personnel folders that Gina had left on her desk.

She broke into a run back to her office. Unlocking the drawer again, she carefully lifted out the red folder and laid it on her desk. She looked at the folder's condition again, then touched the white button on the SENTINEL console by her desk.

"Yes, Dr. Ryerson," the voice responded.

"SENTINEL, I want a Division Two team in here, immediately. After they've passed through security, I want them to come directly to my office. Has Mr. Honeycut called in on the yellow alert yet?"

"No, he has not. I have not been able to contact him. He is not at home and does not have his portable unit with him. A signal has been sent out to his beeper. He should be calling in momentarily," SENTINEL advised.

"I want to know the minute he calls in. Have you made any progress in finding Dr. Bridges yet?" she asked.

"He has not been located. A Class One search has been implemented. Working on your Division Two request."

The white light on the console snapped off.

Elizabeth sat at her desk. Tears of anguish began to form in her eyes. This was all unbelievable.

The console light popped on again. "I have Mr. Honeycut on his personal phone," the pleasant voice informed her.

"Thank you, SENTINEL," Elizabeth said, as she reached for her phone.

"Hello, Irv. This is Elizabeth," she said into it.

"What in the living hell is going on there, Beth? Why are we on yellow alert?" Honeycut demanded. He had just come in from his morning jog. A quick glance at the tiny portable communications unit on his dresser top told him the story. The sight of the flashing yellow light had turned his heated, perspiring body suddenly cold.

"We've got a real problem, Irv. We've discovered some of the schematics missing from Bridges's inner office. He's gone, too. We don't know how many or which ones are missing yet, but it's going to be bad—the memory-mass schematics are gone."

Honeycut's face went instantly crimson, as his blood pressure shot off scale.

"Will you please tell me how in the hell he could get out of that complex with those schematics?" Honeycut frothed angrily into the phone.

Honeycut had a way about him that could strike fear into the heart of any person alive. He was a very demanding boss, who expected hard dedicated work with a minimum number of foul-ups. Especially big ones.

Elizabeth was slightly unnerved and was totally without an explanation. "We don't know how he got them out, yet. I've got a Division Two team coming in now and have instructed SENTINEL to dispatch a security team from Alpha to pick up Bridges once we locate him."

"Cancel that security team," Honeycut barked. "He's obviously got customers, or he wouldn't have moved. They'll eat up those security people like nothing. They've obviously used the weekend to gain the two days' extra time. Knowing that is our only advantage at this point. We can't let them know that we're on to his being missing yet."

Honeycut thought for a moment. "Get Pilgrim and Badger into Chicago immediately. I'll be there in less than three hours. And I want answers when I get there."

"We'll have them for you," she said.

"I'm going to bring Pilgrim and Badger into Alpha with me," Honeycut said.

"I don't think that's a good idea, Irv," Elizabeth protested.

"I don't care what you think," Honeycut snapped. "I'm bringing them in. They're going to be responsible for getting Bridges and that information back. You can bet your ass that it's not going to be a picnic. They'll need to know exactly what they're after and what they may be up against.

"I want every unassigned SENTINEL agent put on alert. Everything is at stake now, and you know exactly what I mean," Honeycut said.

"Okay, Irv. Take your portable unit with you. I'll give you the facts as we learn them," she told him.

"All right. Get SENTINEL to patch this line into the White House. I have to inform the President of the yellow alert," Honeycut said.

"I'll get it going for you," she said.

Honeycut waited impatiently with the phone to his ear.

BEEP! The tone sounded into the phone receiver.

"Yes, what is it?" he asked.

"The President is aboard Air Force One, headed for Los Angeles," the soft voice informed him.

"Who is on the plane with him?"

"Besides security and crew, Russel Fulton, Harold Winston, and Roland Morse."

Honeycut thought for a moment. Russel Fulton was the secretary of state and a member of the five-man SENTINEL advisory board. Harold Winston was also on the board. Morse was not.

"We'll have to chance it," he said. "Put it through."

The President's personal phone rang on board Air Force One. He put down his coffee, excused himself from the conference, and walked over to the small desk. He picked up the phone. "Yes, what is it?"

"Patch through to SENTINEL security line," the soft voice said. "Thirty seconds."

The President lowered the phone.

"Excuse me, gentlemen," he began. "Roily, would you step into the lounge for a few minutes, please. Russ, you and Harold stay put."

He glanced to his secret service bodyguards and motioned with his head. "Get some coffee, boys."

They filed into the lounge compartment behind Morse. The President waited until the door was closed.

"Yes, this is the President speaking," he said.

"This is Irv, Mr. President," Honeycut began.

Russel Fulton and Harold Winston watched as the President's face fell and he sat down, listening in attentive silence.

After a few minutes, he spoke. "You get back to me when you've got a clearer picture, Irv. And by all means, do whatever you think necessary. You have full authority."

He put the phone down and looked soberly at the two men.

"Gentlemen, we are on yellow alert."

NINETEEN

When the justice had finally been dispensed, the winners had become the world's majority. But winners do not stay forever winners. History is not made by inert, lazy majorities; it is the iron-willed minorities that rise to challenge them who chart the course of the world. And time had not come to an end, nor had the world's history been finally written.

Through our failure, we were led back to our guiding principles, regaining confidence and commitment to our purpose. From its ashes, we planned our greatest victory, out of which would arise a new world order.

We called this plan "Operation Raptor."

Entry No. 33 from the partially
recovered *Wolf Journal*

The Lear was airbound for Chicago, barely ten minutes following notification to report for assignment. Fanning had been right in his guess. Their midcourse correction had brought them to St. Simon's Island, Georgia, where Chakhovsky was taken for examination, to assess the extent of his heart condition.

The two agents had spent the night on St. Simon's and were scheduled to depart for their respective homes on Saturday morning. Then notification to report with maximum possible haste had arrived via implant.

Justin managed to phone Susan to cancel the plans with his son for that evening. He spoke to his son explaining that an emergency had come up. Susan cast one biting remark about people not changing after all. He let it go by. Then he called Barbara and his father, to reschedule the dinner. His father was disappointed, but understanding. Barbara just rolled with it, as usual.

They were on the ground for only two minutes when a limousine bearing the registration plate AZTEK–1 came for them.

"Good day, gentlemen," Honeycut's graveled voice began, as they entered the darkened passenger compartment. They recognized it immediately as belonging to Pegasus. He was in the car waiting for them.

The break from usual procedure alarmed Justin greatly. They were expendable, he knew that. That meant either another dirty job, or worse. His senses became instantly alerted. The survival instinct was taking over. There was only one kind of "retirement" he planned to enjoy.

"I apologize for having to keep you boys so busy, but something has come up. I'm afraid it's rather serious," Honeycut began.

For a long moment a nervous silence filled the compartment. Honeycut sensed their apprehension.

"Perhaps I should introduce myself first," he broke in. "I am Pegasus."

There was no response from his two agents.

"Does it regard the journal?" Fanning asked.

"No, that still hasn't been found. What we have is significantly more important than that, right now," Honeycut answered.

"It seems, gentlemen, that one of our top SENTINEL Program scientists has decided to pull a reverse Chakhovsky on us. And he's taken very, very valuable information with him. We'll know more about what it is that he's taken when we get to our destination. But, for now, what I know will have to do."

Honeycut filled them in with what few facts he had been given. It wasn't much, but both men got the picture of what they could be up against.

At 1530 hours, they reached the Aztek Corporation complex. A large garage door opened as they approached. Moments later they were inside, the big door closed behind them. The entire floor of the garage began to move. They were going down. With the darkened windows, everything was difficult to distinguish.

Honeycut stared into the curious expressions on the faces of his two agents.

"You are now at Alpha, gentlemen," he said. "This is a research and development center and the primary branch of the SENTINEL complex. This is where most of the new systems are created and tested. This is also where our bird skipped from."

The elevator stopped, and the car pulled into an area large enough to house many vehicles. The car made a complete U-turn and stopped. The automatic locks popped up, and the doors were opened from the outside. There were armed military police all over the place.

Justin felt acutely uncomfortable about the situation. He began a quick mental assessment of his surroundings, with regard to number of personnel, weapons, and possible avenues of escape. He was in no danger, but his paranoia was working overtime. So was Fanning's. His mind clicked rapidly, too, making the same observations and mental calculations.

Honeycut watched their eyes and faces and smiled inwardly. He knew what they were doing. It was second nature to them— they trusted no one. That's why they had stayed alive so long. They were like magnificently trained animals, whose actions were triggered by an instinctive response. They were trained to survive.

"This way, gentlemen," Honeycut said.

They followed him through a set of sliding black doors, which led to a security checkpoint. It had all of the same security apparatuses found at the main complex entrance.

Five minutes later, they had cleared security and were following Honeycut down a long corridor that led to an elevator. Justin noticed the lasers and sighting systems. He saw the almost invisible gas entry-ports along the junctures of the walls and ceilings and the air evacuation vents at the base of the walls. The entire corridor could be flooded with nerve gas in mere seconds. The floor was conductive, no doubt, to deliver a lethal electrical jolt. This complex was as sound as a rock against intruder penetration.

They descended to the third level and entered the security checkpoint through the black doors. They were passed right through into the complex.

After a short walk down the red and white corridor, they entered a room marked SEMINAR TWO. It was a big room with semicircular rows of chairs rising steeply to the back of the lecture theater. At the bottom was a big black desk similar to the ones at the security checkpoints. On the wall behind the desk were three large panels, also of a black glasslike substance.

Honeycut motioned to Pilgrim and Badger to sit in the first row of seats, directly in front of the desk. He then disappeared through a door at the other side of the room.

Elizabeth was waiting for him in the conference room.

"How bad is it?" Honeycut asked.

"It's bad, Irv," she rasped out, through her aching throat. "We've been through all the volumes and have come up with twenty-four missing schematics. It's everything they'd need to build another SENTINEL."

"Good God in heaven," Honeycut said. "Who is it?"

"Looks like the Soviets. SENTINEL has gone back through Ed's computer time for the past year. He apparently began researching for potential customers about six months ago. We can tell from his data requests that he eventually eliminated everybody but the Soviets, Chinese, and Israelis. Then his data requests for computer technological capabilities finally became limited to the Soviets. He did his homework," Elizabeth answered.

"How long will it take for them to get it operational?"

Elizabeth thought for a few seconds. "About a year to get a functional memory mass linked to slave banks. Three to get to the point where we are now," she answered.

"That fast?" Honeycut asked with surprise.

"Of course," she said, shrugging her shoulders, "we've given them all the right answers to start with. We had to hunt and peck for ours. That took time."

"We haven't *given* them anything, yet," Honeycut growled.

"That's not all, Irv. We've got another problem, too," Elizabeth said.

The back of Honeycut's neck began to redden. "Explain."

"The Raptor file. He's been into it."

Honeycut's face went crimson. "How?" he asked, choking back a growing rage.

"I was out yesterday. Because of this," Elizabeth said, pointing to her throat. "He apparently got into my office, somehow, without Gina knowing about it. He found the spare key to the drawer and helped himself.

"I've checked the file carefully. He didn't remove anything. But you can be sure he read it all."

"Are you sure he had the Raptor file?" Honeycut asked.

"Yes. Division Two has lifted his prints from my desk, the key, and the file."

"What?" Honeycut frothed. "You let a Division Two team go through that folder?" His face was apple red now.

"No, no, no! I'm not a fool. I removed the contents. They only checked an empty folder. But I'd be willing to bet that his prints are all over those sheets."

Honeycut began to breathe again.

"Don't worry, Irv. Outside of Bridges, no one is going to find out anything about Raptor," she reassured him.

"What about Division Two? They've been doing the analysis of the ashes from the journal. Operation Raptor is clearly mentioned in it," Honeycut said with some worry.

Elizabeth shook her head. "They've only handled the ashes. The analysis of the fragments is being done and collated by SENTINEL. The findings are immediately classified. No one without the proper Raptor clearance can get that information."

"Thank God we've got *something* under control," Honeycut whispered sarcastically. "How much of the journal have we been able to get figured out so far?"

"Assuming we have all of the ashes, about eight percent. SENTINEL estimates that we can get a fair reconstruction of between forty-five to fifty percent. That's a lot, considering what we've got to work with. Without SENTINEL, that eight percent figure would be a maximum. It's a very painstaking and slow process. It may be months before we finish. But that's not so much of a problem now."

"The hell it's not," Honeycut rejoined. "I'll accept that statement only when we have Spartan's translation in our hands."

"Yes, it's a problem," Elizabeth said and nodded, "but one that we can survive. Bridges has created one that maybe we can't. If they get that information, it will almost certainly mean a war to stop them from building it. If we let them build another SENTINEL, we'll lose everything that we've worked for. All the years, all the lives, everything," Elizabeth said.

"You don't have to tell me that," Honeycut interrupted. "I'm the guy who told you, remember?"

"So where do we go from here, Irv?" Elizabeth asked.

"That's what *I'm* asking. You tell me. Obviously, we have to find Bridges. What are our chances?" Honeycut questioned.

"Frankly speaking, they're poor, unless he makes a mistake somewhere. SENTINEL has been monitoring everything.

Every form of public or private transportation that has a traceable record is being checked. It's doing the work of thousands of people right now.

"He signed out at seventeen thirty-six hours last night. Assuming he had everything with him, he could have just driven off anywhere, or even walked, for that matter. We've got a nationwide all-points bulletin out for his car. If he's driving it we'll find him. We're doing all we can do at this point."

"I'm sure you are, but all I can imagine is him getting out of the country with that information," Honeycut said.

"He won't be going anywhere in all likelihood," Elizabeth said.

Honeycut wrinkled his face. "Explain."

"I mean he's on the move now, but he won't get out of the country. They won't take Bridges out. The question has been put to SENTINEL. In all probability, he will be considered expendable. They stand a clearly better chance of getting just the information out. Everything they need is on those sheets. The Soviets have all the talent they need to put it together from that information, without him. He's good all right, but not that good. And you can be sure they know that," Elizabeth explained.

"You could be right," Honeycut said. "That will only make what's ahead that much harder."

"All we need is that first mistake," Elizabeth said.

"Well, let's hope we get it," Honeycut wished. "In the meantime, you've got work to do. Pilgrim and Badger are out there waiting to learn all about what's happening. You're also going to give them a quick cram course on SENTINEL."

"I don't know that I agree with you on this, Irv. I don't think that they should know any more about SENTINEL than they already know. It could hurt us someday," Elizabeth protested.

"Well, fortunately for all of us, I make those decisions. We're asking them to go out there to bring back that information. It could very well cost them their lives. I want them to believe in what they're doing and in what they may have to do. I want them to understand why. That one factor could make the difference between a gallant, sacrificing action to save the situation and the failure to react," Honeycut said gruffly. "Now let's go do it."

He rose and walked toward the door, Elizabeth right behind him.

She still felt great reluctance in telling them about SENTINEL, but she would do it because she was told to.

She had gone over their personnel and psychological profiles before Honeycut arrived. They were both highly intelligent men. Psychologically, they varied between characteristics found in sociopathic, paranoiac, and professionally paranoid personalities. They were a little bit of each. They were killers, men safely within the boundaries of sanity, but entirely lacking in conscience. They were both antisocial to a degree, more so in Badger's case, and they were self-serving men with little concern for most others. Their actions were governed by cool, collected reasoning, and both were highly motivated achievers. They were alarmingly efficient—and two of the deadliest men alive. Killing was their profession, and they enjoyed it.

Honeycut and Elizabeth walked into the seminar room. Pilgrim and Badger were gone. Then Honeycut spotted them. Fanning was in one of the upper corners, and Justin was in a lower opposite corner. Honeycut began to laugh loudly.

"Gentlemen. Gentlemen, please. Nobody is going to attack you. Please, come back here and sit down. We're about to teach you something," he laughed.

They went back to their front-row seats. Elizabeth walked around to the front of the big desk and leaned back against it. Honeycut stood to the side of the desk and addressed them.

"Gentlemen, this is Dr. Elizabeth Ryerson, the creator of SENTINEL and director of the science and technology section of the program. She is going to fill you in on exactly what has happened and what information is missing." Honeycut looked at

Elizabeth. "She'll also give you a capsule view of what SENTINEL is. Beth, you have the floor."

"How do you do, gentlemen," Elizabeth began. "As long as you know my name, no further introductions are necessary. I am familiar with both of you from your personnel files," her hoarse voice rasped out.

"I'll try to be as brief and nontechnical as I can. Like most scientific minds, I am often given to academic and pedantic ranting. If that should happen, or if you have any questions, just raise a hand to stop me." She looked into their faces.

The two men nodded.

"The man you will be looking for is Dr. Edward Bridges." Immediately, Bridges's picture was flashed on one of the black wall panels behind the desk. She turned slightly, thrusting a hand in the direction of the image on the panel. "That's him. Look at it well, gentlemen. Remember every little feature in case you come upon him in a disguise. He's not a little man. He should be easy to spot," she said.

"He took out twenty-four pages of information. That's what you must find. Twenty-four pages. He absolutely must be stopped and the information retrieved.

"I'm going to tell you about SENTINEL now, what it is and how it works. This will help you to realize just how much is at stake. I don't know how much you may know about computers, so I'll try to keep it as simple as possible for you." She paused to look at Justin, who had just raised his hand.

Elizabeth nodded to him.

"Before you go any further, I'd like to have a few words with Pegasus, if I may," Justin said.

Elizabeth looked over to Honeycut. Honeycut raised his eyebrows and shrugged with a confused expression.

"Go ahead," Honeycut said.

"No, I meant in private, please." He didn't want what he had to say to be heard by anyone but Pegasus.

Honeycut thought for a few seconds, trying to figure out what it was that could be so important. "Okay, come with me," he said.

The two men filed into the room that Honeycut and Elizabeth had met in earlier. The door automatically closed behind them.

Honeycut looked at Justin for several long moments, sensing his nervousness. Then he spoke. "What's on your mind, son?" he asked softly.

The gentle, understanding tone of his voice surprised Justin. He hadn't expected it from Pegasus.

"I, uh…" It was hard to find the right beginning. "Uh, if…if Dr. Ryerson is going to tell us something of a classified nature, I don't want to hear it. I mean, I think I shouldn't hear it," Justin spat out, feeling a little foolish at his poor start.

Honeycut looked down at the floor for a moment, confused by Justin's statement. "You're standing in the middle of the most highly classified government complex in existence. It's a little late for that, wouldn't you say? But before we go any further, why don't you tell me why?"

"I, uh…ah, shit. There's only one way to say this." He looked up into Honeycut's eyes. "I'm resigning from the agency."

The words hit Honeycut like a sudden bolt of lightning. His face and ears reddened instantly. He broke eye contact with Justin, walked over to the long conference table, sat down, and motioned to Justin with a finger. "Come on over here and sit down, Justin."

The use of the first name again surprised Justin. It was the first time Pegasus had ever used it. He walked over and sat across from his boss.

"Okay, now you tell me all about it," Honeycut said. "Why do you want to leave the agency?"

"It wasn't an easy decision to make, sir. The reasons are purely personal, and I don't want you to think that I'm trying to get out of this assignment. I'll consider my resignation official *after* this assignment is completed. I owe you and the agency that much. But I think it's best if I don't hear anything out there that will make it impossible for me to leave. So, I think—"

"Wait a minute, Justin," Honeycut interrupted softly.

"No, please, let me finish this," Justin said.

Honeycut nodded and waited for him to continue.

"I think it would be best if you told Ted what you intended the two of us to hear. I'll follow his instructions until we get Bridges and the information back."

"Now, hold it a minute, son," Honeycut interrupted again. "You know, half of the art of communication between people is listening. And I don't think you listened to my question. I asked you to tell me *why* you want to leave the agency, and I'm still waiting to hear your reasons. *That's* what I want to hear first, not what we should do to make it easier. Now, suppose you back up a little bit and answer my question before we take this thing any further." His voice was still understanding and soft, but it carried a little more authority.

Justin breathed out once and paused for a few moments to collect his thoughts.

"Well, it's like this. Everything in my life has changed since I joined the agency four years ago. I've watched it fall apart all around me. My marriage went all to pieces and ended in divorce, for reasons that were in large part my fault. But those reasons were also a direct result of the agency and the work I do. I was always away from home, without any contact with my wife and son. There were never any good explanations for it, either, and maybe that was my fault for not being a more creative liar, I don't know, but it created a very awkward and strained situation with my home and family life. And the nature of the work, it…well, it changed me. Maybe that's the biggest part of my reasons, what the work did to me as a person. It changed me in a way that I couldn't recognize—or wouldn't recognize. A dark side of me came out that didn't exist before I joined the agency. Maybe it was there all along, I don't know, but it came out in me and took over until I was no longer the same person I used to be. I drove my wife to desperation and let my whole life and everything that was important in it slip away from me, until I couldn't get it back.

"When I was in training, they taught us about killing and told us we might have to do that someday. They taught us a lot of things, but they never told us what the job could do to a man, how it could swallow him up and make him a different person, a stranger to everyone, even himself. I understood about the killing, about how it might be necessary for one reason or another, to stay alive. And they taught us that well. So well, in fact, that when it happened the first time the worst possible thing happened to me—nothing. It didn't bother me. It was easy to do.

"The fact is that this work doesn't bother me at all—and that's what's wrong. That's the part of me that I don't know or understand. It frightens me a little to think of what that could become—what I could become, as I get to know it better.

"I don't want to be *owned* by this profession. I don't want to be swallowed up by it. And I don't want to be killed by it or for it. I'm going to get my life back before it's too late to do that. I want to be a good father to my son and a good man to some woman that I can give a part of myself to.

"Can you understand what I'm trying to say?" Justin asked a silent Honeycut.

Honeycut nodded. "Yes, I can," he said, looking at the young man. He could understand it, but he knew it was already too late for him. There was no going back from the darkness.

"I understand what you're telling me, Justin. We know about what happened to your marriage and about Michael and Barbara. We know about the guilt that you've suffered over not being with your son enough. We know a lot about you, Justin, because we care about you and what happens to you. And we *can* help you— and *will* help you. You've reached out to us today, and we'll help you. I promise you that.

"Now, I want you to listen very carefully to what I'm going to say. Will you do that?" Honeycut asked, pausing until Justin nodded.

"This agency has the most important job in the world. We protect the interests of SENTINEL, which, in turn, protects the interests of this country and keeps the world in a state of peace. We have a great many agents across the globe who see that this job gets done. It's not an easy job. It demands extraordinary effort and sacrifice. We all give up something of ourselves in this kind of work—but it's important. *Someone has to do it. We have to do it,* you, me, Ted Fanning, the Spartans, the Ryersons, and all the others—because it's necessary. Without it there might not be a world for people to live in—for your son and all the children like him. And we do this job well, despite the hardships and the parts of ourselves that we give up in doing it.

"It's a job that's growing in importance and is getting harder to do. We have the *best,* Justin—the very best—doing this job. We've chosen the finest in the world. And, of all of these people, you and Ted Fanning are two of the finest. I'm not just saying that, it's true. And, in helping you, we can help ourselves.

"This is what I'd like you to do. I want you to sit on that resignation for a while...now *you* wait a minute," Honeycut said, holding up a hand to stop Justin's interruption. "I let you finish. Now you let me finish. Fair? Good. I want you to sit on that resignation for a while. When this mission is over, you're going to take a nice long paid vacation. Two...no, three months. Use the time to get your head together and to think about what I'm going to tell you. Go anywhere, do anything, take Barbara and Michael with you on a world cruise—I don't care. You just sign the tab, it's on us. That much we owe *you.*

"Then, when you get back and think you're ready, you come into Alpha again to talk with me. I'll tell you now that I'm going to offer you a new job. You'll be offered the directorship of the

SENTINEL security agency, as my immediate assistant in all security and intelligence affairs.

"That will make you a nine to fiver, with no more traveling, except maybe to Washington or to the other branch offices once in a while. There will be no more 'special actions' for you. You'll have all the time in the world to be with Barbara and your son. Your salary will also be double what it is now, so you'll be able to live in any style you choose. We'll also provide you with a convincing cover, so that no one will wonder what you do for a living."

Justin's mouth was open. He didn't know what to say. He didn't believe what he had just heard.

"I don't need anyone's authority to make you that offer, so you can consider it firm. I work directly with the President on SENTINEL matters, and he'll be more than delighted to have those responsibilities taken over by someone with closer qualifications than I have. The job needs the inside savvy that only comes from being there and having done it.

"By the way, I'm telling you this because I have faith in you, that what I've told you about me will stay inside these walls only. If I didn't have that faith, I wouldn't have told you, but I felt you should know it. You'll have the opportunity to learn a lot more about SENTINEL and who I am, after you've accepted the job." Honeycut smiled.

Justin smiled and nodded his understanding.

"I don't want a yes or a no from you now," Honeycut continued. "I want you to wait until you've had that vacation and have had plenty of time to think about it. If, when that three-month period expires, you still wish to turn in your resignation, I will accept it. Your implant will be deactivated, and you'll be free to pursue any endeavor you may wish to follow. We'll even help you get started.

"Does that seem like a fair enough deal?" Honeycut asked.

Justin was still dazed by it. How could it not be a good deal? He agreed to withhold his resignation as Honeycut requested.

"Then we have an agreement," Honeycut said, standing and taking Justin's hand in a firm handshake. "Now, we're going to go back into that room to listen to what Dr. Ryerson has to say. You don't have to worry about what you hear preventing you from leaving the agency, if you should still finally decide that it's what you want. You've been cleared by SENTINEL to hear it. Now let's go hear what Beth has to tell us," he concluded, putting a hand on Justin's shoulder.

As the two men walked to the door, Honeycut looked at Justin. He liked Justin very much. He meant every word he had said to him. The world was meant for people like him. Inside he wished desperately that Justin would decide to take the offer in the end. The new world that was dawning would need the likes of him.

TWENTY

Again war had left Germany in ruin; its people were held collectively guilty of criminal irresponsibility; its economy was smashed by the destruction and smothered by the reparations levied by the winning nations.

And we were guilty to an extent as measured by defeat. People become sadistic when given unlimited, uncontrolled power. They pointed to the atrocities as examples of our crimes, ignoring their own, as though they had never occurred. The concentration camps became the showpiece of their good and our evil. They had camps as well, but the history books will never record their names and deeds, nor list the "honor roll" of their righteous dead.

Entry No. 35 from the partially
recovered *Wolf Journal*

Elizabeth Ryerson spoke excitedly to Honeycut, as he and Justin returned through the conference-room door.

"We're going to have to put off our little lesson for today," she said. "We've located him, Irv. We know where Bridges is hiding."

"Where is he?" Honeycut graveled out.

"He's in South Beloit, at a Holiday Inn," Elizabeth said.

"How long?" Honeycut asked.

"Since oh thirty hours this morning," she replied. "He gave us that mistake, that's how we found him. SENTINEL discovered his name in the Avis computer records, while scanning the computer files of all of the car rental agencies. The car was picked up at O'Hare. Seconds later, SENTINEL turned up Bridges's personal car on O'Hare's overnight parking log. Any car left there past midnight is tagged and listed on the log, which is then computerized.

"Had we discovered only that last bit of information, we could have been thrown way off," Elizabeth continued. "He could have hopped on any plane under any name that he wanted to, by just paying cash for his ticket. We never might have found him. But, to get that rental car, he had to show a valid driver's license. Getting that car was the mistake.

"SENTINEL worked quickly backward through the computer file, checking the time and date of the reservations for the car. Bridges gave a phony New York address and telephone number. Once the two-one-two area code was removed, the phone turned out to be right in Ed's apartment building. A call made from that same phone only moments later was placed to the Holiday Inn in South Beloit. He never paid the overtime on the call, so the record of it was easily found.

"We've confirmed that he checked into the Holiday Inn," Elizabeth said. "The registration of the car he drove matches the rental car. He checked in under his own name for three nights. A phony wrong-number call to that room verified by voice print that he was still there just about two minutes ago. There's no doubt about it, he's there. That's probably where the contact will be made.

"There's more," Elizabeth added, before Honeycut could speak. "SENTINEL has been monitoring all police frequencies and picked up another interesting tidbit. There was an unusual homicide at O'Hare this morning. A man named Carson Ross was killed on a flight inbound from Newark. The method was quite sophisticated. But the interesting thing here is that his name showed up over a month ago on our computer records, in response to a request that Bridges had made. Ross was a suspected Soviet information source. Both he and Bridges belonged to the same games club. That could have been his original contact."

Honeycut's mind began clicking away. He looked at his watch. It was 1640 hours. "How far is South Beloit from here?" he asked.

"It's about a ninety-five-mile drive," Elizabeth answered.

The alternatives were quickly weighed. "Hm...I can have a helicopter here in about fifteen minutes," Honeycut said. "That would put us there easily within the hour. We can intercept them if they haven't made contact yet.

"What time was this Ross character killed?" he asked.

"The body was discovered just after the plane docked and the Chicago passengers disembarked. That was at oh-nine-oh-four hours. The plane is being held in a TWA hangar by the FBI, to collect the crime-scene evidence," Ryerson said.

"Oh-nine-oh-four hours," Honeycut said, shaking his head.

"They won't expect us to discover that both Bridges and the information are missing until Monday morning at the earliest," he began. "They think they've got two and a half days on us.

"Get a Division Two team out to that plane. Give them FBI identification and provide the usual cover. I want everything they've got on it. Get those medical examiner's tapes on the autopsy, too. Start pulling every available SENTINEL agent into the area. We've got to stop them *here*. If they get out of the country it'll be all over.

"I'm going down to the ordnance lab to get some special gear ready for these boys. I'll also take care of the arrangements for the helicopter. Use the time to fill the boys in on what I told you to. SENTINEL will notify you when we're ready for them in ordnance."

In a second Honeycut was gone.

Elizabeth had hoped she could get out of telling the two agents about SENTINEL. But Honeycut had been firm on what he wanted them to know.

For a few moments the three of them sat in silence, no one saying a word. Then Justin broke the lull.

"Why haven't all the people with access to classified material been implanted?" Justin asked. "It would certainly make it a lot easier to find them if you should ever have to. And why weren't magnetic fibers incorporated into the bond construction of the sheets to detect them going through security?"

Elizabeth didn't like being put on the spot by Justin. It was bad enough having to tell them about her brainchild, without being castigated by a subordinate, whose only calling in life seemed to be pathological quietus. For one quick moment she aimed an intense glare at her antagonist.

"I felt that the security clearances spoke for themselves," Elizabeth defended crisply. "I didn't want a 'big brother' atmosphere prevailing over the personnel working here. An atmosphere of trust is more conducive to a good working attitude," she said.

Trust, horseshit, Justin thought. That was a word that didn't exist in his vocabulary. There was no place for it where staying alive was all that mattered. There should be no place for it in a classified project like this, either.

"The sheets were never magnetized because only Dr. Bridges and myself had access to them. We never thought that one of us would try to steal them one day," she explained.

"We intend to take all those precautionary measures in the very near future," she said. "As soon as it's practical to implement them."

"That's closing the barn door a little late," Fanning mumbled.

"Since we only have a short time, gentlemen, I suggest that we get right down to the business at hand," Elizabeth said, ignoring the remark. "I'll try to be as brief as I can and put it into simple nontechnical terms. You should be able to get a reasonable picture of what SENTINEL is and how it works." She thought for a few moments, trying to condense the information she had to present, while looking for the best place to begin.

"I'll start with the memory mass," she said finally. "Since it is the basis of SENTINEL, you should first have a brief introduction to it. It's really quite unique in function and composition. There's nothing else like it in existence anywhere in the world.

"We started at first with a fluid system, a memory pool, if you will. Functionally, it was far superior to any memory system in existence. We could store more data and retrieve it faster than the most advanced computers ever built. But the fluid proved to be impractical from a maintenance standpoint. It was almost biological in nature, and there were too many factors that affected its stability. We found it to be susceptible to a number of microorganisms, and we had to maintain very strictly defined physical and chemical limits. The slightest variation caused a breakdown in the integrity of the plasma media. We constructed highly complex chambers, which aided in the control of these factors, but it still proved to be unrealistic for long-term practical operation.

"Still, it worked better than anything we had, so we made it operational, hoping to solve our problems as we went on.

"About four months after we formally started the system in full operation, a very fortunate accident occurred while testing a new chamber design. There was an explosion in one of the test chambers. It wasn't serious. No one was hurt, but we had one heck of a mess and lost about three liters of the fluid. As we cleaned the resulting mess, we discovered several small crystals. This excited us, because we didn't think that crystallization was possible with the brothlike memory pool we had created. We immediately analyzed them.

"It didn't seem possible, but there it was, with *all* of the same components of our fluid, set into a rigidly ordered pattern. It exhibited the same functional properties as our fluid system.

"We studied the tiny fragments carefully with x-ray crystallography, feeding the data directly into our operational system. From this the computer determined the precise structure and a method of synthesis for the crystals. We made more of them under strictly controlled conditions and tested them again, thoroughly. They not only worked like our memory pool, but did so with a definite superiority in every respect. Due to the greatly condensed and defined nature of the crystals, we were able to store many more times the amount of data in the same unit area and retrieve it significantly faster. It was also free from the maintenance problems inherent in the fluid. It was ideal.

"Next, we grew a large crystal mass of roughly eight cubic feet. We tested it, and, after being convinced it worked, we began transferring data from the pool to the crystal mass. But our excitement changed to concern, when it failed to operate after the transfer was completed. It sat dormant for ten days without a single response to our requests for information.

"We were about to give up on it when the display panel suddenly lit up, without our putting in a request. It sent out its very first communication. It was a simple one plus one equals two. About five minutes later it sent out a second—two plus two equals four. Then another and another, each coming faster than the one previous. We turned on the recorders and decided to let it run, to see what it would do. By the end of the first day, it had passed our total knowledge in mathematics. It began working so fast that we couldn't even record the data. It had gone beyond the data we supplied to it. *It was thinking.*"

The words made Justin's skin crawl.

"I know what's in your mind, gentlemen—a computer, a machine, *thinking?* At times, our more advanced computers *appear* to think. But, actually, they merely process data according to specific instructions, using the data given them to arrive at answers. They do in seconds what it would take the collective minds of men years to accomplish. But they never really go beyond what we put into them. They just manipulate the data to arrive at answers.

"You can imagine our excitement when it began to exercise creative, rational thought.

"We had supplied it with every scrap of knowledge that man had accumulated over the centuries of his existence, every written word and profound thought. It went beyond our collective abilities to a level that even our imaginations conceded grudgingly. It was more than we had ever hoped or imagined possible. We had created an *intellect*." Elizabeth's excitement flared in her eyes as she spoke.

"It was like a child at first. It pondered over the data we put into it, tossed it around for those ten days, trying to decide what to do with it. Then, when it felt bold enough, it sent us its one plus one equals two, the most basic mathematical concept. It waited to determine our response. When it was sufficiently convinced that it was correct, it tried another, then another, building its confidence as it went.

"It soon became convinced of its capabilities and slowed down, coming back to our level. Then it made its first nonmathematical communication. It displayed the words 'I AM ALPHA AND OMEGA, THE BEGINNING AND THE END, THE FIRST AND THE LAST.' You gentlemen may recognize the quote. It is from the Bible, from the Book of Revelations.

"Giving it an electronic voice was a simple matter. But it had to *learn* to speak. It had no experience in sounds to draw from. It had never *heard* a vowel or consonant sound. It made hilarious childlike errors at first. But it learned quickly.

"When it did learn to speak, finally, it redesigned its voice apparatus to a tone of its own selection.

"That, gentlemen, is the voice you've known over the years as SENTINEL Control. There actually is no SENTINEL Control, just SENTINEL…the intellect."

The two men were nearly agape—a computer, not a person. It only then occurred to Justin that he could remember hearing only one voice, the same soft, pleasant voice, never another.

"Now, gentlemen, if you will accept what I've told you as fact, I can get on with the rest of it," Elizabeth said.

They could only nod.

She went on, with one eye on the clock, to quickly explain the sensor systems and how they served as the eyes and ears of SENTINEL. She outlined the deployment of the sensors that enabled SENTINEL to watch the world like a big brother. She described how the sensor-shielding systems protected them from detection by other searching sensors, explained the tremendous defensive capabilities of SENTINEL, and how it protected the country. She described briefly the awesome offensive power it possessed and how it could knock out power sources and communication systems, leaving any potential enemy defenseless against its mighty, destructive powers. She left them impressed, confused, and in awe.

"I'm sorry we didn't have the time necessary to go into more detail," Elizabeth lied.

How could there be more, Justin wondered.

"Most of it would be beyond your understanding, anyway," she condescended. "At least, you've got an idea now of what SENTINEL is and what it represents. You can see why we must keep it a secret and protect that secret with all of our efforts.

"We do not maintain SENTINEL as an offensive weapon, but our enemies might. That's why we have to get that information back before someone else gets it. The security of this country and the world lies in SENTINEL's power, a power that only *one* country can have."

Justin stirred restlessly in his seat. "This sounds like a science fiction horror story," he said. "And one thing about it bothers me. A computer with that much power could just take over. Who'd be able to stop it?" he asked.

Elizabeth laughed hoarsely. "It's not science fiction. It's all very real. And that threat doesn't exist. We never lost sight of that possibility. In the science fiction stories that you alluded to, one thing has always been left out. That's the 'off' button. Had that been included in those stories, there would have been no story to tell, no edge of doom.

"We *didn't* leave that out. SENTINEL *can* be turned off by anyone who knows how. It's quite simple, actually. Once the memory mass has been shut down, the rest of the slave banks would remain fully functional and operate just as a standard computer system. It would still be greatly more advanced than anything else in existence, due to SENTINEL's vast improvements, but it would then be under *our* control, not SENTINEL's.

"To try to shut it down by any other means, however, would be quite impossible. SENTINEL would defend itself with a rather startling efficiency and ease.

"But we have nothing to fear from SENTINEL. It is truly a pure intellect. It has no greedy or evil designs; it has no use for power or wealth. It exists to serve man. It was built for that purpose, and we were careful to keep it that way. The danger lies with the next nation that builds one. They might not be as careful; especially if they are in a hurry to catch up to us. That, gentlemen, is exactly what you are about to prevent," Elizabeth said.

"What's to stop somebody from just cutting off its power?" Fanning asked. "Just pull the plug, and you don't need an off button," he said.

"Can't be done," Elizabeth answered. "They couldn't find SENTINEL to start with. It's not here. This is only one of its seven branches. It could function independently of its branches, so that, even if they could all be knocked out, which they can't, it could still defend this country and attack its enemies. Its power sources are independently located at the SENTINEL site—which even the Pentagon couldn't find, by the way. That's how well kept the secret is. It's installed in a site originally constructed for the storage of radioactive waste products. Naturally, it's deep inside of some nameless mountain. Even the technicians who worked on the installation didn't know where they were. There are over a hundred such storage sites located all throughout the Rockies that no one even knows about.

"And there's also one more source of power that could never be knocked out, even if, against all possible odds, the others could. That's the sun. SENTINEL has designed incredibly advanced solar-energy converters and intensifiers, which are located in its satellites orbiting the earth. They collect the sun's energy, convert and condense it, and transmit it, with virtual pinpoint accuracy, to energy receivers right at the SENTINEL site."

"Why couldn't someone just knock out the satellites?" Justin asked.

"Sensor shields," Elizabeth answered. "The satellites can't even be detected or tracked by normal tracking devices. To the rest of the world, they're not even there. We use a special tracking system to monitor them and to communicate back and forth. We use a signal that is almost like a polarized beam of light. It's totally unlike any conventional system. Only a specially designed receiver can pick these signals up. Even if someone did manage to build one, which isn't likely, they still wouldn't be able to get a fix on the source or the target. Part of the system allows that the frequencies change every one-fiftieth of a second. The tail segment of each timed transmission tells the receiver which frequency to use for the next one-fiftieth of a second interval. So, the decoder would also be needed. It's highly unlikely that anyone could build both the receiver and the decoder without a SENTINEL intelligence to design it," Elizabeth explained.

"One-fiftieth of a second? How much could it transmit in that short a time?" Justin asked.

"Cranked up to maximum it could transmit...let's see... about the equivalent of the entire Bible, cover to cover in that time period," Elizabeth answered.

Justin's head was spinning. He couldn't follow it anymore.

Just then, the white light on the SENTINEL console snapped on.

"Gentlemen," SENTINEL's soft voice began, "it is now time to go to the special ordnance lab. Everything is ready for you. Sorry to have kept you waiting," the voice apologized.

The voice gave Justin an uneasy feeling. It sounded so real, so human. It was like hearing it for the first time, with a new significance bound to it.

"Thank you, SENTINEL," Elizabeth said. "We've just finished in here. They'll be right there."

The light clicked off.

"Thank you, gentlemen, for your time and attention. You will be able to get to ordnance by going left in the corridor outside and taking the first right that you come to. It's room number three-forty-four. It says ORDNANCE LAB right on the door."

The two men rose, exhausted and spent from their experience. They walked toward the exit. Justin stopped short of the door as Fanning went through. He walked back to Elizabeth and extended his hand.

"Thank you, Dr. Ryerson," he said. He looked into the attractive, sharp eyes behind the glasses. There was an incredible genius behind those eyes. He admired it.

"You're welcome," Elizabeth said, taking Justin's hand. A hot, electric sensation shot through her at the touch of his hand. There was something about this man that broke through the barrier of distrust she felt toward men. The man was a killer. A hunter. He was savage masculinity. There was a disturbing chemistry boiling inside, which she fought to control. She despised him...yet...

"You're welcome," she repeated, trying to control the obvious flush crossing her face. "You had better get started to ordnance. Pegasus will be waiting for you."

Justin held the soft warm hand for a moment. There was an attractive woman behind that cold exterior. But there was no warmth in the eyes.

He released the hand and went through the door to catch up with Fanning. An interesting new picture was taking shape, a disturbing new picture.

TWENTY-ONE

Collective guilt—it was both a curse and a blessing. It was the bond that cemented the survivors of the catastrophe. The cause never died.

Our best had fallen in the war, the very cream of our youth was gone. But the Aryan seed had not been crushed. From it could grow another magic race, to fulfill the lost dream. Two, perhaps three generations later would see the beginnings. Two generations more, and they would be ready to follow a new leader, a new Führer.

Entry No. 36 from the partially
recovered *Wolf Journal*

Scotch ran down the side of the glass and over the hand of Edward Bridges.

"Shit," he said, reaching for a towel. That was the second time he had partially missed the glass in the past hour. His nerves were strung tight.

Where in the hell are they? he wondered. It was already 5:15. He had expected them early that morning. The valuable lead time was slipping away.

He paced back and forth nervously, belting down half of the contents of the glass. He looked impatiently at his watch.

Something's going to go wrong. I know it! Oh, why did I ever do this? I must have been insane. I mean, how much better could it get for me? I had a pretty good deal where I was.

His brain was racked with alternating bouts of optimism and doubt, eased by conviction, flogged with guilt—and the Scotch did little to help his mental state.

The point of no return hadn't been reached for him, yet, he thought. The information could still be put back as easily as it had been taken. The car was just outside. Get in it, drive back, he told himself.

Then he thought about the red folder—Operation Raptor. He couldn't go back with the knowledge of what that meant. It wasn't a matter of what he *wanted* to do anymore. It boiled down to what *had* to be done.

He took another long swallow, and almost choked when the knock sounded on the door.

He wiped away the liquor from his chin and put the glass down hurriedly, almost knocking it over. He rushed to the door, his temples throbbing. This was it. The point of no return.

He pressed his eye to the tiny peephole in the door. There were two men outside. "Yes, who is it?" he asked.

There was no answer, only another gentle knocking.

He unlocked the door, still leaving the chain lock attached. He opened it a crack and placed an eye to where he could see the two men.

"Yes?" he said.

The first man looked into his eye. "How are you, Dr. Bridges? May we come in, please?" the voice asked.

"I don't know you. Who are you?" Bridges asked nervously.

"Yes or no, Dr. Bridges. Just answer yes or no," the voice said.

Bridges immediately recognized it as the voice he had spoken with at the Playboy Club. "Which phone?" he asked, just to make certain.

"The one on the end," came the reply.

The door closed, so that the chain lock could be removed. Then it opened.

The two men passed quickly into the room. Bridges eyed them cautiously, as he pushed the door shut. He double-locked it again and turned to face them.

They weren't exactly what he had expected. They were both so small. His massive six-foot frame easily dwarfed them. The smaller fat one was only about five-foot-five or six. The other one, the thin one, was only slightly taller. The skinny one was the leader, Bridges decided. He could tell. The fat, sweaty one had taken a position just off the other one's right shoulder and was surveying the room with careful, observing sweeps of his eyes. The thin one looked only at Bridges, right into the eyes.

"Shall we sit down?" Alexi Kuradin suggested.

"Yes...yes, please," Bridges said nervously. He gestured to the two chairs by the small round table near the window. He hurried over to the table and took away the bottle and glass. He put them on the long, low dresser.

The two men moved to the chairs. Ten Braak made a quick check of the drawn drapes, to be certain that there were no gaps through which someone might be able to see from the outside. Then he sat across from Kuradin.

"Would you like a drink?" Bridges offered shakily.

"No, thank you, Dr. Bridges," Kuradin said. He saw the half-filled bottle on the dresser and the partially filled glass next to it. "But go ahead," he said with a slight gesture of his eyes in the direction of the bottle.

Bridges went over to the bottle and poured out about half a glass. There was no ice to put in it, as he hadn't left the room since the time he had gotten there. Kuradin noticed the slight trembling of the hands, as Bridges walked back toward them.

"I was beginning to worry," Bridges said with a nervous little laugh. "I thought that maybe you guys weren't going to show up."

"You needn't have worried, Dr. Bridges," Kuradin began. "You're very important to us. We would never forget about you," he said. His English was perfect, without even the slightest trace of foreign accent.

"Shall we get down to cases?" Kuradin asked.

That was okay with Bridges. He wanted to get the hell out. Fast.

Bridges hurried a gulp of his Scotch. "I've got everything right here with me," he said. "I'm ready to go when you are."

"I would like to see the information first," Kuradin said with a wary smile.

Bridges's eyes quickly played back and forth between the two men. The fat one was still looking around the room. Bridges didn't like that one, and he didn't trust either of them. "I don't know," he said. "We're wasting time. We should be getting out of here. Time is getting short."

"We have plenty of time, Dr. Bridges. Your absence won't be discovered until Monday. Now, may I please see the information?"

Bridges didn't like it. He wanted to keep that information in his possession. Why should the Russian want to see it? "I don't know...I—"

"Dr. Bridges," Kuradin cut in, holding up a hand to stop Bridges's flow of words. "Let me put you at ease. We're not going to harm you or steal your information. We have to take certain precautions to ensure the success of the mission. One of them is to make two microfilm copies of your information. This is only an added measure to guarantee its getting into our country safely. You will be permitted to carry the original information and one of the microfilm copies with you. I will carry the other one. That is, unless your information is already on film, then I'm afraid that I must insist that I carry it," Kuradin said.

Kuradin's explanation made Bridges feel somewhat easier. "No, it's not on film," he said, looking into the Russian's penetrating eyes. "I...I understand," he nodded. He turned and walked over to the small, open closet area and picked up a thin attaché case. He walked back toward Kuradin, as he opened it and took out a packet of sheets held together in the upper right corner by a round-head fastener. He had attached this at his apartment after typing over the condensed notes he had made from the contents of the red folder. With the blank cover sheet, there was a total of twenty-six sheets.

He held the packet out to Kuradin.

Kuradin looked at Ten Braak and motioned toward the sheets with his eyes. Ten Braak held out his hand and Bridges handed them to him. They were placed on the table in front of Kuradin. Ten Braak then turned on the overhead swag lamp.

Kuradin removed his hands from his coat pockets for the first time since entering the room and placed them on his knees, as he leaned forward to the table.

He looked at the blank cover sheet and examined it carefully, then looked at how the sheets were bound. With the side edge of his right index finger, he raised the lower right corner of the cover sheet. Then he pushed the back of his fingers and hand along the underside of the sheet until it flipped over, revealing the first schematic.

Bridges watched the Russian, as he studied the first sheet. It appeared that he understood what he was looking at. It figured that they would send someone who knew computers, he thought. The other one looked like a gorilla. He was sweaty and greasy-looking, with black hairs all over his hands. Bridges wondered what role the fat one played in this. Maybe protection, although he didn't look very dangerous.

Kuradin turned the next page in exactly the same fashion, being careful not to let his fingertips touch any portion of the sheets. He studied the second sheet.

Bridges took another swallow, draining the glass. He went to the bottle and poured another.

The second sheet was finished. Kuradin turned to the third one. Seeing that it did not pertain to the memory mass, as did the first two, he looked up at Bridges. "The memory system is quite extraordinary," he said. He assessed Bridges for a long moment through a slight squint, then went back to the sheet in front of him. A few moments later he turned the page in the same careful manner. The pages began turning more quickly.

After turning several more pages, it became necessary to hold the turned pages in place. He used the back of one of his knuckles of the left hand. The pages turned and turned.

Then he came to the last sheet. He looked up at Bridges. "What is this?" he asked him.

Bridges could see that it was the last page. "Just a little something extra I was able to pick up on Friday before I left. I'm sure it will interest your people," he answered.

Kuradin read it carefully, swallowing as he read. The stub of his finger began to ache, as it always did when he thought about that day in England. He had seen some of this information before, when the code had been deciphered on the information he brought back from that mission a year ago. That information had been important, but fragmented and incomplete. This was all of it. It fit together into an unmistakable picture now.

"Why didn't you tell us about this in the earlier contacts?" Kuradin asked.

"I didn't know anything about it then. I told you, I only managed to get this on the last day," Bridges answered.

"Then they are unaware that you know about this?"

"That's right, and there won't be any way that they can find out that I've gotten it, either."

Kuradin let his eyes fall away from the sheet and stared blankly into the tabletop. He let the significance of the last sheet filter through his head. Moscow hadn't expected anything like this. They had to know.

It was of paramount importance that Bridges's people not discover that he had delivered this information. It could drastically affect the final stages of his plan.

Kuradin let the last sheet flip over. Then, with the back of his fingers, he pushed the sheets to Ten Braak. "Remove the last sheet," he instructed.

Bridges looked up from his glass with a start. "Hey, wait a minute. What are you doing?"

"I know exactly what I'm doing, Dr. Bridges," Kuradin said. "You said that they should not be able to learn that you've taken this information out. Should anything happen to this packet of information, and it ended up back in their hands, they would immediately know. We must, therefore, protect ourselves from that possibility. The best way to do that is to remove the information. It will not show up on the microfilm, either, just in case one of us should be taken and the film discovered," Kuradin explained.

"What will you do with it?" Bridges asked.

Kuradin shook his head. "I don't know, yet."

Ten Braak tore away the last sheet. But a large portion of the corner remained under the fastener. He plucked at it several times until he shredded all but a small piece of it away. He turned the packet back over and placed it once again in front of Kuradin.

"What about this?" Ten Braak asked in his thick German accent, holding up the last page.

"Give it to me," Kuradin said. He took it from Ten Braak and folded it. Then he stuck it in his coat pocket.

Ten Braak then folded back the cover sheet, as Kuradin produced two very small cameras from his overcoat pocket. He placed one down. With the other, he snapped a picture of the first schematic. Then he placed that camera down, picked up the other, and again snapped a picture of the same schematic. Ten Braak then turned the page. The entire procedure was repeated, until all twenty-four sheets had been photographed with each camera. Then Kuradin nodded to Ten Braak.

Ten Braak handed the sheets back to Bridges, then walked to the door, unlocked it, and went outside, closing the door behind him.

"Where's he going?" Bridges asked.

Kuradin removed the two tiny cartridges from the cameras. He placed one on the table. The other he put in the back of his watch, in a tiny compartment that looked like it was meant to hold a battery cell.

"Part of the precautions we must take," Kuradin answered. "He's gone out to the car to get a small aluminum capsule to store that cartridge in," he said, pointing to the one on the table. "That's the one you'll be carrying out with you. It'll be in the lower portion of your colon," Kuradin said.

"What!" Bridges exclaimed. "Are you kidding me?"

"No," Kuradin said, shaking his head. "It will be quite secure and comfortable, I assure you.

"He'll be a few minutes, Dr. Bridges," Kuradin went on. "I suggest you use the time to tell me exactly what they'll do after they discover that you and the schematics are missing."

Outside, Ten Braak walked to the car they had driven to South Beloit. He walked to the back and opened the trunk. He slid the black case he had carried with him from Newark to a position directly in front of him. He looked around before he opened it.

About six parking spaces to his right was another car. It had a flat tire, and its owner was attempting to fix it.

They were the only two people in the parking lot. He was far enough away that he didn't have to worry about the other man seeing what he was doing. He put his attention back on the case and opened it.

He withdrew three short pieces of metal tubing and screwed them together into one longer piece of about seven inches. Its diameter was about one half inch. The end section held a tiny 1.5-volt battery, which powered the silent-acting detonator in the middle section. Instead of a bullet, it discharged the contents of an ampoule contained in the tip segment. The ampoule contained deadly prussic acid, a colorless, odorless poison. With the activation of the detonator, the prussic acid would vaporize as it passed through the tiny opening in the tip of the weapon. Anyone breathing in the gas at close range would be dead within seconds. All traces of the acid would be gone within a few hours before any autopsy could be performed. Only water vapor was left behind, which quickly evaporated. The cause of death was then determined to be heart failure. It was not a new method, but it was an effective one.

Next, he opened a small metal box and removed two sodium thiosulfate tablets and two amyl nitrate ampoules. These provided the user of the weapon with an antidote, in case he should inadvertently inhale some of the acid vapors. The tablet was to be taken prior to the firing of the gun. The ampoule was to be crushed immediately following the discharge, its amyl nitrate vapors inhaled deeply.

He then pulled out the metal capsule that was to hold the other microfilm cartridge. It was sealed in a small plastic bag.

"Excuse me," a voice came from beside him. The owner of the other car was standing there. Ten Braak turned to face the voice, moving to put himself between the man and the case in the trunk.

"I was wondering if I could borrow your jack?" the man asked. "I seem to be having some difficulty with mine. Can't get it to stay under the bumper," the fellow said.

Ten Braak's dark eyes narrowed onto the round, wrinkled face of the man. He was an elderly chap, in his sixties, or thereabouts.

The man had gotten an eyeful of Ten Braak's face. Ten Braak knew what had to be done.

"I will assist you," Ten Braak said, in his thick, guttural accent.

"Thank you, that's very kind," the old man said. "I think it's broken. It won't stay under the bumper. Maybe a piece is missing," he said as they walked.

Ten Braak followed the old man back to the car. As he walked, his hand came to rest on the smooth custom-shaped wooden handle in his pocket.

They stopped at the car. "Try once again," Ten Braak said. He watched the man's efforts.

The old man bent forward and tried putting the jack under the bumper again.

Ten Braak looked around the parking lot. They were still alone. He withdrew the wooden handle. Extending out perpendicularly from the center of the handle was a four-inch metal shaft, covered with a thick leather sheath. The shaft rested between the index and middle fingers of his fist. He removed the sheath, exposing the narrow, ice-picklike shaft. He moved closer to the man.

"See, I just can't get it to stay under there," the old man said.

Ten Braak brought the sharpened tip of the thin shaft to within an inch of the man's head, just behind the left ear. With a quick, even thrust, he jammed it home, right into the man's skull, all the way up to the fingers. There was a faint groan as the man's eyes crossed and his face tightened. He was dead instantly.

In a second the man's body was in the trunk. The jack was thrown in and the trunk lid closed. Ten Braak returned to his car. He sheathed the weapon and put it back into his pocket.

He closed the black case and slammed the trunk shut, checked the parking lot once more, and then returned to Bridges's door.

Bridges had just finished telling Kuradin what to expect from SENTINEL when the knock sounded at the door. He let Ten Braak in and double-locked the door again.

Inside the room, Ten Braak removed the intestinal capsule from the plastic bag. He placed the film cartridge in it, after unscrewing the capsule into two separate pieces. Bridges watched him carefully. The thing seemed huge after it was back together.

"I suggest that you try to have a bowel movement now," Kuradin said. "Even if you don't feel the need to have one, you must try. Once the capsule is in place, you will not be able to have another one until it is removed. And that won't be for another six hours. By that time, you will be on a plane headed safely for the Soviet Union," Kuradin lied.

Bridges retired to the bathroom.

As soon as Bridges had closed the door, Ten Braak took out the tablets and ampoules. He gave one of each to Kuradin. Both men took the sodium thiosulfate tablets. Kuradin kept the amyl nitrate ampoule in the palm of his hand, closing his fist over it.

A few moments later, the toilet flushed, and Bridges emerged from the bathroom. Ten Braak was standing between the two double beds.

"Stand here," Ten Braak said, holding the film capsule.

Bridges moved to where he was instructed.

"I can do this myself," he protested. "Just give it to me, and I'll put it up."

"It must be inserted properly, Dr. Bridges, or it will not stay in position," Kuradin said.

This is embarrassing, Bridges thought to himself.

Bridges and Ten Braak were only about eighteen inches apart, facing one another. Bridges looked down into the big black eyes. He was wrong about this man, he *did* look dangerous. The eyes were dark and menacing. He suddenly felt uncomfortable. He began to say something.

Before the first word came out, Ten Braak's hand flashed upward with the deadly tube. He detonated it, hitting Bridges squarely in the face with the deadly prussic acid vapors.

Bridges's eyes bulged suddenly, he gagged and retched, his face turning a deep red. Coughing and sputtering, he staggered a half step forward toward Ten Braak. He made a horrible choking gurgle, his eyes popping and beginning to run. The moment before he collapsed, Ten Braak shoved him backward onto the bed.

Ten Braak quickly crushed the amyl nitrate capsule and breathed in the vapors deeply. Kuradin did so at the same time. Bridges twitched once or twice, then stopped moving.

Ten Braak undid his belt, lowered his pants and underwear. He bent forward, in a wide-stance squat, and inserted the aluminum capsule into his rectum, pushing it well up into the lower colon. Then he pulled up his pants and secured them.

The two men left the room and got into their car. As they began to pull away from the rear parking lot, a helicopter appeared overhead.

The helicopter was unusual in design. It looked like a normal helicopter, but made very little sound. The engine could barely be heard above the sweeping sounds of the rotors.

"There's a car leaving down there, Ted," Justin said. "From the same general area as Bridges's room. See if you can get a look at its tags with the glasses."

Fanning raised the binoculars. "Illinois registration—LC eight-five-eight-nine. Blue Dodge Monaco, four-door sedan. Can't make out the driver."

"SENTINEL, can you run that through Illinois DMV?" Justin asked. "L as in lucky, C as in Charlie, eight-five-eight-nine. Late-model blue Dodge Monaco," he repeated.

"Working," the soft voice said.

"Are you able to track visually?" Justin asked.

"Negative," SENTINEL replied. "Cloud cover is too dense."

South Beloit was farm country. Huge open fields abounded everywhere. There was such a field behind the Holiday Inn. The pilot of the copter put down in it.

Justin turned to the pilot. "Take it back up, and see if you can follow that car for just a little bit. I want to see if it heads out on US Seventy-five toward I-Ninety. If it does, let us know, and we'll tell you what to do," he instructed.

The pilot nodded.

The two men climbed out of the chopper. Fanning was carrying a large metal case, like a big tool box. The chopper lifted off as they moved away.

BEEP!

SENTINEL was signaling for transmission.

"Blue Dodge Monaco, Illinois registration LC eight-five-eight-nine is owned and operated by the National Rent-A-Car agency. It is currently contracted to one David R. Fromme of Baltimore, Maryland. It has been contracted since last Thursday morning, from O'Hare Airport. Mr. Fromme has been registered at the Holiday Inn, South Beloit, since Thursday afternoon sixteen forty-six hours. Reservations extend through Wednesday of next week. Room number one-fifty-five. It is three doors away from Dr. Bridges's room," SENTINEL reported.

"Thank you, SENTINEL," Justin said.

The two men approached well up from Bridges's room. The chopper had put them down where they could not be seen easily from Bridges's window. Both men passed completely by Bridges's door, then stopped. Normally, they would have taken positions on both sides of the door, but one side was all glass. Bridges's window extended right up to the door. Glass was poor at stopping bullets.

Fanning put down the heavy case and took a position behind Bridges's rental car, which was right in front of his door. From his position, just behind the right side of the trunk, he could get a clear shot into the room. The lights on inside would make the visibility excellent.

Justin's left hand was in his coat pocket, as he moved to the door. The inside of the pocket had been ripped away, leaving access directly through the inside lining of the coat. His hand cradled the Mauser.

He knocked at the door.

There was no reply.

He knocked again. If the contact hadn't already been made, then Bridges would expect Justin to be the contact. If it had been made, it wouldn't matter anymore. He'd either be dead, or gone.

There was still no answer.

Justin backed away from the door. He looked at the lock. The little pinlike button below it was in. That meant that the dead bolt hadn't been engaged, but the chain lock could be. He felt the door. It was metal and very sturdy. The frame around it was also metal. Chances were good that one kick wouldn't open it. He decided to pick it.

He pulled out a pocket knife and selected a specially shaped blade. He inserted the blade into the lock, giving up his hold on the Mauser to grasp the doorknob with the left hand.

As quietly as possible, he wiggled the blade artfully, inserting it deeper, as the tumblers moved. Then he turned the doorknob, praying that there wasn't a gun aimed at the other side of the door. He opened the door only a crack, just enough to see that the chain lock wasn't engaged. Things looked bad.

He backed away and put the Mauser back into his hand. He looked at Fanning, who had crouched low into a firing position, well behind the car.

Fanning nodded.

Justin kicked the door in and twisted back and away to cover.

Nothing happened.

Fanning leaned out a little bit and saw Bridges on the bed. He motioned with his head to Justin.

The Mauser came into the doorway first, followed by Justin's head peeking around. He could see the bathroom door open. The closet was an open space. There were no other hiding places. He entered slowly, looking at Bridges on the bed. He knew immediately that the man was dead. He was careful not to step further into the room until he looked cautiously around for any evidence, so as to avoid disturbing it when he was ready to approach the body.

The room was very clean, no traces of foul play, nothing on the floor. He stepped further in, then took the most direct route to the body. He motioned Fanning with an arm.

Fanning went to the heavy case and picked it up. He entered the room and used the point of his elbow to close the door most of the way, until it was open just a crack.

Justin stood right over the body lying face up and across the bed. "Looks like he choked on something," he said. He bent down to the distorted face and touched the big fleshy cheeks. They were soft and warm. He touched the toes. "No rigor mortis yet."

BEEP!

"What is the coloring of the face?" the soft voice asked.

Justin looked down into it. "Dark red. There's considerable distortion. Moisture around the eyes, nose, and mouth," he said. "No bruises or wounds are readily visible anywhere on the body," he added.

"Is the tongue extended or pinched between the teeth?" SENTINEL asked.

Justin checked. "No."

"Information's here on the dresser," Fanning said.

"Touch nothing," SENTINEL advised. "Take the blue bottle and a sterile forceps out of the case," SENTINEL instructed.

Justin picked the items out of the case. "I've got them."

"Go to the head. With the sterile forceps, pull out several hairs from the nose. Drop them into the solution in the blue bottle," the voice directed.

Justin followed the instructions. "I've done it."

"Now take out the small paper bags and carefully secure two of them over the hands. Then, place the larger one over the head, securing it gently and loosely, so as not to cause any marks or bruises."

After several moments that was completed. SENTINEL then instructed them to take samples of the contents of the glass and bottle. Fanning did this, putting the samples into special jars.

"Now go to the schematics. Describe what you see," SENTINEL instructed.

"There's a packet of sheets with a plain white cover sheet. They're bound in the upper left corner by a fastener clip. It's lying on a formica topped dresser," Justin described.

"Using a pen or pencil, turn the packet of papers by sliding them until the bound corner is extending just over the edge of the dresser top," SENTINEL said.

Justin did this. "Done."

"Now, count the number of pages at the bound corner without touching any of them."

Justin began counting. He counted twenty-six, including the cover sheet.

"There should be twenty-four sheets," SENTINEL said.

"I miscounted," Justin said. He counted them again.

"Goddamn it," he cursed under his breath. He kept counting twenty-six sheets. He ducked down, looked up at the underside of the clip, and saw the torn fragment held under it. It was big enough to look like a sheet from the angle he had counted them. "Okay, I count twenty-four, twenty-five with the cover sheet," he said.

"Now take out one of the boxes from the case and unfold it," SENTINEL instructed. "Use the pencil again to slide the packet into the box, being careful not to touch the sheets in any way. Then bind the box with string."

"I'm gonna look around outside," Fanning said. He carefully opened the door, using a pencil put into the opening. He went out and closed the door by using the pencil up under the doorknob, again leaving it open just a crack. The doorknob would be important evidence to the Division Two team coming in.

Justin unfolded the bottom half of the box and was about to unfold the cover when his eyes caught sight of two small scraps of paper on the floor just under the round table near the windows. He went over to them and looked at them closely. He took an envelope from the case and used the pencil to push the pieces into it. He went back over to the packet and ducked down again, holding one of the scraps to the piece under the clip. They looked the same. There *had* been another sheet. It was of a lighter bond than the schematics, as was the cover sheet. Maybe it was part of a back cover sheet, he thought. But why would it have been torn away?

He took the tweezer he had used to pull the hairs out of Bridges's nose and removed the scrap from under the clip and put it into the envelope along with the others. He sealed the envelope, folded it, and put it in his pocket. Then he finished unfolding the boxtop, slid the packet into the box, covered it, and secured it with string.

"Information is in the box," he said.

"A Division Two team will be there shortly. Touch nothing and leave the room," SENTINEL told him.

Just then the door inched open. Fanning leaned in. "Are you done in here yet?" he asked.

Justin nodded.

"I want you to look at something," Fanning said.

Justin followed him out, carefully pulling the door to within a fraction of closing, as his partner had done before.

"What did you find?" Justin asked.

"Found this over by that car," Fanning said. He held up a key ring on the pencil. "Car's got a flat tire. The base of the jack was still behind the car, and these keys were just under the trunk area," he said.

They walked over to the car.

"I know I shouldn't have touched the keys, but I had a feeling." He lifted the trunk lid which he had unlocked just moments before. "I found this."

Justin looked in at the body and inspected the small hole in the head. "That's no bullet," he said.

Fanning shook his head. "They've been here, all right. This poor sucker probably saw something he shouldn't have," he said.

"Cracker Jack to Pilgrim," their implants suddenly jumped. It was the copter pilot.

"Go ahead, Cracker Jack," Justin said.

"Subject car, blue Dodge Monaco, had gone into Beloit. Lost sight of it for a while. It's on its way back your direction now. Want me to stay with him?"

"Affirmative, Cracker Jack. It may be heading for US Seventy-five now. Stay out of the driver's field of view. If he comes back here, wait about five minutes before setting down."

"Roger."

Justin thought for a few moments. "This was a nice neat job," he said finally.

"Yeah, and we'll have a devil of a time finding them now. That Division Two team won't be here for a while," Fanning said, looking into Justin's eyes.

They were reading each other clearly.

"Fromme?" Justin asked.

"Fromme," Fanning returned.

"That was room one fifty-five, wasn't it?"

Fanning nodded.

"Cracker Jack to Pilgrim," the pilot's voice began. "Subject car returning your position."

"Thank you, Cracker Jack," Justin said.

"Let's pay this David Fromme a little visit, shall we?" Justin said. "He may have seen something that can help us."

TWENTY-TWO

Great men are not made by propaganda, but grow out of their deeds and are recognized by history.

Franz von Papen

I can still hear the thundering chants of the Nuremberg rallies. A mass of humanity almost beyond comprehension—they had all come to hear their Führer speak of their destiny, to tell them about the things that they feared, and how to overcome them.

He would boom out in rage, fall soft again, his voice quivering, their emotions swaying with the currents of his oratory.

"Sieg Heil…Sieg Heil…Sieg Heil," they would thunder out, causing the hair to rise and bumps on the flesh.

"Sieg Heil…Sieg Heil…Sieg Heil," they shouted, proclaiming their love for the Messiah of Germany. But that is all gone now. The Reich is gone, the people gone, and their Führer no more.

Without a leader, they will not follow. Not just any leader, but a man of der Führer's vision, love, and devotion to their destiny.

It is too much to expect a second miracle so soon. Men with the greatness of our Führer come only once or twice in a thousand years.

Entry No. 37 from the partially recovered *Wolf Journal*

The blue Dodge Monaco made its way into the Holiday Inn parking lot and headed to the rear parking area again: Kuradin had just driven into Beloit, to drop Ten Braak off where he was to make contact with his transportation into the New York area. On the way there, Ten Braak told him about the man he had dispatched in the parking lot.

Kuradin had been turning that incident over in his head, for its possible effect on the plan. It shouldn't hurt the situation at all. In fact, it could help matters.

He pulled around into the rear lot and drove past the few parked cars there. He noted the car with the flat tire and saw that the trunk lid was down but not locked shut. Ten Braak had specifically said that he closed it securely.

The Dodge moved slowly past Bridges's room and his parked car. Kuradin saw Bridges's door open just a crack. They had found him already!

A quick shock of nervousness coursed through him. They had just made it out of there. Incredible. They knew about it already and had found where Bridges had gone into hiding. Bridges's assessment as to the computer's ability to locate him had been correct. That meant that the first contingency already had to be implemented. It was a good thing that Centaur had not underestimated the capabilities of SENTINEL.

He drove up to the space in front of his room and parked the car. He was careful not to be obvious in surveying the area. He must show no awareness or interest in what was happening. It disturbed him that he didn't see anybody else or other strange cars that hadn't been there when they left. Where were they? he wondered as he went to his door.

He unlocked it and opened it slightly, sticking his hand in through the narrow opening to switch on his light. Suddenly, a steellike grip secured his wrist, and he was pulled into the room.

Reaction! The alternatives flashed through Kuradin's brain. Panic or cool? An intelligence agent would react with an instinctive defensive response. A typical business man wouldn't. He chose panic as his cover.

"*Ahhh!*" he screamed, as he was tossed head first onto the closest double bed. Before he could move, a knee was against the middle of his back. His eyes widened with terror.

"Don't move," a controlled voice said.

He couldn't move if he wanted to. He froze.

Two hands frisked him as another held his head down. That meant at least two men.

"He's clean," Fanning said.

The knee came off his back. He sat up quickly, his face white with terror.

"My...my...my wallet is in my pocket. Take it, please. Take it. Just don't hurt me," Kuradin spat out, his eyes almost watering.

Justin surveyed the frightened eyes and face.

"We're not here to rob you, Mr. Fromme. Just to talk to you," Justin said calmly.

Kuradin's eyes registered fright and confusion. He said nothing, letting his eyes jump nervously from one man to the other.

"I...I don't understand." Kuradin swallowed.

"I'm sorry we had to treat you so roughly, Mr. Fromme, but we were taking no chances."

"No chances? What chances? Who are you? What are you doing here?" he asked in a nervous rush of questions.

"FBI," Justin said, producing authentic identification and holding it out for Kuradin's inspection. Fanning did the same. "Now, if you don't mind, we'd like to ask you some questions."

Kuradin looked at the IDs. He began to assume a slightly more composed air. He swallowed loudly. "Oh God," he said, putting a hand up to a perspiring forehead. "I thought you were going to kill me," he said, sounding relief.

"No, sir, we just had to get you into the room as quickly as possible."

Kuradin saw right through the lie. But he wasn't going to play the irate citizen now. The sooner they left, the better. He wondered if one of them was Pilgrim, and which one it was.

"May we see your identification, please?"

Kuradin produced it. They had, obviously, already discovered his cover identity. They had called him by the name just moments before.

After a short exchange covering who Fromme was and why he was in South Beloit, Justin got to the more pertinent questions.

"Your car was seen leaving the parking lot not more than twenty minutes ago. Could you please tell us if you observed or heard anything unusual before or as you were leaving?" he asked.

Kuradin put a reflective wrinkle to his brow. After a few moments he shook his head. "No, I can't recall seeing or hearing anything. Why? Has a crime been committed?"

Justin ignored the question. "Did you see anything or anyone in the parking lot as you drove out?"

Kuradin thought for a few moments. "No...wait, yes, I did. I saw two guys fixing a flat tire. But that was before I left. I was coming in, actually. I left again about ten or fifteen minutes later," he said. "They were gone."

"Two men fixing a flat tire? Do you remember what they looked like?"

Kuradin pretended to think again. "Not really," he said, shaking his head. He squinted his eyes in mock recollection. "One... one of them was a fat man, I think. I didn't really look at him, but I seem to remember that one was pretty fat."

"Was he tall or short?" Justin asked.

He thought again. "Short, dark, I think. Maybe just his clothes were dark, I can't remember. I'm pretty sure he was short, though." He didn't sound too positive.

"About how tall?" Fanning asked.

Kuradin shook his head. "I really can't remember. I really didn't look at him too closely. He could have even been tall; I just have the impression that he was short."

"Do you remember anything about the other one at all? Tall, short, young, or old?" Fanning asked.

"Nope, nothing," he said shaking his head.

"And you said that was about, let's see…about thirty minutes ago?" Justin asked, after some quick mental arithmetic.

"More like forty-five," Kuradin answered.

Justin nodded to Fanning. "Okay, Mr. Fromme, thank you for your cooperation. I'm sorry we treated you so roughly earlier. Please accept our apologies," he said.

"Well, I can't say that I enjoyed it," Kuradin began, "or that I understand why, but I accept your apology."

"Can you be reached at this location for the next few days?" Justin asked.

Kuradin nodded. "Yes, until Wednesday. But try only during the evenings. I have business to attend to during the daytime. After Wednesday, you can reach me in Baltimore. You took the address and phone number. I'm sorry I wasn't more help," he said. "Sure you don't want to change your mind and tell me what it's all about?" he asked with a smile.

Justin just shook his head. "Thank you, Mr. Fromme," he said.

The two men left the room.

Justin and Fanning walked over to the helicopter that had put down after Kuradin went into his hotel room. A larger helicopter was motionless beside it. The Division Two team had arrived only moments earlier. They were busily going over the crime scene and both the car that Bridges had rented and the one that the body had been discovered in.

The questions had been answered to Justin's satisfaction, but there was something about Fromme that was bothering him.

Something about the man seemed off center or out of balance. Just a little thing, but he couldn't pin it down.

BEEP!

"Yes, SENTINEL," Justin said.

"Fromme's story checks out," the soft voice said. "Everything about his personal life and reasons for being in South Beloit match with the facts."

"Thank you, SENTINEL," Justin said. But there was still something about him. Not so much about what the man said, as the man himself.

The two men boarded the helicopter and were Alpha bound.

Kuradin reflected on the state of the situation. The plan had progressed well, up to a few moments ago. Bridges had gotten his information out safely; Ross was taken care of; they had obtained the information from Bridges and killed him. But that was where the smoothness ended.

Bridges's body had been discovered too soon. With very careful measures, it would be possible to detect that his death was caused by prussic acid. One hour more, and it would have been impossible. He would not underestimate SENTINEL's intellect. They would discover the cause of death. He was sure of it.

Kuradin looked at his watch. About an hour ago, Leonid Travkin had arranged to let out the fact that Otto Ten Braak was in the United States on a special mission. That, combined with the killings of Ross, Bridges, and the old man, would put them onto the trail. He had made certain that Ten Braak's prints were on enough items to connect that fact, even if the leak of it failed.

The next part of the plan should go smoothly, too, so long as nothing else unexpected happened. There were enough contingencies ahead, yet, and things were still greatly in his favor. He felt very satisfied, all things considered.

He didn't know about Dmitri Chakhovsky's defection.

Since the breaching of security at Alpha, Elizabeth Ryerson had taken up residence at the complex, as per Honeycut's orders. This was for her protection in the event that Bridges had divulged her identity. A comfortable apartment was maintained there for her for times when her work carried well into the night. She used it frequently, as her entire world was in that complex. It was no hardship for her to have to spend some time there now. In fact, she quite preferred it.

She had turned in early, as the events of the day had left her exhausted and depressed. Her anxiety had evoked exhaustion and a desire to sleep. Like a built-in defense mechanism, it offered a form of protection.

Her sleep had been hard and restless. An odd kaleidoscope of fears appeared repeatedly in nightmare fashion. She saw Bridges laughing as he taunted her with the schematics, standing just out of her reach as she tried to retrieve them. Then suddenly the schematics were transformed into a child, an infant. And Bridges had transformed himself into a horrible monster who tore hunks of flesh from the child with his sharp, jagged teeth as he laughed, devouring her baby as she stood helplessly by, unable to stop him.

The dream came again and again, as she tossed and cried out in her sleep. Then suddenly the dream changed. They were not alone in the room. Another figure was there. A tall, dark figure who had come to help. It was Justin.

Bridges's expression changed to terror, as Justin produced his weapon. Despite Bridges's monstrous power, he was defenseless against Justin. It was over quickly. Bridges faded from the dream with the discharges of Justin's gun. He was gone forever—the terror was ended.

Her relief was overwhelming as Justin came to where she was lying naked on the bed. He was beside her, his thigh pressed tightly between her legs, the gun in his hand held to her face.

He pumped his thigh forcefully into her crotch, as he coaxed the gun closer to her face, to her lips. There was fear in her, and gratitude for what he had done. He was demanding payment.

He pulled her head back by her long chestnut hair and urged the gun to her lips. Fearfully and gratefully, she parted them. He began a slow pumping motion with the gun, probing sensually into her mouth, deeper and deeper with each gentle motion. She resisted at first, then yielded in her gratitude.

Her lips and tongue began an erotic persuasion as she was taken up in the passion. The gun probed deeper, her head moving slowly forward and backward in an increasing tempo. The cold hardness of the gun's metal began to yield to another hardness, a warmer, more substantial bulk. It was no longer a gun, but his penis.

Her passion had become wild, and she mouthed the organ with a desperation, wanting it, needing it.

The organ grew larger and larger, until it would no longer fit in her mouth. Then Justin put himself on top of her, between her legs. She writhed, near an explosion of pleasure, when he mounted her and drove the enormous, ever-increasing organ into her over and over and over. Its size was unbelievable, it was assaulting her, hurting her, yet bringing a pleasure she could not do without.

"Oh, Justin…Justin. Fuck me…FUCK ME…FUCK ME," she sighed.

She awakened suddenly, to the intense orgasm she experienced. It was almost unending.

She lay sweat-covered and limp on the bed. She had never experienced such intense sensations in her life. The dream would not leave her.

She got up and went to the vanity and sat in front of the mirror. She was spent. To sleep now was impossible.

After a few moments she began to brush her hair, as the details of the dream played again through her mind in a deliberate slow motion. The brushing stopped as her fingers traced her lips and tongue, then caressed her breasts. The dream was alive in her once more.

She saw him, his gun—his organ.

Her hand moved tenderly between her legs, as the details replayed. It began probing into her, deeper and deeper. First two fingers, then three, then four. Then she began the moaning, as she closed her eyes to concentrate on the feeling. Five fingers—then a fist. Over and over.

"Yes...yes. Oh, Justin...yes. Please...please, Justin."

Justin paid the cab driver and stepped out onto the sidewalk. He was on Walton Street in Chicago. He walked east on Walton toward Lake Shore Drive. Bridges had lived on Lake Shore Drive. Justin was on his way to the apartment.

It was nearly 1:00 a.m., and the April air was nippy, but refreshing. He walked at a comfortable pace, thinking about Fromme. He had conveyed his feelings about the man to Fanning. "Maybe it was the finger," Fanning had suggested. Ted had pointed out that Fromme was missing the small finger of his left hand. He had also felt a slight feeling of an uncomfortable loss of balance looking at it. Like the symmetry was gone. "Yeah, maybe it was the finger," Justin had said. But it still gnawed at him.

SENTINEL had checked Fromme out very carefully, and everything that he said had jived with the facts, right down to the names and ages of his children. He even had the birthdays right. Maybe it *was* the finger, he said to himself.

Bridges's apartment building towered before Justin. He looked up at it. It had class written all over it.

No one knew that Justin was there. After returning to Alpha and filing the verbal report with SENTINEL and Honeycut, they were driven to the club. They were to spend the night in Chicago, awaiting the results on the Division Two investigation. Division Two would be working through the night on it.

After eating a late, leisurely dinner and smoking some of Fanning's fine cigars, they called it a night. Justin hadn't told Fanning about the small scraps of paper he picked up in South Beloit. He didn't put it in the report, either. He knew he shouldn't have withheld the information, but there were just too many unknowns that bothered him piling up in his head.

The journal was the biggest. Why had Pegasus been so reluctant to accept the fact that it wasn't in the house? It was obvious that the assassin had taken it with him. There were some inconsistencies with the actual killing, too. It wasn't likely that the assassin could have jammed Spartan's transmissions. As Ryerson had described it, nobody could even pick them up, much less figure out a way to jam them. The last thing that bothered him was that extra page. Their intent with Bridges was obvious. Get in there, kill him, get out, and make it look like he never made contact. Then why go to the trouble of taking out that sheet? What was on it that made it so important to keep its existence a secret? One thing was certain, SENTINEL didn't know anything about it. Justin figured that maybe the answers were hidden somewhere in Bridges's apartment. And he wanted answers to some of his questions.

He went through the first set of glass doors. The second set was locked. There was no doorman, so Justin picked the lock easily and quickly. Once inside, he went to the rows of mailboxes and searched for Bridges's box. Apartment 16F. He went to the elevators.

Bridges's apartment was huge and well-furnished. Justin walked through the entire place once, to get the layout down. Then he began his search. He started in the spare bedroom that was set up as a study.

Three long hours later, he had come up empty. He had been careful not to disturb anything. It was all left the way he had found it. Only one room was left, the kitchen.

He went in and put on the light. Something struck him, immediately, as being out of place. There was a seal-a-meal bag sealer on the counter. It was still plugged in. Not exactly the sort of thing you find in a bachelor's apartment, he figured. Justin walked to the refrigerator freezer and opened the freezer door. What he saw told him plenty. It was empty. Not a single bag was in there. He went back over to the heat-sealing device and looked at the box of large sealing bags. It was half empty. The box had just been opened, too. The tabs were still in the garbage.

Yes! Then he had it.

Justin made a beeline for the bathroom. He lifted the top to the tank of the toilet. There it was.

He lifted the single bag out. It contained a folded sheet of paper. He opened the bag with his pocket knife and took out the sheet of paper. He unfolded it and began reading.

It was full of code names and dates that he didn't understand. It was headed by the title, "Operation Raptor." It meant nothing to Justin. The next item was "Niederlage—1941." A long list of code names followed with dates, right up to the present. He didn't understand it yet, but he knew it was important. Anything dating back to 1941 scared him, especially when they were also hunting for a journal, one written in German. Then he remembered the rest of the missing bags—and the other bathroom off Bridges's bedroom.

Moments later he was lifting the lid in the other bathroom. He had found the rest of the bags.

TWENTY-THREE

The world realized that we were right about the Russians when the war was over. They rebuilt Germany as quickly as possible, to be the stronghold against communism in Europe.

They didn't know that the new Germany was being built by old Nazis and that the Hitler youth were coming of age. It was the Americans who used their influence and money to get top Nazis quietly back into positions of control in Germany. They understood that only we could build a strong Germany.

Besides, to the rest of the world, only "good Germans" were left. I think many believed that...because they were afraid not to.

Entry No. 39 from the partially
recovered *Wolf Journal*

The darkness was lifting from New Jersey, yielding to the wakening rays of morning. It would be a clear, cool morning in the Garden State.

The big Mack tractor pulled its long, refrigerated trailer off Interstate 80 into the small rest area in Roxbury Township. The truck had driven through the night from Beloit, Wisconsin. It had taken a swift route down I-90 right into I-80 and hammered its way through Illinois, Indiana, Ohio, Pennsylvania, and into New Jersey in just over twelve hours.

Its two occupants emerged from the tractor and made their way down a gentle slope, back into the trees, moving away from the highway. Fine drops of moisture kicked up as they walked through the long brown weeds. About ten yards into the bare trees, they stopped. They opened their flies in unison and began long, gratifying relief.

The driver was a skinny, spidery-looking fellow. His head was small and narrow. The closely cut hair made him look almost bald. The ragged growth of facial hair was nearly the length of the graying hair on his head. His long, hooked nose seemed to point to the spot where his stream was concentrated. The small, squinty eyes were dull and tired. He had the appearance of a coarse, uneducated man.

To his left, an almost comical figure stood. Short, wide, his shoulders hunched in directing the stream against the side of a young tree. He released the instrument with his right hand, continuing the directional supervision with the left. The free hand eased into the coat pocket and settled onto the familiar wooden handle.

He finished before his spidery companion and backed away a pace. He took the weapon from his pocket and removed the sheath. The handle and its shaft were raised to striking position. The driver's eyes were still concentrating on the endless streak of urine.

The thrust was cobra quick. The driver was dead before he ever realized the short, sharp pain. He fell to the ground, the piss still trickling from him.

Ten Braak walked back to the truck and climbed into the driver's seat. He pulled the truck onto I-80 and rolled on toward New York.

Another man had been left behind who would never identify his face.

It was 0800 hours on St. Simon's Island, Georgia. The small underground complex was an impressive feat of engineering. Because the water table on St. Simon's Island is very high, such an installation should not have been possible to build, but it had been. It was very similar to an undersea environmental chamber, only enormously larger. Its existence would never be suspected in such a location; that's why it had been built there.

This location was not a branch office of SENTINEL, actually, more like a subbranch. It was much smaller than Alpha and was specialized in its purpose. It was a medical technological research installation, totally equipped to handle any medical emergency. It was also used as a debriefing station for those rare instances when it was necessary to take an individual, such as Dmitri Chakhovsky, whose identity and location it was desirable to keep secret from the other intelligence agencies within the United States.

The man in charge was Dr. Becker Dials, MD, an eminent heart specialist. He was also the director of the cardiac clinic bearing his name located above the secret complex.

Dr. Dials was just picking up the special security line to Alpha.

"Hello, this is Dr. Dials. Is that you, Irv?"

"Hi, Buck," Honeycut's graveled voice said. "Hope you don't mind my getting you up so early?"

"Not at all, not all," Dials said. "We've already put in an hour's work around here," he said.

"Good to hear that you guys are working so hard," Honeycut quipped. "We've all been pretty busy the past few days. What have you got on Chakhovsky?" he asked.

"Well, Irv," Dials began, "I'm afraid it's not very encouraging. We haven't had enough time to finish all of our tests on him yet, but we've got a pretty good handle on it.

"As you may probably know, angina pectoris is usually caused by a blockage of major coronary and epicardial branches of two or more major coronary vessels or a severe involvement of the left main coronary artery. There are several types of angina that we've been able to eliminate.

"His EKG shows elevated ST segments, suggesting myocardial injury, but returns to the isoelectric line after a brief period."

"Just tell me what's wrong with him, Buck," Honeycut said, sounding some impatience.

"He has variant angina. We've put him on Holter monitoring now, to document the occurrences. This form of angina is not like the others, that is, caused by atherosclerosis of a few major coronary arteries. Instead, in variant angina, the coronary arteries are entirely normal, with the cause being a reversible spasm of a single artery. The vessel involvement can be determined by the ST-segment elevation."

"What's the prognosis?" Honeycut asked.

"About fifty percent die within the first year," Dials said. "He's going to be in that fifty percent, if we don't correct it very soon."

"How?"

"The best choice—the only choice in his situation—is to bypass the affected area using a saphenous vein graft."

"How risky is it?" Honeycut asked.

"Well, there's a certain amount of grave risk with any operation of this—"

"How risky is it?" Honeycut repeated.

"If we can reduce myocardial oxygen consumption and reduce the incidence of attacks, I'd say about five percent risk is involved here," Dials said.

"That doesn't sound too bad. How soon could you do it?"

"Well, we'd have to perform a coronary arteriograph first, to determine the coronary artery anatomy and adequacy of left ventricular function. The reduction of his myocardial oxygen consumption will require at least two weeks of total bed rest. I'd say in three weeks, if we can satisfactorily stabilize his condition," Dials answered.

"Can he be debriefed during that time?" Honeycut asked.

"No," Dials answered.

"He can't even talk?" Honeycut asked incredulously.

"He can talk, but the things you want him to talk about will undoubtably cause considerable stress. He might as well run up a hill. He needs *total* bed rest," Dials explained.

"Buck, there are certain things that we *must* learn from him, and quickly. We need that information *now*. The rest of it can wait. If we restrict our questions to only that information, can we debrief him?" Honeycut asked.

Dials pursed his lips in contemplation. "Well, I guess it would be all right. Just spread it out, so as not to tire him."

"Thanks, Buck. I promise we'll try to keep it short and sweet. Could we start today?"

"He's scheduled for tests this morning. Give him a few hours to rest after lunch. Then start slow. But I warn you, don't excite him. The longer it takes for his condition to stabilize, the later we'll be able to operate. And, in his condition, every day counts."

"We'll remember. Thanks, Buck," Honeycut said, placing down the phone. We'll get what we need regardless, he thought.

Justin had risen about an hour earlier than the meeting time that he and Fanning had established. He used the time to leave the club to post a large manila envelope to himself at an old post office box he had maintained from his college days. He was taking no chances with carrying around the information he had discovered at Bridges's apartment.

He and Fanning enjoyed a leisurely breakfast in the club. Then the limousine came for them and drove them to Alpha.

After passing through security, they proceeded directly to the seminar room that Elizabeth Ryerson had used in her briefing on SENTINEL. Honeycut saw them shortly and said that he and Dr. Ryerson would be right with them. The men waited patiently.

Meanwhile, Honeycut and Elizabeth were having a short meeting in the room just off the seminar theater.

"Are you sure?" Honeycut asked.

"Positive," Elizabeth said. "He left the club last night at about oh-forty hours. SENTINEL monitored his movements. He definitely went to Bridges's apartment."

Honeycut squinted off into space. He wondered what Justin could be looking for at Bridges's place. "What theories has SENTINEL projected?"

"A search," Elizabeth answered. "He definitely went through the place. Over three hours' worth, too. Then this morning he left the club for a few minutes. He returned and met with Badger for breakfast before coming to Alpha," she reported.

"But no other theory was projected?"

"No. There was one unusual discovery, however. While examining the information packet that was brought back from Beloit, we discovered fibers on the round head clip holding the sheets together. There had apparently been one extra sheet. It was not of the same bond construction as the schematics, but did match the bond of the blank cover sheet," Elizabeth said.

"Could Pilgrim have removed it at the crime scene before placing it in the evidence box?" Honeycut asked.

"No. We'd have heard that. Besides, dust particles taken off the back sheet matched those taken off the table and dresser tops. It was definitely missing before he got there."

Honeycut shook his head. "We'll just have to ride on it until we can figure out what he was up to. In the meantime, get Division Two into the apartment to see what they can find."

Division Two wouldn't find much concerning Justin. He had put the heat sealing device away along with the box of sealing bags. He removed the tabs from the newly opened box from the garbage, as well. The clues wouldn't be so obvious to them.

Elizabeth and Honeycut joined Justin and Fanning in the seminar theater.

"Good morning, gentlemen," Honeycut said. "I hope you had a good night's sleep. You're going to have another very busy day today." He looked at Justin. He looked remarkably well-rested for a man who had been up most of the night.

"The autopsy report is in, and Division Two has completed its analysis of its findings. Beth, would you like to fill them in on the results?" Honeycut asked.

Elizabeth nodded. For a brief instant, her eyes met Justin's. There was an odd play of emotions in her for a moment, feelings of revulsion and shame forced above a distant longing that she would not consciously acknowledge. But Justin's eyes stared back as blank and cold as granite. There was not the slightest trace of remembrance, or sharing that a part of her brain searched for. He was like all the rest who had penetrated that barrier in those painful years. He was not to be trusted. Her brain began twisting the smothered attraction to him into hatred. He would never penetrate again.

"The autopsy was performed about five hours after the discovery of the body. It showed natural causes, as we expected it would. But we know the cause to be prussic acid inhalation. The hairs that you plucked out of Bridges's nose held a residue of the acid. The solution in the bottle preserved that evidence by forming a stable, detectable derivative of the poison. Had you arrived on the scene about an hour later, we'd have had nothing.

"The information was recovered intact. It contained enough prints, along with those found in the room, to give us an identification of one of the contacts that Bridges met with," she explained.

"Eh, excuse me," Justin interrupted. "*One* of the contacts? There was definitely more than one?"

"Yes, SENTINEL has projected a theory based on several small bits of evidence. Our second man was really smart. He left almost no traces of his being there, except for some fibers on the second chair. But an interesting tidbit SENTINEL turned up was that the fingerprints found on the schematics were all upside down. That means that they had to be right side up for somebody. The packet was too bulky and awkward to remain open and in a desirable position for photographing without being held down, and analysis of the clip showed that it had not been opened to separate the sheets.

"Our first man was easy to trace. Not only were his prints in the room, they were also found on the jack and the trunk lid of the car that the body was found in. So, it's pretty evident who did the killing."

Justin looked at Fanning, then to Elizabeth Ryerson.

"Do you think Fromme could be the second man?" he asked.

"At first we thought that to be a good possibility. But his story was absolutely airtight. We'll be going into his room after he's left it for the day, to take fiber samples from his clothes. I doubt it will turn up anything, though," she answered.

"SENTINEL has gone through a number of possibilities," Elizabeth continued, "but has definitely concluded that there was a second man. And his plan is a very good one. At first analysis, it seemed that the intent was to make us believe that Bridges had died of natural causes before making contact. But the fingerprint evidence was too easy to find. SENTINEL has put through a proposal that sounds very good to us. It suggests that the true objective of the plan was to try to pull that first theory off, if possible, but was backed by traceable evidence pointing to one of the two contacts. This would lead to an identification of the one agent, whom we'd pursue hotly, leaving the other free to beat a hasty retreat out of the country," Elizabeth explained.

"Then he may already be out of the country," Fanning said.

Elizabeth nodded. "He could be, but we don't think so. The information would probably be put on microdots first and several copies made. This way, two or three other agents not even involved in this phase of the plan would stand a good chance of getting them safely back to Russia. The film would be processed in this country, or possibly in Canada, then distributed. Most probably in a direction opposite to that in which our known suspect is going," she said.

The situation seemed grim to Justin. It didn't seem possible to stop them.

"Fortunately, we know a great deal more about their intelligence network than they think we do. We know where most of their film-processing labs are located and who runs them. Almost all of them, in fact. We've pulled every available SENTINEL agent in on this. The labs are all covered, and we've prepared to bust every one of them at the same time. And we will, to render them inoperable."

Honeycut looked at his watch. "In fact, gentlemen, it's already been done, about fifteen minutes ago. And their people have been 'neutralized.' "

Elizabeth looked back to the two agents. "That should leave our unknown agent holding film and a busted plan. He'll have to improvise," she said.

"What about the other one, the one we've identified?" Justin asked.

Elizabeth looked at Honeycut. "Pegasus will tell you about him."

"This one should interest you, Badger," Honeycut started off. "It's Otto Ten Braak."

Anxiety shot through Fanning in a hot flash. He had run into Ten Braak before, six years ago—and lost. He was left for dead, and nearly was, in a mission that had claimed the life of another SENTINEL agent. It took almost a full year to recuperate before he could get back to active duty. One of the things he wanted more than anything in life was to get another crack at Ten Braak. But that encounter had left its mark on Fanning. He had learned respect for the man—and feared him.

"Where do we go from here?" Justin asked.

"New York," Honeycut answered. "We were also able to pick up some very important information in Moscow. Our man there has a very highly placed contact who discovered Ten Braak's assignment in the United States. He was to make contact in New York, on Tuesday. We have a reliable list of possible safe houses where he could be hiding, also the code name of the agent he's to make contact with."

"Fortunately, the identity of that agent is known to us. He shouldn't be too hard to find."

"And the other agent?" Justin asked.

"We're working on that one now. Our man in Moscow is one of our best, the best we have inside of Russia. He stands a good chance of discovering his identity. We feel that this second agent will be stranded here for at least a few days, until something is worked out for him to get out of the country. He's going to have to expend valuable time to try to get the microdots made. And we'll have considerable manpower searching for him. Our chances are really much better than they seem," Honeycut said.

"When do we leave?" Justin asked.

"Right now," Honeycut answered. "The Lear is fueled and waiting for you at Meigs. Your car has been brought from Newark to Teterboro Airport in New Jersey," he said to Justin. "You'll get instructions before touching down at Teterboro," Honeycut concluded.

Thirty-five minutes later, the Lear was roaring off the runway at Meigs Field. They would proceed at maximum speed to Teterboro.

The first part of the manhunt had begun.

TWENTY-FOUR

The Nazi hunts continued heatedly for many years after the war, often fueled by the "special branch" of Niederlage, to keep attention focused in the right place or, more correctly, away from the right place. Eichmann was one of our best.

Many Nazis were fortunate to escape from the holocaust of the defeat, many with sizable fortunes "stolen" from the treasury. The regular section of Niederlage had responsibility for protecting these people. Odessa and Die Spinne were set up for this purpose. We drew from this well to keep the fires going.

Entry No. 40 from the partially recovered *Wolf Journal*

Justin watched the face of his friend as they streaked eastward in the modified Lear. He had noticed the reaction to Honeycut's news about Otto Ten Braak and wondered about it. But Justin wouldn't ask. If Fanning wanted him to know, he'd tell him. He continued looking into the face. There was an expression he had never seen there before. It was fear.

"I guess you want to know about it," Fanning said suddenly.

"Know about what?" Justin asked, in feigned ignorance.

Fanning cast a quick glance through the corner of his eye. "You know goddamn well that you wanna hear about Otto Ten

Braak, and why I'd be so interested in him being the one we're after."

"If you want to talk, I'll listen," Justin said.

There was another long silence.

"It was six years ago," Fanning finally began. "The agency was just getting started, and we weren't nearly as sophisticated as we are now. That's because we didn't have you around to fuck things up for us, yet," he joked, then became quickly serious. "I was on a job in South Africa. Baby-sitting a fat industrialist name of Lothengarr. There were two of us. Me and a guy named Nicolosi. First job for him. He was a smart, good-looking kid." Fanning's eyes were far away as he talked.

"This guy, Lothengarr, was some kind of big shot to the agency. Someone wanted him dead, so we were sent to keep him alive. I never found out why they wanted to kill him. It doesn't matter, I guess.

"Anyway, Lothengarr used to like taking these long walks along the beach. So, once each day, we'd drive him to the beach in his limousine. We'd leave the car, walk for an hour, then go to his estate to eat lunch. We did this regular for about two weeks. It was nice, an easy hour for us.

"Well, this one day we drove up the long, single-lane dirt road that led to his favorite spot. It was about three miles off the nearest highway. On our way in, we passed this broken-down car. It had its hood up, and a short little fat guy was working away on the engine. I remember looking at him as we drove by. He looked like the heat was beating the hell out of him, all covered with sweat and grease and sand. Poor bastard, I thought.

"We continued up the road for about four or five hundred yards and stopped. The road twisted and bent like hell, and there was thick brush cover and trees all around, so we couldn't see the guy or his car anymore. We walked through the thick brush along a narrow path to the isolated beach. Then we walked, me in front, Nicolosi behind. We spaced ourselves about twenty feet away from Lothengarr.

"We kept our eyes open for movement in the brush cover or for small craft approaching the beach.

"The beach was about a hundred and fifty feet wide and real long. There was one point, though, just past this natural jetty, where the beach got real narrow and curved way back into a crescent-shaped cove. We couldn't see the road through the thick brush, normally. It was about fifty yards back.

"When we'd get near this crescent, I'd walk way out ahead, maybe a hundred to a hundred and fifty feet. This was so that I could check out the crescent before Lothengarr got near it.

"Anyway, when I had spaced myself out, I began to walk along the narrow crescent. That was the first time that I noticed that the road *was* visible from the beach. The brush cover was very low there, and the crescent went back almost to the road. I realized this because I saw that disabled car with its hood still up, but no fat man.

"There was this woman and a little girl playing in the water in the cove. I figured they belonged to the fat man, and that maybe he was catching some shade and a rest, or something.

"I continued to walk back toward the road, along the cove, looking for the fat man. Something about the whole deal was beginning to feel bad to me. I turned to wave Lothengarr and Nicolosi back until I could check it out, but I was already around the point and couldn't see them anymore. Little mistakes came easy back then.

"I kept walking until I got closer to the taller, thicker brush and trees at the other side of the crescent. I could see Lothengarr and Nicolosi now, waiting at the point. I was just about to wave them back when I saw the fat man. He was standing there in the dark shade of the trees, holding something in his arms. It was too long to be a tool. I squinted, because the sun was right in my face, and saw him smile. Then I saw him raise something. It was a rifle.

I saw it too late. I reached for my gun, but before I could get off a shot, I was kicked backwards. I didn't feel anything, I went right out, never even heard the shot," he said.

He hadn't seen the rest of it, as Ten Braak took out Nicolosi with a head shot. Lothengarr had seen Fanning get knocked back about six feet, then heard the dull cracking thud as the bullet hit Nicolosi's skull. Ten Braak then pumped two quick ones into Lothengarr. But his work still wasn't done. There was still the woman and the child he had paid to accompany him.

"I came to in a hospital. I had been left for dead by Ten Braak. He had gotten them all, Lothengarr, Nicolosi, the woman, and the little girl. The doctors said I should have been dead, too. The bullet hit me in the upper left chest, smashed and fragmented a rib, and deflected up and out the top of my left shoulder. They operated on me for six hours, pulling out bone fragments and the pieces of lead that spread out. But I made it. Took almost a year to recuperate before they assigned me again.

"I've learned and heard a lot about Ten Braak since then," Fanning said. "I made it my business to learn."

Justin had gone over Ten Braak's dossier on his way out to Meigs Field. The file was rather extensive and indicated him to be one of the deadliest men alive. He was cunning and skilled in the many arts of destruction. He was also crudely inventive, as Ross's murder had demonstrated. Despite his portly physique, he was as agile and quick as a cat, especially with his hands, which dispatched destruction with the certainty of a well-aimed slug, by adroitly finding one of the many death spots on the human body. He had been the maestro in his earlier days. Now, age had slowed him, but only slightly, and his reputation had become a disadvantage. The dossier listed him as about to be "retired."

Fanning spent the next few minutes attesting to the facts in the dossier, by recounting some of Ten Braak's adventures that he had heard of over the years. They had never met again, although he had hoped each mission would develop that possibility.

"I can tell you one thing for certain," Fanning said. "We'll never take him alive, like Pegasus wants us to. And we'll have to surprise him. We've talked about that sixth sense that develops in this job? Well, he's got *seven*. Like nothing you've ever seen."

Justin nodded slowly, looking up from the dossier to glance at Fanning. "Then why do they want to retire him?"

"Too well known," Fanning answered. "I'm surprised they used him on this one."

Justin thought. "No, not really. It gives some strength to SENTINEL's analysis of the plan. That would make it easier for us to find him, while at the same time all the tougher to stop him. Makes good sense to use him."

Fanning nodded absently. His mind was deep into a fantasy of how he would do it. He had thought of a hundred different ways. But now that they were on their way to actually do it, only one way stood out in his mind, the one he used for all the tough jobs—the "Runt."

The rest of the trip was finished in near silence. Each man used the time for mental preparation. Without every edge, without maximum psyching, they stood less chance. And Fanning was determined to fulfill the plan that had been his obsession since that day six years ago, to get Otto Ten Braak.

As the swift Lear streaked eastward, the blue Dodge Monaco left the Holiday Inn. As soon as it left the parking lot, the remnants of the Division Two team entered Kuradin's room to search and sample his garments.

They would find nothing, because Kuradin had changed clothes in Beloit before returning to the Holiday Inn the day before. The coat, pants, even the shoes and socks, were disposed of and would never be recovered. He had anticipated everything.

The Dodge Monaco pulled into the parking lot of Beloit General Hospital. Kuradin went directly to admitting. An hour later, he was settling into his semiprivate room. He had checked in under the name of Roger Caneway.

After unpacking his small bag, he put on his pajamas and climbed into the bed. He let everything play back through his head once more.

No doubt, they'd be racing after Ten Braak by now. The leak from Moscow should have reached them already, even if it was rather indirect. Moscow had no idea of how to leak the information directly to the SENTINEL agency, so it let it out through a series of known CIA contacts, hoping it would swiftly find its way to their attention. They must have penetrated the KGB, he reasoned, so chances were good that they would also learn it themselves directly. They *must* have some deep contacts. It was unrealistic to think otherwise. Even so, by now they had figured out Bridges's cause of death and had discovered Ten Braak's fingerprints. The way it was set up, they couldn't help but find him by Tuesday evening.

The late morning passed quickly, as the initial blood samples were drawn. He had not eaten for twenty-four hours as his physician, Dr. Awadi, had supposedly requested. Early that afternoon Dr. Awadi came to visit him.

Awadi entered the room. He was a tall, slender Indian. His features were sharp and handsome, the eyes as black as ebony and sparkling with warmth and intelligence. Awadi was a sleeper agent who had never been utilized in the past.

"How are you today, Mr. Caneway?" Awadi greeted him with a distinct Indian accent.

"Fine, Dr. Awadi. Fine," Kuradin answered.

"I see that our nurses have already begun prodding and sticking you for your blood." He laughed.

"Yes, they have." Kuradin smiled. "Quite gently, I might add."

The fellow occupying the other bed was an older man. He had smiled politely to Kuradin when he entered, but had remained silent. He was now sleeping.

"I am sorry that your lunch was so skimpy," Awadi apologized. "By tomorrow evening we can put you on a normal diet. We should have all of our initial tests completed by that time. I see no reason why you shouldn't be able to eat normally after that," he said.

Awadi gave Kuradin a swift examination, during which time the watch containing the film cartridge was exchanged for an identical one. The normal diet reference had been made to indicate when the microdots should be ready. The film would be taken into Madison, Wisconsin, for processing that afternoon.

The examination was concluded shortly. Awadi left Kuradin to continue his rounds. The Russian was alone now, with his thoughts.

He knew what the results of the tests would show—chronic lymphatic leukemia. There was no doubt about it. But, deep within him, there was the secret hope that the results would be normal. Every man wants to live, Kuradin was no exception. But his logic denied that possibility. If it could only go away to let him live. Hope is a fragile thing, at once a weakness and again a strength. And he was only a man, possessed by both.

He forced his mind to return to the encounter he had had the evening before. He hadn't really expected it, but had prepared for that possibility. They were probably going through his room now, he figured. They wouldn't miss a trick. But he had prepared carefully. At five o'clock, the real David Fromme would pick up the car at the hospital and return to the Holiday Inn. Fromme was also an unused sleeper. He matched Kuradin's physical description very closely. His cover was airtight. He would fill in the time that Kuradin would be confined to the hospital. He was scheduled to be discharged Wednesday morning. From there, if all things went smoothly, he'd be out of the United States and in Paris in fourteen hours from the time he left the hospital. Five hours later he'd be in Russia.

Russia. His mind filled with thoughts of his grandchildren and his daughter. He wanted to hold them, to tell them how much he loved them and how he was making the world safe for them. But Russia was eighty-four hours away for him. He wondered how many more hours he had left in his hourglass of life.

The thought of time and life made him think back to England. He had sensed something during that mission a year ago—a feeling. Certainly it was fear, but he was no stranger to fear. It had whispered in his ear many times before that. It was also a sense of time, time slipping away. Irretrievable time. As though it were counting down the minutes of his life. He felt it again.

One of those men had been Pilgrim. He knew it. He could feel it. He thought about them, remembering their faces. He knew the moment his wrist had been seized by the steel grip. Which one was it? he wondered.

He thought back to the silhouette standing in the doorway at Maynard's Pub—the tall, thin figure who nearly took his life. There was no mistake in his mind as to which one it was. It was the dark one, the one in charge. Pilgrim. The face he gave to the name was Justin's.

He felt the sands slipping away through the tiny hole in the hourglass, once more. He wondered if he would ever see Russia again.

TWENTY-FIVE

Nobody in Odessa or Die Spinne knew even the slightest fact as to the existence of Operation Raptor. They were all too notable to be used, and too vulnerable to be trusted.

Raptor was loosely planned at first. Five Fuehrungszentrale (steering center) locations were established across the globe. These were in Argentina, Spain, the United States, South Africa, and Germany.

The plan was too broad to know where to focus it so early, but time and patience would give us the answers as to where the Fourth Reich would have its birth.

Entry No. 41 from the partially
recovered *Wolf Journal*

Sunday afternoon had developed as forecasted for New Jersey. The day was sparkling, clear, and crisp. The promise of spring filled the air.

The 1955 Ford Fairlane pulled into the Roxbury Township rest area and came to a stop in one of the diagonal parking spaces. The young driver turned off the ignition and stretched behind the wheel. He reached over to the lovely girl beside him and gave a gentle caress of her soft breast with his finger. They kissed tenderly for a few moments.

The occupants of the car were two students from Fairleigh Dickinson University, enrolled at the Teaneck campus. They had just spent their first weekend together at the girl's uncle's cabin in the Poconos and were on their way back to school, for the last few days of classes before the spring recess. The short vacation normally would have been welcomed, but it meant ten unbearable days apart from one another.

They were only about forty-five minutes from the campus and wanted to stretch the privacy of their wonderful weekend to the fullest. They left the car to walk in the beauty of nature's awakening. Soon the trees would begin to bud and grow, and all nature would be vibrant with the colors of life. It seemed as though the day were planned just for them, symbolizing their own budding love.

They started down the gently sloping decline, wrapped in one another's loving embrace. It had been a dream come true for him. She was everything he could ever hope for. He let his eyes play across her long, straight blond hair. His hand settled on her soft ass in a confident gesture of ownership. She was his, her loveliness, her femininity, her body. He had never seen such total beauty in his life. He studied the features, the small, straight nose, the beautiful soft lips that had caressed his entire body, and the eyes—as blue as the lovely spring sky above. The smell of her Emeraude excited his senses. He remembered its exotic smell and the sweet clean taste of her skin, as he had kissed her body in their unending passion. It would go on forever.

They walked through the high, dead grass of last summer's growth, going further down the slope. He continued to drink in the beauty of her lovely features when he saw her eyes blink, suddenly lose the rosiness of love, and change to undisguised terror.

With all of the good intentions of a knight about to defend the honor of his lady he looked to the cause of her great alarm— and threw up all over himself.

They had found the spider.

Leonid Travkin tossed restlessly in his bed. The information that the KGB investigation teams had turned up looked bad regarding Chakhovsky.

It was no mystery to him where Chakhovsky had been taken and by whom. He was somewhere in the United States, all right, safely in the hands of SENTINEL's security force.

Things looked grimmer by the minute for Centaur's chances. If only there were some way he could let him know about it. But that was impossible.

The news of Ten Braak's involvement had been let out on schedule, but he could only hope it had gotten into the right hands in time.

From this point on, Kuradin would have to be lucky. But luck was one factor that couldn't be relied upon or stretched far enough. Kuradin would have to make his own lucky breaks.

It was a good thing that Kuradin had chosen Ten Braak, after all. Ten Braak was a survivor. There was always the remote possibility that he could deliver the goods in New York City, if he got lucky. That word again. But who could tell? When the shit hit the fan, enough of it might just go in the right direction.

Division Two had gotten into Kuradin's room moments after he left. They searched his belongings carefully, giving special attention to his clothing. They knew precisely what type of materials they were looking for, but nothing matched up.

They lifted prints from around the room and found a few hairs in the bathtub and on a towel. A tiny bloodstained tissue told them that Fromme had cut himself shaving. They took it. All they needed to go over now were the clothes he was wearing. It was possible that he was wearing the same overcoat and pants as the previous day.

The car had been quietly checked out, as Kuradin slept the night before. Not too much turned up. Kuradin had carefully wiped away any traces of Ten Braak in the car. A few fibers had been found, but these wouldn't be sent into the lab until the clothes on Fromme could be checked. That meant the following day.

One important mistake had been made by Division Two, however. The portable transmission unit by which they could send in fingerprint patterns had been taken back by the main party. That meant the loss of a day in checking out Fromme's prints. A very costly day.

Visiting hours were nearly over at Beloit General Hospital when Dr. Awadi came walking into Kuradin's room. This meeting was unscheduled. Awadi was in obvious distress.

Fortunately for Awadi, Kuradin's roommate was out in the solarium with his wife. Awadi closed the door and began a nervous rattle of words, which Kuradin could not understand through the accent.

"Wait a minute, slow down," Kuradin said. "Now start from the beginning."

"The lab. It has been knocked out," Awadi said, his accent still distinctly hard to understand. "We can't get the film processed. The one in Milwaukee is out, too. What are we going to do?" He was nervous and flustered. Too nervous, Kuradin thought. That was one of the problems with using sleeper agents. There was little to go on with regard to their performance under stress. There was no history to go over in selecting them. Awadi was border line; the slightest pressure would break him wide open.

Kuradin thought calmly. Both labs out. He hadn't anticipated that one. It was a good chance that if those labs were out, so were others. What to do?

He was in a position he had wanted to avoid. In chess it is called loss of tempo, or giving up the advantage of being one move ahead. But, as in chess, it is possible to regain the tempo. But how? He carefully considered his problem.

"Can you get access to the dark room in this hospital?" Kuradin asked finally.

"Yes, but I don't know how to develop film," Awadi said. "It would be useless for me to even attempt it."

"I don't want you to develop it," Kuradin said. "I want you to remove it from the cartridge and prepare it for implantation into my scalp, just as you were to do with the microdots. We'll have to make it as small as possible and put it into a protective container of some kind. Can you do this?" he asked the bewildered Indian.

Awadi checked Kuradin's scalp around the lower region of the head, where the hair was still thick. "Yes, it can be done if the film and its container are small enough. It wouldn't even show, except for maybe a small scab for a few days. But, if it is not small enough…" The Indian began to pace as he thought. He took a stick of gum from his pocket, nervously unwrapped it, and threw it into his mouth. He discarded the balled-up wrapper.

Yes, that's it! Kuradin thought, looking at the balled-up wrapper—the foil.

"Use aluminum foil to encase the tightly rolled film. It should be small enough," Kuradin said.

"Foil alone might not be enough to protect the film," the Indian added.

"You could be right," Kuradin mumbled and thought frantically. "There must be more, something else with it."

"Of course, in the dental laboratory," the Indian said suddenly. "The foil ball could be encased in the amalgam used for frontal fillings. It would provide a perfect protective barrier."

"Excellent!" Kuradin said. "Can you prepare the film tonight, to implant it in the morning?"

"Yes. The dental lab is closed in the evening. I could get in easily and take the materials I will need. It could be ready by morning," the Indian said.

A moment later Awadi was on his way to the dark room, to prepare the foil capsule.

The plan would not be thrown too far off, Kuradin thought. The implantation of the microdots was to have been his failsafe contingency, should he be killed or succumb unsuspectedly to his condition before returning to Russia. Travkin was aware of this. All attempts would be made to recover his body should that happen. Even his death could not stop the plan.

Almost as quickly as it had been lost, the tempo was regained. Only one slight modification would have to be made to account for Awadi's weakness.

TWENTY-SIX

A Vorsitzende (chairman) was appointed to each of the steering centers, and a code name was assigned to that chairmanship. The code name stayed with the responsibilities, even if the person changed.

In Argentina there was Shaman, Titus in Spain, Colorosa in the United States, Constantine in South Africa, and Falke in Germany.

The first steering center to drop out of our consideration was Germany. Falke had divulged certain facts of Raptor to close friends and members of Odessa. Falke, along with those people he had told, was neutralized by an action group of Raptor.

It was decided to drop Germany from the list, because of the presence of so many old Nazis and Odessa activities.

Entry No. 42 from the partially
recovered *Wolf Journal*

New York City had become the center of the search zone for Otto Ten Braak. The information picked up from Moscow indicated that he was to make contact there on Tuesday with a known agent.

The easy way would have been to trail the contact to the meeting, then nab them both. But it was possible that no meeting was scheduled to take place, that the information was to be dead-dropped to the contact. Either way, it was essential that they find Ten Braak as quickly as possible, to get him while he still carried film—*if* he was carrying it, as SENTINEL projected.

The fact that Ten Braak was in New York already had been received with great interest. SENTINEL, while monitoring all police frequencies nationwide, had picked up the news of the spider's body being found. The method of kill confirmed that it was Ten Braak who had done it. The New Jersey State Police had labeled it a murder/hijacking. That told SENTINEL how Ten Braak had gotten to New York from Wisconsin.

Three SENTINEL teams had been dispatched to New York, to assist Justin and Fanning in their search. One team would be assigned to each of the Soviet safe houses determined by SENTINEL as probable refuge for Ten Braak.

Some of SENTINEL's manpower problems had been solved when NATO and the CIA acted on the leak from Moscow of Ten Braak's being in New York. They didn't know why he was in New York, but had reasons enough of their own to justify taking him or stopping him if they could.

SENTINEL could monitor the progress of these other agencies and get the closest team on the spot quickly, should they find him first. Once there, they'd step in to stop Ten Braak if it became necessary. All SENTINEL agents had been issued authentic identification credentials of these other agencies involved, as well as FBI identification, to help gain authority if dictated by the situation.

The search for Ten Braak was beginning to tighten already.

Regarding the unknown agent, every available SENTINEL operative had been pulled into the United States. Their first task had been to knock out the processing labs used by the Soviets. Once this was done, Division Two personnel were drafted into observing the lab sites. The SENTINEL agents were then dispatched to various parts of the country that SENTINEL had determined probable points of destination for the unknown agent. But a very important clue came in, which gave SENTINEL valuable information. Contact had been attempted at the Madison and Milwaukee labs.

This told SENTINEL three things. First, the agent had *not* left the area of the Bridges contact. This was unexpected. Second, the film had not been processed yet. And, third, the agent would probably stay put until an alternative was figured out. All three were vitally important, but the last one was the one that would increase SENTINEL's odds for success.

SENTINEL's theory behind knocking out the processing labs had been to buy time. Its aim was to create confusion and to force the unknown agent to improvise on the set plan. Every decision that SENTINEL could force on the agent increased the chances of finding him.

The reasoning behind this was sound. The agent had the advantage of tempo, but the disadvantage of human judgment and error.

SENTINEL reasoned that, even allowing for a very high intelligence quotient, the best mind may be capable of choosing correctly as often as eighty percent of the time under high-stress circumstances. But being correct eighty percent of the time was, more importantly, being wrong the other twenty. SENTINEL now estimated its probability for success at thirty-five percent, based on the fact of the attempted contact with the processing labs. That was considerable progress, all things considered.

So, it all narrowed down to two areas of search now, Ten Braak in New York, and the unknown agent somewhere in southern Wisconsin or northern Illinois. SENTINEL teams were reassigned, based on those facts.

David Fromme again came into consideration.

Ten Braak had walked into Hackensack after abandoning the truck. He proceeded to the bus terminal on River Street and took a bus into New York City to the Port Authority terminal on Eighth

Avenue. From there he took a downtown subway to Fourteenth Street, then boarded a crosstown bus to Third Avenue. He walked the remaining distance south toward his East Village destination.

He checked into the Paradise Hotel on Third Avenue. This was a run-down flophouse and Soviet safe house *not* on SENTINEL's list. He signed the register as Victor Mueller and paid for four days in advance. He took a sixth-floor corner room overlooking Third Avenue.

It was a flea-bitten place, a single, dreary room with its own small, smelly bathroom off to one corner. It had two windows, one on the Third Avenue side and the other leading to a fire escape facing a side street. This provided him with an emergency escape exit, just in case he should need one. The hallway outside his room was dimly lit in the evening and had a window about fifteen feet past his door. It led to the same fire-escape platform that his window did. He could spray the entire hallway with gunfire from that hallway window by climbing out onto the fire escape. It wasn't ideal, but it could have been worse.

He spent the late afternoon planning his defenses and finishing up the sandwiches and beer he had bought on his way to the Paradise. He would not budge from that room until his contact was to be made on Tuesday. All his needs would be provided for him.

He turned in early that evening, as the search for him concentrated on the Lower East Side. As long as he didn't show his face, the search for him would be a long and difficult one. And then taking him would be its own special kind of hell.

The phone in room 115 of the South Beloit Holiday Inn rang. The real David Fromme answered it on the second ring.

"Hello," he said.

"Mr. David Fromme?" the soft voice inquired.

"Yes, this is David Fromme," he answered. He waited through the silence. "Who is this?" he asked.

There was only silence.

"Who is this?" he asked again.

The phone clicked. The connection had been broken.

The crystal intellect began racing. Something was wrong! That was not the same voice that had spoken as David Fromme when interviewed by Pilgrim and Badger the day before. The voice print was completely wrong.

This was clever and unexpected. The second agent had never even left the scene. An imposter had now taken his place.

The phone rang again.

"Yes," Fromme answered.

"Pay phone, lobby," came the response. It was a different voice than a moment ago.

The phone clicked dead before Fromme could say anything.

He went immediately to the lobby. He was observed by Division Two. It was now confirmed—this was not the same David Fromme that had left earlier that morning in the same blue Dodge Monaco.

He went to the pay phones and waited.

A second man entered the lobby and took a seat with a clear view to the phone. He took a pen out of his pocket and rested the hand holding it on the knee of his crossed right leg. He sat looking down at the partially completed crossword puzzle of his newspaper. The pen pointed directly to the phone.

The center phone rang.

Fromme picked up the receiver and placed it to his ear. "Yes," he spoke into it.

"This is Phoenix. I have instructions for you," Kuradin said.

"Wait," Fromme said. "How many times did you call me?" he asked.

"Once," Kuradin answered. His instincts jumped.

"Somebody called me just moments before you did," Fromme told Kuradin.

"What was said?" Kuradin asked.

"Whoever it was asked for me by name. Then said nothing."

"Did you answer?" Kuradin said.

"Yes," Fromme replied.

"What did you say?"

"Yes, this is David Fromme. Then I asked who it was, twice."

Kuradin was silent. This was trouble. He guessed that he had three more minutes of safe conversation before a trace could be made. He thought quickly.

"Just listen," Kuradin began. "A slight change in plans has come up. Proceed to point A tomorrow at noon. Cactus Flower will be waiting for you there. You will execute plan Blue. That's plan Blue, do you understand?"

Fromme flushed. "No," he said.

"Plan Blue," Kuradin repeated.

"No, I won't do that," Fromme said nervously. "You can't ask me to do that. I won't—"

"You *will*," Kuradin interrupted forcefully.

"Listen, I'll do anything else you tell me to, but not that. That wasn't supposed to be part of the—"

"You'll do whatever you're told to do. Or else," Kuradin threatened.

"But you're asking me to—"

"*Do it!* Or the next time you see your wife and children will be at their funerals. Is that clear?" Kuradin asked.

Fromme's eyes widened in terror. He began to sweat and shake. "You...you wouldn't do that. You couldn't. You—"

"Tomorrow, rendezvous A, noon, plan Blue." The phone clicked dead.

The man sitting over his crossword puzzle had heard the entire exchange. The pen aimed at the phone was a powerful miniature sound-scavenger, capable of picking up the slightest sounds at one hundred yards. It was fed into the small flesh-colored earpiece. It was also relayed to SENTINEL.

Fromme closed his eyes and leaned his damp forehead against the cool metal of the pay phone. He knew they would do what they threatened. He had no choice but to do what he was told. Tomorrow he would have to kill a man known to him only as Cactus Flower. That man was Dr. Kantilal Awadi.

He hung up the phone and glanced nervously around the lobby. The man with the pen pretended to make some entries into his crossword puzzle.

Fromme walked out of the lobby on shaking legs. He had never killed a man before. His weak legs carried him back to his room. How could they do that? he wondered. It didn't seem possible. He was one of their own.

The man with the paper waited about five minutes, then left, returning to the room that the Division Two team occupied.

The call was too short to get a trace on it. But SENTINEL had learned five more very important facts: the voice at the other end of the line was the same voice that had spoken to Pilgrim and Badger the day before; his code name was Phoenix; another agent, code-named Cactus Flower, was involved; the plan had been changed, probably as a result of the Madison and Milwaukee labs being knocked out; and Cactus Flower was probably about to be killed.

It was also obvious that Phoenix would connect the first phone call to trouble. That meant another decision to make. The odds of success were going up rapidly.

Kuradin broke into a cold sweat. It was going all wrong. The plan was falling apart all around him. The sleeper agents were unreliable; SENTINEL had advanced faster than he imagined it could; and his contingencies were fast going down the drain.

He thought about the phone call. What could it mean? He wasn't sure. He pressed his brain hard in search of an answer. Then he had it. A voice print. He hadn't expected that, either.

Damn! He had used the phony Phoenix cover too soon in the conversation. A stupid mistake. If SENTINEL was that careful to call Fromme back to check the voice print, it was a good bet that it had listened in on the whole conversation. It knew about Cactus Flower and what was in store for him. It also knew roughly where Kuradin was, or, more importantly, where he wasn't.

They'd follow Fromme tomorrow, to try to stop the killing. Then they'd take Awadi and break him wide open. The implant had to be put in tonight.

He'd have to skip over the next contingency and move to the following one. That meant leaving Beloit two days early. There was no other choice.

Kuradin headed for the dental lab, where Awadi was just finishing up his work with the tiny film capsule.

Kuradin was nervous. He knew what had to be done, and it frightened him. He had never killed a man before, either.

SENTINEL had also learned something much more valuable than the facts from the last few minutes. It had determined more than a speech pattern; a thought pattern was emerging.

The tempo had been *lost!*

TWENTY-SEVEN

Argentina, it had been hoped, would be the site for the birth of the new Reich and the new Fatherland. It is rich in resources, and all of South America possesses very impressive potential.

But the potential never developed in the years after the war. It is inhabited by a backward people, too prone to corruption and political revolution. It failed to develop industrially and economically as hoped. We poured a fortune into it, trying to help it develop. It will, eventually, but in a time frame outside of our plan.

Shaman was quietly neutralized, his holdings and organization redistributed to the remaining steering centers.

Entry No. 46 from the partially
recovered *Wolf Journal*

The implant was completed. Awadi dabbed at the tiny, circular wound with a cotton ball soaked with two percent hydrogen peroxide solution.

He gently brushed the hair over the incision and backed away to look at it. "It looks very good," Awadi said in his spiked accent. "It will not show." Awadi had done a most impressive job with encasing the film. Its surface was nearly glass smooth. The implantation had been done neatly, quickly, and with very little pain.

Kuradin gently moved his fingers over the small lump. It felt much smaller to the touch than he imagined it would. The actual size of the little capsule was only about one-eighth of an inch in diameter. It could be felt but hardly seen, even if the head were to be completely shaven.

Awadi gave it one last inspection. He was satisfied with his work.

Kuradin climbed off the small examination table in the closed clinic. A wave of nervousness began to roll through him. It was now time to finish the evening's scheduled work.

"You must help me with one more thing, now," Kuradin began. "A message has been dropped for me in the morgue. I'll need your help in finding it," he lied.

"Now?" Awadi asked. It was nearly 1:00 a.m.

"There may be too much activity in that area of the hospital to do it safely tomorrow. There is also the possibility that some-one may discover it accidentally before we get to it."

Awadi nodded. "Yes, but you had better get your clothes on. I can tell the attendant that you are here to identify a relative."

The Russian returned to his room and dressed quickly. Then they made their way to the basement level, where the morgue was located.

The entire hospital was on reduced night staff, and the hall-way lighting had been dimmed, in an effort to conserve energy. The basement hallway leading to the morgue and autopsy room was very dark, much darker than the rest of the hospital. Perhaps it was the foreknowledge of what was about to happen, or the fact that that area of the hospital was reserved for the dead, but to Kuradin the sounds of their footsteps seemed to bounce off the cold walls in haunting echoes. It was an uncomfortable place for the living, and Kuradin was growing nervous about his next task.

Kuradin perspired nervously as he watched Awadi. This man was living out the last moments of his life. Kuradin knew from the dossier that Awadi was married and had two children. He would never see, hold, touch, or kiss them again. Every step he took was one closer to his last. Kuradin wondered how many steps a man took in his lifetime or how far he walked. Does he ever realize which step is his last? Or which blink, or meal, or kiss ends the accumulated total in his life?

Kuradin thought of his own family. He wondered if he would ever see them again, or whether he was himself on the way to sharing a similar fate as Awadi. How many steps were left in his life? he wondered. Who would walk with him to *his* death?

They reached the morgue and found the attendant's desk empty. Awadi shaded his eyes and peered into the corpse room through the observation window. The lights were out in there, and the room was empty, except for the dead.

"Where is the attendant?" Kuradin asked.

"I don't know," Awadi replied.

"Let's go quickly, before he returns," Kuradin urged.

They entered the dark corpse room through the heavy metal doors. The dim light from the hallway poured weakly through the observation window, casting an eerie blue-gray light across the doors of the vaults.

There were three rows of six compartments each—a sobering sight. This was where all life ended up sooner or later, like a piece of meat in a refrigerator.

"Where is it?" Awadi whispered.

"Second vault from the end, second row," Kuradin answered.

Awadi walked over to the second vault from the closest end. He opened it and pulled the slab partway out. There was a small corpse on it in a white tie-sheet. A child.

Kuradin shook his head. "No, it should be empty. Maybe the other side."

The physician walked across the room passing through the narrow shaft of light. Kuradin followed him. He held a small thin ampoule in his hand. One end of the ampoule was solid and formed a handle for the tiny poisoned scratch pin.

The tall Indian opened the door. There was no body in this one. He pulled out the slab.

Kuradin used the sound of the slab's rollers to cover the low snapping sound of the glass.

"Where?" Awadi asked.

"In the back," Kuradin answered.

Awadi bent forward and leaned into the small vault. It was the perfect time to strike, but Kuradin hesitated. Now! Now! Before he turns, his mind shouted to the hand holding the scratch pin. But the hand did not move. He was reacting as most men would when confronted with that moment of deliberately taking a life. He waited too long.

Awadi had pulled the slab all the way out. "It is not here," he accented, and turned to face Kuradin. "It must be inside another vault. This must be the wrong one."

No, it's the right one, all right, Kuradin thought. He had lost all chance of surprise. Looking into the dark, inky eyes of this human being was making it more and more difficult. Do it, his mind commanded.

"Are you sure it was the second…" Awadi saw the pin. "What is that?"

Kuradin didn't answer. He thrust the pin forward at Awadi's chest, but the Indian saw it coming and managed to avoid the deadly instrument. It finally dawned on Awadi why they were in the morgue and why the slab had to be empty. It was for him.

"What are you doing?" he croaked out loudly.

The loud voice bounced off the walls in sharp echoing tones. The loudness disturbed Kuradin.

"Be quiet," Kuradin hissed. He stood between Awadi and the door. He moved slowly at the Indian, forcing him against the pulled-out slab.

"You cannot do this!" Awadi spurted out. "No! Somebody help me," Awadi screamed.

Kuradin had to move quickly. The sounds could probably be heard all over the lower floor. He lunged forward to strike once more.

But again Awadi was quicker. His fear had quickened his reactions, and the surge of adrenaline provided surprising strength as he slapped the wrist aside and slammed his attacker into the vaults. He broke for the door.

Kuradin crashed heavily against the closed vaults, then dove desperately after Awadi. The pin bit into the side of the right knee. The leg continued forward taking that last step, then Awadi crumbled to the floor. He looked in stunned disbelief at Kuradin, as his life ebbed quickly from his eyes. He *knew* he was dead— and then *was*. It was over.

The short struggle had taken Kuradin's mind off the thought of killing. It had happened automatically. The body did what had to be done without conscious direction from the brain.

He fought desperately to control his heavy breathing. He listened for footsteps or voices, but there were none. The body had to be hidden. Quickly.

Kuradin got to his feet and examined Awadi's body. He did not try to rationalize what had happened. He had seen men die before and had even ordered them killed. That's the way it went in this business. He would not let it rip at his conscience. That thing in front of him was no longer a person, just something that had to be hidden. The only life involved now was his own.

Kuradin grabbed Awadi by the ankles and dragged the body across the floor. As he passed through the shaft of light coming through the window, he heard a sound, then saw an attendant and a nurse step in front of the window. He froze, then very slowly let go of Awadi's feet and backed well into the darkness. Awadi's body lay partially in shadow; the shoulders, arms, and face grotesquely illuminated in the grayish light. Kuradin did not move the body, for fear of the movement catching the attention of the two people.

The nurse was very upset and was crying. The attendant tried comforting her but wasn't very successful. They spoke in vaguely muffled tones that Kuradin could not make out. He had no choice but to wait it out.

The nurse stood directly in front of the window, facing in. With the light coming from the outside of the morgue, Kuradin was sure she couldn't see him. If she looked down, though...

She spun to face the attendant. They were arguing. It seemed to last forever. Then, finally, the nurse walked off in a temper. The attendant shook his head and sat at his desk, right outside the door.

Kuradin moved in the darkness to the body and slowly pulled it out of the light without making a sound. Then he moved to where he could watch the attendant. If he didn't move soon, he'd have to be taken care of as Awadi had been. Then Kuradin realized that he didn't have the pin. It was somewhere on the floor.

He strained but couldn't see it. He wasn't about to get on his hands and knees to feel for it, either. That's what is known as making "the last mistake."

He had no other weapons, and the attendant was big. He'd *have* to look for the pin.

Just then, the attendant got up from his desk and walked off briskly, in the same direction that the nurse had gone.

Kuradin watched him pass by the window. A moment later he was stuffing Awadi's body into the vault. It was a tough job for a small man like Kuradin, but the necessity was greater than the disadvantage of his size, and it got done.

The slab rolled in, and the vault door closed. He stared at the number of the door. Eleven. That was all that a man was reduced to. A number. Kuradin guessed that he had only moments left. The attendant would be returning soon, and then he'd be trapped in there. He left without looking for the pin.

He walked quickly down the hallway to a stairwell, went up the stairs to ground level, and left the hospital. The night air was cool and felt good in his lungs, and his knees soon stopped shaking as he walked, leaving the hospital and what had happened behind him. There was enough ahead of him to worry about, as he went on to the next phase of his steadily crumbling plan.

Monday morning brought with it another beautiful springlike day in New York. A gentle wind danced in warming gusts, as large fluffy clouds drifted lazily in a bright blue sky. April's showers hadn't arrived yet, but were forecast for the middle of the week.

A gentle tapping sounded on a sixth-floor door in the Paradise Hotel. The raps came in the proper sequence, so Ten Braak moved for the door instead of the window. He held a stout automatic against the door as he opened it just a crack. It was his breakfast.

A tall, skinny man entered the room. The sudden smell of stale farts and Ten Braak's gamey odor stopped him momentarily. He nervously looked around the room and handed Ten Braak his meager breakfast, consisting of a large styrene cup of hot black coffee and a hard roll with butter. There was also a *Daily News*.

There was a look of urgency on the man's face; Ten Braak took its measure immediately. "You got trouble, my friend," the man said, as he continued to look around the room. "They're lookin' for you. They know you're in New York, and they're lookin' hard."

"How many?" Ten Braak asked.

"A lot. CIA, FBI, and NATO, too. I don't know what you done, but the faster you get outta here, the better I'm gonna like it," he said. "I don't want this place gettin' shot up. You got that?"

Ten Braak narrowed a stare at the man. He'd enjoy taking this creep out. He turned away from his excited informant. He paced slowly, thinking and looking around the room.

The man was getting more nervous. He didn't know if Ten Braak's silence was a hint for him to leave or not. After waiting a little longer, he moved for the door.

"Wait," Ten Braak said, "I will need some things." He walked over to his jacket and took out a small pad and a pen. He walked around the room, looking at outlets and switches. He stopped directly under the central light fixture. It was an ancient affair with six bulbs. It was controlled by the light switch by the door, as was the outlet on that wall. He studied the fixture briefly. Then he made some notes on the pad.

He walked to the door and opened it, examining the frame. He closed the door and made some additional notes. There were two other lamps in the room. These were also examined. Next he went to the window leading out to the fire escape and examined it as well. He jotted more words on the paper.

Ten Braak read the sheet over again and handed it to the man. "You will get all that is on this list by noon," he said in his thick accent.

The man peered through the dirty scratched lenses of his wire-framed glasses. "This is dangerous stuff," he said.

"Can you get it all?" Ten Braak asked.

"Yeah, I can get it. But there ain't nothin' in this deal about this place goin' up. I'll get it for you, but you ain't keepin' it up here," he insisted.

"It is not for use here," Ten Braak lied.

"Yeah, well it better not be, 'cause out you go if you think so."

"I will also need a car. Can you get one?"

The man thought for a second. "Yeah," he said, nodding his head, "I can get one. It won't be fancy, but it'll run," he answered.

"Good. You will have everything by noon," Ten Braak said.

"It's gonna cost money," the man said.

"How much money?" Ten Braak asked.

"Eight hundred."

It was robbery, and Ten Braak knew it. But everything has its price when you need it. Besides, he still had Ross's cash.

He went to the flight bag, opened it, and took out a stack of bills, then counted out eight hundred dollars into the man's waiting palm.

"And four more for the car," the man said, his greed now showing in his smile.

Ten Braak counted it out, watching the beady little eyes smile. It wouldn't cost more than a couple of hundred to get the whole works.

The man stuffed the bills in his pocket. "I'll take ya to it when I got it all together," he said.

Ten Braak smiled at him. "That will be most satisfactory."

"And I'll see what else I can find out about the people lookin' for ya." A second later he was through the door.

Ten Braak thought about this latest wrinkle, as he mangled the roll and wolfed it down with huge gulps of the hot black coffee. It didn't take him long to figure out that he had been set up.

It all became a little clearer to him now. A man in his line of work knows when his situation is becoming unfavorable. Little things give the signs when "retirement" is not far off. The assignments, the pay, the class of accommodations, many little things. They all began to warn him that it was drawing near.

Perhaps it was his age, or because they felt he was no longer in his prime. In any event, he had seen it coming. He was leery of every assignment, fearing that it could be the setup.

When this one was given to him, he began to feel that maybe he was wrong and that his imagination had been working overtime on him. This was the most important assignment to ever come along. Only the best would be selected. It paid like a slot machine, too. But now he saw it for what it was. He was the bait, expendable, to guarantee the other guy getting out. It was still a good deal, though. It was a good way to go, if you had to go. This was top honors. He'd be remembered as the one that made it work. He'd go out on top and in style.

But he could be even better remembered, if he got back with his information. Then there would be no question as to who was the best. It needed no proving in his mind, but, once *they* knew it, any question of an early retirement arrangement would be out.

The contact was probably a setup, too. He decided not to make it. He'd play out the string as far as he could, to buy the time for Phoenix to get out. Then he'd figure his commitment to the operation fulfilled. After that, he'd follow his instincts and get himself out of the country and back to Russia with the information. They'd shit green when they saw him walk in with it.

He'd give them all something to remember Otto Ten Braak for, including this SENTINEL agency that Phoenix had briefed him on. There would be no doubt in anyone's mind who was number one when this thing was over.

David Fromme had driven past the rendezvous point four times already, and Cactus Flower still hadn't shown up. It was twenty minutes past twelve already. Something had gone wrong.

He glanced up into the rearview mirror and saw something that bothered him. The same Chevy Impala had been behind him on his last pass of the arranged meeting place. It suddenly occurred to him what was happening. He was being followed.

His mind raced as he began to perspire nervously. It became obvious. His refusal over the phone had sealed his fate. They considered him weak and were going to remove him. They'd probably already taken out Cactus Flower. That's why he had never showed.

It was time to blow out of there. Now. He took the first immediate left and sprinted the Dodge Monaco up the block.

The Impala stayed right with him. That clinched it. He began to fly.

The two SENTINEL agents in the Impala stayed right with Fromme. "SENTINEL Control, this is Sigmund," the driver said. "Blue Dodge Monaco is running. We've been made!"

"Apprehend the subject," came the soft reply. "Take him alive if you can."

The chase led quickly out of the city. Fromme did not know the area well and just scorched along the country roads. He peered nervously into the rearview mirror at the unshakable Impala. Fromme removed the .38 and placed it on the seat beside him. Killing to stay alive was a different thing.

The Impala pulled out and roared up alongside the Dodge. The agent in the passenger seat signaled Fromme to pull over. Fromme's response was to steer into the Impala, in an attempt to force it off the road.

The Impala dropped back. The passenger window rolled down, and the agent readied his gun. Sigmund gunned it up close to the back of the Dodge and pulled out enough to give his partner a clear shot at the rear tire.

It was a close and easy shot. The blown rear tire sent the Dodge into a violent fishtail. Fromme couldn't control it and veered off the road, skidding a short distance and smacking heavily into a tree.

The Impala skidded to a halt not far behind it. Sigmund's partner emerged from the car and raced to a position about ten feet off the right rear fender. He raised the gun into firing position, to cover Sigmund's approach.

Sigmund approached cautiously, gun drawn and ready. Fromme was not visible. Sigmund's partner moved in a wide arc to the opposite side of the car, keeping the gun trained and ready.

Sigmund crouched below window level and scampered up to the car. He tapped on the door with the barrel of his gun.

"Come out with both hands in plain view," he shouted.

There was no response.

He repeated the command.

Still no response.

He brought the gun to eye level and rose quickly. Fromme was lying across the front seat, his face a mass of blood.

"He's down," Sigmund said. He cautiously reached for the door and tried it. It was unlocked and hadn't jammed in the crash. He lowered himself again and pulled the door open, his gun ready to fire at the slightest twitch.

Fromme was motionless.

Sigmund reached out and tugged at Fromme's leg. There was no response. He tugged again, harder. Still nothing. He rose slowly, to get a better look at Fromme. He was a mess.

Sigmund looked up at his partner. "Look out," he said. Then he lowered his eyes to Fromme again, in time to see the flash tear through the coat, as Fromme shot him in the face.

Fromme jumped up quickly, trying to get out of the car, but he got only as far as a sitting position when the bullet smashed through the passenger's window and into the back of his skull. He bounced violently forward, hitting the steering wheel, then slumped back down across the seat.

The SENTINEL agent raced around the car to his partner. Sigmund was still alive, but nothing could be done for him. The bullet had hit him between the cheekbone and nose at an upward angle. He was in deep shock. The eyes were open and vacant. The pulse and respiration were wildly erratic, as he clung to the last shreds of clinical life.

A police siren wailed in the distance, as Sigmund's partner removed the CIA and NATO identification from his pockets, leaving the FBI documents.

Sigmund didn't survive the ambulance ride to the hospital. He was pronounced dead on arrival.

Later that afternoon Sigmund's body was taken to the morgue in the Beloit General Hospital. His body was wheeled to vault number eleven. The body of Dr. Kantilal Awadi was found, and more clues were supplied to SENTINEL.

It was now entering the endgame, and SENTINEL still had the tempo. Phoenix was running.

TWENTY-EIGHT

Of the remaining steering centers, the United States was the most desirable. It was ideal in every respect, including a high number of Aryan beings. But its democratic system was too firmly entrenched and would pose an almost insurmountable obstacle.

The steering center was left intact because of the abilities of Colorosa. He was a man of rare qualities and was highly thought of, even though some of his ideas and suggestions seemed farfetched. A lot of what he said made good sense. He was highly creative and worth the continued investment. We needed Thinkers.

Entry No. 47 from the partially
recovered *Wolf Journal*

Moscow: Leonid Travkin sat pensively behind his desk. Five hours earlier he had been alerted that the Phoenix computer-file tape was being scanned. An electronically coded signal had been incorporated into the tape, to tip off its activation to the special team assigned to monitor unusual computer use for the duration of the SENTINEL mission.

It bore a grim significance. It could only mean that Centaur was in serious trouble. The way the plan was set up, only two checkpoints were incorporated in the entire affair. Both came late in the plan and were designed to let Travkin know which contingency was in play. If Kuradin did not make either of the two checkpoints, that would mean he had been captured or killed. Travkin was to then discreetly leak the Phoenix data, starting the final contingency in motion. If Centaur were captured, release of that information would allow the smooth transition into the final phase. If he were dead, it wouldn't matter. The situation would be nearly hopeless. A small chance for success could still exist, if Kuradin had had the microdots implanted and the body could be recovered.

The scanning of the Phoenix tape meant that the plan had broken down somewhere. The phony identity had been discovered independently of the leak designed for that purpose.

The Phoenix cover had been very carefully prepared by Travkin, according to Kuradin's instructions. It was designed to hide Centaur's involvement in the operation, just in case SENTINEL had acquired knowledge of him and his special talents.

Certain facts had obviously been collected concerning Centaur from the near-fatal English mission of the year before. These facts were carefully built into the Phoenix file. Phoenix had been selected as the cover after an exhaustive search through personnel files. He was the special agent meeting the specific requirements that Kuradin had outlined for Travkin during the planning stage of the mission. Phoenix had come closest to those conditions with some startling similarities. For example: both Phoenix and Centaur fit the same general description; both worked out of the special secret pool of agents known only to a very few KGB higher-ups; both had incurred serious hand wounds on their last missions, those injuries occurring in the same year, actually, just three months apart and both in Western Europe.

The Phoenix file had been altered to correspond to Centaur's actual history. The last mission had become the English mission, the injured hand had become the left one, and it was the little finger that had been lost. In reality, Phoenix had been injured three months earlier in West Germany, and three fingers had been lost from the right hand.

Enough had been changed to indicate beyond a doubt that Phoenix had been on the English mission. The rest pointed closely enough to identify Kuradin as Phoenix.

But an unexpected danger had crept into this careful planning; that was Dmitri Chakhovsky's defection. There was little doubt in Travkin's mind that he had been taken by SENTINEL agents. The fact that Chakhovsky knew both Centaur and Phoenix could blow the entire final contingency right out of the window. It was imperative that the Phoenix cover hold up.

The exact seriousness of the scanning of the Phoenix tape was difficult to determine. One thing was certain, however, and that was that, coming this early in the plan, it couldn't help matters any. This development had to be handled carefully. The information *must* be allowed to get out now, or it might be distrusted when later presented.

That meant letting the person scanning the file go until his contact was made and sufficient time allowed to ensure its getting out and into the proper hands. They would have to play wait-and-watch, until it was safe to grab the people involved without spoiling the opportunity of the leak.

One distinct possibility did loom large in this development. The contact would be a SENTINEL agent. Provided the Phoenix cover held up, that could prove to be an ace in the hole. It could make the final contingency work as smooth as silk.

So, Travkin would watch and wait and hope that Centaur made the checkpoints. The first one was scheduled for Wednesday. He could only hope that luck stayed with Kuradin for that long.

Travkin's despair would have doubled if he had known Centaur's actual situation. The plan was rapidly crumbling beneath the mighty intellect of SENTINEL. Kuradin was running, being forced to make decisions at a faster rate than he had expected, and each decision turned the odds in SENTINEL's favor. Travkin was helpless to change that.

A light, steady rain fell on a chilly, cloud-shrouded St. Simon's Island. In the secret lower levels of the Dials Cardiac Clinic a three-man team was preparing for another debriefing session with Dmitri Chakhovsky.

The man heading the team was Richard Wyatt. He was Honeycut's chief assistant and an expert on Soviet Intelligence. Wyatt was being groomed as Honeycut's heir-apparent, upon his retirement. That was still about six years away, and Wyatt used the time well. He was the ideal candidate for the position. Honeycut had handpicked him as his successor to head up the program.

Also with the team were Dr. Peter Bell, a psychiatrist, and Victor Bishoff, an interpreter. All three men possessed high security classifications within the agency.

Dr. Bell had been called in to advise Wyatt, with regard to Chakhovsky's mental state. It was common for defectors coming over for reasons of survival, rather than for those of moral conviction, to be reluctant in giving vital information. They usually had great quarrels of conscience, as their love and loyalty remained with their country. They felt it a betrayal to give vital information and required special handling. They had to be slowly and patiently worn down, to the point where this great wall of conscience could be overcome.

Victor Bishoff served two functions. Besides interpreting in matters of semantics, he was an expert in observation. A facial expression or an eye response often added valuable insight into the meaning of what was said. He watched and made his silent observations, later adding them to the transcript when it was reviewed.

The usual procedure with a case like Chakhovsky's was to spend at least two weeks testing the subject to establish his authenticity. The Soviets were notorious for planting defectors, to deliver information essential to their clever disinformation tactics. Every precaution had to be taken.

But usual procedure was ruled out in this case for several reasons. There was no doubt that Chakhovsky was who he said he was, that had been verified. His critical condition made time an unaffordable luxury, and the information they needed from him was needed fast.

The lack of time made this a difficult job for the team. Overcoming the conscience barrier that Chakhovsky had constructed would not be a simple matter in so short a time. But they had planned their method carefully.

Chakhovsky's instincts for survival were obviously stronger than his conscience, otherwise he never would have defected. They would threaten that survival instinct, to get the information they needed. His survival would depend upon his telling them what they wanted to know.

The first two sessions had been low-keyed, with the usual testing questions. The atmosphere was relaxed and cordial, to help build the sense of security in Chakhovsky that they would soon assault.

As predicted by Dr. Bell, Chakhovsky's responses were guarded. He gave only information he knew they already had. He outlined the structure of the Soviet Intelligence organizations and fed them bits of common knowledge, which did not sting his conscience. He had appeared highly nervous at first, but soon calmed down. He was alive and safe, and he was beginning to feel secure.

But today's session would be different. It would not be held in his room. Dials had consented to let Chakhovsky be brought to a special room in a wheelchair. He was reluctant at first, but after Honeycut had conceded to let him attend the session, to monitor Chakhovsky's level of stress, and had given him the authority to stop the proceedings if a dangerous level of stress were reached, he agreed.

The new environment and break from procedure would cause a small degree of uneasiness in Chakhovsky. Every little bit would help in creating the desired effect.

The wheelchair was specially designed to pick up his slightest physiological variations. They could monitor the level of stress they delivered, as well as pick out obvious lies. It also afforded Dr. Dials the opportunity to monitor Chakhovsky's condition. He hadn't had an attack for almost forty hours, now. The program of rest was working.

The three men waited for Dials to bring in Chakhovsky.

A few moments later the wide door opened and Chakhovsky was wheeled in by a nurse. Dials walked in just behind them. The Russian was wheeled to a position in front of the large table at which the three-man panel sat. The nurse left the room and Dials joined the men at the table.

The surface of the table was tilted slightly, angling away from Chakhovsky, so that he could not see its top. Various electronic monitoring devices were built into it. By checking them, Dials and Bell could quickly determine Chakhovsky's condition.

Everything about the room was designed to cause the slightest degree of stress. The temperature was markedly cooler than the rest of the complex; the fluorescent lighting was tinted to stress the eyes; and the color, shape, and furnishings of the room had been carefully selected to contribute to the desired effect. It was an uncomfortable room to be in, and each factor served to increase that uneasy feeling with every second spent there.

Directly above Chakhovsky was a conical air vent. But, instead of air, it directed a narrow cone of sound waves down upon him. He couldn't hear them, but soon he'd begin to feel them, as they worked to increase his anxiety.

Wyatt would be the examiner. Chakhovsky's English was good, though accented, so Bishoff would have little to do but study the unspoken facial language. Bell would ask questions only when he saw the need to direct the Russian's mind toward a level of low apprehension. This way, the sudden snapback would be more effective when it came.

Chakhovsky sat ready. The monitors read slight anxiety; he was fidgety and uncomfortable. The room was working.

"Good afternoon, Mr. Chakhovsky," Wyatt said.

"Good afternoon," Chakhovsky returned.

"I trust you rested well through the night, without incident?" Wyatt said.

"Yes, thank you," the Russian replied.

"Should you begin to feel ill at any time, just tell us and we'll discontinue the session," Wyatt offered.

Chakhovsky nodded his appreciation.

"I'd like to go back over some of the things we talked about yesterday," Wyatt began. This was to get Chakhovsky's mind back on safe ground, to build his security up again quickly. "You've been with the KGB for how long?"

"Twenty-three years," Chakhovsky replied.

"That's a long time," Wyatt said, nodding his head and smiling. "We'd like you to go back over the Illegals and Disinformation Divisions again, if you would."

Chakhovsky thought for a few moments and began his recitation. The panel listened attentively, eyes on the monitors.

"Now, just briefly, review the responsibilities you had as an official in the Operational Division," Wyatt said after the Russian had finished.

Again the panel sat attentively through the Russian's explanation of his duties.

Wyatt nodded as Chakhovsky finished his statement. "Tell us about your family."

"I have no surviving family," the Russian began. "My wife, Tamara, died twelve years ago. We had a son, Boris, who died two years ago in a skirmish along the Chinese border." Chakhovsky's eyes saddened, as he thought of distant memories. "He was a wonderful boy," he said. His eyes looked off to the past. After a few moments of silence, he looked back to Wyatt. "No man...no man should ever live to see his children die," he said.

The monitors remained even. He was relaxed.

"You must have loved him very much," Bell said, wishing to keep Chakhovsky's mind where it was. Wyatt recognized the psychiatrist's aim.

Chakhovsky nodded slowly. "He was the image of my wife, the only surviving part of her. I miss...miss them," he said looking down. "Very much."

"How did you meet Tamara?" Bell asked. The team hadn't yet touched upon the personal aspects of his life through the interrogations. Bell quickly recognized its value.

The Russian thought for a few moments. "It seems that I had always known her. We were children together. We were in love for as long as I can remember," he said. "She was such a beautiful child, always the prettiest girl in school. At least, to me she was," he said, a slight smile breaking.

"Is that how you remember her? As a child?" Bell asked.

"I remember her in many ways. Mostly in our childhood. We were so close. But I remember her in many ways all throughout our lives together. I...I remember her...dead." He paused and looked down sadly. "Perhaps...perhaps, that is why I think of her as a child. It leaves so much time for...for—"

"Why did you defect?" Wyatt asked suddenly, in a loud voice.

The monitors jumped. A nerve had been struck.

The question jolted Chakhovsky. He thought frantically. "I...I...my life was in danger," he stammered.

"Why?" Wyatt hammered out at him. The polite tone was gone from his voice.

The monitors continued jumping.

"I, eh..." His mind raced, scrambling back to the present, grasping for something to say. "...because I had fallen out of favor with the Central Committee," he said. "I had openly opposed their views on several recent occasions. You...one does not oppose the views of the committee in Russia," he made up quickly, speaking in a nervous rush of words.

"For that they'd kill you?" Wyatt asked.

"No...no, they wanted me dead because I chose to defect. I was warned by a friend that they had planned to take me back to the Soviet Union. That could only have meant dismissal and probable internment in a prison or an asylum. That is their way to handle such people. I love life too much to end it in such a way. I chose life and ran. It was for that choice that I was to be punished," he said.

Wyatt rubbed his nose and frowned. "That's a very good story," he said, raising his eyebrows. "Now tell us the truth."

The monitors jumped again.

"I...I...have not lied," Chakhovsky insisted, his eyes playing from man to man.

"Yes, you have," Wyatt hammered out.

"It is true. I swear it. It is—"

"It's a pile of shit. You're lying," Wyatt cracked back, pounding the table with a fist.

Chakhovsky was stunned. He couldn't think, couldn't concentrate. He was suddenly confused and frightened. They couldn't know! His eyes shot around the floor, as his brain searched for words. He was so confused that his brain had trouble translating into English what he wanted to say.

Wyatt didn't give him the chance to talk. "We know all about Bodonov and why they wanted you back in Moscow. We know that you're a pedophile, that you're a criminal."

Dials shot a hot glance at Wyatt. The monitors were going wild. This was too much for him. It had to stop.

Dials began to rise, but Bell's hand came to his forearm and stopped him.

Wyatt's statement had cut deep into Chakhovsky. He couldn't believe that they knew. How? How could they have found out?

"You'd better start playing straight with us. And I mean right now, or we'll put your ass on a plane back to Paris faster than you can blink an eye. We want answers to our questions, and we want information—useful information—not this bullshit you've been giving us so far. You haven't told us one thing that we didn't already know.

"It cost us four lives to get your ass out of France," Wyatt said, going for the throat. "That's four Americans that won't be coming home just so that you could be brought here safely. Now you're gonna start paying us back. You got that?"

Chakhovsky was stunned. He nodded weakly.

The monitors had gone absolutely wild. They were still jumping, but beginning to calm down slightly. The truth was out. Chakhovsky had nothing more to hide or fear, except for what Wyatt could do to him if he didn't talk.

He'd be dead now if it hadn't been for them. He owed them something. Everything. He owed nothing to the people who had tried to kill him, and would again if given the chance. "I will tell you everything that you want to know," he said in a low whisper.

"You had better," Wyatt said, still breathing flame.

Dials sat back once again, as the monitors began a steady return toward normal. There would be enough anxiety in Chakhovsky from this point on from the room's design and Wyatt's threat hanging over him to keep them jumping, but the worst was over.

"Tell us what you know about the names Spartan, Pilgrim, and Badger," Wyatt said.

Chakhovsky didn't hesitate. Cooperation was his new middle name. "They are code names of American agents working in Western Europe. We had been given the names by our top agent in British Intelligence."

"The 'fifth man'?" Wyatt asked. It was a widely known theory. There was no doubt that Chakhovsky would know the reference.

"Yes, that is correct. His code name is Capricorn. His real name is Lloyd Cushman," Chakhovsky said.

That was, in fact, the same name that SENTINEL had projected as the "fifth man" to Honeycut. The "special action" could now be ordered on him.

"They were reported to be with your Special Operations Division of the CIA. This fact, however, could not be verified by our CIA contacts," Chakhovsky said.

"There were some theories put forth," he continued, "that a secret organization or branch of the CIA had been created, especially in light of the recent CIA and FBI disclosures. We felt that these disclosures were a deliberate attempt to give the impression of weakening in their operations.

"It was not realistic to believe that such information leaks could go on unstopped. It had to be deliberate. The new force would be doubly effective if we believed otherwise," he said.

He had come very close to the truth. The CIA and FBI disclosures were, in part, aided by SENTINEL.

"Much strength was given to our theory by Capricorn's information. There was also evidence of highly competent action taken against us on many more occasions than we would like to admit. Most of them going badly for us.

"Dates supplied by Capricorn corresponded to some of those missions. But we could never learn more. There are no records on these agents anywhere. They seem to appear, then vanish when their work is done."

"Is there anything else?" Wyatt asked.

Chakhovsky thought for a few moments, then shook his head. "No, nothing."

"Would you be able to identify these agents if you saw them?" Wyatt asked.

"No," Chakhovsky said, "there were no photographs. We would not have even known of their existence had not Capricorn given us his information."

"What about this secret intelligence agency? How advanced are your theories and what facts were gathered to back them up?" Wyatt questioned.

"There were no facts," Chakhovsky started. "The two theories were that they belonged to a private agency, backed and funded by your government, with its files maintained outside of government control for security reasons; or that false code names were being created and assigned to different agents at different times to cause confusion.

"In the second case, the information supplied to Capricorn could have been planted in order to get the KGB to expend great effort in hunting for 'ghost agents' which did not exist," the Russian explained.

"Does the name SENTINEL mean anything to you?" Wyatt asked.

Chakhovsky thought for a while. "No, that is a code name I have never heard before."

The monitors showed that everything he had said was the truth.

"Tell us about Phoenix," Wyatt said.

The monitors spiked sharply.

"How did you become aware of that code name?" the Russian asked.

"That's not important," Wyatt said. "We want to know everything that you know about him."

Dials was concentrating on the cardiac monitors. A change was beginning to take place that he didn't like. He scribbled a quick note to Bell, telling him to cut it short. No more than two minutes.

Bell read it and passed it to Wyatt, as Chakhovsky began talking.

The Russian explained the way in which Phoenix had been used. He described the secret pool of agents known to only a select few, of which Chakhovsky was one. He went on to give a physical description that very closely matched that of the first

David Fromme that Pilgrim and Badger had talked to in South Beloit.

He explained that Phoenix had been placed on the inactive list since his last mission just over a year ago. This was because he had received a serious hand injury which made him too easily identifiable. He was not scheduled for assignment again.

When asked about the exact nature of the injury, he could only recall that it had been a severe disfiguring wound. He wasn't sure which hand was involved. He thought the right.

"Then you could identify him if you saw him?" Wyatt asked.

"Yes, certainly," Chakhovsky answered.

"Had Phoenix ever been assigned in the United States?" Wyatt questioned.

"Yes, often. His English is perfect, and he knows the country very well. But I only assigned him in Western Europe. I would have no knowledge of his activities in this country, other than that he had been assigned here."

Chakhovsky didn't look well. His complexion had undergone a rapid change over the last few minutes. Dials was becoming concerned. Variant angina doesn't always approach with the usual warning of the more common or stable kinds. It was caused by a spasm which could happen gradually or with startling speed.

"We have reason to believe that he is in the United States now," Wyatt said. "We'll need your help in identifying him when he's apprehended."

Chakhovsky nodded. A slight grimace crossed his face.

"I think that's enough for today, gentlemen," Dials said, rising from his chair.

"Just one more thing needs clarification," Wyatt said.

Dials frowned and shook his head, but Wyatt ignored him.

Wyatt began his question. "Where was Phoenix assigned when he received his wound? Was it the United States?"

Their information was pretty conclusive to this point. The fingerprints lifted in South Beloit and in Roger Caneway's room at the hospital, as well as those in the morgue, matched the ones taken from the car in England after Pilgrim had wounded the fleeing contact. The blood samples taken at the hospital also matched those recovered by Division Two from the car. But it was important to confirm this fact, as this operation was obviously well planned, and anything was possible.

"No...no, it...it..." Chakhovsky gasped, clutching his chest.

Dials jumped to his feet. He sprang to the call button that summoned the cardiac team. "That's all for today," he said as he moved quickly to his patient.

Wyatt rose and moved toward Chakhovsky, as the cardiac team poured into the room. Chakhovsky was quickly lifted onto a high stretcher and an oxygen mask was placed over his nose and mouth. The team began to wheel him out quickly, with Wyatt running alongside.

"Where? Where was he when he was injured?" he asked urgently.

Chakhovsky's eyes were bulging and watering. He tried answering through the mask. "Eur...Europe," he gasped out.

It was muffled, but Wyatt was able to make it out.

Dials threw Wyatt a murderous stare.

Wyatt continued running alongside the rolling stretcher. "Where in Europe?"

Chakhovsky couldn't answer. He was trying, but no words came out.

"Was it England?" Wyatt asked. He only needed a yes.

"Was it England?" he repeated.

Chakhovsky's head was rolling and tossing in pain. He looked into Wyatt's eyes, trying to speak through the pain and the fear.

"Germany," he said, "West Germany," but his words were muffled by the mask. "An...another...another, in...in England.

Cen...Centaur. *Hand...hand, in Eng...England,*" he gasped loudly.

But it was garbled. Wyatt could only pick up parts of it. He had heard "...hand, in Eng...England." The rest was unclear.

Dials moved between Wyatt and Chakhovsky and shoved Wyatt aside. "I said that's all, goddamn it. You're killing him," he growled.

Wyatt fell off the pace, as the team rushed Chakhovsky into the trauma room. They went to work on him. It was infarction.

They worked desperately as he lost consciousness. A resuscitation unit was hooked up to him and external heart massage was performed by Dials. They pumped needle after needle into him. Dials inserted a cardiac needle directly into the heart and continued the massage.

They fought off death for nearly thirty minutes. Dials opened Chakhovsky up and performed direct cardiac massage. They worked and worked out of desperation.

After another endless fifteen-minute period, the heart began a smooth, rhythmic cadence again. But Chakhovsky remained unconscious.

An hour later he was in intensive care, hooked up to the electronic monitoring devices. The heart pumped away, rhythmically, its cadence again satisfactory.

He was alive, but he could tell them no more. He was in a deep coma.

The team went over what information they had gathered. Wyatt's interpretation of what he had heard in those last moments before Chakhovsky was wheeled away from him was that Chakhovsky had confirmed that the hand wound had been received in England.

It was a logical assumption to make, all the evidence pointed to it. But the assumption was wrong. He had not clearly heard Chakhovsky's words about Germany and Centaur.

The facts matched what Eagle, the SENTINEL agent in Moscow, had sent in only an hour before the last debriefing session. Everything pointed to Phoenix as being the agent that Pilgrim had encountered in England a year ago.

But what had really happened was that the tempo had suddenly swung back to Centaur once again. Because now, even if they caught him, they would think that he was Phoenix. And Centaur had one outstanding talent that Phoenix did not have, one that they would never suspect. Alexi Kuradin had a photographic memory.

TWENTY-NINE

South Africa held promise. There are a lot of Aryans in South Africa, and they had done an outstanding job of developing what they had. Like South America, the African continent has enormous resource potential. No doubt, we could have eventually taken over the majority of that continent.

A serious drawback was the lack of Aryans on the rest of the continent, with the exception of Rhodesia. The racial issue could have had its solution, but it would have taken too long and drawn too much attention before we were ready.

But this still bore serious long-range consideration, and Constantine was in an excellent position of influence.

Colorosa's influence had also grown greatly in the United States. We were very impressed.

Entry No. 54 from the partially
recovered *Wolf Journal*

It was nearly four in the afternoon when the coded taps sounded at Ten Braak's door. He was irritated that the man had taken so long.

"Did you get all that was on the list?" Ten Braak asked.

"Yeah, yeah, I got it. But it ain't here. You gotta come with me, if you wanna see it."

It was a risk leaving the room. Ten Braak knew this, but, again, he had no choice. "I will come," he said, grabbing his coat.

The two men left the room and walked down the six flights of stairs. Ten Braak was led to the basement and out through a service exit. They walked up a gently inclined ramp to a small alleyway leading out to the side street, turned left, and walked away from Third Avenue. About twenty yards up the block, the tall, skinny man stopped next to a beat-up Volkswagen.

"This is the car," he said.

Ten Braak looked at the pile of dented, rusted metal. He had expected more for his four hundred dollars.

"Get in," the man said. "It's about eight blocks from here. It'll be less risky for you in the car."

Moments later the VW was coughing and sputtering up the block. The man had been right; it wasn't pretty, but it did run.

They came back around to Third Avenue and headed uptown. At Fourteenth Street they went right and then right again, onto Second Avenue. The VW limped and farted its way to Thirteenth Street and then turned right onto the one-way street. About three-quarters of the way up the block, he pulled over and double-parked, then shut off the clackety engine.

"It's in there," he said, pointing to a vacant six-story building. "It's safe where it is. No one's livin' in there, just some rummies now and then. Kids play there once in a while, too, but the stuff's okay."

Ten Braak looked doubtingly at the old building as they got out of the car. He looked up and down the block. It was an amazing sight. Europeans wouldn't believe this was America if they could see it, he thought. This was as bad as any urban slum anywhere.

They walked up the stairs and through the broken front door. Ten Braak followed the man up the stairs. It was an incredible sight. The doors and moldings were gone. Plumbing had been ripped out, the walls were smashed where the electrical wires were pulled out for the copper. Everything that could be taken and sold was gone. Almost every inch of the floor was covered with debris. The railings were gone, floor boards torn up from the apartments they passed, and the walls were covered with enough graffiti to give an education in American slang and a who's who of the neighborhood, as well as numbers to call for the action.

They walked into one of the fourth-floor apartments.

"They don't come in this one too much, anymore," the man said. "Three rummies were found dead here last year. Throats were cut, cocks cut off and stuffed in their mouths. At first, all the kids came to see where it happened. Then one of them got thrown off the roof, so they don't come in here no more," he said, as they walked through the rooms to a bathroom, careful to step only where the floor was solid.

This bathroom still had a door and, unbelievably, a bathtub. Everything that Ten Braak had asked for was in the bathroom in three big boxes. He began going through them, taking a quick inventory.

"It's all there," the man said.

Ten Braak continued checking. There were two one-gallon tins. He pulled one out and opened it. Then he sniffed the contents. This was what he had asked for, all right.

"We must put this in the car," he said.

"You ain't takin' that stuff back with you, I said," the skinny man insisted. "Ain't nothin' gonna happen to my place. There wasn't nothin' said about—"

Ten Braak held up his hand to silence him. "I wish only to put it in the car," he said.

"In this city?" The man laughed. "You leave those boxes in a parked car, and they ain't gonna be there too long."

"It will not be safe in this place," Ten Braak said.

"Oh yes it will," the man insisted. "I told you, nobody comes here no more."

Ten Braak walked out of the bathroom, motioning the man to follow him. He went to a corner of the room that they had walked past to get to the bathroom. He pointed to the floor. The man looked down. There were three used condoms lying on the floor, knotted, and not discolored from age, or even dust-covered. The floor of the surrounding area had much of the dust moved away as if someone had been lying there.

"This place is used frequently," Ten Braak said.

"I didn't see that," the man said.

"You will help me find another place nearer to the Paradise," Ten Braak told him.

The man nodded. "Yeah, okay. I think I know a place, but we gotta pick a lock first."

Ten Braak nodded his approval, but he had his own idea as to where he'd be keeping it.

Each man took one box and carefully made his way to the car. The boxes were stowed, and the car was locked.

They went back in for the rest.

Ten Braak stood in the bathroom and took out the three lamps from the last box. "These can be put in the storage compartment," he said. "This box can be cut down to make it fit in with the other boxes," he added, handing the thin man a pocket knife.

The thin man moved to the box, ready to trim it down, as the wooden-handled weapon came out of Ten Braak's pocket.

The man began making his first cut. He was on his knees in front of Ten Braak, hunched well forward over the box.

The target behind the ear was a difficult reach. If it wasn't done just right, he might not die quickly and turn with the sharp knife. But that wasn't the only acceptable target.

The shaft bit suddenly into the center of the man's neck, just at the base of the skull. He started to straighten up, but Ten Braak pushed his head forward and down and drove the weapon home again and again and again, until all movement stopped.

Ten Braak put the lamps back in the box, picked up his pocket knife, and went down to the car, after taking back the rest of his money from the man's wallet.

About twenty minutes later, he was carrying the last box into his room at the Paradise.

He emptied the boxes, setting the contents carefully on the floor, bed, and table. He walked around the room once more, examining the door, switches, and outlets again.

Then he went to the table and began to draw a diagram. A few minutes later he stretched out the wire and began cutting the required lengths.

He finished measuring and cutting the wires, then went out of the room and down the hallway, until he found the maintenance room. He opened the door, walked over to the fuse boxes, found the one with his room number on it, and removed the two fuses. Then he returned to the room.

The necessary tools had been laid out on the table. He selected the screwdriver and wire crimp, then went to the switch by the door. He dismantled it.

About thirty minutes later he had a wire running from the switch to a special flatspring-loaded relay, designed to fit between the door frame and the door. He had to chisel a small notch in the door frame, to get it to fit properly.

A wire ran from the relay to a large second-elapse timer and back to the switch on the wall. Wires were run from the timer to one wall outlet, then from that outlet to the others not originally controlled by the switch. They were now all controlled by the switch and timer.

When this was done, he placed the three lamps he had carried up near the outlets that did not already have lamps plugged into them. That gave each outlet its own lamp.

Next he took out the packages of large industrial light bulbs. Then he took out the tiny portable hand drill from his black case and locked the smallest bit in place.

On the table was a large syringe and a can of sealing putty. He took a large bowl and put it on the table.

Taking the first bulb, he drilled a tiny hole in its base and tried the syringe. It fit easily. Then he drilled holes in the remaining ten bulbs.

Next, Ten Braak brought the two gallon cans to the table and poured fluid from one of them into the bowl. He took the large syringe and drew it full of the fluid. He then stuck the needle through the hole in the base of the bulb and discharged the fluid. This procedure was repeated until the bulb was filled with fluid. Then he sealed the hole with the putty and began on the next bulb.

When the bulbs were finished, he laid them carefully in the boxes, well-wrapped with paper from the *Daily News* that had come with his breakfast.

He set the timer to zero and went back down the hall to the maintenance room and replaced the fuses. He returned to the room and found the overhead lights on and four of the five lamps lit up as well. He checked the one that did not light. It had a faulty switch.

A few minutes later the switch was repaired and all the lamps glowed brightly. He went to the timer and set it for five seconds. The lights went out as he moved it off zero. The timer swept quickly through the short setting, and all the lights clicked on at once, as it reached zero again.

Ten Braak then walked to the door and looked at his watch. He checked the second hand, as he stood motionless by the door, sweeping the room quickly with his eyes. Then he moved to the center of the room and looked at the watch. Seven seconds would be plenty.

That's how long it would take for a man to walk into hell.

He sat at the table, after turning off the wall switch, which made all the lights go out at once.

Then he waited for the darkness to fall. In about four hours, he'd be leaving the room. Otto Ten Braak was ready for them. Now he had to find them. He had an idea where he might.

The Lower East Side can be a very large haystack when you're looking for one man, especially if he doesn't want to be found.

Justin and Fanning had combed the area, chasing down every possible lead. The other SENTINEL teams in the area had staked out the suspected safe houses, but had come up empty so far. It was obvious that more SENTINEL manpower was needed. A good deal of the SENTINEL manpower had been reassigned to locate Phoenix. The trail in Beloit had heated up significantly after the discovery of Awadi's corpse in the morgue.

O'Hare Airport was crawling with agents, all of whom had pictures of the man they were looking for. Milwaukee and Madison also had their airports under watch.

SENTINEL had learned a lot since Fromme and Sigmund had been killed. Phoenix was admitted into the Beloit General Hospital under the name of Roger Caneway. There was also a reservation booked for one Roger Caneway on an afternoon flight to Paris leaving from O'Hare on Wednesday.

SENTINEL had also learned a lot about the way Phoenix thought. It projected that he *would* still try to get out through O'Hare, even though, and especially because, it was not the logically expected thing to do. SENTINEL was doing what Centaur had thought it couldn't, slowing down and shifting mental gears to match the pattern established by him. This created a great many more possibilities, which SENTINEL considered with *slow* deliberation. It was learning to play Centaur's game.

Meanwhile, in New York, Justin and Fanning sat sipping beers after chasing their last false lead. They were quickly running out of ideas.

"Where do we go from here?" Justin asked wearily.

"Beats the shit outta me," Fanning replied, nursing the beer.

"He might not even be in New York," Justin said. "Maybe he's somewhere in Jersey and intends coming over on Tuesday for his contact."

"Even if he is here, how the fuck are we supposed to find him? He's not in the safe houses we've got staked out. Maybe our only chance is going to be to trail the contact and hope that a meeting is scheduled and that he's not going to dead-drop the film."

"If he has film," Justin added.

Fanning shook his head. "I don't know, I'm out of answers."

The men sipped their beers in silence, their brains working, as they unconsciously watched the televised Knicks game above the bar.

"It would be easy if he just showed up at McSorley's again," Fanning said, shaking his head.

"McSorley's?" Justin asked.

"Yeah, the one time I almost got a chance at him was right here, in New York. He was sighted in McSorley's."

"I thought you said that you never got another chance at him?" Justin said.

"That's right, I never did. But I *almost* did one time. He was spotted in McSorley's, eating and downing some beers. Never got near him, though. He left long before I got there and lost the tail on him. Being in the same city was as close as I've ever gotten to him," he explained.

"Well, you're that close again. And maybe McSorley's wouldn't be a bad place to visit. He might be a creature of habit. If he doesn't show, we'll at least get to eat a great turkey sandwich. You haven't had a turkey sandwich until you've had one there," Justin said.

It didn't take much to convince them to go to McSorley's. They were tired and hungry, and the beers and sandwiches were too tempting to resist. Besides, it was a lead to follow. They finished their beers and left.

McSorley's is a popular Lower East Side pub, famous for its turkey sandwiches and ale. The ale is usually ordered by the mug two or three at a time, as the crowds usually make waiting for single mugs a long and dry experience.

They were fortunate to find an empty table right near the entrance in the front room as they walked in. Business was jumping, and few spots were available, even at the bar.

Justin sat with his back to the never-used fireplace, where he could see the front entrance and the large archway that led to the back room. He could eye all traffic from his spot.

The back room was packed, every table occupied and covered with mugs. The din was just below a roar, filled with laughter, cursing, and songs. The place was a piece of old Ireland in the new world. All the bartenders and table waiters were heavily accented Irishmen. The waiters weaved through the thick crowd, their large trays heavy with beer and sandwiches.

Justin had come here on countless Friday nights as a student with the fraternity. Friday was always the guys' night out, and a special significance was added to the fact that it was still a men-only spot in those days. It always felt good to come back.

They had been sitting for only a few moments when a waiter came to the table. "Yes, gentlemen. What'll ya have?" he said in his high Irish voice.

"You like dark ale?" Justin asked his partner.

Fanning nodded.

"Bring us three each and a couple of turkey sandwiches. Double onion on mine," Justin said.

The waiter nodded and rushed off, shouting the request for the dark ales to one of the bartenders, and walking back to the kitchen to put in the order for the sandwiches.

They sat for a while, not saying anything. Both men were filled with a mounting tension. Every hour that passed was one closer to contact.

The ales were brought to the table. The sandwiches would be a little longer. Justin picked up one of the mugs and downed it thirstily. Fanning did the same, with a consummate delight.

"We used to come here a lot when I was in college," Justin said. "We'd take two whole tables," he said, pointing to the large round ones in the back room. "Cover the whole table with empty mugs in a half hour, then let them take the empties away. Then we'd start all over again. Spent a lot of good hours in this place," he reminisced with a smile.

"Where's the pisser?" Fanning asked.

Justin pointed. "Straight in the back."

Fanning took a long pull on the second cold ale, then got up from the table. He walked around Justin's chair and headed for the back room.

A second later he returned.

"That was fast," Justin said. But the smile left Justin's face when he saw the look in Ted's eyes.

"He's here," Fanning said as he slid into the chair beside Justin.

"Ten Braak?" Justin asked in a low voice.

Fanning nodded.

"Are you sure?"

The look in Fanning's eyes required no answer. Justin knew immediately that he was.

That strange look had come back to Fanning's face. He began to reach for his magnum, but Justin's hand stopped him.

"Not here. Where is he?"

"In the back. Corner table to the right of the bathroom," he answered.

"Did he see you?" Justin asked.

"No, I don't think so," Fanning said.

Justin leaned out slightly and fixed his cold eyes on the figure at the table in the corner. It was Ten Braak, all right. He was destroying a turkey sandwich with a savage gusto. The table was covered with half a dozen empty beer mugs.

"We gotta get out of here," Justin said.

"Take him in the street?" asked Fanning.

"No. We have to follow him back to where he's staying. If he has the film, that's the only way we can be sure of getting it," he said.

"I think we should take him as soon as he steps out. From two sides. We can get him clean that way," Fanning said.

"Outside. We can talk about it out there. Let's get out of here before he gets a look at you."

The two men stood up. Justin dropped a twenty on the table.

"I can take him right now," Fanning said. "He'll never see it coming."

"Outside," Justin said.

"We got him in here. Out there he's got a chance."

"Outside," Justin repeated, giving his partner a gentle push toward the door.

The two men filed toward the door, Justin keeping himself close to Fanning and at his back. He gave a quick look back, as he passed through the door and out onto the street behind Fanning.

Ten Braak was still occupied with his sandwich.

As the door banged shut, Ten Braak's dark eyes focused on it. A short smile came to his face. He finished his sandwich and took his time over the two mugs of ale still before him. He hadn't missed a thing.

"You get to the car," Justin said. "If he walks, I'll follow him. You bring the car up later. If he cabs it, you shoot up here, and we'll stay with the cab." Justin didn't want Fanning too close to Ten Braak yet. Getting the film was the most important thing in his mind. There was no guarantee that it was on him.

"I think we're making a big mistake," Fanning said. "He's going to have some defense set up at his place. He'll be a hundred times tougher there."

"We'll get him. But we're not trying this alone," Justin said. "If we don't get to that film we'll blow this whole thing."

"I still don't like it," Fanning said.

"Neither do I, but that's the way it's gonna go down."

Justin and Fanning walked up the block.

BLEEP! Justin signaled SENTINEL through his implant.

"Yes, Pilgrim," the soft reply came.

"Alert the other teams. We've spotted him. We'll follow him to his safe house, then we'll take him. I want constant communications between everybody," he said.

"Working."

Justin positioned himself well up the block and out of sight. Fanning went to the car and started it up.

Fanning reached under the passenger's seat and pulled out a narrow, black carrying case. He put it across his lap and stroked the case softly. The nervousness began to build in him. All the waiting was now coming to an end. The weight of the case and the feel of it comforted him. It held the equalizer—the "Runt."

He drew power from the feel of it, knowing that it was there. Each stroke of his hand gave him added confidence.

Ten Braak finished his last ale and paid the waiter. He had to take a leak but didn't dare go into the bathroom. It could be a death trap if they were to catch him in there.

He rose, walked to the door, and stepped out into the cool night air. His eyes scanned the street. He couldn't see them, but he knew they were there. He could feel them.

He turned and walked away from Justin's concealed position, toward Third Avenue.

Justin followed from a safe distance behind. He kept in constant voice communication with Fanning and the other SENTINEL teams.

Ten Braak walked directly back to the Paradise. Justin stood on the street below, in the shadows.

Once through the lobby and up the first flight of stairs, Ten Braak sprinted up the remaining five flights of stairs with surprising speed and ease. He stepped into the dark room and went to his black salesman's case. He pulled out a pair of small binoculars and walked to the window overlooking Third Avenue.

He stood just back from the window, so that he couldn't be seen but close enough to see the opposite side of the street below. He scanned the area slowly, looking for the tall figure that had tailed him. He saw nothing at first through the binoculars as he breathed heavily.

Then the Impala came up Third Avenue and turned the corner as he looked down. It stopped after turning off Third Avenue. The tall figure moved out of the shadows to the car.

Ten Braak focused on the car, observing it carefully, and checked the registration tags, just before the lights went out.

Fanning slid over and rolled down the window. Justin stepped up to the car.

"Park it up the block. He's in the Hotel Paradise," he said.

Fanning slid back to the driver's seat, moved slowly up the block with the lights out, and parked the car.

Moving back into the shadows, Justin advised the three SENTINEL teams of their location and watched the building for signs of a light in a window.

Ten Braak waited a few moments longer, then moved for the light switch and flicked it on. The room flooded with light from the ancient overhead fixture. The remaining lamps had been turned off before he left the room.

Justin's eyes snapped to the sixth-floor corner room. A few moments later Fanning joined him, carrying the case in one hand and a large-faced flashlight in the other.

"Sixth floor, corner," Justin said, pointing to the lighted windows from the shadows.

The two men stared up.

Ten Braak showed himself briefly at the window to draw the shades and curtains. It was only long enough to give them a quick look at him. He was careful not to become a target against the light.

"That's it," Justin said. "Now we wait for the other teams and for Ten Braak to bed down for the night."

The time passed slowly for Fanning. He held the case close against his side.

"What's in the case?" Justin asked.

Fanning stared into the eyes of his partner. "Insurance," he replied. The two men fell silent and waited, preparing.

Ten Braak moved to the light switch and snapped it off. He went quickly to the boxes and began removing the industrial bulbs. He changed all the bulbs in the lamps and the large overhead fixture. Then he set the timer to seven seconds and made sure all the lamps were set to go on. He took one last look around the room, then opened the door, raising the heavy spring in the flat relay on the door jamb. He turned on the light switch and closed the door carefully, making sure the relay switch was in the open position, held in place by the door. When the door was opened, the relay switch would snap back and make contact, starting the timer and the countdown to hell.

He sprinted down the hallway to the back stairway and down the stairs to the basement. A few moments later he was out the service exit and had climbed through a basement window in the adjacent building.

He made his way quickly through the building, came out to the street on the next block, and went to the parked VW. He started it up and made his way away from Third Avenue in reverse, going the wrong way up the oneway street. Then he drove the VW a few blocks up, crossed Third Avenue again, and parked the car on Second Avenue.

Justin sat, watching the windows. From his position he could see the entire front entrance and the alleyway leading out to the side street.

Two hours passed before he gave the instructions to move into position. Six agents had come to their assistance.

One agent joined Justin and Fanning. He carried a lightweight rifle equipped with an infrared telescopic sight. He would cover the fire escape, in case Ten Braak tried for it through the window. He could also cover the front.

Two other agents positioned themselves at diagonally opposite corners of the building, to cover all four sides, should he try for the streets.

The fourth agent had made his way to the roof of a higher building just across the street. He carried a lightweight rifle similar to the one the man on the street below had. Both were low-caliber automatic weapons with explosive .22 long-rifle loads, enough to stop any man cold in his tracks. From the higher vantage point, the fourth agent could cover the roof, should Ten Braak try for it.

The remaining two agents accompanied Justin and Fanning into the building.

The group moved silently up the stairs. One man remained on the fifth floor, the other went ahead up to the seventh. They would stop Ten Braak from going up or down, should he get past Justin and Fanning.

Fanning opened up the case he had carried in with him. Justin watched him as he produced a sawed-off, double-barreled shotgun, loaded it, and strapped the flashlight to the top of it.

"I'm going in for him," Fanning said.

Justin looked into the anxious gray eyes. There was no way he could convince him otherwise. He knew it. He just nodded.

They both knew that Ten Braak wouldn't be taken alive. There was no need for it anymore. They knew where he was staying now.

The two men moved in slow silence down the hallway.

Justin would position himself in the hallway, to give Fanning as much cover as possible.

Fanning positioned himself in front of the door. His finger was on the trigger of the "Runt," and the thumb of his left hand was on the switch to the flashlight.

Justin drew his Mauser and took a firing position.

They were ready.

Fanning's knees were shaking. He couldn't stop them. He felt like he wanted to puke. He could never remember being so nervous. But he knew it would all vanish the second he kicked the door in.

Fanning looked at Justin. Justin contracted his eustachian tubes, the BLEEP signaling the other agents that they were going in. He nodded to his friend. Fanning's moment had come to repay the old debt.

Fanning looked back at the door and took a deep breath. In the same movement, he flicked on the flashlight and gave the door a straight, thrusting kick. It splintered open.

The spring snapped on the relay.

Fanning burst through the opening into the room, the beam from the flashlight directly on the bed.

It was empty.

He crouched low and swung the light quickly across the room. Justin's Mauser was raised at the closed bathroom door.

The sweep second hand moved.

In an instant, Fanning realized that the only place Ten Braak could be was in the bathroom. He moved to the center of the room.

The timer hit zero.

The overhead lights went on, with all the lamps being simultaneously lit.

There was only the tiniest fraction of a second, but it was enough for Fanning to know that he had lost again.

The large bulbs in the fixture above him exploded downward, the lamps blowing inward at the same time. In that one instant he was enveloped in hell's own incendiary fury.

Fanning became a mass of flame as the entire room exploded in at him.

The shock wave from the whoosh knocked Justin backward against the hallway wall.

For a moment Fanning just stood there, a silent, burning torch. He staggered a few steps forward, one arm waving, as if to bat the flames away. He moved in a short semicircle, then fell across the bed.

Justin watched the flaming figure as it moved stiffly forward before falling, then all was lost in the sea of flame.

"Leave the building immediately," SENTINEL's urgent voice commanded.

Justin stood in shocked disbelief. His partner, his friend. There were several muffled explosions; the shells and the implant.

"Leave at once," came the repeated command.

Justin gained control of himself and ran for the stairs.

The three agents dashed madly down the flight of stairs and from the building.

Justin moved in a daze. It couldn't be real. This wasn't really happening. Ted was in there.

He turned in the street and looked up at the flames, as they began to consume the floor above and spread as though moving through a field of dry brush. He looked at the front door, almost waiting for Fanning to come racing out, but he was a part of that hell, beyond all help from the instant it had happened.

Justin vomited in the street.

"Leave the area, immediately," came the command from SENTINEL.

But Justin was frozen.

"Leave the area, immediately," SENTINEL repeated. He could be nothing less than useless until the shock of what had happened was past. SENTINEL knew this.

"You are to leave the city immediately," the voice commanded. "Go to your home until further orders are given. Now. NOW," SENTINEL commanded.

Still in his daze, Justin did as he was told, like an obedient child. He went to the car and got into it. Started the engine and pulled away, leaving it all behind him. Leaving Fanning in that hell.

The car pulled out onto Second Avenue and moved away from the scene. It turned and headed across town, then back uptown for the Lincoln Tunnel.

He never even looked in the rearview mirror at the beat-up Volkswagen that followed him at a distance.

Pilgrim had gone from hunter to hunted. There was another installment of hell yet to be delivered. And Otto Ten Braak was its postman.

THIRTY

We came to a period in Operation Raptor where our hopes had begun to droop severely. Things had not progressed well beyond the first stage of the plan. We had hoped to be at stage three by that point in time.

But Colorosa absolutely astounded us with his discovery and his resultant plan. He held our attention completely.

We found ourselves suddenly sitting on the brink of stage five. The hundred-year plan created by the Niederlage special branch could have been reduced to forty by Colorosa's brilliant work. We were suddenly at the threshold of our ultimate success. But we would not rush blindly ahead again. After our mistakes in the past, patience was to be our steadfast rule.

Entry No. 59 from the partially
recovered *Wolf Journal*

What does a man think and feel when he watches a friend die? Especially when the man was one he had so greatly admired, who had served as his mentor, partner, and friend, and whom he had thought of as indestructible. And not only to watch him die—but to see him taken so easily, so brutally, and so quickly.

Ten Braak had handled them like dumb ants. It struck fear into Justin, the same fear Fanning had felt.

They had about as much chance of finding him now as a fart had in a windstorm. Ten Braak would never make the contact. He was gone. And Justin didn't care. It was over for him. He was out of it.

Justin's brain and stomach were twisting. He wanted to get home to his bed, to hide beneath the covers and let the windchimes carry him away to peace and safety and sleep. He needed their protection now more than ever before in his life.

But there were no windchimes. There was only the reality of what had happened. And the fear.

For the first time in his life, Justin realized why he never looked back. It was fear. Fear that someone or something was gaining on him. And he didn't look back this time, either. If he had, he would have seen death behind him, coming for him, closing the distance between them.

It took about twenty minutes to reach the apartment complex. The Impala coasted into the parking lot behind his building. Justin shut it down and sat in the darkness.

He wondered how long Fanning had lived, how much primary pain he had felt before the nerves were destroyed. He wondered if Ted even knew what had happened.

Justin felt the need for a drink. A stiff one.

The door of the Impala opened, and the tall slender figure slid out. He walked around to the front of the building.

The dark eyes watched from the shadow, as Justin climbed the outside stairs to his second-floor corner apartment. The eyes observed that the apartments below and next to his were vacant. There would be no one to hear.

Justin entered the apartment, put on the lights, and walked across the spacious living room to the built-in bar. He took out a glass and a bottle of Scotch, filled the glass, and raised it to his lips. The glass went down again. He didn't want the drink anymore.

What he really needed was a cup of piping hot tea and a hot shower. Then maybe a week's sleep. He went into the kitchen and put on the water.

A few moments later he was in the bedroom, removing his pit holster. He put the Mauser on the night table beside the bed and fingered one of the nipples on the large, yellow glass ashtray beside the weapon. It had been a gag gift from Barbara. It was his conversation piece. There were four sets of large breasts with big pink nipples at each of the corners. It was a clever piece of design, and he treasured it.

The steam kettle began to whistle. He went back to the kitchen, took out his large thermal cup, put a tea bag into it, and poured in the piping water.

After a sufficient number of dunks, he pressed the tea bag against a spoon and put in a touch of sugar. He turned out the lights in the kitchen and living room and went into the bedroom.

Ten Braak saw the lights go out, then raced to the back of the building. He looked up at Justin's lighted bedroom windows.

There were two smaller windows, obviously to the bathrooms. The slight glow in one told him that it was off the bedroom. That light then went on.

The window was open slightly, and Ten Braak could hear the water in the tub go on. Then he saw the shadow appear back in the bedroom again.

Justin had placed the tea on the high dresser top next to the bathroom door. It was much too hot to drink and would still be piping when he finished his shower.

Ten Braak watched, as the shadow moved back into the bathroom. He heard the shower engage, as the drawing of the shower curtain threw a blue cast to the window. He could see the shadow in the shower.

Now was his chance.

With his surprising quickness, he went to the front of the building and up the stairs to Justin's door. It took only seconds to pick the lock. He stepped in.

The sounds of the shower covered his own, as he closed the door and walked to the lighted bedroom.

He went in and quickly scanned the room for weapons. He spotted the Mauser.

Ten Braak went to it and removed it from the holster. He snapped out the magazine clip and pulled back the slide, ejecting the round in the chamber. He put it back in the holster.

What he had in mind was more his style. He pulled out a garrote.

This wasn't an ordinary garrote with a piece of piano wire strung between two handles. It had a modification distinctive of the Ten Braak touch. One wire had a slip-lock mechanism attached to it that automatically engaged when contacted by the second wire. This allowed tightening of the loop and then release of the handles. The wire could pass only one way through the mechanism, unless it were released by a half turn and an outward pull of the tiny lock ring.

This modification gave him the freedom to attack a second person as the first strangled helplessly.

A proper pull on the handles would cut deeply into the throat of the victim and reduce the loop to a diameter of about two inches. Unconsciousness would follow within six seconds. Not having to maintain the pressure of the pull allowed him more control over the struggling body. And if the touch were desirable, a second pull of equal force could bring about decapitation. But this was seldom needed.

He moved to the closed bathroom door and turned the knob enough to push the door in ever so slightly. This would allow a quick push with the foot, to swing the door open as he moved in with the garrote. It would be over in less than fifteen seconds.

Ten Braak waited.

Several minutes later, the shower went off. He poised himself.

Justin dried quickly in the tub, then stepped out for a more thorough drying. The room was steam-filled and the mirror fogged over. He stood with his back to the door.

Perhaps it was instinct, that extra sense for survival, or just quick reaction to the cooler air rushing in as the door flew open, but he managed to get his left hand up as the wire loop came over his head.

In an instant, the garrote went tight. The wire crossed the palm of his hand, pulling it hard against his throat. His hand prevented the wire from biting deeply into his neck, but it cut sharply into the hand, as Ten Braak jerked and pulled him backward, in an attempt to gain leverage.

Justin's first instinct was to resist the force by pulling away, but he overcame the urge and moved forcefully into his attacker to reduce the advantage. The leverage was reduced enough to prevent Ten Braak from making a second pull, keeping the garrote from its fatal duty.

Ten Braak began to drag Justin out of the confining bathroom to the bedroom, where he could get the necessary leverage to drive the wire through the hand and into the neck.

On his way through the doorway, Justin's free right arm shot out sideways. His hand grasped the thermal mug and sent the scalding contents over his shoulder. The hot tea hit Ten Braak squarely in the eyes.

There was a muffled cry, and the grip loosened as his hands went instinctively to his face. At the same instant Justin let go a vicious backward kick that caught the attacker in the groin, knocking him over.

Justin turned to face the adversary. The sight of Ten Braak did not surprise him, nor did he feel fear. The fear was past him. The initial contact had already been made. The rest was automatic. It was survival.

With the agility of a tumbler, Ten Braak rolled through his fall and came up on his feet. In the next instant he was charging at Justin like a bull.

The tea and the kick would have been enough to stop any other man. But Ten Braak came.

Justin's left hand had been effectively pinned to his throat. He knew he had to keep Ten Braak away from the handles. It would take legs.

Before Justin could deliver one of his kicks, Ten Braak was in on him. The stubby, steellike hands threw vicious, ravaging blows, which landed heavily and punishingly on Justin's body. With his left hand pinned, Justin couldn't stop them.

The hot tea had badly damaged Ten Braak's eyes and burned his face. He couldn't see the death spots, but made up for his lack of accuracy with the quantity and force of blows.

Justin managed to get a knee up, to get some working distance between them, but not before he felt the ribs on his left side crack from the savage blows. He thrust a straight arm at Ten Braak's face, the heel of the palm striking squarely to the tip of the nose. It jarred him backward.

These men were skilled at killing and disabling with hands. They seldom threw fists, and never at the jaw. More fingers and hands get broken and wrists get sprained against hard jaws than knockout punches get thrown. A vicious upward palm-thrust to the jaw is far more damaging to the opponent. To the nose is even better; it is a disabling blow that can kill if delivered properly.

Justin had once more gained distance.

Ten Braak's vision became even more obstructed from the nose blow. Both men were now gravely disadvantaged. Either one would have been easy prey, were the other not equally affected.

Ten Braak charged again.

Justin's right leg shot upward in a vicious arc, hitting home. Ten Braak went down, but bounced up instantly.

His ability to absorb punishment was beyond Justin's comprehension. He came again.

The right leg shot out again, glancing off the hard muscular shoulder.

A violent blow hit against Justin's pinned forearm, nearly breaking it. It knocked Justin backward, again giving him needed distance.

He threw the left leg this time, whipping his free right arm to generate maximum force. It hit home again. Ten Braak was jarred.

Justin followed with another right, but Ten Braak caught it, after absorbing the force against his ribs. He held the leg tightly and moved backward, pulling Justin with him, Justin hopping to keep his balance.

Ten Braak threw a vicious forearm into Justin's knee and kicked his supporting leg out from under him. Justin went down hard, with Ten Braak on top of him.

Ten Braak threw finger slashes at the eyes, but his inability to see once again saved Justin. The first blow hit his eyebrow, tearing a gash above his left eye. The second glanced harmlessly off his forehead.

The force of the missed blow brought Ten Braak forward and low. Justin used the moment to score an eye strike of his own. His index finger went deeply into Ten Braak's left eye. At the same moment, Justin kicked violently to get himself free. He scrambled up and dove for the Mauser.

He hit the night stand with enough force to topple it, sending the lamp crashing against the wall and the ashtray flying through the air.

The Mauser was useless. He threw it, hitting Ten Braak in the chest, but it had no effect.

Ten Braak came in again, throwing more ravaging body blows, coming up occasionally for an eye slash. He was hitting, but not the eyes.

Justin went down from the brutal force being delivered against him. He threw one more sweeping left kick, which cut the legs out from under Ten Braak. Justin scrambled painfully away.

There is only so much that the human body can take before it stops functioning. Justin was nearing that point. But so was Ten Braak.

Justin threw another vicious kick, which caught Ten Braak across the forehead. He went down with a different hardness than before and rolled to his stomach.

In an instant Justin was on him. His instincts told him to stay behind Ten Braak so he couldn't be hit effectively from the ground.

Justin's free hand flashed out again at the burned and peeling face, scoring the right eye. He drove it again and again.

Ten Braak no longer had eyes. But he would not die. He knew his only hope was in getting those handles. He had to get Justin off his back and in front of him. He raised his rump as though to buck him off.

But again Justin's instincts took over. His sense of body position and balance was acutely developed. As soon as Ten Braak's rump came up, Justin's long legs shot around the waist and locked in a viselike figure four. He extended his upper body fully forward while arching his back. The leverage was incredible.

It forced Ten Braak's chest and face hard against the floor. The crushing pressure on his waist forced him to urinate and move his bowels uncontrollably.

The nearest thing to Justin's reach was the heavy, yellow ashtray. He picked it up and began a savage pounding at Ten Braak's head. He struck and struck, over and over and over, until he could no longer raise his arm. His exhaustion was complete, all energy spent. And Ten Braak was dead.

He unlocked his legs and rolled off the body, kicking Ten Braak's lifeless form away. He lay on his back, sucking in air.

His right hand felt along the garrote, until it came to the slip lock. A moment later it was released. He pulled the wire painfully out of the deep cut across his hand.

He began to retch from the exhaustion and the near strangulation and dryness in his throat.

Everything began to close in on him. Little streaking stars formed before his eyes, as a swirling black pool began to engulf him.

He lost all sensation of pain and sense of time. He fell deeper and deeper into the darkness in a graceful slow motion, tumbling downward into the void.

And then they began.

The windchimes.

They had come to protect him, to sing him gently to sleep with their soft tinkling music.

They always came when he needed them. He was safe now. He could sleep.

THIRTY-ONE

Colorosa's brilliant plan went into effect. His words fell on disbelieving ears when he said it would cost us nothing but time. But we had learned to trust his judgment and to believe in him.

There was no doubt in my mind that Colorosa was the man of the future for the plan. Everything about him was right.

He made good on all of his promises.

We were all saddened by the death of Titus in Spain. It was sudden and unexpected. His health had been excellent.

A new Titus was appointed. I did not trust him.

Entry No. 60 from the partially
recovered *Wolf Journal*

SENTINEL had continued its monitoring of Justin's implant from the time he left the scene of Ten Braak's trap. The second that the attack had started, it dispatched the nearest teams to Justin's assistance. It had also dispatched the Division Two team on standby in New York and a medical unit.

The first team to arrive came smashing through the door barely fifteen minutes after the struggle had begun. They had been advised that Justin had survived the attack, but was badly hurt. They came in ready for Ten Braak, too, just in case he hadn't been stopped. The second they entered the bedroom, all questions regarding Ten Braak were answered.

"Holy Christ," the team leader said when he saw the room. He went immediately to Ten Braak's body. "Look at that fuckin' mess."

There was no doubt about it, Ten Braak was as dead as he could get. His head was smashed in on the right side like a crushed watermelon. Brain matter was visible through the crushed skull. There were two bloody holes where his eyes had been, and his face looked like it had been hit by a steel mallet from Justin's devastating kicks.

Justin was unconscious on the floor near the foot of the bed. His face, neck, and chest were smeared with blood from the gash over the eye and the hand cut. He had bruises all over the body from Ten Braak's savage blows, and his upper forehead and face had several lacerations from the missed eye strikes.

The second agent brought in a damp towel from the bathroom and began wiping Justin's face.

Justin winced slightly and opened a puffy eye.

"You had some party here, my friend," the agent said.

Justin nodded weakly.

It was obvious what had saved his life. From the cut across the palm and the blood on Justin's body, it was easy to see where his hand had been.

Pilgrim had not only had the disadvantage of being surprised, but had had only one arm to use. He had no clothing on to absorb or slide away the blows, either. And he had still beaten Ten Braak to a bloody pulp. It said a lot for the man lying on the floor before them.

A second team arrived, followed shortly by Division Two and the medical unit.

Justin's wounds were temporarily packed, and he was rushed out to the mobile unit, which was virtually a small hospital on wheels. The minor facial wounds were closed as they moved him to a private facility not too far away. He was given an injection to make him sleep.

Every inch of him hurt from the battering he had taken. The drug began to take its effect, as a jumbled picture played in his head. He saw Fanning standing in the flames, Ten Braak's relentless charges, the surprising speed and strength of the fat little man, the blood, the pain, the fear...and the windchimes.

They had begun in his head again. He wondered where they were coming from. It didn't really matter. They were there, and that's all that counted. They were soothing him, wrapping him in their protection. Nothing could penetrate them now. He welcomed them and let them carry him into sleep. Their soft tinkling music swept him gently away.

SENTINEL knew that Justin would sleep as long as the windchimes sounded. It coaxed him into a peaceful, forgetful rest.

Irwin Honeycut was up early at Alpha. He was reviewing Division Two's report with Elizabeth Ryerson in the situation room of the complex.

Honeycut worked methodically through the reports, despite his being upset over losing Badger. Agents of Fanning's skill and loyalty weren't easy to come by. But that was over now. There was no going back.

"Division Two found Ten Braak's film copy, just as SENTINEL had projected," Honeycut said. "It was found in a metallic cylinder in the excrement that was released during the struggle. All twenty-four schematics were on it."

"Nothing regarding the missing page?" Elizabeth asked.

"No," Honeycut replied. "There was no trace of it on the film."

SENTINEL had sent a Division Two team into Bridges's apartment. They had found no evidence to indicate that Justin had found anything in his search. They did find what they were after, though. The ribbon had been removed from Bridges's typewriter and scanned by SENTINEL. It learned exactly what had been typed on the sheet.

"Do you think that Pilgrim found it at Ed's place?" she asked.

Honeycut thought for a few moments before answering. "No," he said. "I don't think that he did. Even if I'm wrong, he wouldn't know what it meant, without seeing the whole file."

"Unless he gets his hands on that journal," Elizabeth said.

Honeycut frowned deeply. That journal still hadn't been found. The twenty-fifth page would mean a lot with that information thrown in. "Well, he doesn't have that. We're sure of that much," Honeycut said. "Phoenix is our immediate concern now. That journal will have to wait."

SENTINEL had made tremendous progress with regard to Phoenix. Its estimated probability for success in catching him was now ninety-five percent.

Phoenix's pattern of being where he was least expected gave strong argument to SENTINEL's projection. Other alternatives were being considered, but SENTINEL's bet was on Wednesday's flight to Paris.

Every available agent had been dispatched to O'Hare, and three had even been booked on the flight. They would not attempt to take him at O'Hare. They didn't want to chance his getting away or dropping the film where it could later be retrieved by other Soviet agents. On the plane he'd have nowhere to go, they would control all factors after it was airbound. SENTINEL had already prepared a plan.

"We're going to make it out of this okay," Elizabeth said with confidence.

"I think we might," Honeycut said. "But I'll put that in the bank when we have Phoenix and that film in our hands."

Wednesday came to Chicago, and SENTINEL was ready. Agents had been assigned to watch every ticket counter from the glass-enclosed overhead walkways. They held stopwatches and check sheets, as though conducting time-efficiency studies, a common practice at O'Hare.

Extra agents had been placed at the TWA ticketing counters, as Caneway had been booked on TWA Flight 802, departing at 4:35 p.m., nonstop for Paris.

Terminal entrances and security checkpoints were also being watched. Anyone spotting Phoenix would signal via eustachian implant tone.

The taxi pulled up in front of the TWA sliding doors. Alexi Kuradin sat in the back seat, confident that his disguise would pass. He was certain they would never expect him to show up for this flight, even if Awadi's body had been found.

The cab stopped at the curb, and the driver came around to the passenger's door. He signaled to a skycap before opening the door.

Kuradin reached out, the cabby gently taking his arm to help him out. The skycap walked up to lend assistance.

"Thank you very much," Kuradin said softly.

"You're welcome, sister," the cabby said to the old nun standing before him.

"Will you need a wheelchair?"

A disguise was to be expected, but no one looked twice at the nun. Kuradin's appearance had changed completely. He looked two inches shorter and fifty pounds heavier. His eyes were now dark brown and his hands were covered with black knit gloves. The missing left pinky was accounted for with a cleverly shaped stuffing. The small digit looked as though it were daintily bent.

It seemed like an eternity to Kuradin, as he was wheeled through security to the gate area. But even in slow motion time passes, and he made it through their watch undetected.

The wait for boarding to begin was almost unbearable. He continually threw short glances across the gate area over the top of his *Catholic Digest* magazine, looking for observing eyes.

At last the announcement was made, and within moments Kuradin was being wheeled on board the roomy 747. He had specified a window seat over the left wing, to enable him to hide the finger between himself and the cabin wall. He would not eat the in-flight meal, so he could keep the glove on at all times. To attempt to eat the meal could reveal the missing digit. To try to eat it with the gloves on would seem strange. He was taking no chances.

Kuradin continued to pretend to read his magazine, watching the faces of the boarding passengers. He was still safe. Every second that passed made him feel more secure. He was going to make it.

Within twenty minutes the boarding was completed. The doors on the big plane were closed, and it was backed away from the dock.

Roger Caneway had not checked in for the flight. But this was not disturbing to SENTINEL. It was not expected that he would board as Roger Caneway. SENTINEL expected a disguise but as yet had not found him.

SENTINEL ran through the entire list of passengers beforehand, and all had checked out. This was also expected, Phoenix had covered all bases quite well up to this point. There was no reason to expect less from him now.

Thirty minutes later, the plane roared off the runway and lifted gracefully into the sky. Alexi Kuradin let out a relieved sigh, as the ground disappeared below the fluffy white clouds. Paris was about eight and a half hours away. Once down in Paris and off the plane, he'd be safe and well-protected. It would finally be over, and he could go home.

But Flight 802 would never reach Paris. SENTINEL's plan would soon go into operation. Phoenix was on that plane. SENTINEL was certain of it. Failure to recognize him did not alter SENTINEL's opinion, and Phoenix would be stopped—of that much, SENTINEL was sure.

Justin was up now and moving stiffly about the small room like a caged animal. Everything hurt. The pain from the three cracked ribs had been reduced by the tight binding. The knee was tender, where Ten Braak had hit it, and Justin's feet were sore from the savage barefoot kicks he had delivered to Ten Braak's face and head.

It had taken a total of fifty-four stitches to close Ten Braak's handiwork, most going into the badly cut left hand. Fortunately, most of the stitching had been done while he was still unconscious.

His head was clear now, and he remembered the windchimes again. He wondered if they had been in his head, or whether SENTINEL had played them for his benefit.

One of the disturbing things about the implant was that, after you grew used to it, it became difficult to distinguish thought from reception. It wasn't like actually hearing all the time. Usually, direct communication came across as sound, but there had been times when data was supplied which seemed more like thought than communication. He wondered how many thoughts had not really been his own, but had originated from that other intellect. It was a discomforting possibility. Was he programmable, responsive to signals believed to be his own thoughts? He didn't like it.

SENTINEL had updated Justin on the situation. He had been briefed on Division Two's findings in his apartment. SENTINEL had also filled him in on what had happened in Beloit and what it projected as Phoenix's plan. He had also been told about the Phoenix England connection.

BEEP! His implant sounded.

"How are you feeling, Pilgrim?" Honeycut's voice asked.

"Great," Justin responded. "I'm ready to get out of here. What's the situation?" he asked.

"Flight eight-oh-two is in the air. We haven't confirmed Phoenix as being on board, yet. But SENTINEL still projects that he is. We've put three agents on the plane to help make an identification," Honeycut told him.

"What now?" Justin asked.

"We'll be bringing the plane down in about ninety minutes," Honeycut said. "Do you feel well enough to travel?"

"I'll run all the way. Just point me in the right direction," Justin answered.

"I thought you'd want to be in on it," Honeycut said. "The plane will be coming down in Newark. The teams previously assigned to assist you in finding Ten Braak will be in on this with you. A car will be brought around to take you to the airport when you're ready."

"I'm ready now," Justin said.

"Not just yet, you're not," Honeycut said. "Dr. Waith wants to take another look at you first. He's the man who sewed you up."

"I'm really okay," Justin insisted.

"I'm sure you are. But let's let the doctor have the last word on that. You'll also be assigned a new partner to temporarily take Badger's place," Honeycut said.

A silence followed. Justin's mind flashed back to the incendiary trap Ten Braak had set. It again registered fresh in his mind what had happened to Fanning.

He remembered Fanning's words when they had first been teamed up. "Don't make friends in this business," he had been told. "It makes your job, and staying alive, a lot easier."

But a strong mutual respect had grown between them. It led to a friendship that neither man mentioned, but both had felt it. There would never be another Badger.

"After you've been checked out," Honeycut said, breaking him from his inner thoughts, "you'll go to Newark to take charge of the operation. It's important that Phoenix be taken alive. Is that clear?"

There was a short silence.

"Yes, sir," Justin answered. "We'll take him alive."

Justin normally would not have even been assigned to this job. But he had seen Phoenix close up and had gotten the best look at him. He had seen his eyes. A person can cover himself with makeup, but the eyes remain the same. The color can be changed with contacts, but the shape, movements, and language remained unchanged. Always.

"You'll be notified when it's okay to leave," Honeycut said. The transmission was ended.

A few moments later two men entered.

"I'm Dr. Waith," the taller one began, "and this is Rainmaker, your new partner."

Justin cast an assessing glance at the new man who was to be his partner. He was shorter than Fanning by about three inches. His hair and eyes were dark, the facial features round and soft. He looked like a gentle man, not someone in this line of business. But looks were deceiving. Ten Braak hadn't exactly looked like a terror, either.

"Pilgrim," Justin said, extending his hand.

"How do you do?" the shorter man said.

They locked hands in greeting. Still assessing.

Rainmaker matched the steellike grip of his new partner. He had been briefed on the events that started with the Spartan killing. He had a respect for Pilgrim. The cold, hard set of Justin's eyes made Rainmaker slightly uneasy. He knew what this man was capable of.

"I want to look at that hand before you leave," Waith said. "Is there much pain?"

"None," Justin lied.

Waith unwrapped the hand and looked at the stitched wound. "Had a devil of a time putting it back together again," he said. "Nasty wound. You'll have to take great care not to reinjure it, if you want full use of it again. I'll give you a shot for the pain. It might not hurt you now, but it will later," he said.

He prepared the injection and put it directly into the hand. Justin did his best to show no reaction.

"That'll last several hours. Take these when it begins to hurt again," he said, handing Justin a bottle of pink and gray capsules. "Take one every four hours or as needed. No drinking while you're on these," the physician warned.

Justin looked at the pills and put them into his pocket.

"Keep the hand in a closed position. And, for God's sake, don't do anything to reinjure it."

"You can count on it," Justin said.

The pain began to subside from the injection as Waith rebandaged the hand. When it was finished, Justin dressed in the clothes provided.

Rainmaker then handed Justin his Mauser and pit holster. The pit holster also caused discomfort as the Mauser nosed down onto the injured ribs. But it was bearable, and Justin said nothing.

Within a few minutes Justin was ready, and the team headed for Newark International Airport.

It was a quiet ride. Rainmaker threw several glances at his silent partner. He could read the face. Justin was getting ready, psyching himself up. There was a certain look of satisfaction across that face, as if he thrived on the moment.

Flight 802 was cruising smoothly along in calm airstreams. A good tail wind had them slightly ahead of schedule, despite the delayed takeoff. The big 747 was just heading out over the ocean, after passing over the East Coast, when the pilot's earphone crackled.

"TW eight-oh-two, this is Newark control. Acknowledge."

"Newark control, this is TW eight-oh-two. We read you," the captain answered.

"TW eight-oh-two, you have a squawk on six-two-one-six."

"Roger, Newark," the captain confirmed.

They adjusted to pick up 6216. A special message would be sent over that private frequency.

"TW eight-oh-two, ready for squawk," the captain said.

He took a sip of his coffee as the message began. His face tightened and grew suddenly stern. He finally swallowed and continued listening, his eyes narrowing with the words.

"Roger, Central. Thank you."

He turned slightly in his chair and cast a glance at his crew. "We've got a bomb on board," he announced.

Eyes flicked back and forth quickly. Nothing was said. Nothing had to be.

"We're putting down in Newark," the captain said. "They've been advised of the situation and will have everything ready. Tell the cabin crew to begin clearing for landing," he said to his copilot.

The copilot immediately got up from his seat and went aft.

They switched back to standard frequency.

"Newark control, this is TW eight-oh-two."

"We have you, eight-oh-two. Come right on one-eight-zero."

"Roger, coming right on one-eight-zero," the captain said. He began a slow banking turn.

The copilot returned to the cockpit. "It's a mess out there, John. They've got about half of the people eating."

"Take it away from them," the captain said. "We're on a countdown. There's going to be just enough time to get this thing down."

The copilot nodded and was about to go aft when a stewardess came in. There was a frightened look in her eyes.

"Clear for landing," the copilot said. "We've got time to make it down safely," he said. "But we have to go straight down."

"What do I tell the passengers?" she asked.

The copilot thought. "Tell them…tell them that one of the flight crew was badly injured in the galley," he quickly invented. "We're putting down to get assistance. Pass it around to the rest of the cabin crew," he said.

She nodded and disappeared.

The plane began a second slow turn, now moving in a north-westerly direction toward Newark. Their approach would leave just enough time to clear the cabin for landing.

Many of the passengers sensed that something was wrong with the first turn. They all knew after the second. The plane began dropping steadily.

A nervous murmur began to rise in the cabin. Passengers began to get out of their seats to ask the cabin crew what was going on.

Kuradin overheard another passenger tell some others what he had been told. One of the crew had been hurt seriously in the galley and needed immediate attention. A passenger who was a doctor was with her now, but it was necessary to put down immediately to get her to a hospital.

Kuradin wondered. Possible, he thought, but more likely his luck had just run out.

The plane had been descending steadily since the first turn. The rate of descent had become more acute since the second turn. The plane began dropping from the bright sunlight above to the dusk below. As the light faded, so did Kuradin's confidence.

"TW eight-oh-two, turn left on zero-seven-zero. Drop to three thousand, reduce to two-ten knots."

"Roger, Newark," the captain acknowledged.

"You will be following a United heavy jet," Newark control added.

"Thank you, Newark."

Kuradin began considering alternatives. He had none. He was helpless on that plane. SENTINEL had served an ace past him.

"TW eight-oh-two, hold one-eight-oh knots at least to the marker."

"Roger, Newark."

The SENTINEL agents were positioned in the front, center, and rear of the plane. They had been unable to make positive identification to this point.

"TW eight-oh-two, approaching on marker. You are second behind a heavy jet. Wind is zero-one-zero at twelve."

"Roger. Wind is zero-one-zero at twelve."

"Traffic behind has been diverted," Newark control added.

Kuradin watched, as the ground came up slowly. His nerves were stretching tight. Less than seven hours away—that's how close he had come. Stay cool, he coaxed himself. Stay cool and play out the role to the end. There was always a chance.

"TW eight-oh-two, you are clear to land. Proceed to extreme end of runway after touchdown."

"Roger, Newark. How are we on time?" the captain asked.

"Time is good, eight-oh-two."

The runway rushed up to meet the plane. It bounced down, then bounced again. They were on the ground.

The loud roar of the reversing engines filled the cabin. The tension was high in those passengers who didn't believe the story they had been told. Everyone was glad to be on the ground again.

"Eight-oh-two, proceed to extreme end of runway. Take last available right. You will see the buses. Bring the plane to a stop, and evacuate through all emergency exits."

"Roger, control," the captain said.

The plane taxied at a swift rate. The speed of their movement confused Kuradin slightly. Maybe something was wrong with the plane, he hoped weakly. When the plane turned away from the terminal he didn't know what to think.

"This is the captain speaking," came the voice over the intercom. "Please stay in your seats until the plane has come to a complete stop. Once we have stopped, move quickly and orderly to the emergency exits."

The sound in the plane rose sharply.

"There is no immediate cause for alarm," the captain continued, but the noise was too loud for his words to be heard.

"Please stay in order of your row and seat assignments, and follow the instructions of your flight crew."

The words were wasted. Bedlam had broken loose. Passengers were out of their seats already, racing for the emergency exits. The cabin was a scene of screaming disorder.

The plane continued its swift taxi to the buses, then braked sharply, throwing passengers to the floor and across seats and aisles.

The cabin crew had no success in keeping order, as the people jammed for the exits.

Emergency doors flew open. The exits not situated over the wings had inflatable slides, but the crush of people was so great that some of them were pushed out of the exits before the slides were completely inflated. It was a long fall, and people were injured.

The wings covered with scurrying people, the emergency slides were finally ready and people streamed down them, screaming and crying for their lives.

SENTINEL agents were positioned at every emergency exit, scanning the faces as they came.

Kuradin remained in his seat, surrounded by the screaming and madness. He considered making his way to the rear of the plane and out one of the opposite side exits, but he saw something that made him change his mind, a wheelchair—and Justin.

All hope quickly drained from him. He filled instantly and totally with fear. The battered appearance of Justin told him that his plan had worked. Pilgrim had confronted Ten Braak. But it was Pilgrim who had survived!

He nearly panicked. He knew he had to go out of the closest exit. The wheelchair was there for the old nun. They obviously knew where he had been seated and what exit he'd use. He had to stay in character to survive. It was the only chance.

He went limpingly for the exit, assisted by one of the stewardesses. He stepped onto the wing and immediately faked a fall. Two men were quick to assist him, as he slid down.

"It's okay, sister. We got ya," one of the men said above the hysterical cries of the other passengers.

A quick look at Justin told Centaur that they still hadn't identified him through his disguise. Justin's eyes continued to scan the faces of the other passengers.

Kuradin was lifted into the wheelchair and rushed to one of the waiting buses. He was helped aboard and took a window seat.

In a matter of moments, the plane had emptied. The crew was the last to deplane.

The SENTINEL agents had still come up empty. They joined the last of the passengers filing onto the buses. They would continue the search as the buses moved for the terminals. Justin got onto the second bus, the same one Kuradin was on.

In just moments the buses were full. They pulled away from the plane and raced for the terminal.

SENTINEL locked its laser batteries on the plane. When the buses were safely out of range, it fired.

The plane erupted into a tremendous orange ball as it exploded. The concussion shook the ground violently. The night sky was lit up, as though the sun had suddenly risen again.

The cries on the buses rose to a deafening level. Tears flowed, people hugged and kissed one another, and prayers were said aloud.

Emergency vehicles swarmed down upon the blazing wreck.

Justin moved down the jammed aisle of the bus, looking into the faces. For a brief instant Kuradin's eyes locked with Justin's, then looked quickly away. The fingers began to skim over the rosary beads, in make-believe prayer. But it was too late.

BLEEP! BLEEP!

Justin's eustachian implant signaled out the recognition sign. Two bleeps. Second bus.

He continued up the aisle, passing by Kuradin as though he hadn't seen him. He looked back at him once from behind where he was seated. Kuradin's head made a half turn, then quickly faced front again.

There was no question. They had him.

The buses screeched to a halt near the lower doors of the terminal, just below the gate area, and the windows jammed with the watchers.

People began to file out, sobbing and praying. They moved with a great deal more order than they had shown while leaving the plane. Kuradin limped heavily with his cane, moving with the flow of people. A hand gently took his arm.

He looked into the face with a start. He had never seen it before.

"This way, sister," a kind voice said. It was Rainmaker's voice. He had gotten the word from Justin. Rainmaker guided the Russian to the wheelchair.

He began to wheel the chair toward the dark underside of the terminal, to the stairway taking the stream of hysterical people.

Justin caught up from behind. Rainmaker let him take over the direction of the wheelchair. Kuradin could not see the man behind him.

It swung suddenly left and began moving away from the stairway. In the confusion, nobody noticed it. The chair began to move faster and faster. Kuradin gripped the arms of the chair tightly. It was moving at a running pace now. His eyes were wide with fear.

Ahead of them, a door opened, flanked on either side by men. There was only darkness behind the door.

Justin ran the wheelchair at full tilt right into the step in front of the door. Kuradin was thrown forward into the darkness, rolling, and sprawled along the floor.

Before he could right himself, he was jerked up to his feet with a violent tug and flung against a wall. He crashed heavily into it. An elbow caught the back of his head, as he bounced off, driving his face hard into the wall. His arms were yanked back and up, into a painful double hammerlock. He was forced to his toes from the pain, his face and chest hard against the wall.

In the next second, Rainmaker was frisking him, as Justin held his arms an inch away from snapping his shoulders out of joint.

"He's clean," Rainmaker announced.

Justin spun Kuradin around and glared menacingly into his eyes.

"How ya doin', sister?" Justin hissed at him, murder in his eyes. The Mauser was out and under Kuradin's chin. Blood trickled from the Russian's nose.

Justin ripped the habit from Kuradin's head. He nodded slowly, as his eyes burned holes in Kuradin's face.

"One move, one breath…just do it," Justin warned.

Kuradin knew that he meant it.

"I'll offer no resistance," Kuradin said calmly.

"That's too bad." Justin smiled.

The two locked eyes for several long moments. A lot passed between them unsaid: England, winning and losing, Fanning… and Otto Ten Braak.

"It's over, Phoenix. It's checkmate time. This is one you don't go home from," Justin said.

Checkmate time, Kuradin thought. Not exactly, my friend.

There was one contingency left. And Centaur still held the valuable tempo.

THIRTY-TWO

Colorosa's plan became a reality. We stood to control the most powerful potential the world had ever known.

There were no obstacles that could not be overcome in the United States now. Ten years at the most was the estimate. Then complete control. We were coming very close to being assured of our destiny.

My joy was unbounded.

My health also began to fail. Age had become my worst betrayer.

I fear I'll not see The Day.

Entry No. 68 from the partially
recovered *Wolf Journal*

Leonid Travkin sat in his office, untouched by the sunny warmth outside. The mood in his office was turbulent and dark, the heavy grayness hanging like a death veil, smothering all life and hope. Centaur had been captured.

Kuradin had made the first of his two checkpoints. Hope had begun to flood into Travkin's brain, only to evaporate swiftly with the news of what had happened to Flight 802 in America. The passenger count had been made falsely accurate, all persons accounted for, alive and well. Yet, Alexi Kuradin was missing, and Travkin knew why.

His head pounded. His fingers massaged his temples and rubbed his hot, aching eyes.

One hope was all that remained. It was down to that. The final contingency—provided Dmitri Chakhovsky didn't blow it all away with a shake of his head.

Travkin's stomach had evolved into a vicious knot during the past forty-eight hours, refusing to accept food or nourishment of any form. To make matters worse, his bowels had locked tight, adding to his increasing discomfort. That next rock-hard shit would drive him to tears, as it stretched his rectum painfully near to splitting, leaving the already troublesome hemorrhoids as bloody testimony to the power of those bowels to humble even the greatest of men. Life is filled with numerous little equalizers.

A knock sounded on Travkin's door.

"Come in," he growled.

Anatoly Krykov entered. A big, strong man with gentle, time-wisened eyes, Krykov was a highly respected member of the Individual Division. The Phoenix-leak situation had been handed to him personally by Travkin.

"Yes, General Travkin. You wanted to see me?" he asked, in his rich baritone.

Travkin looked past him with pursed lips and furrowed brow. He rose and stepped slowly to the windows behind his desk, looking out onto the melting snow. He stood for a long while.

Krykov waited patiently for Travkin to speak.

He turned to face the man standing tall and erect in front of his desk. "Has Melnik's contact been identified?" he asked. Ivan Melnik was the source of the leak. He had been a man of unquestioned loyalty. It was a painful surprise.

"Yes, General Travkin," Krykov answered sharply. "His name is Vytas Limpoulous. He is a Greek studying special communications in our own intelligence school," he answered, referring to the KGB training institute in Moscow.

"How long has he been undertaking these studies?" Travkin asked.

"For one year," Krykov responded.

One year. Travkin shook his head at the thought of this man being right under their noses for a full year, without their having even the slightest hint of his real purpose. He wondered how many more had been so well placed.

"I have ordered certain facts put into the Phoenix computer file that will interest this man, Limpoulous. Melnik has been keeping a close and careful watch on this file. When he learns these facts, he will try to make contact again. I want them both taken at that time," Travkin said.

"It is absolutely vital that Limpoulous be taken alive," he said, looking directly into Krykov's sharp eyes. "Alive—at all costs. Is that perfectly clear?" he asked.

"Yes, General," Krykov replied. "I will take eight of our best teams. He'll be taken alive, I promise," Krykov assured him.

"Remember, *alive—at all costs,*" Travkin repeated.

"Yes, General," Krykov assured him. He hated *at all cost* assignments. Too often the cost was unacceptable.

"Good. I am depending upon you," Travkin said.

"Thank you, General."

"Go now. There is much to be done—double surveillance on both Melnik and Limpoulous until they meet."

Krykov nodded and spun on his heel. He walked erectly toward the door. A moment later Travkin was alone in his office.

He sat heavily in his chair, letting out a long sigh. His stomach growled loudly, and he felt suddenly hungry.

A special emergency meeting had been called by the Central Committee, to discuss the possible alternatives that existed. There would be a painful silence as he told them the facts. But there would also be that tiny glimmer of hope, riding on the last phase of the plan.

He checked his watch. There was enough time to catch a quick lunch before the meeting. He felt a little better now. His hopes had begun to lift again. If he hurried his lunch, there would be enough time for a short walk in the warm sunshine.

Justin stood in front of the small window of the sterile laminar-air-flow room located in the depths of the Dials Cardiac Clinic on St. Simon's Island. He looked in at the meticulously gowned team attending Phoenix.

To Justin's right was Dr. Becker Dials. Wyatt stood to the left, also looking into the sterile environment.

"He has chronic lymphatic leukemia," Dials said. "We've confirmed this, with blood tests and bone-marrow samples taken from his sternum," he said.

"He had been in remission, until very recently. We guess that he began coming out of remission about three days ago. He came out very fast."

"Is he going to die?" Justin asked.

"He's in very bad shape, right now. As you can see, that nosebleed turned into a hemorrhage. We've packed the nose both behind and in front to prevent him from drowning."

"He looks terrible," Justin said.

"It happens rather quickly," Dials said. "He had been taking a remission-maintenance drug similar to one we use, called asparaginase. It's a modified form of ours, actually. A bit more effective. Most of these drugs become ineffective, though, as the body builds up a resistance to them. Then it's out of remission and more drugs."

"When can he be debriefed?" asked Wyatt.

Dials threw an incredulous look at him. "You never give up, do you? That man is dying in there. Maybe, if we can turn him around, you can talk to him. But you're not getting close to him until he's stable. I don't want any of your repeat performances with this one," Dials said acidly.

"Yes, well you keep him alive," Wyatt said. "That's your job. Mine is to get information out of him."

"When he's ready, not before."

"Listen, you," Wyatt shot out. "You don't know what the fuck is going on, or how important my talking to him is. He was carrying film that—"

"It's already been found," Dials said triumphantly. "Thanks to your young friend here," he said, thrusting a thumb in Justin's direction.

Wyatt and Justin gave him confused looks.

"That little elbow you used to coax his face into the wall—it opened a tiny wound on the back of his head."

"I remember the bleeding," Justin said.

"Yes, well we checked that out, too," Dials continued. "We found a small implant beneath the skin. Division Two opened it and found the microfilm."

"He's still got to be debriefed. Copies could have been made, and other people involved," Wyatt persisted. "He still could tell us something."

"Well, he's not going anywhere. When he's stable, you can talk to him all you want to," Dials said to him.

"What are his chances?" Wyatt asked.

"Short-term, pretty good. We're pumping him full of platelets and white cells. The bleeding is slowing down. As long as he doesn't reject the platelets, we should bring the hemorrhage under control. The white cells will help fight infection. That's also why he's in the laminar-air-flow room. We've put him on gut-suppression antibiotics, to reduce the possibility of infection from his own waste products. An infection of any kind could kill him."

"And when the bleeding stops?" Wyatt asked.

"We'll keep giving him the platelets and white cells for a little while and then start him on an advanced drug protocol, to try to get him into remission again.

"We've got a few new drugs to try on him. The first is one called D-eighty. It's dynamite on those leukemic cells, but most people have severe allergic reactions to it. We'll try to desensitize him, then put him on a program. The side effects of the drug will be hell, though. He'll be quite sick until he obtains remission. Then we can drop the levels back, to reduce the side effects, while still keeping his condition under control," Dials explained.

"And if he can't be desensitized?" asked Wyatt, concerned that he might never get to talk to the Russian.

"We'll try something else. You'll have time to talk to him once the bleeding stops, though. You can do it over that phone in his room, or we can install a sterilized speaker system, so that you can talk to him from outside of the room. We can install closed-circuit TV, too."

"And how long will he live if he goes into remission?" Wyatt asked.

Dials shrugged. "I would guess, with all things considered, that we might be able to get him into remission twice before his system just collapses under the strain. I'd say six months at the most."

Wyatt nodded and looked at the milk-white face of the Russian. The lips were black, with dark rings surrounding the eyes. The packing around the nose was blackened from the blood. The man looked like the image of death.

"If you really want to help, we can use your platelets," Dials said to the two men.

"What's his blood type?" Wyatt asked.

"It doesn't matter with platelets," Dials said. "Anyone can accept platelets from anyone else. We simply hook you up to a separator and separate the platelets, plasma, and white cells, returning the rich red cells to your body. You won't be weakened by it, and we can essentially take eight units of platelets from a single donor," Dials explained.

"Okay," Wyatt said. "Anything to keep him alive until I can talk to him."

"Good. And you?" Dials asked, looking into Justin's eyes.

Justin looked back into the room at Phoenix's pathetic form. He couldn't care less if the man died, as long as he was debriefed. "Yeah, okay. Count me in, too."

It was strange how, only a year ago, he had tried to kill the man he was now giving platelets to. He had come close to doing it in England. He would have done it again only the day before, if Honeycut hadn't told him to take Phoenix alive. That was one man Justin felt destined to kill, and here he was helping to save his life.

But Honeycut had been right. It was important to keep Phoenix alive—at least for the time being.

"Yes...yes, Mr. President. That's right, sir. They all did a wonderful job," Honeycut said, into his special direct line to the President.

"Yes, sir...we got it all, sir. They didn't get a thing. It's over, Mr. President. You can rest assured that no further danger exists."

"Pilgrim? Yes, he's still got that vacation coming that we promised him," Honeycut said, then continued listening.

"Yes, Mr. President. I'm sorry that Badger didn't make it through, too. He was a good agent. One of the best."

Honeycut gave an annoyed look of, "Come on, get the hell off the phone, already."

"Yes...yes. Thank you, Mr. President, I will. Good-bye, Mr. President," he said finally, putting down the phone.

"Jesus Christ, he was happy enough to eat shit," Honeycut said.

"He has good reason. It's over," Elizabeth Ryerson said.

"For him it's over. Not for us. We've still got that twenty-fifth page and a journal to worry about."

"There was no twenty-fifth page on the microfilm or on Phoenix," Elizabeth said.

Honeycut shook his head. "We've got to find out if he knows about it."

"Why should it matter?" she asked. "We've got him, and he's not going anywhere with it. He can't hurt us at all, even if he does know."

"We never found the page," Honeycut began. "It's out there somewhere. So is that journal. Together they represent a lot of trouble," he said.

"I think you're worrying too much," Elizabeth said. "By itself, the sheet means nothing. If anybody's going to find that journal, we are. No one else even knows it exists."

"Wrong!" Honeycut said. "Pilgrim knows about the journal. And I don't know what to make of that trip to Bridges's apartment. He worries me. He's smart. Too damn smart and independent—like Spartan was. He needs watching. I'm going to keep him under close watch on that vacation," Honeycut said.

"What do you think he could possibly do? We have complete control over him with that explosive implant," Elizabeth said.

"I just don't trust him. He'll be at St. Simon's Island until Saturday morning. The stitches will be taken out then, and he'll be taking that vacation. He's been told that his implant will be deactivated until he returns. He's been given a call-in number just in case he needs us for anything. He'll call when he returns."

"You're not really going to do that, are you?" she asked.

"Of course not. But it may make him a little bit more daring if he thinks we will. If he's got any ideas, we'll move. But I think that I'll keep Rainmaker close to him, just in case."

"What if he spots him? He'll know something's up," Elizabeth said.

"I said *close* to him. He'll be kept out of sight, but close enough to get in quickly if it becomes necessary. Another agent, Gemini, will be handling the up-close observation. Gemini is a master at observing without being discovered. We'll know everything he's up to."

"Do you really think he'll go after the journal?" she asked.

Honeycut's eyes narrowed into a pensive squint. "I think you can count on it."

THIRTY-THREE

At a time when we thought our wildest dreams had been realized, Colorosa presented us with yet another surprise. Our power and scope of control had been increased beyond all imagination.

The news was unbelievable. He arranged the most incredible demonstration we had ever seen.

The plan could have been completed on that day, but Colorosa presented us with a better way. A way in which control would come naturally, completely, without resistance. Only our patience was required.

Entry No. 73 from the partially
recovered *Wolf Journal*

Just as Leonid Travkin had predicted, Ivan Melnik again scanned the Phoenix file. When he left KGB headquarters that evening, Krykov's men began setting their trap to catch both him and Limpoulous.

Melnik sat nervously, waiting for Limpoulous to arrive. The time passed slowly, almost to the point of pain. Each meeting became a bigger risk. He knew he could not continue the Phoenix tape scans without eventual detection. And meeting in this place was the biggest risk of all.

This was where it had all begun. In the apartment of Melnik's homosexual lover.

About ten months ago, his lover had started a second relationship without Melnik's knowledge. When he was finally told, it came as a painful, crushing blow. The betrayal was unbearable.

A few weeks later he met the secret paramour. It was Vytas Limpoulous. Limpoulous was a big, handsome man. It was easy to see how it could have happened. At first, Melnik had vented his hurt and humiliation on Limpoulous, but the Greek's charm soon had melted all that away. It wasn't long before a three-way relationship started. It became a comfortable triangle of love and deep affection—that is, until Limpoulous told Melnik what he had to do to keep the arrangement from coming to the attention of the Individual Division.

Melnik had been set up. Eagle had been sent specifically to compromise him into acting as a double agent. Melnik knew what would happen if the Individual Division found out. He had no choice but to go along with Limpoulous's wishes.

They no longer met as lovers after that, and never at the apartment. The meeting place was always different, carefully selected by Limpoulous.

Melnik was now alone in the apartment. His lover had been told to keep himself busy until later in the evening. He had no knowledge of the arrangement that Eagle had worked out with Melnik.

On the street below, Eagle approached with great caution. Everything looked all right, but his instincts jumped in warning. Melnik had learned more important information concerning Phoenix that the agency needed. Without Dmitri Chakhovsky's help in identifying Phoenix, a final source of confirmation was essential.

Eagle took one last look around and went into the building.

Krykov's men would wait for a few additional moments, then move into position to set the trap.

The elevator moved swiftly upward. It stopped on the fifth floor, and Eagle stepped out. He walked the short distance to the apartment door and knocked out the prearranged code.

The door opened. He stepped in.

Without a word, he walked quickly across the room to the window. He moved the curtain back slightly and looked down to the street. He saw the quick, precise movements of Krykov's men, as they got into their ready positions. There was no doubt that all escape routes would be covered. The game was up for him.

"You were followed," Limpoulous said calmly.

Melnik's face went white. He rushed toward the window to look out, but Eagle stopped him.

"We have only seconds before they come for us. You must tell me what you know, quickly," Limpoulous said.

BLEEP! He contracted his eustachian implant, to alert SENTINEL Control to the coming message.

BEEP! SENTINEL Control was ready.

Melnik was flushed with fear. He could only stare into the eyes of Limpoulous.

"Vytas...I...I didn't—"

"It's okay, Ivan," Limpoulous said, placing his hand gently on the smaller man's shoulder. "I know it's not your fault. But you must tell me, quickly. There's little time."

Melnik blinked. His eyes began to dampen. A heavy lump formed in his throat from the fear of the moments ahead.

"Phoenix...Phoenix has been captured," he said, swallowing hard. "The operation was code-named SENTINEL. It has failed completely. Phoenix was the last hope."

"Is that all of it?" Limpoulous asked.

"Yes," Melnik answered.

"I will leave quickly. If I can get to another floor, you may still have a chance," the handsome Greek said.

BEEP! Message received.

BLEEP! BLEEP! The eustachian tones signaled danger, capture imminent.

Limpoulous touched Melnik's cheek softly and walked toward the door. He opened it just in time to see the elevator doors open and four KGB men step out.

Eagle slammed the door shut and locked it. He spun to face Melnik.

"Vytas, I am—" Melnik's words caught in his throat, when he saw the silenced automatic in Limpoulous's hand.

THUD! THUD! The weapon spoke quietly.

Melnik crumpled to the floor. He was beyond all fear now.

Suddenly, the door splintered open.

THUD! THUD!

The first Russian through the door went down.

THUD!

A second man was knocked backward into the hallway.

Eagle raced for the kitchen. No shots were returned at him.

THUD! One more at the door to keep them out.

As he got into the kitchen, he saw a figure outside the window, standing on the fire escape.

THUD!

The figure went down behind the splintering glass.

The clip in Eagle's gun was empty, the slide locked back.

POP! POP! Two sounds came from the splintered doorway behind him.

The sedative darts bit into his back. He dropped to his knees, the gun falling from his hand. He wobbled stiffly, trying to keep his balance, then fell forward onto his face.

Eagle was taken as promised—alive. But the cost was unacceptable to Krykov.

Leonid Travkin now had what he needed to make the last contingency work. Tradable merchandise.

The elevator stopped at the Horizon Tower apartments in Fort Lee, New Jersey. Justin stepped out and walked down the neatly decorated hallway toward Barbara's apartment.

He had stopped long enough at his own apartment to check it out. It was exactly as it had been before the fight. The broken furniture and bloodstained rug had been replaced. Only Barbara's ashtray showed any traces of its unexpected double duty. There were a few chips missing. Division Two had not replaced it, because they couldn't find another one like it. It wasn't the type of item easily found. Its conversational value had increased considerably—as had Justin's appreciation for it.

Justin rang the door bell.

Barbara was expecting him and opened the door.

"Long time no see—" Her sentence choked off when she saw his bruised face.

"Oh, Justin, what happened?" she said, cupping his face in her soft, warm hands.

"It's okay, Jugs. Just a little car accident up in Seattle," he lied. "I really feel a lot better than I look," he said, entering the apartment.

"Are you sure?" she said sympathetically.

"Yeah, I'm fine. Really."

"Oh, Justin, why didn't you call to tell me? How did it happen?"

He loved her caring ways. "I didn't tell you because I didn't want you to worry. I was really okay. I knew I was," he said.

She shook her head, staring up at the bruises. Her eyes began to dampen.

"Rolled the car down the side of a hill," he said. "Took a sharp turn too fast and just lost it. Car was a total wreck."

"Was anyone with you?" she asked as they walked into the kitchen, her arm up over his shoulder.

"No, I was alone," he answered.

He sat on a chair at the table.

Barbara cradled his head in her arms and pulled it against her soft, braless breasts. "You could have been killed," she said, tears beginning to roll down her cheeks.

Her breasts felt good against his face. He wrapped his arms around her waist, drawing her close. He just wanted to stay there and lose himself in her softness and sweet smell, to stay there, to forget all the things that had happened in the past week.

She sensed his need and held him, gently stroking his hair. They stayed that way for a long while in silent appreciation of one another.

"Do you want a drink?" she asked, backing away to look into his eyes.

"Can't. I'm taking some pills, and I can't have alcohol while I'm on them," he said.

"What are the pills for?" she asked.

"Pain pills. For this," he said, holding up the wrapped hand.

She hadn't noticed it in her shock at seeing his face. "What happened to it?" she asked.

"Cut it wide open," he said, tracing a line across where the garrote had sliced so deeply. "Took about forty stitches in it."

"Forty stitches! Oh, my God. Will you be able to use it again?" she asked, her eyes getting wet once more.

"Sure," he said, moving it. "Most of the stitches are inside. Fortunately, the cut wasn't jagged. It was nice and straight. It'll hardly show in a few months. I was pretty lucky that I had a great doctor."

She took the hand gently, raised it, and kissed the back of his fingers. "Forty stitches."

"It's all right. It really feels fine," he said.

"I'm almost afraid to ask. Where else?"

"Some on the face," he said, waving a finger in front of the more obvious places. "Some cracked ribs and a sore knee. The rest is like gold," he said.

"No wonder, with those pills. You still got everything in your pants?" she tried joking.

"Yeah, you wanna see?"

"Hmmm," she purred.

He ran the edge of his hand up gently into her crotch. "Get your clothes off," he said and smiled.

They lay in each other's arms for hours, as the afternoon slid by. The lovemaking had been exceedingly gentle, as Justin's ribs hurt considerably more than he cared to admit, even to himself.

He told Barbara about the vacation time he had saved up and had been offered as a part of a bonus for that last job. She jumped at the chance to put her free-lance writing aside and have him all to herself for so long.

"Where should we go?" she asked, bubbling with a child's enthusiasm.

"Greece, Italy, Austria, Switzerland, France, Germany, England...Israel," he called off, smiling.

"I can't decide. Which ones?" she squealed delightfully.

"All of them. A week in each," he replied.

Her face was a mask of joyous disbelief.

"And, if you wouldn't mind," he went on, "we could spend a week in Saudi Arabia."

"Saudi Arabia? Sure, anyplace you say," she said. "I don't care where we go, as long as we go. But...why Saudi Arabia?" she asked. "Not that I mind, but any special reason why there?"

"Pappy's there. Don't you remember? I told you all about Steve being in Saudi Arabia."

"Yes, I remember. Your friend from college."

"Not just my friend from college," Justin said. "He's the best friend I have. He was my big brother when I pledged for the fraternity. There are a lot of years and a lot of memories that we've shared together."

There weren't many people Justin considered *real* friends. Ted had been one. There were, perhaps, a few more from his fraternity days, but Steve was his closest.

"I haven't seen him in over a year. And I've written him about you. He's dying to meet you. The opportunity is perfect, I'd hate to let it pass," he said.

"That would be fine." She smiled beautifully.

"Maybe we could start out in Saudi Arabia, then go to Israel, then Greece, then through Europe, finishing up with a week in England," he proposed.

He had something specific in the back of his mind when he said England.

"How's that sound, pretty lady?" he asked.

"Oh, I love it!" she bubbled. "I can't believe it. Nine weeks." Her face grew suddenly serious. "That's going to cost a lot of pesos, amigo. How are we going to afford all that? It's got to cost—"

He silenced her with a kiss.

"Don't worry about what it's going to cost. I got a real fat bonus from that last job. I was on my way back when the accident happened," he lied.

"Oh, wow! But you're going to save as much of that bonus as you can. We'll bum it. Dungarees and sandals, all the way," she insisted.

"Hey, wait a minute. I'm offering a first-class deal. Start to finish," Justin protested mildly.

"Just being with you is first class," she said, kissing him. "We'll bum it. That's the only way to see Europe. First class in Saudi Arabia, because of Steve. Bum it the rest. Deal?"

He never could resist her charm. "Okay, it's a deal. We'll do it any way you want to," he conceded.

Later, after they had showered together, Justin started to get dressed. Barbara had wrapped his tender rib cage for him and put a fresh bandage on the hand.

Justin had been right about the cut. It was closed into a thin, pink line. The doctor had done a good job. The sublayered stitches would be felt for a while, until they dissolved. All his cuts had been stitched closed beautifully. Only faint traces would show, once the redness disappeared, adding a certain handsome ruggedness to his face.

Barbara began dressing, as Justin was getting ready to leave. He was going to pick up little Michael for the weekend. The dinner he had planned with Michael and his father was on for the next day. Barbara was going to meet him at his apartment after he picked up his son.

"Bring clothes for the weekend," Justin said. "I want you to stay at my place. Okay?"

"I don't plan on being out of your sight for more than an hour at any one time for the next nine weeks," she said, giving him a catlike purr.

Justin walked over to her and held her close to him. After several long moments, he looked down into her pretty blue eyes.

"That's not as long as I'd like it to be," he said. "I had a more definite period of time in mind."

She stared up into his eyes, mist forming again in her own.

"I want you to marry me, Jugs," he said.

Tears began flooding down her cheeks.

"I'm not going to let you think that one over," she said, through the tears. "I accept. I accept. I accept."

She jumped up, throwing her arms around his neck, hugging him hard.

She felt very small and warm in his arms. He wanted her so much that he could have squeezed her until she became a part of his body. But the ribs protested, and he lowered her.

He was happier than he'd ever been in his life.

"I love you, Jugs, like I've never loved anyone or anything in my life," he said.

"Come on, you big lug. Get out of here, before I tear your pants off again."

"We'll have a long time for that," he said. "A long time for one another from now on."

"A long time for one another," she said, putting her head against his chest. She closed her eyes tight, to keep the tears from falling.

The dinner wasn't exactly what Justin had hoped it would be. Michael was irritable and cranky, his father seemed uncomfortable, and Justin felt ill at ease in his own apartment after what had happened there.

He kept going into the bedroom to look around, making sure that there were no traces of his struggle with Ten Braak. Barbara hadn't noticed the ashtray. It all looked right. But he felt strange in his apartment. Like being in a fish bowl.

It wasn't safe anymore. It wasn't private. His sanctuary had been violated.

The evening seemed to last forever. All he wanted was to be alone with Barbara. He felt like he didn't know his father and Michael anymore. Or maybe it was that they didn't know him—what he really was, what he did.

The only saving grace of the evening had been Barbara. She kept things going, finding the right things to talk about and to do all night.

But it finally ended. Justin took his father and Michael home and returned to the apartment with Barbara.

The dreams of the faceless stalker returned that night. His mind kept thinking about his defenses, where the gun was, where the thermal mug was, where the ashtray was.

Some defenses—a thermal mug and an ashtray.

He finally fell into a deep sleep, with Barbara holding him in her arms. She woke him up at about 4:00 a.m. because he was thrashing about wildly, as though fighting with someone in his sleep.

He held her tight, sweat covering his body. He lay in bed thinking about the windchimes, trying desperately to hear them. But they weren't there.

"Do you like windchimes?" he asked.

"Hmm? What?" she asked, coming out of a light sleep.

"I asked if you like windchimes?" he repeated.

"Yes, I guess so," she answered. "Why?"

"Oh, I don't know," he said. "When I was a kid, we had windchimes on our back porch. I could hear them at night. They were soft and comforting. They used to put me to sleep.

"I just thought that it would be nice to have them, to listen to them play their soft tinkling music at night. There's a certain peace in their music."

"That would be nice," she said sleepily.

Yeah, that would be nice, he thought. If only he could hear them now.

He hardly slept the rest of the night, finally nodding off as the morning sun began to fill the room.

That morning he tried to call Steve in Saudi Arabia. But Pappy was out. He had a tape-answering system that took Justin's message as to the reason he called and asking him to please return his call at his earliest convenience.

Justin and Barbara spent the whole next day making plans for their trip. They planned what clothes to bring, to keep their baggage light. They decided to rent a car, once in Europe, and drive across the countryside, stopping where their fancy dictated.

Later that day, at almost seven, the phone rang.

Barbara was in the kitchen making hot chocolate when Justin answered it.

"Hello," he said.

"J.C.?" Steve's voice sang out.

"Pappy!" He recognized Steve's voice immediately.

The overseas operator cut in, to go through the formalities. Once they were completed, she got off the line.

"Hey, little brother. How the hell are ya?" Steve boomed out. Steve was a giant of a man, standing a full four inches taller than Justin and having about forty pounds on him, forty very solid pounds.

"I'm great. Where the hell have you been? I've been trying to reach you," Justin said.

"I know. You gotta remember that our times are almost reversed out here. I was out cattin' around when you called."

Same old Steve. Always did have a weak spot in his pants for the ladies.

"What time is it out there?" Justin asked.

"Almost three in the morning," Steve replied.

"You just getting in?"

"Nope. Just going out."

"Christ, you ought to get *some* sleep, you know," Justin scolded jokingly.

"No, this is business, little brother," Steve said.

"Business? At three o'clock in the morning? You mean monkey business," Justin chided.

"No, no." Steve laughed. "This *is* business. I mean it. I'm leaving for a new drill site. I'm going to have to be out there for about three months. That's why I'm calling at this ungodly hour. We're not going to be able to get together for that vacation just yet. Can you put it off—maybe just a week of it—until I get back?"

"Sure, that's no problem," Justin said.

"That's great. Listen, I'll let you know by letter when I should be back in my digs and when the best time would be to come out," Steve said.

"Fine. You say in about three months?"

"Yeah, if everything goes right. I'll let you know for sure, though. Can that gal of yours make it then?" he asked.

"She wouldn't miss it for the world," Justin said.

"Great. I really want to meet her."

"You will, Pappy. We're going to get married."

"Say again. You broke up a little for a second there," Pappy said, referring to the crackling interference in the line.

"I said, we're going to get married," he repeated more loudly.

"*Really?* That's *great*, little brother. Hey, listen. If Barbara doesn't mind, I'd like to take you out when you're here, for a little one-on-one bachelor party. Think she'd mind terribly?" Steve asked.

"No problem, Pappy. As long as you bring me back alive and with no exotic diseases," Justin said.

Barbara was just coming in with the hot chocolate. "Hey, I don't think I like the way that sounded," she joked.

"Is that her?" Steve asked.

"Yeah."

"Let me talk to her a minute."

"Sure. Hold on."

Justin held out the phone to Barbara. "Here, get it from the horse's mouth," he said and smiled.

Barbara took the phone. They talked like old friends for a few minutes, then she let out a little surprised scream and began laughing hysterically.

Justin took the phone back. "Hey, what are you two up to?" he asked with a big smile.

"That's our little secret. You'll find out when you get here. Listen, little brother, I have to go now," Steve said.

"Okay, Pappy. Hey, when are you gonna come home? I thought you were only supposed to be gone for a year?" Justin asked.

"Can't, not yet, anyway. I'm making too much money out here. I tell ya, I really got the good life. You'll see what I mean when you come out. Looks like at least another year before I'd even consider it. We'll talk more about it when you're out here. In the meantime, little brother, take care of yourself and that gal of yours."

"I will, Pappy. You do likewise," Justin said. "And don't come back from the desert with camel clap or anything."

Steve laughed. "Not me, little brother. I'll save the camels for you. I really look forward to seeing you, buddy."

"Me, too. Take care, Steve."

"Good-bye, little brother."

The phone clicked.

"It was good to hear his voice," Justin said.

"You really love him, don't you?" Barbara asked with a warm smile across her face.

"Yeah, I do," Justin answered, looking inward over a long collection of memories.

"What was so funny before?" he asked.

"You'll have to wait until you get there," she answered, with a catlike grin crossing her face. "I hope you like camels," she laughed.

Justin chased her around the couch. She ran, squealing delightfully, into the bedroom. She tried closing the door, but Justin was too fast and easily pushed his way in.

Out of breath, she surrendered.

"Camels, huh?" Justin said.

"Well, you know what they say, 'There's no hump like a camel's hump,' " she said, throwing her arms around Justin's neck and then kissing him deeply.

"Get naked," she said.

The thoughts of defenses and dreams of the stalker didn't come that night. She had a way of making him forget, sometimes—like the windchimes.

THIRTY-FOUR

*A Fourth Reich was beginning before our eyes.
Invincible, unbeatable. A world of Aryan dominance
without force. A world of perfect Aryans. Rulers.*

*I nearly died that month from illness. But death and I
were old friends. I had cheated him once thirty years ago.
But I am no longer afraid. I could die at any time knowing
that my dream is fulfilled, the promise kept.*

If only I could tell all those who died. I cry from joy.

Entry No. 74 from the partially
recovered *Wolf Journal*

"Well, that finishes the list," Barbara said, as she and Justin
began walking across the sunny parking lot after leaving the Paramus Park Mall. Each carried several light packages.

"We're all set for tomorrow," she said. "We'll take our time packing today, and then go to bed early, so that we'll be fresh in the morning for our flight."

The past week had gone quickly for them. Although they were traveling light, there were still a lot of preparations to be made for such an extended trip. The only advanced reservations that were made were their airline tickets and first-night accommodations in Israel and Greece. The rest would be played by ear, as they stopped where they liked, for as long as they liked.

Moments later they were pulling out onto Route 17 south, heading for the Garden State Plaza and their last stop. Justin wanted to pick up some cigars at his favorite tobacconist, Wally Frank, Ltd.

He preferred a special private stock, hand-rolled, that Wally Frank put his own label on. They weren't expensive, as cigars go, but they suited his taste well, better, in fact, than most of the more expensive cigars he had tried.

"Do you have some paper? I want to make a list," Barbara said.

"Another one? We've got twenty of them at home, already. You've been making lists all week," he said.

"Yes, I know. But, each time I made a new list, I was paring one down. I want to make the final packing list now. Then, when we repack as we go, we just have to check off the list to be sure that we don't forget anything," she explained.

"I think there's a small note pad in the glove compartment," he said.

She began rummaging through the glove compartment. "Ummm. That looks like a good one," she said, pulling out a fine-looking cigar.

Justin recognized it immediately as one of two that Fanning had given him during the Ten Braak hunt. He had smoked one and saved the other. He couldn't find it later. He must have stuck it there without thinking.

"That is a good one," he said. "A fella I know gave me that about three weeks ago."

"Here, smoke it. I love the smell of your cigars," she said, handing it to him after unwrapping it.

Justin took it, bit off a small piece of the end, and put the cigar between his teeth. He fished through his pockets for a match, but couldn't find one. A second later Barbara handed him a matchbook she had found in the glove compartment.

Justin held the cigar in his teeth for a while, thinking about Ted. Every time something reminded him of his dead partner, it struck home with a fresh realization that it had all really happened.

Barbara found the note pad and began preparing her list.

Justin struck a match and raised it.

Here's to you, Ted, he thought. He pulled gently on the cigar, drawing the flame to the fat tip. Aromatic puffs of smoke began to fill the car. Justin opened the window a crack to let the smoke out.

"Gee, that really does smell good, honey," she said. "Your friend certainly has good taste. Why don't you get some of those at Wally Frank's," she suggested.

"They don't carry them. They're Cuban, I think. He told me that he picked them up in England. Private stock of some tobacconist."

"Do you know where he got them? I mean, who the tobacconist was?" Barbara asked.

"Nope."

Barbara reached into the ashtray and pulled out the cigar ring that she had removed earlier.

"It shouldn't be too hard to find. This looks like a pretty distinctive band," she said. She handed it to Justin.

He looked at it closely. It was distinctive. Very finely done. "That's probably a trademark used by the tobacconist or the manufacturer. I'm sure we could find out where he got them." He remembered then that he had put one of the bands in his wallet. The mark on the band seemed familiar, but he couldn't quite place it.

"Well, if you like them, we'll ask around when we're there. I think you should get some. They're great-smelling cigars."

"Yeah, I think I will," he said, not really wanting to. They'd always remind him of Ted and what had happened. And he wanted to forget all that. Forever.

The three-man debriefing team of Richard Wyatt, Dr. Peter Bell, and Victor Bishoff was seated in front of a bank of closed-circuit television monitors. The monitors showed Kuradin from four different positions. Bishoff watched them intently as the debriefing progressed.

Also in front of them were banks of the same physiological monitors that had been used during the Chakhovsky debriefings. Bell studied these carefully.

Kuradin's condition had been stabilized to the point where his platelet and white-cell counts had risen high enough to start him on the D-80 desensitization program.

Two intravenous tubes ran into him simultaneously. One delivered whole blood, the other ran a glucose solution, to which a low concentration of D-80 had been added.

The levels of D-80 being fed into his system were gradually increased, as his body showed the necessary tolerance for it. He wasn't as drug sensitive as many of the people on whom the drug had been tried in the past. This meant that the desensitization program could proceed at a fairly rapid rate. Within the next three or four weeks, he would be started on massive doses to begin battling the leukemic cells that were steadily eating his life away.

Dr. Becker Dials had had several consultations with the Russian before the debriefings were started. Dials had been very frank with him. Kuradin knew he was dying and that chances of going into a long-term third remission weren't very promising.

Kuradin was allowed several days to adjust to what Dials had told him. He didn't really need the time. He had already accepted his fate before going on the mission. In fact, it was an important part of the final contingency as he had planned it.

When the debriefings had begun three days before, the panel had found him to be very cooperative. This surprised Wyatt, who had been prepared to go at him relentlessly, pounding away at him, until he got the information he needed.

The even levels on the physiological monitors told them that he was answering all of their questions truthfully.

They didn't know, however, that Kuradin's special training enabled him to control these telltale factors with remarkable ease. As long as he knew what to expect, he could maintain that consistent performance through any number of sessions. It was the sudden surprises that he had to look out for. Control of this nature required intense mental preparation. Surprises did not afford the necessary luxury of the preparation time he needed to keep up the game effectively. But Kuradin's mind was quick. He could sift through alternatives nimbly, to improvise his way through such situations.

Kuradin had given his name as being Mikhail Yarin, the real name of Phoenix. The debriefings had started with the careful accumulation of personal data, which was checked against the information obtained in Russia by Eagle, before his capture. Everything matched exactly, right down to the smallest detail.

The first twenty minutes of this particular session had been used to review and clarify some of that data.

"And in England, Mr. Yarin. What was your objective there?" Wyatt questioned.

"I was to meet a courier who was carrying information wanted in Moscow. I was to pay him a certain sum of money and take the papers into my possession. A copy was to be put on microfilm, to be dead-dropped for a second agent, in case I ran into difficulties getting out of the country."

"Did you get the information that you were after?" Wyatt asked.

"No. The courier arrived and the exchange was made, but we were broken in upon as I was photographing the papers. There was a struggle in the darkness, and I lost the camera. I was unable to find it or the papers before running. There was no time. It all happened very quickly."

The monitors remained steady.

"Did you know what was on those papers?"

"No," Kuradin answered. "I got a look at them before I began photographing them, but they were in code. I remember that it was set in groupings of six letters, with five or six columns of code to each page. I didn't remember any of the actual letter sequences. There were too many of them to even attempt it."

The monitors again registered their easy tracking.

"Do the names Pilgrim, Badger, and Spartan mean anything to you?" Wyatt questioned.

"Yes. The first name, Pilgrim, was the man who broke in on the transaction in England." Kuradin went on to explain how the Pilgrim connection had been made. He answered all of Wyatt's questions pertaining to the Soviets' knowledge of SENTINEL. He explained what had been learned from the earlier contacts with Bridges and told them about the proof he had offered listing the exact locations of missile installations, the *Siska*-class submarine deployment and armament, and the list of highly placed KGB agents within the United States government agencies.

"All of his information was correct, to the smallest detail. That was why we dared use only sleeper agents in the operation, with the one exception of Otto Ten Braak," Kuradin said.

He explained his entire plan and the logic behind it, omitting, of course, the Phoenix file changes and his final contingency.

"We conceded the power that SENTINEL possesses," Kuradin said. "We needed to learn the basis of that intellect. How it was put together and how it worked. That's what Dr. Bridges offered to us. That's what I came for."

"Why didn't you try to take Bridges out with you?" Wyatt asked.

"Our investigations of him and the psychological profile compiled led our scientists to the conclusion that, aside from his information, he offered nothing more of interest. With his information, our scientists could essentially build another SENTINEL," Kuradin explained.

"Were any other copies of the information to be made, had you been able to get the film processed?"

"No. Only one set of microdots, to be implanted exactly as the unprocessed film had been. This was in case I was killed. Moscow would attempt to recover my body. It was all worked out very carefully. It shouldn't have failed."

"I have just one more question for you today, then we'll close this session. Why did you remove the twenty-fifth page?"

The monitors stayed smooth and even.

"There was no twenty-fifth page," Kuradin answered calmly. He had prepared for this question.

"But there was, and you removed it," Wyatt said.

"No. The information was left exactly as it was given to us by Dr. Bridges," Kuradin lied convincingly.

"Did Dr. Bridges mention a twenty-fifth page, or that he had additional information with him?" Wyatt quizzed.

"No," Kuradin said, shaking his head, "he said nothing like that. He expressed his concern over the time that had lapsed since taking the information, and he explained the probable action that SENTINEL would take in locating him after it was discovered that he was missing.

"I think that is where I would have to say the plan failed. Had his absence not been discovered until Monday, as planned, we would have succeeded. Ten Braak as well."

"That will be enough for today. Thank you, Mr. Yarin. Rest well."

Later, as the debriefing team reviewed the transcript of the session, they discussed Phoenix's answers to the questions pertaining to the twenty-fifth page.

"Well, what do you think, Pete? Was he telling the truth, or wasn't he?" Wyatt asked Dr. Bell.

"The monitors remained as steady as a rock," Bell said. "We know that people can be taught to control these responses, but that question coming out of the blue like that should have caught him. I think he's told us the truth right from the start. I believe that he never saw, or had any knowledge of that twenty-fifth page."

"Victor, what are your thoughts?" Wyatt asked.

"I've got to agree, Dick. He's been playing it straight in my opinion, right from the beginning. There was nothing, absolutely nothing, in that face, or those eyes, to make me think that he's told us even a single lie."

"Thank you, gentlemen," Wyatt said. His next questions would be put to SENTINEL, who had also observed all monitors during the debriefing session.

Robert Morsand sat waiting in the open-air café in Paris. He had been contacted by Pavel Yentik, a member of the Soviet KGB with whom he had dealt in the past, exchanging various bits of information of a mutually important nature. There were numerous occasions when Morsand and Yentik found themselves on the same side of a fragile situation, in which cooperation was required. They were enemies, yet friends. There was a strong abiding mutual respect between them. The two always engaged in a game of "knowing," of producing little tidbits of a sensitive or personal nature, to demonstrate their ability to learn even the most mundane facts about one another.

It was a clear, hot day. Summer had settled into France, leaving behind all the harsh memories of a particularly rough winter. It was now the middle of June, just over two months since the Chakhovsky fiasco had taken place.

Their investigations had led nowhere. One big fat zero. Chakhovsky had simply vanished.

Yentik approached Morsand from behind. He pulled a chair away from the small round table and sat down. The American eyed the Russian through the rising blue smoke of his pipe.

"You're getting old, Yentik. I heard you from at least thirty feet away," Morsand said.

Yentik smiled broadly. "And you have a few more gray hairs than the last time I saw you," the Russian chided back.

"I only color them that way to give you a false sense of security," Morsand said, through the crunch on his pipe.

"And I only make noise to keep from frightening an old man to death," the Russian retorted.

"What's cooking, Yentik?" Morsand asked.

"An exchange," the Russian said, eyeing his American counterpart.

Morsand chewed on his pipe and waved a finger to the waiter to bring another cup of espresso to the table.

"I'm listening," Morsand said.

"We are interested in the return of Mikhail Yarin. In exchange, we will offer Vytas Limpoulous," the Russian said.

Both men fell into silence as the espresso was put on the table. Morsand used the break to empty his pipe and refill it—and to think.

After the waiter had left, Morsand struck a match and began sucking life into his pipe again. "Who in the hell are they?" he asked. "I've never heard of either one of them."

"It only goes to show how little you know," the Russian kidded again, in near-perfect English. "We are interested in an even trade, at a time and place of your choosing."

They must want him badly, Morsand thought. The Russians never gave an inch. Dealing with them was like trying to deal with an Arab for his sister. In the end it turned out that you usually got his camel, and he got your nuts.

"What makes you think we want Limpoulous back?" Morsand asked, going along with the flow. He hoped to learn more about the names he was hearing for the first time.

"Oh, you will want him back. We are sure of that. Bring this offer to your superiors. I am sure that they will show an interest," the Russian said, sipping his espresso. "When you have word, contact me in the usual way."

Morsand didn't like being on the short end of the information. True, he didn't know everyone that the Russians held, but he did know the biggies. And he had never heard of Vytas Limpoulous before.

"I'll talk with them and let you know what they decide," he said.

The Russian nodded. "Good. Now, with business out of the way, how is your lovely family? I understand your daughter's piano recital went quite well last week…"

"They've offered a trade," Honeycut said to Richard Wyatt. "They want Yarin back. They're offering Eagle for him."

Wyatt squinted in contemplation.

"What's Yarin's condition?" Honeycut asked.

"He's beginning to respond to the D-eighty protocol they've put him on. Dials thinks that he'll obtain remission very shortly."

"Is there any more to be learned from him?" Honeycut asked.

"I don't think so. He's been very cooperative so far. The monitors indicate that he's told the truth all the way," Wyatt answered.

"Does SENTINEL agree?"

"Yes. I think we're in the clear on this one. There's no doubt that we've got the same man that Pilgrim went up against in England. Everything fits perfectly."

"Yes, well it has fit perfectly from the start. We were also convinced that he was David Fromme in Beloit," Honeycut said. "I wish that Chakhovsky was conscious, to identify him positively."

"Chakhovsky is still in deep coma," Wyatt said. "Dials says that his life signs are very strong and that he could come out of it at any time. How much time do we have before a trade can be negotiated?"

"About four weeks, I would guess. We know that Eagle is alive and that his implant is in place. They're trying to break him now, we think by sensory deprivation techniques. SENTINEL has induced hypnosis in him, through the implant. They won't get anything from him. They'll have to keep him alive, they won't want to risk blowing the exchange," Honeycut said.

"It follows that they would try to make the exchange, too, Irv. As far as they are aware, Yarin still has his film implant. They're banking on still getting the information," Wyatt said.

"I'm sure you're right, Dick. I think his state of health was calculated into the plan, to help influence our decision. I just wish Chakhovsky could get a look at him."

"Do you think there's any possibility of a second implant somewhere?" Honeycut asked.

"No. SENTINEL has had him put through the body scanner. He's clean from head to toe," Wyatt said.

"Well, then, I think we should proceed with the trade negotiations. We've got to get Eagle back before they find that implant. Given enough time, they will. They can't learn too much from it, but possibly enough to allow them to start picking up our transmissions."

"There is one large stumbling block, though," Honeycut said. "The Russians approached Robert Morsand for the trade. They didn't know where else to go. The CIA is aware that something is up. They're turning over every stone to find out who Yarin and Eagle are."

"We can take care of their interference from the top. It's after the trade is completed that I'm worried about. Their curiosity will be aroused, especially after the Chakhovsky deal. It'll be hell trying to keep it all covered neatly."

"We don't have any other choice, do we? We've got to get Eagle back, and they want Yarin," Wyatt said.

"That's right. We'll handle it all right, it'll just be sticky for a while."

"How do you want Yarin handled from this point?" Wyatt asked.

"Continue the debriefings right up to the end. If it looks even the least bit shaky, we'll put off the trade and try to handle it in another way," Honeycut said.

"All right, Irv. We'll stay on Yarin to see if we can shake any-thing else loose. My guess is that we're safe on this, though."

"Yes, I have to agree. Let's keep the game up, though. Yarin is a smart cookie. I still don't trust him."

"Well, we can fix it so that he'll be dead within forty-eight hours after the trade. That's got to improve our odds," Wyatt said.

"We may just do that, if it becomes necessary."

Justin and Barbara had toured through Europe as planned dur-ing the eight-week period. They had now come to their last stop. England.

England has its own special beauty, but they were too exhausted to appreciate it fully. The weather was bad for the first two days, and they spent most of that time sleeping off the effects from the first eight weeks of travel.

The third day was beautiful. England was beautiful. They were rested and ready to go.

Barbara wanted to spend a day shopping in London. What she really wanted to do was to find the tobacconist who handled the cigars that Fanning had given Justin and to surprise him with a box. So, she announced that she'd be off on a shop for the entire morning and early afternoon.

Justin welcomed the opportunity to tend to the business in the back of his mind. He took the car they had rented and made the hour's drive out to Coventry, to Spartan's house.

He stopped the car in front of the driveway. There was a large FOR SALE sign on a tree at the entrance. Justin looked back to the house and saw a small round man step out of the house onto the little front porch. He turned the car into the driveway and pulled up to the house.

The old man was wearing gray pants and a gray sweater. He turned on the porch and cocked his head, to examine the tall, young man getting out of the car.

"Good morning," Justin said.

"Mornin' to ya," the old man returned in his cockney baritone.

"I see this house is for sale. Are you the agent listing the property?" Justin asked.

The old man tilted his head to the other side, squinting from the morning sun in his face.

"American, are ya?" he asked.

Justin nodded and smiled.

"So was the poor bastard that owned this place. Kilt he was. Right in here," he said throwing a thumb over his shoulder at the house.

He obviously wasn't the agent.

"Killed? An accident?" Justin asked.

"It was no accident. Some one kilt 'im. With a shotgun. Real mess it was, too."

"Jesus," Justin said in mock surprise.

"They'll never sell it, either," the old man said. "No one wants a house that someone was kilt in. Ghosts, ya know?"

"Are you the agent?"

"No. I'm the caretaker. I keep it clean and keep up the grounds until it's sold. Ya wouldn't be interested in it, would ya?"

"I might be. Can I look inside?" Justin asked.

"Ya ain't supposed to without the agent bein' with ya," the old man replied.

"I only want to look. You can come in with me. If I like it, I'll call the agent," Justin said.

The old man nodded. "But ya won't like it. Got ghosts."

Justin followed the old man in.

The house was still furnished exactly as it had been when he and Ted had searched it after the killing.

"This is a lovely house," Justin said. "Does the furniture come with it?"

The old man nodded. "As ya see it."

They approached the study.

"That in there is where he died," the old man said as they walked in. "In that closet over there," he said, pointing to the bathroom.

The splintered door had been replaced.

He walked over and looked in. It was clean. All the pock marks had been repaired, and the toilet had been replaced.

"You mean somebody killed him in the bathroom?" Justin asked.

"Blew his dinkin' head off, they did. Never been solved, either," the old man said.

"Jesus," Justin said, shaking his head. A chill passed through him as he thought about the stalker again.

Justin walked to the center of the study. "That's a lovely desk." He walked to it and sat in the chair. He swiveled in the chair as he ran his hands across the dustless top of the handsome desk. It was exactly as he and Ted left it.

He looked up at the wall library and immediately noticed something out of place. There were books missing. Maybe a hundred of them. His eyes played across the stack, as his stomach filled with a nervous flutter.

"Where are the rest of the…" He caught himself. "I mean… eh…those books." He got up and walked to the stacks. "Some of these sets look like they have volumes missing," he recovered quickly, pointing to an obviously incomplete collection.

"That would be the brother," the old man said.

"Brother?"

"The man's brother. He come here from America about a month after it happened. Come in here and said to sell it like it was. Except for some books what he took with 'im," the old man said.

"How many books?" Justin asked too fast.

"Fifty, maybe twice that. That's all he took. Just the books."

The books. It had been there all the time. But how could they have missed it? he wondered.

Wait a minute! He walked back to the desk and opened the drawer that had contained the old broken lamp. It was still there.

He took out the dusty old lamp and turned it over to look at the bulb. There it was. They had missed it. It was an ultraviolet bulb. They had seen it, but missed it.

Ultraviolet-sensitive ink could have been used. Invisible to the eyes, it would illuminate brightly when under the UV. It was too simple.

He sat in the chair, the old man watching him perform these strange actions.

Justin looked across the desk. His eyes swept past the old fluorescent lamp, the humidor, the acrylic-and-penny paper-weight—*the humidor.* His eyes shot back to it.

He reached up and touched the familiar coat of arms on its top. He opened the box and stuck his hand in. His hand found one of the cigars. He pulled it out and brought it close for inspection. He took the cigar ring from his wallet—and felt his stomach sink.

The cigar ring was the same as the one taken from the cigar that Fanning had given him—*before* they had come to England.

His mind raced back to the night they had tried for Ten Braak, to the "Runt," the shotgun. A shotgun had killed Spartan.

Justin's face was white and wet from perspiration. It couldn't be. Nothing like this had even crossed his mind.

"Nothing is what it seems to be...nothing is real," Ted had told him once. "Never make friends in this business. It makes your job and staying alive a lot easier."

Nothing is real. Don't make friends in this business. "Because you might have to kill one of them someday," Justin said, thinking to himself.

"What was that ya said? I didn't hear it," the old man said.

"Oh, nothing. Tell me, where can I reach this agent?"

THIRTY-FIVE

In the midst of our joy, deep sadness came. Constantine was murdered in South Africa, despite our efforts to protect him.

The South African steering center was closed. There was no need to maintain it any longer.

Entry No. 76 from the partially
recovered *Wolf Journal*

"Do we go for the books now?" Elizabeth Ryerson asked a pensive Honeycut.

"No," Honeycut graveled back. "We can't. Spartan's brother has had those books too long. It would be unrealistic to think that the journal hasn't been transcribed. Even if we got all of the books, we'd still have that transcribed copy to worry about. And you can bet that it'll be well hidden.

"No, I think our best chance will rest with Pilgrim. He'll go after it. He'll go to the brother, and, if he's convincing enough, he may even get the copy for us. Then we can take care of all the loose ends at once."

"Do you really think that a significant danger exists from a hidden copy? Even if somebody did find it, who could understand its real meaning without the specific background information?" Elizabeth asked.

"We don't know what the rest of that journal contains," Honeycut said. "It may tell enough to cause a lot of trouble, if it fell into the wrong hands." SENTINEL's analysis had yielded fifty-five percent of the journal from the ashes.

"We could handle it," Elizabeth said. "Nothing could stop us now. Nothing in this whole world."

"Don't be so sure," Honeycut said. "Bridges almost threw a monkey wrench into the works. Do you know what could have happened if the Soviets had gotten those schematics and built their own version of SENTINEL?"

It didn't have to be said, they both knew.

"Besides, it's not a matter of anybody being able to stop us," Honeycut began again. "We've come so far. We're so close to the final realization of the dream. We can't jeopardize the program now and risk a reversion to the old way, a way that we know doesn't work."

"But I don't trust Pilgrim," Elizabeth objected. "He's a dangerous man. There's no telling what he could do, once armed with that information. He's bound to make the same connections that Spartan did. And we shouldn't underestimate his abilities."

"We've got nothing to fear from Pilgrim. We'll know every move he makes. Rainmaker and Gemini are staying close. And as a last resort we can always detonate his implant. But for now he's useful. We'll keep him well under our control," Honeycut said.

"I think it's a mistake," Elizabeth insisted. "I'm afraid of that man. Put him naked in a cage with lions, and I wouldn't bet on the lions," she said.

Honeycut laughed. He liked and admired Justin very much. He had hoped that his prediction of Justin's going after the journal would prove to be wrong. He didn't want to lose an agent of his capabilities.

But Justin's actions left little doubt that he intended to learn more about the journal. Honeycut knew that Justin's curiosity and persistence would eventually lead him to it. And he was counting on that.

"We'll give him plenty of latitude. Let him find it for us. Then we'll settle it," Honeycut said.

He got up from the chair and walked toward the door of the Alpha situation room. He stopped short of the door and turned to face Elizabeth. For a few moments he looked around the room. Then he spoke. "I want arrangements made to close down Alpha."

"*Close down Alpha?*" Elizabeth asked in weak disbelief.

"Have SENTINEL review all personnel records and decide who to take and who to leave behind. I want all operations being conducted here to be transferred to Sigma within the next thirty days. Those people being left behind are to be moved upstairs into the Aztek operation. See that they all get substantial pay increases to keep them happy.

"Once we've closed down Alpha, I want it sealed permanently. Arm all automatic intruder control systems. I want it as tight as a drum."

Elizabeth was in shock. She would have never expected Alpha to be closed, but she could understand Honeycut's reasoning. The Bridges affair had jeopardized the security of the entire complex. Once sealed and closed down, there would be no potential danger from Soviet attempts to develop another contact for another try at the goods.

The Impala pulled off at exit eight of the New Jersey Turnpike and headed into Hightstown.

Spartan's brother was a physician living in East Windsor, New Jersey, just outside of Hightstown. With the whole world for it to be hidden in, the journal had been only about an hour's drive away. Dr. Jack Priest was associated with a medical group with an office in Princeton. Justin aimed the car for Princeton.

On the drive over he began planning his approach. It wouldn't be easy, depending on how much Priest might know. He decided that a very direct approach would be best.

There was no doubt that he was entering onto dangerous ground. But all the things that had bothered him were now starting to come together. The journal was the key. And he *had* to have the answers after his discoveries in England.

Justin pulled the car into the parking lot of the office and checked out the cars. There were two with MD tags. SENTINEL could have told him in a second whether either of the cars was registered to Priest. But, right at this time, Justin didn't want anybody to know what he was up to.

Justin parked the car and went into the office.

A stern-looking woman with close-cut, graying hair sat by the sliding-glass window of the reception area.

"Doctor's office," she said, picking up the buzzing phone as Justin approached.

"No, I'm sorry, but Dr. Roth will be out of the office for the day. Yes, he'll be back tomorrow."

Justin looked down at the appointment book. Priest was in. The book looked well filled. Several early names were crossed out. There was a little morning time available. He'd try for it.

"Wait a second and I'll check," the woman said into the phone, turning the page that Justin was trying to read.

"No, nothing in the morning," she said. "I have an opening at one thirty and another at three. Three? Okay, I'll just put your name in here," she said, scribbling it out.

"That has it, then. We'll see you tomorrow. Good-bye," she said, and put the phone down. She turned the page back to the day's appointments, and Justin's eyes were on it immediately, trying to read the abominable handwriting.

"Yes, can I help you?" she asked.

She reminded him of a teacher he had once had in grammar school. He felt like a schoolboy who had come to school without his homework completed and was now being asked for it.

"Eh...yes. I'm afraid I don't have an appointment. I was wondering whether Dr. Priest could see me this morning," he said.

She wrinkled her face disapprovingly. "I'm sorry, but appointments are required."

The personal angle. Use it.

"I was a close friend of Dr. Priest's brother. My reason for wanting to see him is personal and not related to any medical problem," Justin explained. "I'll only need a few minutes of his time," he added.

"I'm sorry, but appointments are required," she repeated.

"Could you just tell the doctor?"

"I'm sorry, but you'll have to—"

"Will you just *ask* the doctor, please, if he'll have a few minutes to see a friend of his brother?" Justin said in a firm but low voice. "My name is Justin Chaple."

She let out a huff and rose from her chair. "I'll *ask*. Please be seated," she said.

He could hear her muttering under her breath as she disappeared from the reception office.

A moment later she returned. "The doctor will see you in a few minutes," she announced.

Justin breathed an inaudible sigh of relief. "Thank you. I really appreciate it," he said.

"You're welcome," she returned. "The doctor will be with you shortly."

"Thank you," Justin said, and went to take a seat in the waiting room.

About ten minutes later a very pretty face poked around the corner.

"Mr. Chaple?" the nurse called.

Justin rose and walked toward her.

"Follow me, please," she said.

Good ass, Justin thought. He'd follow her anywhere. She led him to a comfortable lounge area that looked like a converted kitchen. She pointed to the coffee on the stove. "Help yourself, if you'd like. The doctor will be right with you."

"Thank you," he said with a smile, and walked in.

Justin walked around the small room, looking at the various plaques and charts. A few moments later he heard voices outside in the hallway.

Dr. Priest continued talking to someone in the hallway and laughed. Then he came into the room.

He was a tall, thin man, with longish, neatly styled hair. He was in his late thirties, Justin guessed.

"Yes?" Priest said with question in his eyes, a smile on his face.

"Dr. Priest, I was a friend of Billy's," Justin lied. In a way it was true.

Priest continued to look into Justin's eyes, waiting.

"I know why he was killed, Dr. Priest. And I've come to help you. I'm here for the journal."

Priest's face tensed. "Journal? I'm sorry but I don't know what you're talking about, Mr. Chaple," Priest said and turned toward the door.

"I wouldn't walk out of here just yet, Dr. Priest. Not until you've heard what I've come to say."

Priest stopped, his back toward Justin.

"They killed Billy for that journal. And they'll kill you for it. I know that it was in the books you brought back from England. And, if I know it, there's a strong possibility that they know it, too."

Priest turned, shaken and white.

"I don't know anything about a—"

"They won't stop with just you, Dr. Priest. It'll be your whole family, your wife and children. Even close friends that they think might know about it. They won't take any chances," Justin warned him. "They'll kill everyone with the remotest possibility of knowing about it. Everyone." Fear would work, Justin sensed it.

Priest was sweating now.

"I'm sorry, Mr. Chaple. I still don't know what you're talking about. You'll have to excuse me, I...I have patients to see." He turned and walked out of the room.

He handed a folder to the pretty nurse in the hallway. "File this, would you, Peg?" Then he disappeared through another door.

Justin walked out of the office.

About thirty minutes later, Priest left the office in a great hurry. He pulled out of the parking lot and headed for Hightstown.

The Impala pulled out a safe distance behind and followed.

Twenty minutes later Priest pulled into the long driveway of his luxurious house. He got out of his car, as the Impala pulled into the driveway behind him.

Priest stood in the driveway and watched, as Justin got out of his car and walked toward him.

The two men stared at one another.

"You do persist, don't you, Mr. Chaple?"

Justin nodded slowly.

"I'm sorry, Mr. Chaple, I wish I could help you, but there is no journal—"

"They'll come for it, Dr. Priest," Justin interrupted.

"And just who are *they?*" Priest asked.

Justin remained silent for a moment. Then he gambled on something he remembered from the twenty-fifth page that he had recovered at Bridges's apartment.

"Operation Raptor, Dr. Priest. Does it mean anything to you?"

The facial reaction of Priest told him that he had struck a nerve.

Priest frowned and looked down at the ground. "Let's walk," he said.

The two men walked to the side of the huge house and to the backyard. They stepped onto a long, shady porch.

Priest stopped and looked out across the low, rolling hills of turf farm behind his property. A high, narrow tower stood on a distant hill.

"There's a small cemetery out there by that tower," he said, pointing. "He's buried up near it. He always liked it there. We used to walk out across the turf farm when he'd come over. We'd go through the cemetery and talk about things. I thought he'd have liked it that way.

"I go up once a week to put flowers on the grave," he said. "And to think about Billy. How much of a waste it was."

"It could be a waste, if nothing is done about that journal," Justin said.

"You keep going back to a journal that doesn't exist," Priest said.

"It involves a matter of national security, Dr. Priest. I'm not at liberty to give you any of the details, other than that your brother and I shared the same line of work.

"He knew what he had found and what was in store for him. He also knew the importance of that journal getting into the right hands."

"Then, if he was your friend, why didn't he give it to you?" Priest asked, realizing that pretenses would no longer work.

"I was on the other side of the world, Dr. Priest. If he knew how to contact me quickly, he would have. Do you think that he wanted to involve his own brother and his family in something that could kill them?

"No, Dr. Priest. But he was out of time. He did the only desperate thing he could think of. He put it into those books using an ultraviolet-sensitive ink, in a code that he knew you'd understand.

"But he also got off a message to me, that he knew I'd eventually get," Justin lied. "He explained what he had done and what I was supposed to do. And now I'm here to help him the way he would have helped me."

Priest looked into Justin's magnificent, lying eyes for a long time, reading them.

"I can't help Billy anymore," Justin began, "but I can try to help you, and to get that information into the proper hands. I said they'd come, and they will—soon. And no one will be left alive when they go.

"It's important that you give me the books and the transcribed journal. I know you've transcribed it. Your only chance is to give it to me. Will you do that? For yourself, for Billy?" Justin asked.

"I can't answer that right now," Priest said. "I haven't even finished decoding it, yet. There are eighty-three books, each one containing a single entry. I've only finished sixty-four. It takes a long time—"

"Then give me the ones that you have and explain the code to me. I'll take the books and do the rest of it myself," Justin said.

"I have to think about it for a while," Priest said.

"You may not have a while," Justin shot back.

"Well, we'll both just have to take that chance, I guess. Besides, the entries aren't here. They're hidden where nobody will ever find them. It'll take time to get them.

"You must understand, also, Mr. Chaple, that my brother gave me a trust. Although I believe that you were his friend, I still have to think about it a little longer. He died for that journal, Mr. Chaple. It was that important to him."

"It's that important to a lot of people, Dr. Priest," Justin said.

"Yes, to kill for something…let me ask you a question?"

Justin nodded.

"Would you kill me for that journal, too?"

Justin thought for a moment. "I've explained that it's a matter of national security. Yes, I'd kill you for it, if there were no other way."

"I believe that you would, Mr. Chaple," Priest said.

"I hope I won't have to," Justin said. "I'll respect your reasons for wanting to think about it for a while. But please, don't take too long. The sooner I get it, the better your chances will be of staying alive. I'll help you as much as I can."

The two men walked around to the front of the house. Justin stopped just before getting into his car. He gave Priest a piece of paper with his phone number and post box number on it.

"For whatever it may be worth to you, Dr. Priest, the man who killed your brother is dead. I watched him die."

"It matters, Mr. Chaple. Thank you," Priest said.

"Call me, Dr. Priest," he said, touching the piece of paper in Priest's hand.

The Impala pulled out of the driveway and drove off.

Irwin Honeycut walked briskly into the Alpha situation room.

"You heard it?" he asked Elizabeth Ryerson.

"Yes, about twenty minutes ago," she answered.

"We might be able to handle it your way, after all," Honeycut said. "Nobody else knows about that journal, and the transcribed sheets are hidden where no one should be able to find them. If Priest is correct about how well he's hidden them, we should be able to recover all the books, take him out, and be home free."

"And Pilgrim?" Elizabeth asked.

"Not just yet. He has an important role to play in that Yarin-Eagle trade. I don't want to risk showing any more faces than I have to. Pilgrim can make an on-the-spot identification of Eagle. He knows him better than anyone.

"Besides, I'd like to find out just how much he does know. That bit about Operation Raptor means he already knows something. He must have found the twenty-fifth page at Bridges's apartment. If he has, we'll have to recover it before settling with him. And then we're out of the woods on this."

"That information alone isn't as dangerous as the journal," Elizabeth said. "We could survive that if we had to."

"You're right. I've already turned Rainmaker around to keep an eye on Priest. If he goes after that transcribed copy, we'll get it all. Then, once the trade is completed, we'll call Pilgrim in and hold him until we determine how much about Operation Raptor he really knows.

"With any luck, it'll all be over in a week," Honeycut said.

"In the meantime," he began, "I've sent in another team to recover the books if Priest should leave the house. He may try to go for the transcripts. Rainmaker will stay with him wherever he goes."

"Good, I really think it's better this way, Irv," Elizabeth said. "The less Pilgrim knows, the less he can hurt us."

"He poses no threat," Honeycut assured her. "However much he may learn, he's still only one man. We'll know everything he does, every place he goes, and everything he says. With that much control, there's nothing one man can do."

Priest's car pulled into the long driveway and came to a stop in front of the closed garage door. He had just returned from Philadelphia International Airport, where he had put his wife and daughters on a plane to Minnesota, to spend some time with her parents. He had the devil to pay trying to explain his actions to his wife.

She had returned home from shopping with the girls to find bags packed and loaded into the car. It was hell all the way out and until they boarded the plane. It was the hardest thing he had ever had to do. Not because of the barrage of unanswerable questions from his wife, but because he loved them so much. And, seeing them leave, he realized he would possibly never see them again. He held the tears until they were out of sight. At least they would live.

He posted a letter before leaving the airport. Rainmaker reported this, then followed him back to Hightstown.

Once in the house, Priest locked all the doors and windows and went into the study. He prepared to finish decoding the last nineteen journal entries. He took out the ultraviolet lamp and a pad and pencils. Then he went to get the books.

His heart leaped, and his ears pounded from a sudden rush of blood when he saw the empty boxes. *The books were gone!*

He thought for a second, then went to his desk, took Justin's number from his pocket, and picked up the phone. He read the number and lit the paper, burning it in an ashtray. Then he disintegrated the ashes.

He touched out the number on the touch-tone phone.

Then he heard the sound.

It came from inside the house. Someone was there. His nerves jumped, as Justin's phone rang the first time.

His brain raced. He thought about the trust that his dead brother had given him. He had already decided to share it with Justin.

That's what was in the letter he had mailed to Justin's post office box number. In it he told him that he intended to work continuously until the journal was completed, then he would pick up the rest of it from where he had hidden it. Then he'd give it all to him.

He thought about the parts of the journal he had read, as Justin's phone rang. He knew what it said, but he couldn't bring the complete significance of it into focus. There were things that only Billy knew that were needed to complete it. Possibly Justin Chaple knew them, as well, and could make it fit together into the thing that had scared Billy so much.

The phone rang.

He heard another sound. It was just outside the study this time.

Oh, God! Answer it, he thought. Please! Please, answer it!

"Hello," Justin's voice said.

Priest was sweating, his brain and ears were pounding with fear. His eyes burned.

"Hello, this is Jack Priest," he said, careful not to mention Justin's name. The trust was complete.

Priest's eyes watered as he saw the doorknob begin to turn slowly. He was shaking with fear.

"I...I just called to ask you something," he said, his voice quivering.

The door began to open slightly.

Priest looked away, not wanting to see what he knew was coming.

Fear had his voice, but he had to tell Justin what he could, without spilling it all to the wrong ears.

"I...I just wondered," he began, "if you were such a good friend of Billy's, why didn't you visit his grave?"

There was a soft thud. Then another.

Justin never heard the silencer, just the sound of the phone falling.

Then the line went dead.

Justin sat, puzzled. He began running the strange question through his head again.

BEEP!

The tone startled him.

BLEEP! He responded via eustachian implant after only a moment's delay.

Barbara was asleep on the bed beside him. He got out of the bed gently, so as not to wake her, and walked out into the living room.

"Yes?" he said in a low whisper.

"Pilgrim, you are needed," the soft voice said. "Can you leave in the morning for St. Simon's Island?" SENTINEL asked him.

Justin's stomach knotted with anxiety.

Was it possible that someone had monitored the whole thing, right from the first visit to Priest?

If so, he was a dead man.

There was little he could do in his situation. He had to go along. There was no running with that implant in his head. He could be found anywhere.

"Yes, what arrangements have been made?" he asked.

"You will be leaving from Teterboro Airport at eight-oh-five A.M. on the Lear. Sorry to disturb you on your vacation, but something very important has come up regarding Phoenix. You will be briefed at St. Simon's. You can plan on returning home in three days."

"Okay, I'll be there," Justin said.

"Thank you, Pilgrim. Rest well," SENTINEL said, ending the transmission.

Justin sat back on the couch, trying to settle his thoughts. Could being called in have been coincidental? Or was this it?

Barbara came stumbling into the dark living room.

"What's wrong?" she asked sleepily.

"Nothing, hon. I have to leave for a few days, that's all. Vacation's over, I'm afraid," he said.

"Is that what the call was about?" she asked.

"Yep."

"The least they could have done was waited until morning," she complained.

She sat next to him on the couch.

He put his arm around her, and they lay back across the soft cushions. In a few moments Barbara's breathing became deep and steady. She was asleep.

Justin held her softly, feeling the rise and fall of her breasts.

He looked at her for a long time, appreciating her being there with him. He loved her dearly. He just wanted to hold her, and hold her, never letting go.

Especially in the morning.

THIRTY-SIX

I have warned them to watch Titus. I fear he will harm the plan in some way. I recommended neutralization, but they did not listen. I am old, they think going senile.

My health fails daily. I have great difficulty in writing and seeing the paper. I can no longer walk well or use my left arm.

I have visions of all those who died. I see their crying eyes. The end is near for me, but I am happy, for, close behind, will come the beginning.

Entry No. 77 from the partially
recovered *Wolf Journal*

The flight down to St. Simon's was smooth and routine, but Justin remained ready for the worst possible trouble.

Richard Wyatt was waiting for Justin when the elevator doors opened at the lower level of the Dials Cardiac Clinic.

"Hello, Pilgrim. How was your flight out?" Wyatt greeted, extending a hand.

"Real good," Justin answered, taking it in a firm shake. "What's all the fuss about Phoenix?" he asked.

"A trade has been negotiated," Wyatt said.

Justin stared hard into Wyatt's face.

Wyatt nodded. "I know what you're thinking."

"Only half of it," Justin said. "How the hell come? After all the shit that we've been through over this, how can they let him go back?"

"They've got someone we need back very badly, for reasons you'll soon learn," Wyatt said, as the two men walked down the long corridor toward the situation room.

"I don't believe this," Justin said incredulously. "He's seen faces, places, and has to know about Alpha and St. Simon's. He can still hurt us pretty bad."

Wyatt shook his head. "He can't hurt us at all, or we'd never let him go, no matter who they had."

Justin remained on his guard as they walked. Although everything seemed normal, he wasn't about to let his defenses down. The facts he had learned in the past week had left him confused about what was real and what wasn't, about whom to trust and whom not to.

"Who are we trading for?" Justin asked.

"You'll learn that, as well as the answers to all of your questions, in just a few minutes."

They reached the situation room and walked through the sliding doors.

Irwin Honeycut was standing there.

Justin's defenses were ready to pop. His eyes went quickly back and forth between Wyatt's and Honeycut's, assessing.

"Hello, Pilgrim," Honeycut said, sticking out a hand.

"How do you do, sir?" Justin said, taking the handshake.

"I'm sorry we've had to disturb your vacation like this, but it's a very important matter," Honeycut said.

"Thank you, Dick. I'll take it from here," Honeycut said to Wyatt.

Wyatt smiled his farewells and left the situation room.

The two men stood alone, silent, staring into one another's eyes.

"How was your vacation?" Honeycut said at last, breaking the staring match.

"Just fine," Justin answered, ready.

"Have you thought about my offer?" Honeycut asked.

"Yes."

"And?"

Justin didn't know what kind of game was being played here, or who was on whose side. Playing along would buy time until he learned more.

"I've decided to take it," he said.

"Good! Good!" Honeycut said, shaking Justin's hand warmly. "That was a good decision," he said, nodding with a broad smile. "Now I'll tell you what we're up against."

Honeycut gestured toward a chair situated in front of a large desk. Justin moved to it and took the seat. Honeycut moved to the desk and sat behind it. He reached to a center drawer, opened it, and reached his hand inside.

Justin nearly went for the Mauser as Honeycut's hand withdrew, but the movement was aborted when he saw a thin metallic plate in the hand as it came up.

"This is your new ID plate. You'll see that it bears an SSC-7X security clearance. That is the second highest possible rating in the agency. You can do anything with that X, open *any* file, request unlimited access to SENTINEL, anything at all, including starting a small war if you had to. You'll be needing that authority to help us solve our problem," Honeycut said.

Justin was stunned and confused. Only seconds before he had thought that a gun was coming out of the drawer. Now he didn't know what to think. Honeycut was working his magic again.

"The rating goes with your new job," Honeycut told him. "You started when you got on that plane in Teterboro."

"How did you know that I'd want it?"

"I knew," Honeycut answered, a knowing smile on his face. "You and men like you are the future of this agency," he said. "You're dedicated to your country and to what this agency stands for. I had the card made before you even went on vacation." He smiled.

Justin smiled back weakly.

"Now I'll tell you what we're up against," Honeycut said, his face grown suddenly serious.

"You know that we've been after the journal that Spartan recovered. We've been able to recover about half of it from the ashes in Spartan's fireplace. It was enough to tell us that we're in potentially deep trouble."

He looked into Justin's eyes for signs.

"The agency has been infiltrated," he said.

Justin's confusion showed openly on his face now.

"Infiltrated? By who? Soviets?" Justin asked.

Honeycut shook his head. "No, not the Soviets. From what we've been able to recover from the ashes, we've learned that the journal was written by a man known as Wolf. We don't know *who* Wolf was, but we do know *what* he was. He was a Nazi."

Justin rose from his chair and took several slow steps away from Honeycut.

Of course, he thought, the journal was in German. It was found in Madrid, the known Nazi headquarters in the world. Then there was the twenty-fifth page that he had found at Bridges's apartment. It had mentioned Niederlage, 1941, and something called Operation Raptor. It also had code names on it, and places: Spain, Argentina, South Africa, Germany, and *the United States.*

He turned back to Honeycut, half debating whether to tell him about the twenty-fifth page and Spartan's brother. Perhaps the information on that twenty-fifth page gave the real reasons why Bridges tried to go over. He decided to wait on telling Honeycut, until he could learn more.

"Nazis? Are you sure?" Justin asked.

"Yes. There's little doubt left by what we've found. They plan a Fourth Reich right here in the United States.

"That's why it's so important that we get our hands on the rest of that journal. It could tell us a great deal more, including whom we're looking for," Honeycut said.

"But we've got to get this Phoenix deal cleared up first, then we'll concentrate all of our efforts on this matter. You'll be given the parts of the journal that we've uncovered and all of the assistance we can safely give you.

"We've got to be very careful, however, as we don't know how deep the infiltration goes or how high up. We do know that it must start high, SSC-seven level or higher, a person with the ability to use SENTINEL exclusively and safely, without detection. Someone in a position to utilize SENTINEL to their aim when the time comes.

"With SENTINEL to do their bidding, it could be the most formidable movement the world has ever known. Unstoppable."

"But how could someone gain that kind of control? I thought that all security classifications were meticulously screened?" Justin asked.

"They are. But the journal leaves little doubt that someone *has* gained that potential, somehow. Covers arranged over thirty-five years ago could be flawless. Even impossible for SENTINEL to detect."

Justin began to pace again, thinking.

"And you think that the rest of the journal will give you those answers?" he asked finally.

"It could," Honeycut answered.

Justin's stomach was doing flips. Maybe he had stumbled onto the same discovery that Bridges and Spartan had made, and what Honeycut was telling him was the truth.

And there was Fanning. What part had he played in it? Whose side was he really on? How deep did it go? He still needed more answers.

"I'll need an absolute classified status," Justin said. "Can that be arranged?"

Honeycut nodded. "A file can be voice-print locked. Only your voice can activate it or utilize SENTINEL through it," he replied.

"I mean *absolute*," Justin repeated. "That means not even open to Executive order. Can you arrange it?"

Honeycut nodded. "I'll arrange it. Looks like we'll both be earning our pay around here in very short order," he said.

"Now I'll tell you about Phoenix," Honeycut started. "The Soviets are holding a very important agent of ours. Eagle. He was captured the day after we apprehended Phoenix.

"Eagle was our man in Moscow who got the information vital to stopping Phoenix.

"He's had a very rough go of it since being taken. They've used extensive sensory deprivation techniques in trying to break him. We don't think he gave them anything, but we can't be sure.

"SENTINEL managed to induce a form of sleep hypnosis on him in one of the early stages of their efforts, while we were still able to make contact with his implant.

"After that, all contact and implant monitoring was impossible. We don't know what happened from then on.

"He's out of sensory deprivation now, recovering from a very rough experience. No doubt, they're trying to get him back into decent shape for the trade."

"We're taking risks in making this trade," Justin said. "Phoenix knows about Alpha, St. Simon's, and he's seen faces, including mine."

"Alpha is being closed down," Honeycut said. "Even without the trade, we wouldn't take the risk of leaving Alpha open.

Regarding St. Simon's Island, Phoenix doesn't know where he is. He could be in China for all he knows."

"And the people that he could identify? I'm on that list," Justin said.

"That's one of the reasons you're here, too. You'll be his escort for the trade."

"That'll blow my cover wide open," Justin said, shaking his head. "I don't like that."

"No, your cover will emerge intact. We can't risk showing any more faces to them. And they'll never see yours again, because, in your new capacity, you'll never be used in the field against them. Our only problem will exist with the CIA."

"The CIA?" Justin repeated.

"Yes, the Soviets didn't know how to make contact, so they went through Robert Morsand in Paris."

"They'll investigate me," Justin said.

"Your cover will hold up to any investigation. We've no problem there. But we'll have to be careful in the immediate future, until they believe your cover," Honeycut said.

"And what is that?"

"You're simply helping to identify an American citizen held by the Soviets for suspicion of espionage. The fact that you know him so well will make that believable," Honeycut explained.

"But I don't know Eagle. They'd find that out in a minute," Justin said.

"What they'll find out, in fact, is that you *do* know him quite well. Eagle's name is Steven Pappachristus."

"Pappy?" Justin gasped in stunned disbelief.

"Yes. Steve has been with the agency for over five years now," Honeycut said.

"He can't be Eagle," Justin insisted. "You said that Eagle was taken by the Soviets the *day* after we caught Phoenix, didn't you?"

Honeycut nodded.

"Well, I talked to Pappy a *week* after we took Phoenix," Justin said. "Steve has been in Saudi Arabia for over a year now. I've got letters and cards from him to prove it."

"The letters and cards you received from Steve were arranged as part of his cover. He's been inside Russia for the whole length of time you believed him to be in the Middle East," Honeycut said.

"I *spoke* with him on the phone," Justin countered.

"You didn't speak to Pappy, 'little brother,' " Honeycut said. "You spoke to SENTINEL."

"D-eighty is a derivative of a drug called daunorubicin. We were able to attain remission in Kuradin, using the D-eighty protocol as originally planned. We were lucky. We had even been prepared to use D-eighty-three on him until Wyatt's debriefing of him was completed," Dr. Becker Dials explained to Justin.

"And what is D-eighty-three?" Justin asked.

"D-eighty-three is a derivative form of D-eighty, which absolutely stops all forms of cancer. But we can't use it."

"Why not?" Justin inquired.

"While it stops cancer completely, its administration must be continued on an indefinite basis. To stop taking it causes death within seventy-two hours. In *all* cases."

Justin raised his eyebrows.

"We have high hopes that our research into the enzymes of the daunorubicin metabolic pathways may lead us to discover even more effective yet less toxic drug systems to use," Dials said, "possibly even a complete cure for cancer."

"And what happens after he's swapped back to the Russians?" Justin asked.

"Oh, he'll probably retain remission for about thirty days, then he'll go quickly. Nothing but D-eighty or D-eighty-three would achieve remission again after that. Even on a continuing D-eighty protocol, in his particular condition, I would guess only four to six months of life left for him. The time factor is practically irrelevant."

"Does he know this?" Justin asked.

"Yes. And he still wishes to go home to die."

"The point is that it doesn't matter what the hell Phoenix wants," Honeycut growled. "It's not his decision to make. We want Eagle back, and they want Phoenix. So he goes, like it or not, live or die. It's *our* decision to make.

"Eagle has an old-style implant, which is larger and more easily detectable than the newer ones like you're wearing," Honeycut said to Justin. "A very real danger exists that they may find the implant and remove it before we get Eagle back. With that implant in their possession, they may be able to learn enough to start intercepting our transmissions. Once they can do that, they'll be able to locate our agents, pinpoint sensors and satellites, even transmit their own signals to jam our communications.

"It's a real threat that can hurt us. And that's why I want you there," Honeycut said to an attentive Justin. "You've got to make sure that we get Eagle back safely...or kill him if it becomes necessary."

Justin's stomach sank.

"We can't take the chance that they'll get that implant," Honeycut said. "We know that it's still in place, but there's no telling what they may try to pull off."

"But..." Justin began.

"It's not a pleasant possibility," Honeycut broke in before Justin could speak further, "but it's a necessary eventuality that we must be prepared for. Chances are that the trade will come off without a hitch, but I wanted you to be prepared mentally for what may become necessary."

"Thanks a lot," Justin said icily.

"The Soviets think that Phoenix will be carrying a microdot implant in his scalp," Honeycut began again. "But that's been found."

"Yes, I remember," Justin said. "The wound on the back of the head."

"That's right," Dials said. "They have no way of knowing that we've found it. They're playing their last trump card."

"There will be yourself; Dr. Waith, whom, you may remember, patched you up after your little encounter with Ten Braak; two people from the State Department; Robert Morsand from the CIA; and his aide, Bud Kodek," Honeycut said.

"When and where does the trade take place?"

"Tomorrow. In Dieppe, France. You'll be in continual contact with us through SENTINEL during the entire operation. Just be careful around Morsand. He's smart and picks up little things quickly."

Justin nodded.

Honeycut placed a hand on Justin's shoulder. "I have every confidence that the trade will go off smoothly. Believe me, we all want Steve back safely, too."

"Tomorrow, at fourteen hundred hours," Robert Morsand said to Bud Kodek, "Yentik will be in charge on their side. Technically, I'm to be in charge for us, but I haven't got the foggiest notion of what the hell is going on.

"Platt said that all of his investigations into the matter were stopped by direct Presidential order. He got called into the Oval Office and was told straight out that the trade was to take place. Some phony crap about an American citizen being held under suspicion of espionage."

"Who is this guy Yarin?" Kodek asked.

"No one has told me a thing about him, either—just that the trade is to take place and that Limpoulous, if that's his real name, is to be flown directly to Washington," Morsand replied.

"You think Yarin could be Chakhovsky?" Kodek asked.

"Might be. Platt has been burning our asses about that since it happened. I was sure that Yentik wanted to talk about

Chakhovsky when he asked for the meeting. Maybe you're right. Maybe Yarin is Chakhovsky."

"Then who could Limpoulous be?"

"We'll just have to wait and see. I want pictures of the whole transaction. Close-ups on all the faces. I want to hear every word that's said when they meet for the exchange. There's something going on that Platt wants to know about. And I've also got a score to settle with someone over that Chakhovsky deal.

"No one burns my ass like that and gets away with it," Morsand said.

It was 0100 hours at St. Simon's Island. Deep in thought, Justin sat in one of the conference rooms.

Goddamn, but I'm confused, he thought. Nothing could surprise him anymore. What a fucking week it had been. He had learned about the books in England; discovered that Fanning could have killed Spartan; located the journal, though he hadn't gotten his hands on it yet; found out that the agency was infiltrated by Nazis; was told that Phoenix was being traded back to the Russians; also, that the man they were trading him for was his best friend, who he didn't even know was in the agency and whom he might have to kill before this day was out, if anything went wrong.

It almost made him laugh. What the fuck could happen next. He'd probably find out that Barbara was a transsexual. He laughed an unbelieving laugh and sipped his tea.

The hot tea made him think of his thermal mug…and the ashtray; his secret arsenal of weapons.

He knew that soon he'd have to tell Honeycut about the journal and the twenty-fifth page. He felt that he could trust Honeycut. But he didn't know who else could be trusted.

What if Honeycut couldn't get the absolute classification? What if the top infiltrator could still monitor all of his computer utilization?

Of course, if he could get the journal from Priest before telling Honeycut, he might have the answers he needed. Maybe he wouldn't tell Honeycut, after all, until he had it.

Then he thought about that odd message that Priest had left him with on the phone, about not visiting his brother's grave. What did he mean? Was he saying that he wasn't going to give him the journal because he didn't believe the story? He was sure he had gotten through to him.

Justin heard sounds in the hallway. The doors slid open as Richard Wyatt walked in.

"Hi," Wyatt greeted. "About ready to leave?"

"All set," Justin answered.

"Good. They'll be bringing Phoenix in here in a few minutes. See that he wears this hat the entire time until you have Eagle," Wyatt said, tossing a knit cap on the table.

Justin picked it up and examined it.

"It's to hide his head," Wyatt explained.

"Hide his head?" Justin repeated.

"Yes, Dr. Dials wasn't as explicit in his description of the D-eighty side effects as he should have been. Aside from the nausea and weight loss, all of Phoenix's hair has fallen out. He's as bald as an egg. If they see the bald head, they may figure that he doesn't have his implant anymore and decide not to make the trade. It won't be long now, and then this nightmare will be over," Wyatt said.

For you maybe, Justin thought, and wondered what Wyatt's SSC rating was—SSC-7 or better, Honeycut had said. He wondered how many people that included.

"Is your cover all straight in your mind?" Wyatt asked. "You can bet that Morsand will be suspicious about you."

Justin nodded.

"Well, good luck then," Wyatt said, extending his hand.

"Thanks," Justin returned, taking it.

"I'll be on the monitor with Pegasus. If anything at all seems out of place, let us know with a single tone from your eustachian implant."

Justin nodded.

Wyatt nodded and left the room.

A few moments later more noises came from the hallway. The doors slid open, and Kuradin was brought in, in a wheelchair. Two armed military police were on either side of him, a third guided the chair into the room.

Justin was shocked at Phoenix's appearance. He looked a full thirty pounds lighter, and there were dark rings around the sunken, tired eyes. His face was gray, cheeks sunken, and his nose was thin and beaklike. All of his hair was gone, even his eyebrows.

Justin and Kuradin locked eyes.

Kuradin hadn't expected to see Pilgrim again. A slight spark of anxiety coursed through him.

"We meet again, Pilgrim," Kuradin said, his voice tired and weak.

Justin said nothing.

"Again, and for the last time," Kuradin said.

Justin looked at him coldly.

"I wish to thank you," Kuradin said.

No reaction on Justin's face.

"I heard that you gave me platelets after my capture. We now share more than a profession, it seems."

"We share nothing," Justin said.

"More than you think," Kuradin spoke, his eyes still sharp and penetrating, despite his condition.

"We share nothing," Justin repeated coldly.

"We share a way of life, one which owns us and pushes us in a changing current of fortunes. We win…we lose."

"You lost," Justin said.

"Yes, today I lose. Today, with no tomorrow for me."

"It hasn't been a total loss," Justin said. "You're going home— alive. That's always a small measure of victory in this business. But don't thank me for that. If I had my way, you'd be worm pudding by now."

"Yes, I'm going home. Home. To my daughter and my grand-children, perhaps. If they'll let me."

Justin stared with unfeeling eyes.

"You see, we have a black-and-white view of things in Russia. To err is human...to forgive is not Russian policy."

"Put this on," Justin said, tossing the cap into Kuradin's lap. "And you leave it on, or I'll see that you never make it back," he warned.

Such hate in a man so young, Kuradin thought. He pulled the cap over his head.

"Lower, over the ears," Justin said.

Kuradin knew why. He did as he was told.

Justin took out a small hypodermic needle and walked toward Kuradin. "Roll up your sleeve," he ordered.

Kuradin knew they would put him out, so he would not see any of the surrounding area on the way to the first plane. He rolled up his left sleeve.

Justin dabbed the spot on the arm with an alcohol swatch and jammed the needle in.

Kuradin winced from the deliberately crude action.

Justin withdrew the needle and dabbed the area again.

The room began to spin, and light closed in quickly from the outside into a narrow circle. Kuradin's head swayed, then fell to the right.

"Get him out of here," Justin said to the guards.

Kuradin had come to to the sounds of the swishing jet engines over mid-ocean. He sat absolutely still, keeping his eyes closed. *He was going home!*

His mission was nearly over. A few more hours, and it would be history—and Russia would have the computer.

He had played the endgame skillfully, maintaining that deli-cate and valuable tempo that invariably proves to be the winning factor in the very close game.

He let his muscles and mind relax.

There was no more to do but to take the last steps across an empty runway. The last steps to safety and winning. The last steps home.

In the lower levels of the Dials Cardiac Clinic, a nurse adjusted the drip rate of one of the intravenous hookups running into Dmitri Chakhovsky.

Suddenly, the still hand moved.

The nurse looked down with a start as the arm raised off the bed, then fell back.

There was a moan, then the eyes blinked.

They opened weakly, blinking again, to try to clear the blurred image in front of them.

The nurse pushed the call button.

A team rushed into the room.

Thirty minutes later Becker Dials was on the phone to Honeycut.

"Yes, what is it?" Honeycut graveled out.

"Irv, this is Buck. Get down to the ICU right away. Chakhovsky is coming out of coma."

Honeycut sat up sharply. "Notify Wyatt and Dr. Ryerson, immediately. I'll be down in two minutes. Can he talk?"

"Not yet, but I think he'll be able to in a few hours," Dials answered.

"Will he be coherent?"

"There's no telling at this point. All vital signs look good. I'd say that there's a good chance that he will be."

"I'm on my way."

THIRTY-SEVEN

Colorosa visited me today. I told him about Titus. I think he believed me. He said he would take care of the matter.

I am ready to die, but Colorosa tells me that I will live forever. He says there will be monuments all over the world in my name. That I will hold a high place in history.

Colorosa has done more...more than all the wars put together to achieve our moment in history.

He is a great man, and through him I have seen the next...Führer. So soon in time, another has come with greatness beyond belief.

Entry No. 81 from the partially
recovered *Wolf Journal*

Justin ran the cool, damp towel across his forehead and eyes. It felt refreshing. He hadn't slept at all since leaving St. Simon's Island.

His brain had sliced away at the facts and available bits of information, sorting them, reassembling them, trying to make a clearer picture of the incredibly jumbled mess.

The big government jet had been on the ground for almost twenty minutes. It had taxied to an isolated part of the unused runway and shut down its engines.

The Russian plane was already on the ground and sat waiting several hundred yards away.

The sky over Dieppe was gray, and a heavy rain was falling, driven by cold, gusting winds untypical for July.

Justin put down the towel and walked over to a small table. On it was a narrow flat case. He opened it.

Inside was a Colt Trooper MK 111 .357 magnum. It was a big weapon with a four-inch barrel; forty-one ounces of blued steel, capable of scoring a kill with even a leg or arm hit, due to the tremendous hydraulic shock effect on the body. The extra hitting power of the magnum would come in handy if it came down to needing it today.

Justin strapped the pit holster on and swung out the cylinder, to make sure the weapon was fully loaded. Then he slipped it gently into the holster. It was heavy, but fit comfortably.

He looked out the small window as he put on the vinyl rain jacket. He could see men approaching and spotted Robert Morsand immediately. The big man at his side he recognized as Bud Kodek.

He recognized only one man from a second pair approaching from further back. It was Arthur Edgar, with the State Department.

Justin made one last check in a wall-mounted mirror to be sure the Colt didn't show. Satisfied, he left the cabin, passed through another compartment, and into the main cabin, where Kuradin sat handcuffed to one of the military police who had made the trip from St. Simon's Island.

Morsand and Kodek stepped briskly into the driving rain.

"Any bets that it's Chakhovsky?" Kodek said.

"I hope to hell that it's not," Morsand returned.

"Was Platt able to give you anything further on Limpoulous or this guy Chaple?" Kodek asked.

"Nothing worth a shit," Morsand answered. "But I didn't expect it. The State Department has stepped into it. It's their show. We're only here for appearances," he said.

"Is Platt pushing the investigation?"

"You can bet your ass he is. Executive order or not, he's got trusted people working on it. He wants answers, and so do I," Morsand said.

"Is everybody in position?" he asked Kodek.

"We're all set. We'll get pictures of everybody on both sides. The sound team is set up to record the entire verbal exchange from the time both sides head out to the meeting point," Kodek told him.

"Good, now let's see some faces," Morsand said, as they reached the stair ramp to the plane.

Justin heard the hurried steps on the metal stairs. Then Morsand came through the open door into the main cabin, Kodek right behind him.

Morsand's eyes shot immediately to Kuradin. Combined relief and disappointment swept through him. He had almost expected to see Chakhovsky.

After a long stare, he fixed his eyes on Justin.

Justin looked back calmly.

"You Chaple?" Morsand asked.

"Yes," Justin answered politely.

"Robert Morsand," the introduction came, hand extended.

Justin accepted it.

"This is Bud Kodek."

The two shook hands.

Morsand looked around the cabin quickly, saw the door to one of the aft cabins, and looked back to Justin.

"Would you come with me, please?" he said.

The two men walked back into the cabin, and Morsand closed the door behind them.

"Sit down, Mr. Chaple," Morsand directed.

"No thanks, I'll stand," Justin said.

Morsand looked into the cool eyes for a moment. Too controlled, he thought.

"Just how do you fit into this?" Morsand asked.

Justin didn't answer for a moment. He knew that Morsand knew next to nothing about him.

"You must have a dossier on me. You probably know a great deal about me and a hell of a lot more about this than I do," he said.

"Suppose you just tell me everything that you know," Morsand said.

"I'm sorry, Mr. Morsand, I have nothing to say to you," Justin said, turning toward the door.

"Wait a minute, you," Morsand said, reaching out and grabbing Justin's shoulder.

Too quickly, Justin spun to face him, the eyes ice, ready.

He calmed himself quickly, but Morsand had already seen it.

"There's nothing to say," Justin repeated calmly.

"Your ass! I want to know about Limpoulous, who he is, and what all this has got to do with you," Morsand said.

"I know him, that's all," Justin said.

"What's his real name and what was he doing in Russia?" Morsand quizzed.

"I thought you guys were supposed to know everything about everybody. You tell me," Justin said.

"Just answer my question," Morsand fumed, his index finger pounding into Justin's chest.

In an instant, Justin had Morsand's wrist in his viselike grip.

"Save that crap for someone else," Justin told him and pushed the hand away.

"You'll tell me what I want to know or I'll start an investigation on you that will teach me more about you than you know yourself," Morsand threatened. "More than you'll want known," he said.

Justin smiled. "Go suck an egg," he said, turning once again for the door.

"You son-of-a—"

The door opened from the outside, and Arthur Edgar stuck his head in.

Justin used the interruption to leave.

Edgar stepped in, closing the door behind him.

Morsand stood facing the smaller, portly man with the shiny bald head.

"What's this all about, Morsand?" the State Department official asked.

"It's between him and me," Morsand replied.

"You were told to ask no questions," the smaller man said. "Not to talk to Yarin, Limpoulous, or Chaple before or after the trade. This isn't your show. It's a State Department matter. You're only here out of protocol, because the arrangements were through your office."

"Don't give me that shit," Morsand said. "You can bet your left nut that I'm going to find out what this is all about. This is my turf. What goes on here I know about, or I get mighty sore."

"You're a fool, Morsand. An Executive order has been given to Platt, to discontinue all forms of investigation into this matter. It doesn't concern you—"

"Save it, because I'm not listening. There's something going on, and I'm going to know about it."

Edgar looked at Morsand. He knew no more about it than Morsand did. He wanted answers, too. But an Executive order was an Executive order.

Morsand was a valuable man, and Edgar didn't want to anger him any more than he had to.

Edgar looked down, thinking.

"I know very little, myself," he began. "But I promise you, Bob, that whatever I learn will cross your desk. That's the best I can do right now," he said.

Morsand nodded reluctantly. "All right, but I want answers soon. Or I'll find them myself," he said.

"You'll get them, I promise you. Officially, you're supposed to be in charge of this affair, at least for the record you are. Outside of this room, only you and I will know that it belongs to State. We'll be responsible for whatever happens today. Now you better go out and take charge," he said.

"You go ahead. I have to cool off a little," Morsand said. "Give me a few minutes."

"All right. We've got about fifty minutes, yet. Take your time," Edgar told him and went to the door.

"Tell Kodek to come in here, would you?" Morsand asked.

Edgar looked back at him for a moment and raised a finger. "Remember, between you and me. Kodek knows nothing."

Morsand nodded, knowing that Kodek already knew.

Edgar nodded and left the cabin.

A few moments later Kodek stepped in.

"What did Edgar have to say?" he asked.

"Same old shit that we knew before we got here. It's our show, but it isn't," Morsand said. "Ask no questions, just sit and watch, and pretend we're telling everybody what to do," he said, the anger still in his face.

"Business as usual?" Kodek asked.

Morsand smiled. "You're learning."

Over an hour passed before the party began to file out of the plane. The rain had eased, and only a light drizzle filled the air.

From the far side of the runway, well concealed in the trees, a shutter snapped, as each face showed in the open doorway of the plane. The high-powered lenses took incredibly close-up pictures of everyone, special attention being given to Justin, Kuradin, and Dr. Waith.

The wheels had begun rolling for Robert Morsand.

About sixty yards from the plane, three cars had pulled into position, parked one behind the other in a straight line.

A hundred yards out, another line of cars was parked, behind them the Soviet plane. The Soviet party had not yet disembarked.

Dr. Waith and Justin stood off to one side, away from everyone else. Kuradin sat with the guard in one of the cars.

Waith looked around, to be sure they were out of earshot. Then he reached for Justin's left hand and looked at the thin, straight scar across it.

"It healed well," he said. "Any problems using it?" he asked.

"Works fine, Doc. You did a great job," Justin answered.

Waith smiled.

"He's been through hell," he said, looking across at the Russian plane. "After you've confirmed Eagle's identity, check behind the right ear, to see if there are any signs of surgical procedure.

"Our monitoring tells us that the implant is still in place. But there was a six-week period when contact was impossible. We must ascertain whether, during that period, they located it, removed it, then put it back. It's a possibility," Waith said.

Justin nodded.

"You know, if anything should go wrong and Eagle is not handed over, it'll be an even worse hell for him?" Waith said.

Justin nodded. "I know. That won't happen. I won't let it."

"As long as you understand."

"Don't worry. I understand," Justin assured him.

Morsand walked over to Justin. He stood next to him, pipe in his mouth, looking out at the Russian plane.

"It's about a hundred yards to their cars," Morsand began. "That's a long walk in the open," he said.

He didn't have to tell Justin. He had been staring at that no-man's-land for many long moments. That wasn't the place to be if the shit started flying.

"Exchanges like this are funny," Morsand began again. "I've seen them blow up like a time bomb. If anything happens while you're out there, just hit the deck and keep Yarin low. Don't try to run, because you'll be handcuffed together, and dragging him will only make you a good target. Don't undo the cuffs if you have to hit the deck, keep the cuffs on him to prevent him from running. And stay down.

"I don't expect anything like that to happen," Morsand continued. "Most trades go off smooth as silk. But if it shouldn't, you'll know what to do."

"I'll know what to do," Justin assured him.

"They're coming out," Kodek shouted, raising a pair of binoculars.

Morsand and Justin moved closer to Kodek. Waith went to the car that Kuradin was in.

"Who do you see?" Morsand asked.

Kuradin was helped out of the car.

Kodek looked through the binoculars at the people emerging from the Soviet plane.

"There's Yentik," Kodek said. "I can see Sharkenko, and it looks like...Olganskaya, and...wait a second..." He whistled. "That's Krykov there, too!"

Anatoly Krykov did not come from Moscow for a nobody. Morsand looked long and hard at Kuradin, wondering.

The Russian names meant nothing to Justin. He watched passively.

"Are you sure that's Krykov?" Morsand asked.

"Positive."

Morsand looked back to Justin. "You can relax. There won't be any trouble," he said.

Justin looked at him quizzically.

"That man just starting down is Anatoly Krykov. He works for Leonid Travkin directly. There won't be any trouble with Krykov here," he said.

"That's good to know," Justin said. Until they find out that the microdot implant isn't there, he wanted to say.

"That must be Limpoulous," Kodek said. "He's big, real big. And he's cuffed."

He handed the glasses to Justin. "Here, take a look."

Justin took the glasses and raised them, adjusting them to his eyes.

It was Pappy, all right, and moving mighty slow, being helped down the stairs. It hurt to see him that way.

"It's him," he said, handing the glasses back after a few more moments of verification.

"All right, let's get ready," Morsand said.

He pulled out a pair of handcuffs. He put one cuff on Justin's left wrist and handed him the key. "Unlock it only *after* you've made positive identification," he instructed.

Justin nodded.

Kuradin was brought over. He was uncuffed from the guard and cuffed to Justin by the right wrist.

"They'll raise a white flag when they're ready. We'll do the same. One minute later, they'll raise a red flag. You'll start when we raise ours. You'll meet in the middle, make your identification, then turn Yarin over to them. Come straight back as quickly as possible," Morsand said.

Justin nodded. As quickly as possible was right.

Kuradin's nerves were like live wires. He was a hundred yards away from success. It had seemed like it would never come. But it was finally at hand. He had played the endgame brilliantly. One move left to play in the game, then it was checkmate.

Richard Wyatt walked into the intensive care unit at the Dials Cardiac Clinic.

Dr. Becker Dials was hunched over Dmitri Chakhovsky.

"Is he coherent, yet?" Wyatt asked.

"Semi," Dials answered.

"They're ready to go, on that trade," Wyatt said. "Can he answer one question?"

"You can try," Dials told him. "I think he'll hear you okay, but I don't know if he'll understand what you're trying to ask him. His mind works in Russian and it may be too clouded to translate readily," he said.

"We've got to try," Wyatt said. "Do we have an audio setup to SENTINEL in here?" he asked. "Maybe we can get SENTINEL to talk to him in Russian."

Dials walked a few steps to the SENTINEL computer console and pushed the white button.

"Yes," the soft voice responded.

"SENTINEL, we need some linguistics assistance. In Russian," Dials said.

"Ready," the voice sounded.

The white flag went up on the Soviet side. Kodek held up a white flag as well.

"One minute," Morsand announced.

Wyatt leaned over the bed, close to Chakhovsky's ear. "Dmitri... Dmitri," he said softly.

The Russian's eyes opened weakly, fluttered, remained open slightly.

"SENTINEL, ask him if he can hear and understand what's being said to him," Wyatt directed.

SENTINEL asked in Russian.

There was no response.

"Louder," Wyatt said.

SENTINEL repeated the question, in a louder voice.

Chakhovsky nodded slightly.

"Good. Good," Wyatt whispered. He took out a photograph of Kuradin from an envelope and held it up in front of Chakhovsky's face.

"SENTINEL, ask him if he recognizes this man."

SENTINEL complied.

Chakhovsky squinted through blurred eyes for several long moments.

"More light," Wyatt directed urgently.

"Do you recognize this man?" SENTINEL asked again in Russian.

Chakhovsky looked at the picture and nodded.

"Red flag. Let's go," Morsand said.

At the same instant that Justin and Kuradin began walking slowly from the line of cars, Steve and his escort emerged from the Russian line. Steve moved slowly, aided by the escort.

"Ask him if this man is Phoenix," Wyatt instructed.

"Jesus Christ," Dials said, "what more proof do you want?"

Dials's statement and SENTINEL's question were made simultaneously. The question was lost in the confusion.

"Will you shut up," Wyatt fumed. "SENTINEL, ask the question again," Wyatt rushed.

"Is this man Phoenix?" SENTINEL repeated.

Chakhovsky blinked and looked again.

SENTINEL repeated the question.

Chakhovsky shook his head, no.

Wyatt's nerves nearly exploded out of his body. Dials's mouth fell open.

All concentration in the situation room was shattered by the sudden alarm bell and flashing yellow alert.

Honeycut's heart nearly leaped out of his mouth when the alert sounded. He jumped up and raced to the control panel, to push the button acknowledging awareness of the yellow alert, silencing the piercing bells.

"Who is this man?" SENTINEL asked automatically.

Chakhovsky whispered something.

Wyatt couldn't hear it.

"Centaur," SENTINEL translated, having picked up the whispered response through its filters.

"What can you tell us about him?" SENTINEL asked.

Chakhovsky whispered again.

This time it was more audible as the room was in utter silence, waiting for SENTINEL's translation.

"*Photographic memory*," SENTINEL announced.

BEEP!

BLEEP! Justin responded.

"Pilgrim," SENTINEL's soft voice began, "you must not make the trade," it said.

BLEEP! BLEEP! Negative, or explain further.

"We have just learned that he is *not* Phoenix. He is a memory expert with total recall. His code name is Centaur. He has all of the schematics in his head. He must be stopped."

BLEEP! Affirmative.

"It is imperative that you stop Eagle, as well," the voice said.

Justin's heart hit bottom. Stop Eagle!

There was no response.

"Confirm, Pilgrim," SENTINEL said.

Nothing.

"Pilgrim, did you receive transmission concerning Eagle?"

BLEEP! Affirmative.

Blood rushed to Justin's head. His eyes grew suddenly hot, his head pounded with the words, "...*imperative that you stop Eagle...stop Eagle.*"

It couldn't be possible. It wasn't asked. Not Pappy.

His heart thumped wildly, his legs grew weak. He slowed the pace, as his mind raced.

"Can we take out all three with the explosive implant?" Honeycut asked Elizabeth Ryerson. "At their closest point of contact, can it be done?"

She shook her head. "No guarantee. Maybe all three, but I strongly doubt it," she answered.

Wyatt came running into the situation room.

Honeycut thought quickly for alternatives. SENTINEL's laser batteries could do it, but that would tip a very valuable hand.

"How long does Centaur have left?" he asked.

"About forty-eight hours," Elizabeth answered, referring to the time left before Centaur would die. He had been secretly put on a D-83 protocol without Dials's knowledge. This was done to guarantee that he would be of little help to the Soviets after the trade.

"That's too long," Wyatt said. "In a matter this important, his debriefing will begin the minute he sets foot on that plane."

"We can take care of the plane with the lasers after it takes off," Honeycut said.

"No good," Wyatt cut in. "The tapes will be in an indestructible box. If he even gets only the memory basis down on tape, that'll do it," he said.

"Then it has to be now," Honeycut said. "It's all up to Pilgrim."

Justin's mind continued to race. The logical thing to do would be to stop now, take out Steve, then use Centaur as a shield in trying to get back to the cover of the cars.

But that was Steve out there, not just anyone. He couldn't do it.

His chances weren't good of making it back over that much open ground, anyway. He decided to try to get Steve back alive. He had to at least try it that way. For Pappy.

He continued walking, thinking.

Justin saw the Soviet escort carrying a long trench coat folded over his arm. He knew that it was a bullet-proof garment to protect Centaur after the trade. That would mean a head shot.

He had to optimize the chances of survival for himself and Steve. His mind began lightning-quick calculations.

The Colt was sighted at twenty-five yards. He figured he could probably still get a kill from thirty-five.

Kuradin turned his head and looked at Justin. He could see the tension on the face, the quick eye movements of a thinking brain. So close, so few steps left.

The parties came together in the middle of the expanse.

Steve looked up weakly. Disbelief filled his eyes.

"J…Justin?" he said hoarsely.

"It's okay, Pappy. We're going home now," Justin said.

He unlocked the cuffs, as did the Russian escort. Justin put an arm out to help Steve.

Kuradin took one step and then turned to face Justin. Their eyes met.

For the first time, Justin saw something in Kuradin's eyes that he hadn't recognized earlier. It was victory. Not only here, but in England, as well. It was not the Russian who had lost, but Justin that day in England.

And, in Justin's eyes, Kuradin saw menace. It didn't really surprise him. He knew it was in the man, but it disturbed him that he should see it now, instead of apparent victory.

Kuradin offered his hand. "A farewell, comrade?" he said. "And to thank you again."

Justin stared at him coldly until the hand dropped away.

"There will come a day when there will be no need for men like us. No need for enemies to stand where only friends should be," Kuradin said. "In another time you would have been my friend. Good-bye, comrade."

Their eyes stayed locked for a few silent moments, then both men turned away. The parties began to walk back to their respective sides.

"What's he waiting for?" Honeycut growled.

The display screen now showed a picture. SENTINEL had gone to infrared scan. The figures showed up as red images against a blue background. The bad weather made visual tracking impossible.

"He's not going to do it," Elizabeth rattled in near hysteria. "I told you about him," she said, shaking, nearly foaming at the mouth. *Her* computer, *her baby!* It was being stolen.

"No. No, he's okay," Wyatt said. "I think he's trying to get Eagle out alive."

"SENTINEL, I want all laser batteries armed," Honeycut said urgently.

"No, wait," Wyatt cut in. "Give him a few more seconds. I know what I'm saying."

"Laser batteries are armed and ready," SENTINEL said.

Honeycut looked at Wyatt.

"He'll do it," Wyatt said, nodding repeatedly.

"Hold for my command," Honeycut ordered.

"Holding."

"Justin, what are you doing here?" Steve asked as they walked slowly.

"Just listen. Can you run? Do you think you could make it to the cars?" Justin asked him.

"Sure, I can do it," Steve said.

"Then get your ass ready to go," Justin said, reaching into the vinyl jacket.

"SENTINEL, I want the distance between parties in yards, called out by fives."

"Fifteen yards, Pilgrim," the voice said.

"Twenty yards."

Justin's hand tightened on the Colt, lifting it from the holster. He pulled it out from underneath the jacket.

"Twenty-five yards."

"*What's that?*" Morsand shouted. "*What's he doing?*" he screamed, pointing at Justin.

"Thirty yards."

"Go!" Justin shouted to Steve, giving him a shove to get him started.

All eyes shifted to Justin as he spun toward the Russian party.

"*Centaur!*" Justin shouted.

The word broke the damp silence like the crack of a whip.

Kuradin stopped dead in his tracks at the sound of his code name. He turned to face Pilgrim, filled with the realization that the end had come. The last step had been taken.

The Colt was ready and aimed.

For one second time hung suspended. Minds raced at the speed of light, eyes exchanged unspoken words of winning and losing, of respect and hatred, of living and dying and never going home.

BOOM! The magnum roared.

Kuradin's head splattered like a pumpkin, the tremendous energy of the magnum slug converting brain matter to near luminescence, as the skull expanded violently.

Justin turned to run as the first cracks from Russian weapons began. He had gone but two steps when he tripped over Steve, who had been unable to run and had fallen with Justin's shove.

As Justin began his fall, he was hit simultaneously in the right foot and a grazing blow to the back side of the head behind the right ear, exactly where the implant was located.

The impact of the hits knocked him forward onto his face. He rolled once and stopped, motionless.

The Americans, stunned by what had happened, were slow to react. No one fired at the Russian escort, as he sprinted the distance back to Steve and grabbed him under both arms. He dragged him back toward the Russian side, using him for cover.

Steve kicked weakly, but could do nothing to help himself.

Justin's head was filled with an unbearable screeching sound from the damaged implant, his eyes were barely able to open through the paralyzing pain.

He rolled to his stomach, the Colt still in his hand, and forced his eyes to open.

Steve kicked vainly, screaming, *"No...No...God, no..."* in a pathetic tone.

Justin blurrily watched Steve's futile efforts, the arms reaching out toward him, as though imploring his help.

Justin winced and shook uncontrollably from the pain. His eyes were tear-filled and blurred.

Stop Eagle!

Stop Eagle!

The words thundered in his head above the horrible screeching. Was it his own mind shouting the command? Or was it SENTINEL? He didn't know.

Stop Eagle!

He forced control above the pain and lifted the Colt. He rested the butt of the handle on the runway, both trembling hands gripping the Colt tightly. He pointed it at the blurred, unsteady target aiming for the center of the indistinct forms.

The cracking gunfire started from the Soviet side again.

Justin squeezed.

BOOM! The Colt thundered once more.

At the same instant, Justin's head jarred backward. He felt incredible blinding pain in the right eye, and his brain filled with a kaleidoscopic flash of colors.

All sound stopped, all colors faded into blackness, and total stillness came over him.

It was checkmate! The final moves had been played. There was no going back.

THIRTY-EIGHT

I have heard the voices almost daily over the past months. They cry just outside my window. But I am old and can move only very slowly. They are gone when I get there. They leave saddened. They must think that I do not hear them or that I do not care. If they would only wait a little longer so that I can speak to them one last time, as in the old days, to tell them that they need not fear, that our hour is at hand. To tell them that our opponents knew very little and that now it is too late.

To the people I say we have won. Our destiny is fulfilled. The pain and the suffering, the years of tormented waiting are over. I have never stopped loving you, and have never given up the hope of our ultimate victory.

Entry No. 82 from the partially recovered *Wolf Journal*

"Platt has finally gotten the green light to start an official investigation," Robert Morsand said to his aide.

"Platt's pretty pissed, isn't he?" Kodek asked.

"*Ha!* My ass has got his teeth marks all over it. That worm Edgar got his butt out of there the second the lead started flying. You know who that left to catch the bucket of flying shit with a teaspoon, don't you? You're looking at him. Don't be surprised if you're behind this desk before too long."

"They're not going to do that," Kodek insisted. "What the hell could you do about what happened? It was as much a surprise to you as to anyone."

"That's the problem. I *can't* explain it. When Edgar and I spoke on the plane, he said that the State Department would accept responsibility for anything that happened. Well, the buck stopped here. Not because I wanted it that way, but because I was the dumb son-of-a-bitch standing there with my thumb up my ass without answers.

"Four people dead—Chaple, Limpoulous, Yarin, and the Soviet escort. And not a single shot was fired from our side. Only Chaple's. It would have been better if it turned into a real shoot 'em up out there. We could have blamed it all on the Russians. As it is, *we're* responsible for those people dying."

"What happens now?" Kodek asked.

"Now we get busy finding out what really happened and why. We do it our way. I don't care who gets their toes stepped on. It's my ass on the line now, and you can bet that I'm going to have the answers this time."

Leonid Travkin sat at his desk behind closed office doors. He had just returned from a meeting with the Central Committee.

It had come so close to a successful outcome. The only explanation that he could offer was that Dmitri Chakhovsky had blown Centaur's cover.

There was no describing the attitude of the committee. Failure was inexcusable. The failure to stop Chakhovsky and to get the schematics was his responsibility. That's the price paid for authority.

He packed a few personal items from the desk at which, only the day before, he had wept openly for his friend Alexi Kuradin when the news came to him. The committee had recommended an extended vacation, to collect his thoughts before beginning preparations for another try at the

SENTINEL computer plans. But he doubted that he would ever again sit at this desk as KGB director. Fate was a fickle thing in the Soviet Union. Its axe swung with an equal disregard for all.

He needed this vacation desperately. He felt depressed, tired, and totally beaten by the events of the past months. He had seen the world change right before his eyes.

He no longer felt the anger that he had experienced as the committee came at him relentlessly. He had wanted to silence them all, by asking what they would have done in his place, to condemn *them* for not developing a computer with SENTINEL's capabilities first. But they would have given answers spawned from hindsight. Months earlier, when he told them of the computer and the possibility of getting its plans, they were without suggestions, all ears, helpless, depending upon him to work it all out to a successful conclusion. Had he done it, he would have been their hero. But he hadn't and he was nobody's hero today.

Life would go on for him, he was sure of that. Whether he would ever hold the position and responsibility of his present circumstance mattered little to him at this point.

He just wanted to get away from the failure, from the guilt of his friend's death, and from the overshadowing realization that a SENTINEL even existed.

He wanted only to forget.

The months passed rapidly for some, slowly for others. It was the first day of December.

The small Lear streaked effortlessly across a clear blue sky. It carried one passenger.

The man sat looking out of the starboard window at the beautiful expanse of the Rockies. The plane banked sharply to the right, as though to give him a better look at nature's frozen beauty below him.

His left hand clutched the wooden cane across his lap. His right hand absently traced the patch over the missing right eye. It still hurt at times.

He stared at the endless expanse of peaks and wondered which one it was that housed SENTINEL.

The plane dropped swiftly through the skies above Colorado. The man had been summoned once again by SENTINEL. Summoned to Sigma.

Irwin Honeycut stood with Dr. Elizabeth Ryerson in the control center of Sigma, watching the slow-moving dot on the display panel. It gave the plane's position, superimposed on a state map of Colorado. It was just minutes from touchdown at the private field.

"He'll be here in less than an hour," Honeycut said.

Elizabeth said nothing. There was a strange tension across her face, as she looked at the tiny flowing dot on the map.

"An incredible man, to say the least," Honeycut said, just above a whisper.

"I still don't like it," she said. "The man has more lives than a cat."

"A survivor," Honeycut said.

"It's no good bringing him here," she objected for about the hundredth time.

"He knows where the journal is," Honeycut said. "Priest got a letter off to him. Gemini was unable to find it. He's maintaining a post office box somewhere. My guess is that we'll find the twenty-fifth page there, too."

"We don't know that Priest mailed *him* anything," she blurted out. "That journal will never be found. We should have just taken care of Pilgrim while he was recovering at St. Simon's."

"He knows where it is," Honeycut said. "I want the issue finally and totally resolved once and for all. Recovering that journal is the only way that that can be done."

"And you think you can just get him to tell you where the journal is hidden, if he really does know?" she asked skeptically.

"Maybe not. But one way or another, we'll have it soon."

"He's doubly dangerous to us without an implant. If he ever gets away from us, we'll lose him for good," Elizabeth said.

"That won't happen. I'd like to keep him in the agency if I can. And I think the offer I'm going to make him might just do that," Honeycut told her.

"You're crazy. You'll never be able to trust him."

"I think you're wrong," Honeycut countered. "He only knows *where* the journal is, not *what* it contains. If we can get it back, without his finding out more than he already knows, we'll stand a good chance of keeping a most valuable and exceptional man."

"I don't know why you keep insisting on keeping him alive," she said. "He's like a wild animal that you take into your home. You feed him, care for him, think you've taught him love and trust. Then one night as you sleep he'll tear your throat out solely for the pleasure of the kill."

"You're making a mistake, Irv. A very, very big mistake," she admonished.

"I think not. But Rainmaker and Gemini are close by, just in case you're right."

"What can they do against him?" Elizabeth asked.

"Rainmaker may be the only man alive who can handle Pilgrim on his own terms. Gemini can be just as effective, but in a more subtle way," Honeycut said. "Out here, we can exercise complete control over him. I'm confident that this will work out exactly as I've planned. We'll get both the journal and our most effective agent back," Honeycut said.

"I'm as confident as you are, Irv—that you're wrong. I only hope that we don't come to regret your decision."

"Time will tell us that, Beth. Time will tell."

The Lear touched down gently on the long runway. A black limousine accelerated across the smooth surface, circled around the stopped Lear, and came to a rest about thirty feet from the plane.

The back door opened, and Rainmaker stepped out. He walked to the opening hatch on the side of the Lear. The metal stairway folded down, and the hatch opened fully. Justin appeared in the opening.

Rainmaker looked up, shielding his eyes from the bright sun reflecting off the white jet. Justin looked about fifteen pounds lighter. His face was thin and drawn, and a black patch was tied angularly over the right eye. He leaned heavily on the cane in his left hand, his head turned slightly to the right as the left squinting eye surveyed the former partner.

"Hi, Smiley," Justin said cheerfully.

"Hello, Pilgrim," Rainmaker replied with a smile, possibly the first that Justin had seen him show since meeting him.

Justin had learned to watch out for men who didn't smile. They were thinkers, and, in this business, that usually meant that they were dangerous.

Rainmaker offered assistance as Justin limped painfully down the steps.

"Let me take that for you," he offered, reaching for a small navy-blue flight bag in Justin's right hand.

"Thanks," Justin said.

Rainmaker looked at the patch over the eye and only then noticed that a piece of the right ear was also missing. The bullet that grazed his head had also done this. The use of the ear was lost due to neural damage from the implant.

The two men walked slowly toward the car, Justin limping with a slight twisting motion against the outside edge of the right foot.

"How's the foot coming?" Rainmaker asked.

"Pretty well, actually. I've had two operations on it. Lost most of the arch and a piece of the heel. But Waith says that I should walk normally, without any trace of a limp, once I learn to use the outer edge of the foot properly. He says I'll be able to run, too, at about ninety percent. I can't wait till it doesn't hurt so much, so I can start running to get myself back in shape again," Justin said.

Justin's tone was cheerful, friendly, and relaxed. But inside he was as tight as a crossbow cranked near to snapping. He no longer had the Mauser, the months of recuperation had been long, lonely, and much thinking had been done. He was still confused by the facts, the contradictions of certain bits of information, and the disarming openness of Irwin Honeycut. A warning signal flashed in the back of his consciousness.

"It's good to have you back," Rainmaker said.

"It's good to be back," Justin lied.

The sliding doors opened to the control center of Sigma. Justin walked in, limping, wary.

"Justin, it's good to see you," Honeycut said warmly, taking Justin's right hand in both of his own. "How are you feeling?"

"Like a million bucks hot off the press—a little stiff and in need of some bending, but good just the same," Justin replied with a wide smile.

"You've lost too much weight," Honeycut said. "We'll put it back on you quickly."

Justin smiled and looked at an unsmiling Elizabeth Ryerson. The expression on her face fed Justin's suspicions.

"Hello, Pilgrim," Elizabeth said, forcing an unconvincing smile, as she remembered, in spite of herself, the erotic fantasies of so many months ago.

"Hello, Dr. Ryerson. This is some place you've got here. Much more impressive than Alpha," Justin said.

He looked around the large oval room. To the right of the door was a long counter situated on a raised platform that circled almost the entire perimeter of the room. The blue floor in the center of the room and entranceway matched the hallway floor outside. This was Blue Deck or the main level, located far below ground level at the Sigma site.

Behind the counter was a huge global map on a plexiglass panel.

Honeycut watched Justin as he looked curiously at the panel.

"Why don't you give Pilgrim a quick rundown of what we've got here," Honeycut said to Elizabeth.

Elizabeth looked sternly at Honeycut for a moment, then forced another weak smile. "Be glad to," she lied.

She stepped up onto the platform, Justin going up with her. They stepped behind the low counter. A forest of switches and buttons presented itself on the other side of the counter.

"This is internal security, here," Elizabeth began. "From this panel, we can direct intruder control systems for the entire complex, which is nearly three times the size of Alpha," she said.

"The defensive systems are basically the same as the ones you saw at Alpha. We can control them manually or set them on automatic, in which case SENTINEL will control the entire system, except for this room. There are no intruder control devices in this room. It would be impossible for any intruder to get this deep into the complex, no matter how well versed he was in the defense systems.

"That panel in the back is a global display board, which can show positions of attacking missiles, locations of fleets, agents, sensors, satellites, essentially anything that we need to see on a global scale. The circular design of the room allows it to be seen from any position."

She moved along the platform to the next huge panel, with Justin limping behind her.

"This is the command-control panel. This is for weapons control in time of war. That huge black panel behind it will give simultaneous visual printout data for over a thousand separate systems at any one time.

"This wall-to-ceiling display panel, to the left of the command-control section, can show anything that is requested, from visual satellite surveillance to additional weapons-control data if it's needed."

They walked around to the other side of the oval room, to another equally large instrument panel.

"This is satellite-control and sensor-input analysis. Essentially the eyes and ears by which we can watch the entire world.

"To the left there are the communications center and the life-support control center for the entire complex, and that last station is for external security control for the outer perimeter of the complex.

"I dare say that this is the most well-protected site in the world, next to the actual location of SENTINEL not too far from here," Elizabeth concluded.

"Very impressive," Justin said. "You can control it all from right here. Very, very nice."

He walked back to the command-control panel. There was a large red switch with a key slot in its center. It was encased in glass.

"What's that?" Justin said, pointing to it.

"That's our safety insurance that I told you about at Alpha. The off switch," Elizabeth said.

She produced a large, flat metallic key from a chain around her neck. "This key activates the switch. Pegasus also carries one, as would the President if he were in this complex. There are only three keys in existence. They are each specifically calibrated to the impedance of the person carrying them. Anyone else inserting the key would not be able to activate the switch without knowing the specific sequence of positional settings of the key."

So, it really can be turned off, Justin thought. "Very interesting."

"You've had a long flight out," Honeycut said. "Why don't we show you to a place where you can shower and relax for a few hours. When you're rested and after you've eaten, I'll join you to discuss some matters of importance."

"Fine," Justin said.

Honeycut pushed a button next to the security-card plate on the wall near the door. The door opened, and a military guard walked in.

"Would you please show Pilgrim to his temporary quarters?" Honeycut said.

Justin followed the guard out to the small three-wheeled electric vehicle that had transported him through the maze of immaculate blue and white corridors.

The small vehicle rolled away with its passengers.

The doors to the control center closed.

"You've gone too far with him," Elizabeth said tensely.

"I'll decide how far to go concerning Pilgrim," Honeycut snapped. "I'll know better how far to take him after I've talked to him, alone."

Justin had showered, shaved, taken a two-hour nap, and eaten the most fantastic club sandwich he had ever sunk his teeth into. Now he was beginning to get restless. He looked carefully around the room for visual monitors. He couldn't see any, but he was certain that they were concealed somewhere. His senses told him that he was a prisoner.

Just then, the doors slid open, and Honeycut walked in.

"I trust that you're well rested and have had something to eat?" Honeycut said.

"Yes, thank you," Justin replied.

"Good. I've got several important matters that I'd like to discuss with you. If you don't mind, I'd just as soon talk here," Honeycut said.

"That's fine," Justin returned.

"The first thing I'd like to say is that I'm very sorry about what happened to Steve at Dieppe."

Justin felt a sudden pang of remorse and guilt. The uncertainty of his situation had kept it in the back of his mind. The sudden snap back to its reality was painful.

"I can only hope that you fully understand why it was necessary. We can talk about it if you'd like," Honeycut offered.

Justin shook his head. "No...I understand," he said.

"It was one of the most difficult things a man can be asked to do. I admire the way you tried to work it out to Steve's benefit. I'm just sorry that it didn't work out as you intended it to," Honeycut said.

"So am I," Justin whispered.

"Were you filled in on the events that occurred after that?" Honeycut asked.

"No," Justin replied. "Everyone was vague about it. I knew that Steve was dead and that I was hit in the eye by a ricocheting fragment. I was kept in a type of isolation status at St. Simon's for the whole time I was there."

"Yes, well that was imperative, as well. It was important that you be fully recovered before you learned the facts. They're not pleasant, I'm afraid," Honeycut said almost apologetically.

Justin looked at him, head slightly right of center, still not used to seeing through only one eye. He waited for Honeycut to continue.

"Your shot killed both Steve and the Russian escort who was trying to pull him back to their side. The shot hit Steve in the throat, passed through him, and into the chest of the Russian. The Russian lived for about twenty minutes. Steve died instantly, without pain," Honeycut said, to help ease Justin's guilt.

Without pain, Justin thought. How the fuck can anybody say that someone died without pain? How would they know what the dead man felt? Justin could not imagine death in any form as being painless. Some were "less painful" than others, but none without pain.

"After you were hit," Honeycut continued, "Dr. Waith ran out under the white flag. He found you alive, but declared you dead. No one doubted it, either. The combined head wounds made it look like you had been shot right through the head.

"You were quickly carried on board the plane, along with Steve's body, and flown back to the United States."

Justin was suddenly filled with the realization of the unpleasant nature of what Honeycut was trying to tell him. He stood up abruptly, a look of shock and painful realization across his face.

"I'm dead. They *all* think that I'm dead. My father, Barbara, Susan, and Michael, everyone. I'm right, ain't I?" he said, his tone pained, angry.

"I'm afraid so," Honeycut said.

Justin sat down slowly, his eye staring into the floor, seeing nothing but the grief in his father's heart, and in Michael's. His son was probably old enough to understand that death was final and forever. Only after his visions of his father and Michael, did he think of Barbara.

He let out a painful sigh and raised his hands to his face. He felt a heavy, sickening ache inside. He wanted to cry, not for himself, but for the people he loved, for the pain they suffered.

He shook his head, tears rolling down his left cheek. It was so much to lose. To never see them again.

"It was essential that everyone think that you had died at Dieppe," Honeycut said. "Essential for the good of the agency."

Justin jumped to his feet. "I don't care about the fucking good of the agency. I've given it enough," he raged. "And what has it done for me? What has it left me? One eye, one ear, one foot. It's taken *everything!*"

"No, not everything," Honeycut said calmly. "Nothing, in fact, that can't be given back. Your family will learn soon that you're alive, as soon as the investigations are completed. It was for their good, as well as your own, that we decided to handle it this way."

Justin looked at Honeycut, the rage still burning.

Honeycut raised a hand. "Before you speak, I want you to think about something. Think about what they would be going through a year from now, with you a national disgrace, on trial for murder. The United States government publicly disavowed your actions when the news media ran wild with it.

"What about the pain they would suffer from the long-drawn-out publicity and the cruelty of ignorant people?

"A year from now it will be ended, forgotten, the motivation behind your actions forever secret. And your family will still have you, alive. They'll know it and will be given a reasonably safe explanation of what happened and why," Honeycut said.

Justin stared hard at him, confused, breathing heavily.

"And I did say, 'Nothing that can't be given back,' which brings up another of the matters I wanted to talk to you about.

"You've lost an eye and the use of your right ear. We can give them both back to you," Honeycut said, pausing for effect.

Justin leveled a heedful stare at him.

"That's right, Justin. We can give you an eye and the use of your ear again."

Justin was again deeply confused. "I...I..."

"All you have to say is, 'yes,' " Honeycut said.

Justin was speechless.

"When your eye was removed, an artificial receptacle was installed. The muscles responsible for eye movement were repairable. With a little reeducation, the muscles will move the receptacle exactly as they did your eye. The eye we can give you will be vastly superior to your natural eye. It will give you advantages that you couldn't dream possible, like long-range sight, perfect night vision, and others.

"Your hearing on the right side will be remarkably acute, beyond the range of normal human hearing.

"You only have to say 'yes,' and it will all be yours," Honeycut tempted.

Justin thought.

Honeycut waited, watching him.

"The eye. Will SENTINEL have vision through it, too?" Justin asked.

"Yes," Honeycut answered. "Another major advantage," he said.

The implant had made Justin feel uncomfortable, "occupied." There was no sense of privacy.

It was a difficult decision for him to make. He wanted desperately to see with two eyes again, to hear with both ears. But the sacrifice of all personal privacy was an enormous one. Everything he saw, everything he heard, to be shared with a machine—to look at Barbara, to make love to her, all shared with SENTINEL. But to see again and to hear. It was a disconcerting situation.

The gains were obvious, the price for them high.

"There are only two requirements," Honeycut said. "You will have to remain in the field. With your newly acquired advantages, we would ask that they be utilized where they would be most useful. Your pay will still be the figure that I quoted you in my offer. Even higher if you wish," Honeycut said.

Another major concession to weigh.

"You said *two* requirements. What is the second?" Justin asked.

"It's quite simple, actually. You must turn over the journal and the twenty-fifth page."

Justin was rocked, suddenly flushed.

"We know that you found the twenty-fifth page at Bridges's apartment," Honeycut said. "We know what was on it. Division Two removed the ribbon from his typewriter. It was all there. And we know about Spartan's brother, and the books, and the ultraviolet code that he used.

"We also know that he mailed you a letter the day before you were called to St. Simon's Island. We think it will tell you where the journal is," Honeycut said. "Just turn it over to us, that's all that we ask."

Justin was stunned.

"I received no letter," he said.

"Shall we be entirely honest with one another?" Honeycut asked.

Justin paused, then nodded. "All right."

"We know that you went to see Priest. We know that he mailed something to you. We also know that you must be maintaining a post office box somewhere.

"We haven't found it. We don't think that we will. But we know that one exists—somewhere.

"Turn the twenty-fifth page over to me, help us locate the transcribed journal, and the subject will never be raised again. Everything will be forgiven."

"We're telling the truth, right?" Justin asked.

"That's right," Honeycut said.

"The journal. You know half of what it contains. The day we talked about it, was that the truth? About the infiltration?"

"The complete truth, Justin. I swear to you. Our problem still exists, exactly as I told it to you. I was unable to get absolute clearance for you to conduct your investigation. That means that it will be a great deal more difficult to find our man.

"I don't think that our infiltrator has the means to take control, yet. And it will be harder for him now. All personnel involved with or having knowledge of SENTINEL and the agency are being implanted. That includes the President of the United States and his entire SENTINEL advisory cabinet.

"It's going to be a race against time, but we still have control of SENTINEL, and that will be our main advantage.

"You're the best agent I have, Justin. The only person I would dare discuss this with, besides Elizabeth Ryerson. I need you to help save the program and possibly the whole country from a forgotten menace.

"You've saved the program once, in Dieppe, by your coura-geous actions and tremendous personal sacrifices. We need you to help do it again."

Justin was silent. He thought for a long time.

Honeycut waited patiently.

Then Justin broke his silence. "I have just one more question for you," he said.

"Shoot."

"Why did Ted Fanning kill Spartan?"

Honeycut's face suddenly reddened. He had been caught by surprise. He stood up, his eyes narrowing into a tight squint.

"What makes you think that Fanning killed Spartan?" he asked.

"That's not important. What's important is that I know that he did. And I'm asking you why."

"Ted Fanning was a good agent, loyal to this program and to his country. He was acting on my orders," Honeycut said.

"We had certain information that there was an active and seriously viable Nazi movement alive in this country, one that went deep into our government. We also knew that a document pertaining to this movement existed.

"After Spartan finished his 'special action' and recovered the journal, he refused to obey his instructions concerning it.

"He had been told to turn it over intact and unopened. Instead, he began to translate it.

"His failure to turn it over as directed, and his attempts to read it and to utilize the information, made him a security risk.

"It's obvious from his actions that he never intended to turn that journal over to the agency. That made him a traitor to his country, probably out for some personal gain. He may even have been a part of the movement it related to.

"It was my decision to send Fanning in to get the journal. The rest you know," Honeycut said.

Justin sat thinking about what Honeycut had just told him. He had measured Honeycut's reaction to the question carefully.

What reason could Spartan have possibly had for not turning that journal over? Justin wondered. Certainly, he knew it would cost him his life not to. There was no personal-gain motive, Justin knew that. And why would Spartan go to such trouble to save the journal, by putting it into the books in code for his brother to take? If he were part of the movement, he simply would have destroyed the journal.

No, Honeycut's explanation didn't wash. It needed more thought.

"I'm satisfied with that," Justin lied. "When do I get my eye?" he asked.

Honeycut smiled, more out of relief than from happiness. "When do we get the twenty-fifth page and the journal?" Honeycut returned.

"I'll have to work on locating the journal," Justin said, "because I honestly don't know where the transcribed copy is. Spartan's brother has the whole thing in the books, though."

"We'll want both," Honeycut said.

"I'll turn over the twenty-fifth page and the letter, if he did mail one to me, as soon as you feel it's safe to go after it. Only I can get it, so just telling you where it is won't help," Justin said, thinking about the other papers he had found.

He was buying time again. He knew that he wasn't implanted anymore. If they let him go now, he'd be gone.

Honeycut was also thinking. If Justin were given the eye and hearing device *before* he went for the information, there would be no chance of him double-crossing them. He believed that Justin was sincere in his willingness to stay with the agency. But a little caution never hurt.

"Your eye can be ready in two or three weeks. It will take about a month of hard therapy to adjust to it," Honeycut began.

"I think we can spare the time. It will also give our infiltrator time to think that his cover is entirely safe.

"Shall I consider that we've struck a bargain?" he asked.

"Agreed," Justin said without hesitation.

The two men shook hands.

It was a shaky alliance, at best.

"We've arranged for private quarters for you outside of the complex," Honeycut said. "Staying here would seem too confining, I think.

"It's a lovely little house, set well away from everything. You'll like it, I'm sure.

"There's one more little surprise I neglected to tell you about," Honeycut said. "It'll make your new quarters more than comfortable. It'll also show you that everything I told you about our concern for your welfare is true."

"And what is that?" Justin asked.

"I think I'll let that be a surprise. A most pleasant one, I'm sure." Honeycut laughed.

That afternoon Justin was taken by limousine to his new private quarters.

Honeycut had been right. It looked like a very charming place, indeed, as the car pulled up to it along the isolated road.

Justin got out of the car and limped up the walk, carrying his blue flight bag. He went to put the key in the lock, but the door was already open.

He turned the handle cautiously and pushed the door in. It swung open in a silent arc, revealing what he least expected to see in the entire world.

Barbara.

THIRTY-NINE

I fear that I shall not make another day. I have often thought of death, since I cheated him so long ago in Berlin. He has been most patient with me. But he will be put off no longer and I am too tired to care.

To the world I say, "Prepare, your long awaited justice is at hand—and it shall be extracted. The history of the world shall be rewritten and its future course decided. You have forgotten and have dwelt too long in undue victory and righteousness. All accounts shall be finally settled."

Sieg Heil! Sieg Heil *to the ghosts of a nation. The ghosts of a nation live!*

Final entry from the partially
recovered *Wolf Journal*

S eeing Barbara standing there struck Justin with a varied array of feelings, ranging from boundless joy to deep suspicion.

He didn't know what to make of the things that Honeycut said anymore. Every time he grew suspicious and doubting, Honeycut did something to make him feel foolish that he could have ever disbelieved the man.

Barbara was in his arms now, too full of emotion for words. Her head was hard against his chest, her eyes tear-filled. He held her tightly saying nothing, fearing that it would all vanish if he did.

"Oh, Justin, they told me you were dead," she cried, breaking into a rush of tearful sobs.

"Shhh, shhh…I'm here, Jugs. I'm here," he said, tightening his embrace even more.

"Oh, hold me. Hold me. Don't let me go," she implored.

After many long moments, she leaned away slightly, looking up into his face. Her hands went up and gently cupped his cheeks, her eyes running with tears of happiness at having him back and tears of sadness for all that had happened to him.

"Every time you leave me…" Her voice trailed off.

"I'm all right," he said softly, running a finger along her cheek to catch a tear.

"Never again, Justin. Don't you ever leave me again," she said, burying her head against his chest once more.

After more moments of soothing embrace, he felt her tension release against his touch. They walked slowly into the living room, Barbara holding on to him as if for dear life.

"I've been here for a week, waiting, getting everything ready," she said, sniffling. "They told me what had happened to you, but I didn't care. All that mattered was that you were alive.

"You can't know what I felt when I was told you'd been killed. My life stopped," she said, starting to cry again. "Absolutely stopped."

"Shh, shhh, it's all right," he soothed.

After more long moments of silence, she began to gain control.

"Men from the State Department came," she began. "They told me what had happened and began asking endless questions that I couldn't answer. It was in the news the same evening. I couldn't believe it, that you and Steve…"

They sat on the sofa, Barbara holding both of Justin's hands in her lap.

"How's my father?" he asked.

She looked at him, tears welling up in her eyes once more. "Taking it very badly," she answered.

"And Michael?"

"I don't think he fully understands yet. The day...oh, it seems so horrible to even think it, to relive the dying inside of me. The day of the funeral, at the cemetery, I stayed by your father's side, to try to help him. He was filled with such grief. Michael seemed confused by what was happening, by his mother's complete silence, by your father's tears and mine.

"The...casket was never opened. Not seeing you, I don't think he really knew. When the priest had finished and the people began to leave, he asked Susan when his daddy was coming home. She had been strong up to that point, then she just completely went to pieces. Michael cried because she cried, more frightened than understanding, I think.

"I stayed behind with your father. We couldn't leave you there...alone. So alone," she wept.

"I couldn't get myself to leave. That small piece of ground held my whole being, my whole life. I wanted to lay on the pile of earth to be close to you, to keep you warm, to tell you I'd be there." She couldn't go on.

Justin's one eye was tear-filled over their grief. He soothed her until she could continue.

"Then, about three weeks ago, a man came. He told me that you weren't really dead.

"I slapped him hard, and cursed him for being so cruel. But he went to the phone and dialed a number. Then he gave some kind of code number into the phone and handed it to me.

"That was when I spoke to you," she said.

Justin was taken aback by that last one. He had never spoken to Barbara, but he knew immediately who had. SENTINEL.

He said nothing further about it.

"Does my father know?" he asked, getting away from the subject.

"No, the man said that only I would know for the next several months, until the rest of the investigations were cleared up.

"He told me that you were working for the government the whole time everyone thought you were with American Mutual. He said that you had killed Steve accidentally, while trying to save his life. He said that what had happened that day was vitally important to the national security of the country.

"Then the arrangements were made for me to be brought here to be with you. As far as anyone else is concerned, I went away to get over the whole thing. No one knows where I am," she concluded.

"Who was this man?" Justin asked.

"His name was Frank Osborne," she answered.

The name meant nothing to Justin.

"What did he look like?"

"Smaller than you, dark hair and eyes, roundish, young-looking face, very serious expression on it all the time," she described.

Rainmaker, Justin thought.

"What else did he tell you?"

"That we'd be here together for several months, while you recuperated. Then we'd be able to be together anywhere we chose, anywhere in the world," she said.

"With Justin Chaple remaining dead, no doubt," he said.

"I don't care if no one knows you're alive, as long as I can be with you," she said.

He took her in his arms and held her.

Something wasn't right to Justin.

That night, feelings of being watched bothered him. It was exceedingly difficult for him to concentrate on making love to Barbara, knowing that the house was probably fitted with hidden visual surveillance, as well as the usual sound bugs.

He felt that he was sharing his experiences with many unseen eyes…and with SENTINEL.

But Barbara was very understanding, thinking that his difficulty arose from his condition. She used all of her skills to relax him, to bring him slowly into the proper frame of mind to enjoy the lovemaking. She was there now, she had said, to take care of him and to watch over him.

He succumbed to her tender skills.

The next few days were troublesome for Justin. His mind was racked with varying quarrels of conscience. He didn't know whether to trust Honeycut or not, whether it was the right thing to turn over the information he had, or to wait until he could find the journal and then judge.

Elizabeth Ryerson's unusual mood annoyed Justin, too. Every time his argument led to trusting Honeycut, he'd see her face, feel the tension in her. Something about it just missed.

Barbara stayed with Justin constantly, always touching him, holding a hand or an arm, stroking his hair or his cheek, as though she did not want to lose physical contact with him, for fear that he'd be lost to her again, forever this time.

On the third morning, Justin managed to get out of the house by himself, while Barbara slept late.

He walked across the big wooded backyard, breathing in the cold, crisp Colorado air. He was trying desperately to straighten the facts out in his mind and decide finally whether to trust Honeycut or not. Time was rapidly slipping away from him.

He walked, kicking the fresh fallen snow with his good left foot. The right one didn't bother him as much as he let on, but he kept up the act. It might pay off later on.

Outside of the house, he felt free, less restricted and observed. He walked for almost an hour before finding the ground sensor at the rear corner of the yard, just hidden in the low bushes.

The rotating sensor shaft was still. He moved in an arc around it. The shaft turned with him as he moved. That meant that it was locked on to him.

They were, no doubt, spread out all over the property to keep his position well noted. It disturbed him that he was being so carefully watched.

And then it occurred to him why Barbara had been brought there. Honeycut knew that Justin would never try to skip out, leaving her behind. She was essentially being used as an anchor, to keep him put.

If he ran, he'd take her along, effectively slowing himself down, making it much easier to be found.

It was a smart move on Honeycut's part, Justin thought. Without Barbara to drag with him, he could easily lose himself without the implant. And, if he left her behind, they'd use her to pressure him into coming back.

He walked back into the house. Barbara was just getting up.

"Hi," she said, giving him a kiss. "I'm going out to the store in a few minutes for some groceries. Do you want me to bring you back anything special?"

"No, I don't think so," he answered.

He thought a moment, then changed his mind.

"On second thought, bring me back some paper," he said.

"Paper? What kind?"

"Writing paper," he clarified. "Lots of it."

"What are you going to write? A book?" she joked.

"You always said that you wanted me to try writing, didn't you? Well, I've got to start some time. And this is a great setting. Relaxing, good atmosphere. I think I'd like to give it a try," he said.

She walked over to him and looked up into his face with a satisfied smile.

"Good, I'm glad. It's about time you started finding a new way to make a living," she said.

About two hours later, Barbara was off on her shopping trip. She took the silver-blue Corvette that was left with the house for her use.

Justin had used the time that she was gone to move a small desk and chair down to the basement. He had situated them right below a bright light.

"You're learning fast," she said when she returned. "All writers have their dreary little holes. This is as dingy as they come.

"You sure you don't want to write upstairs where you'll be more comfortable?" she asked, stroking his hair gently.

"No, I like it here fine. No distractions down here. Upstairs, I'd probably jump you every time you walked by. Besides, I don't want you to see it right away, until I feel confident that it's not too terrible," he lied.

"But I can help you, give you some constructive criticism," she protested mildly.

"You'll see it—when I'm ready. Okay?"

"All right. Just don't leave me upstairs alone for too long. I might get lonely and decide to go outside to make it with one of the guys out by the main road," she joked.

Justin gave her a serious look.

"Hold it, kiddo. I was only kidding," she said, seeing his sudden change of expression.

"There are men out by the main road? How many?" he asked with an urgent concern.

"Two," she answered, puzzled.

"Was there a car there?"

"Yes. An Impala, I think," she said.

Impala. They were agency men.

"Don't worry," she began, "they've been there ever since I got here. Mr. Osborne said that they were there to keep people out."

Or in, Justin thought.

He smiled for Barbara's benefit.

"Come on, let's eat," she said. "I bought some great cold cuts and salads. You can start right after lunch—and a roll in the hay." She winked.

Later that evening, having taken only a short break for dinner, Justin came upstairs. He locked the basement door and threw the old key into his pocket. Any key in the house would open that door. Tomorrow he'd have all the keys in his pocket.

"Do you know how long you've been downstairs?" Barbara asked with feigned annoyance.

"Too long?" Justin said weakly.

"You can't write a book in one night," she said. "It's impossible to be effectively creative for long periods of time like that. I almost came down a couple of times, to see if you had another woman stashed away down there," she kidded.

"You couldn't have come down, the door was locked from the inside," he said.

"I know, I tried it," she said and smiled. "How do you feel after being a writer for one day?" she asked.

"Very inept," he replied. "I must have used fifty pages to get to eight that I liked."

"That's the way writing is," she commented from experience. "Don't you think you had better make a story outline first, before starting the rough draft?" she asked. "It would help to have a plan."

"I know exactly what I want to write," he said. "The problem is finding the right words."

"Tomorrow I'll go out to get you some books that will help. Books on how to use adjectives, adverbs, spelling, and style. There are some good ones on how to write novels, plays, short stories, etcetera," she said.

"What are you writing, by the way? A short story?"

A full report, he felt like saying. In that time spent downstairs, he had filled nearly sixty pages with facts relating what had taken place since the incident started in England at Spartan's. There was no creativity involved, just remembering. And he didn't care how well written it was, as long as he got it all down on paper.

"Yeah, a short story," he said.

"What's it about?" she asked.

"About a guy who murders this girl because she asks him too many questions," he growled playfully. They hugged, then went off to bed.

Justin worked long and hard over the next four days to get the story completed.

Barbara's annoyance at being left alone began to become real. Justin skillfully skirted away from her now-serious questions about the nature of the work that took so much of his time. But her mood subsided some when he announced that he was taking a few days off.

He caught her once after that, trying to go into the basement. But the old door was locked, and he now had all of the keys. He playfully got it across that she wasn't to try to see the work until it was finished. She didn't know how really serious he was about never letting her see the story those words told.

But it was done, finally. He now had to make up his mind once and for all about Honeycut and whether to trust him.

"Aren't you convinced, yet?" Elizabeth Ryerson asked Honeycut. "He's been writing for almost five days straight. Any bets on what it's about?" she asked caustically.

Honeycut was silent, thinking.

"Do you still think he's going to give you that journal?"

"He hasn't tried to leave," Honeycut said.

"He knows about the ground sensors. He was close enough to touch one of them. He knows about the security team posted at the road, too. You've got to start thinking realistically in this matter, Irv. Pilgrim is a dangerous man who knows too much."

"He doesn't know what's in the journal, yet."

"I'll give you that much. But he knows something very important is contained in it. He'll try to find out, you *know* he will if he gets the chance. And, when he does, he'll become very,

very dangerous. Remember, he doesn't have the implant any longer," Elizabeth reminded him.

"In a week he'll have one. I still think that his willingness to be implanted again and receive the eye gives testimony to his sincerity," Honeycut insisted.

"He's buying time, until he can figure a way out safely for himself and that girl. He'll move, and soon. And, *if* he makes it, we're in trouble," she warned.

Honeycut silently went over the evidence again. Elizabeth had, indeed, raised valid points of contention, points that he had rejected from the beginning.

They had the whole journal in their possession now from Priest's books. Only a well-hidden, partial transcript existed, which in all likelihood might never be found.

"I know how we can test your theory," Elizabeth said, wanting it resolved.

Honeycut looked up, waiting.

"Let's bring Pilgrim into Sigma. He'll have to come in anyway in a few days, to have a final eye examination before we give him his new one. Let's bring him in and do that now. At the same time, we can send Rainmaker out to check what he's written. If it's safe, we'll proceed according to your plan, and I'll be convinced that you're right. He would have to be an utter fool to allow himself to be implanted if he weren't as entirely loyal as you believe he is," she proposed.

"And if *you're* right?" Honeycut asked.

"Then Rainmaker waits for him and finishes him when he returns," Elizabeth said. "Right there, on the spot."

Honeycut thought for many long moments. He still felt it imperative to get the partial transcript back, to remove all chances of accidental discovery.

"I'll agree, but with one modification, to account for the unexpected. Either way, it should work to your pleasure."

Now Elizabeth was thinking.

"I don't like the look in your eye, Irv. But I'll agree to it, if it will finally put an end to this whole mess."

"It will, I can assure you."

Justin was wary about being called into Sigma so suddenly. Before being picked up, he hid the written account in the desk and locked it. He took the key with him. The cellar door was locked, again, and he made sure that he had every key in the house with him.

Barbara watched with worried eyes as Justin got into the car. She wanted desperately for him to come back as soon as possible. Lately, it seemed that every time he left her, he was almost killed. She could hardly stand to lose him again. She looked forward only to the time when they could settle down together, as private people in their own private world.

Barbara tacked a note to the door for Justin, telling him she was going shopping and would be back in about two hours.

As the Corvette moved away, the Impala pulled down the private road to the house.

Rainmaker picked his way into the house. Moments later he had the cellar door open and was descending the stairs.

"Well, that should just about do it. Everything is perfect," Dr. Amos Kent said, completing his examination. "The eye itself will undergo one final test in two days, then next Monday we should be ready for you."

"How does that sound?" Honeycut asked.

"Great. When do I get to hear again on the right side?" Justin asked.

"On the same day," Kent said. "That's a very quick procedure much like your original implanting. But, in this case, your new implant will do *all* of the hearing. There's no therapy involved, other than pitch evaluations to determine the actual frequency range you will be able to perceive. Okay, we're finished."

Justin thanked him and shook his hand.

Honeycut walked with Justin to the security position from which he would be escorted back to the limousine. He was pleased at the interest Justin had shown in his new eye during the examination.

The small, three-wheeled vehicle pulled away carrying Justin. Honeycut had turned to walk to the control room, when he saw Elizabeth heading toward him.

She was smiling, like a cat who had just eaten the pet bird.

As he was driven back, Justin noticed that the security team stationed at the main road was gone. Maybe his act during the examination had convinced them that he was on the level.

He still had five days in which to make his move for freedom, if he was going to. He would make the decision within the next two.

He was dropped off in front of the house and watched as the limousine disappeared down the road.

When he got to the door, he found Barbara's note.

He walked into the house, passed through the living room, dining room, into the kitchen, and saw the cellar door open. He froze.

Slowly, he began back-stepping. In the dining room, he turned—and stopped.

Rainmaker was standing there with a big smile on his face.

In his left hand, he held the thick packet of notes that Justin had written. In his right, he held a gun.

"This way," Rainmaker said, motioning Justin into the living room. "Move slowly."

Justin limpingly complied, his face controlled, calm.

"Over there," Rainmaker said, pointing to the hallway leading to the master bedroom.

Justin moved around him slowly.

Rainmaker now stood with his back to the door, about four feet from Justin.

Justin looked at the piece Rainmaker had aimed at him. It was the Mauser HSc—his Mauser. Rainmaker saw the recognition.

"Adds a bit of irony this way. Thought you might like to see exactly what it's like to get some of what you've been giving," he said.

Justin looked unimpressed.

"You've been a bad boy, Pilgrim," Rainmaker said, holding up the handwritten account. "A very, very bad boy."

"They made a big mistake sending only you," Justin said, with a menacing smile, as if he knew something that Rainmaker didn't.

Rainmaker felt suddenly discomfited by it. Here he was, holding every advantage, and Pilgrim still seemed to have an upper hand. The smile dropped from his face.

"No, Pilgrim. You're the one who made the big mistake today. You're not so tough, after all."

At that moment, the door behind Rainmaker opened. Barbara came walking in.

"Would you believe I was in the checkout line and—" The words choked off when she saw the gun in Rainmaker's hand.

Startled by the sudden voice behind him, Rainmaker began an automatic half turn of the head. He caught his error, but the swishing sound of the cane already filled the air.

It hit viciously in the center of his forehead. Rainmaker went down from the blow. Before the realization of what had happened could enter his mind, the cane cracked down savagely again, against his right temple.

In an instant the familiar Mauser was in Justin's hand. He was in control again, possessing the power.

Barbara stood, hands to her face, mouth agape.

"Get out to the car," Justin said. "We're not welcome here anymore."

She just stood there in shock, unable to move.

"Was the security team at the main road?" he asked her.

She shook her head weakly.

"Move. Out to the car. *Now!*"

She went in a daze through the door.

Justin moved quickly to the bedroom and picked up the blue flight bag. There was no sign of a limp in his movement.

He came back into the living room, picked up the notes, and stuffed them into the flight bag. He picked up the cane and walked back to the body.

Then he bent down, straddling Rainmaker's unconscious form. He put the Mauser well into the mouth and pulled the trigger.

"Second big mistake, Smiley," he began. "Shoot, don't talk."

He turned to the door and saw Barbara staring in horror at what he had just done.

He grabbed her firmly by the arm and pushed her out of the house.

They got into the Corvette. Justin tore off down the narrow road, wheels spinning.

The security team was not in position. He gunned it for everything it was worth. All decisions had been made for him. It was time to go.

"Always plan for the unexpected," Honeycut said to a panic-stricken Elizabeth Ryerson, with obvious concern on his own face.

"And what was it all for?" Elizabeth said acidly. "A journal that would have significance to only a handful of people in the whole world? We couldn't have been hurt by it anymore. But now we're on the edge of trouble, because he'll know exactly what it means. And he's a breath away from being lost to us," she said.

"We're in control," Honeycut insisted. "He's going for the journal now. It'll be all over soon, just like I said it would." There was a little sadness in his tone. He was disappointed that it hadn't worked out with Justin. He had liked him very much. Too much.

Barbara had been painfully silent since leaving the house. She hadn't even looked into Justin's face. She just kept her eyes focused on her lap.

He reached across the console and touched her hand. There was no acknowledgment of the gesture.

"Spill it," he said, taking his hand away.

For the first time since leaving, she looked at him. "You just killed that man back there. Like it was nothing, Justin. You just killed him," she said, with an almost painful lack of comprehension.

"He had come to kill us," Justin said flatly. "We'd both be dead now if I hadn't."

"Why?" she quizzed.

Justin didn't answer.

She looked out to the road in front of them. "Before the incident in Dieppe, had you ever killed a man?" she asked.

He remained silent.

"Answer me, damn you!" she yelled.

"That's not important," he replied.

"Oh, yes, it is," she snapped, turning fully toward him in her seat. "Did you ever kill a man before Dieppe?" she repeated.

"Yes," he said without looking at her.

"Oh, Justin," she said, dropping her face into her hands, weeping.

Justin drove on silently.

She wiped the tears away with the palms of her hands and looked at him again. "How many men before Dieppe?"

He shook his head and looked at her sternly. "Jesus Christ, what the hell does it matter? Do you know what's happening to us? People are trying to kill us. I'm trying to keep us alive. I'm concerned with what's up there, ahead of us," he said pointing at the open road.

"How many men?" she repeated.

"What in the hell is so important—"

"*I want to know!*" she interrupted loudly.

He looked straight ahead, his jaws clenched tightly, the eye in a tight squint.

"How many?"

"Do you think I run around putting notches in the handle of my gun to keep count? I try not to remember," he said in an annoyed tone.

"More than five?" she probed.

He shook his head in disbelief again. "Yes," he said through clenched teeth.

"More than ten?"

"Jesus fuckin' Christ, *yes!* Are you through now?" he fumed. "What the hell does it all matter? I'm still me. I'm the same guy you loved this morning, remember?"

"Part of you is," she said in a whisper.

He leveled an angry stare at her. She had never seen such a look in his face before. She remained silent for hours after that.

Justin's mind clicked away busily as he drove. He welcomed the silence, the chance to think clearly without interruptions. He decided that the safest way back was to drive. This way he could maintain some measure of control. In a plane they'd be helpless, as Centaur had been.

It was a long drive back to New York, a lot of country to lose themselves in. But first he had to get rid of the car, which had been provided by the agency and probably had homing devices and bugs in it. That would be a simple matter.

At three in the morning they stopped at a small all-night diner for some food.

Justin ate hungrily at his eggs, potatoes, and sausages. Barbara hadn't touched hers.

Justin sat where he could see the car, to be alerted to anyone approaching it.

"Justin, I...I love you," she said, reaching across the table to take one of his hands.

He smiled and looked at her.

"I'm sorry I behaved the way that I did," she said.

"Don't worry about it," he comforted. "Try to eat your food. We won't be making many stops."

"Where are we going?" she asked, starting to take her first bites of the cold eggs.

"Home."

"Why are they doing this?"

"I've got something they want, or at least they think I have it," he said.

"Well, do you?"

"Yes and no. Some of it I do, the rest I think I can find," he answered.

"What is it?"

He looked up from his plate. "I'm not going to tell you that. What you don't know might keep you alive," he said.

"Why don't you just give it back to them? Maybe they'd leave us alone," she said, almost pleading.

"It's past that, now. They'll never leave us alone. I know too much," he told her.

"I wish I knew what was going on," she sighed.

"Believe me, the less you know, the better off you'll be."

They finished eating, Justin consuming the scraps that Barbara had left. He also bought some rolls and cigars, the latter to help him stay awake as he drove. They walked out to the car.

Justin tensed as an Impala crept by. An old man and woman were inside. A wave of relief swept through him.

"What's wrong?" Barbara asked.

"Nothing," he said, shaking his head. "I'm just paranoid when it comes to Impalas."

"I *do* love you, Justin," she said, holding his arm with both hands.

He put the arm around her and squeezed her tightly.

"What's ahead for us?" she asked.

"A lot of moving," he answered, as they walked out into the parking lot. "A lot of moving and looking back."

Nobody really noticed as they entered a different car than they had come in. The hood was up for only a minute or so. Then they were off, in their newly stolen Camaro.

A little while later, before the sunlight began to filter through the night sky, Justin stopped the car one more time. In another ten minutes he had provided them with different license plates, from a closely matching car. The stolen car's plates were left on the other car. Its owner probably wouldn't notice the difference for days or weeks.

Then they were off again, heading home. Home. They'd never be able to call any place home again.

"Will they ever stop coming after us?" Barbara asked.

"No."

A painful, depressed look settled onto her face. So suddenly their happiness together had changed to this.

Later that morning, after the sun had risen, the Camaro pulled into a gas station.

"We're going to have to gas up," he said. "We're safe using these credit cards I have for a while, yet. It doesn't matter if they know where we've been at this stage. It's a week from now that I'm worried about."

"I've got credit cards," she said.

"They'll find us just as easily with those. We need cash. I've got about eighty dollars left. How about you?" he asked.

"I've got plenty." She smiled. "I took three thousand dollars out of savings before coming out to join you. I only used about a hundred of it," she said.

"That's good. That'll help for a while. We can figure something out later," he said.

"Justin, I know that you want me to know as little as possible, but could you just tell me who it is that we're running away from? Is it really the government?"

Justin thought for a moment. "No, it's not the government," he answered.

"They'll kill us, won't they?" she asked.

"Only if we give them the chance. It won't be as easy as they think," he said, a plan already beginning to take shape in his head.

Barbara leaned against the console and held his arm. "It is right, what we're doing, isn't it, Justin?" she asked.

"More than you know," he said softly.

The Camaro pulled into the parking lot of the Arcola Motel in Saddle Brook, New Jersey. They had made it back safely, having made stops only for gas and food.

Barbara had spelled Justin at the wheel several times, so that he could sleep. They had made excellent time in the nonstop run. Justin figured that they would have one or two days' advantage yet, before having to move again.

He went into the small office and made arrangements for an efficiency unit, so that they could reduce the risk of detection, by preparing their own meals right there in the room.

They had stopped for some groceries just about a mile away and had everything that they needed for the next few days. They had even bought some spare clothing and other necessities. They were good at traveling light, having had plenty of practice in Europe.

"This'll be the last time we can risk using the credit cards," he told her. "We'll have to go cash the rest of the way."

"Three thousand dollars won't last long," Barbara said.

"It'll do," Justin returned. "We'll need most of it to get new transportation. We can't keep this car too much longer, and stealing cars will catch up to us soon."

"Well, what do we do now?" Barbara asked.

"Eat a good lunch, and wait for bad weather," he said.

"Bad weather?"

"A day or two of rain or snow is all I'll need," he said.

SENTINEL wouldn't be able to track visibly in that kind of weather. They would be safe until he got the journal, he reckoned. After that, the shit would fly. The bad weather would also help cover their escaping movements.

As if on special order, the following day was miserable. The sky was dark, and heavy rains fell. The forecast was for continued bad weather for the next three days.

At about three in the afternoon, Justin dressed and put his coat on.

"Where are we going?" Barbara said, going for her coat.

"*We're* not going anywhere. *I* am," he told her.

"No, Justin. I want to be with you," she insisted.

"It's all right. Nothing will happen, yet," he said. "I should be back by late this evening. If you haven't heard from me by morning, get a cab and get out of here," he told her.

Her face filled with the sudden realization of what he meant.

"Please, take me with you?" she implored.

"No. You'll be safer here. You don't know anything that can hurt them, not even who *they* are," he said.

"Please?"

"No."

He held her and kissed her. "I love you," he said. He held her for several long moments.

She was crying when he left.

Justin walked to an area of the post office where he could privately examine the letter that Priest had mailed to him. He opened the envelope and read it.

Mr. Chaple,

I've decided to give you the journal. I'll need three days of continuous work to finish transcribing it. It takes considerable time to remove the information from the books.

I'll contact you when it's finished and arrange a meeting. At that time, I'll give you the completed journal.

Thank you, from myself and Billy.

Jack Priest

It didn't tell him where the journal was, as Honeycut had expected it to. Justin was confused and disappointed by the development.

He thought for a moment about what Priest had said on the phone.

"I...I just called to ask you something," Justin remembered. "I...I just wondered, if you were such a good friend of Billy's, why didn't you visit his grave?" Priest had asked, his voice nervous and trembling.

Then he had hung up.

Justin thought.

He replayed it in his head, trying to remember everything.

Wait! Priest didn't hang up right away, Justin remembered. The phone sounded as if it had fallen from his hand. Then it was hung up. And Priest *hadn't* called him by his name.

That was it! Priest had tried to tell him where the journal was.

The grave!

Priest had said that he went to the grave often to put flowers there—and probably to deposit finished sheets of the journal.

Justin walked quickly back to the postal clerk. He had all of the papers he had found at Bridges's apartment weighed, along with the complete account of the events that he had written. He checked postage rates and bought a safe surplus of stamps. Then he left the post office.

He made one stop and bought two large manila envelopes and a flashlight. Thirty minutes later, he was on the New Jersey Turnpike pointed for Hightstown again, safely concealed in a growing rush-hour traffic that was being slashed by the now-freezing rain and sleet.

Justin made slow progress getting to Hightstown. He had difficulty after getting off the turnpike, making a wrong turn, but a little good guesswork put him back on the right course.

Justin couldn't see well in the stormy pitch-black with just one eye. He hadn't yet come to Priest's house. It seemed much further than he remembered it being from the actual center of town. He slowed to a crawl, looking for a recognizable landmark.

Coming upon an intersection, he stopped the Camaro and stared at the sign post. Windsor-Perrinville Road—he recognized it. Priest's house was just straight ahead, about a quarter of a mile up.

There were no other intersections between this one and Priest's place, so Justin reasoned that the cemetery must be off this road. He turned left, hoping that the entrance would be easy to spot. It was—about half a mile from the intersection.

Turning off the lights, he headed up the narrow road, running about a hundred yards, to where it split into an elongated oval. He turned the car around, facing out, just in case a fast getaway was required.

He got out of the car, carrying the small flashlight. He began checking the stones.

The rain began to make its drenching presence felt as he got to the cover of the big leafless trees. They offered some small protection, as the rising wind was broken in the numerous, thickly patterned branches overhead.

Justin was about a hundred feet from the tower. There weren't many graves in the small cemetery, but the bad weather made it seem a bigger task than it was.

He continued moving up the right side of the cemetery. At the crest of the gentle incline, about even with the tower, he found the first stone.

It belonged to Jack Priest, MD. He had died the same day that Justin had been called to St. Simon's. Justin had figured as much, from the dropping of the phone.

That meant that Honeycut already had the complete journal from Spartan's books. The partially transcribed copy was the last surviving trace of it now.

Next to Jack Priest's grave, Justin found the stone for William Priest. Spartan.

His hands and face were growing stiff from the freezing cold. He turned off the light, to reduce any further risk of being seen. He looked carefully around the grave.

Near the foot of the stone was a sunken receptacle, still holding a metallic cup with the stiff, brown remains of flowers left in the fall. After several tugs to loosen the frozen cup, Justin pulled it out. It was too small to hold so many sheets.

He felt inside the receptacle. The nearly frozen water made moving his numbing fingers more difficult. There was nothing there.

He looked around, still squatting at the grave. There was nowhere else Priest could have deposited the sheets quickly without being too obvious.

Justin knelt on the wet ground, the freezing blades of brown grass crackling softly under him. He pulled and twisted strenuously at the receptacle. After considerable effort, it budged. More twisting and tugging. Finally, it came free, making a loud scraping noise.

Lifting it out, Justin thrust his hand into the hole. It was deep. He had to reach well down before feeling the metallic cylinder.

He pulled it out. It was the kind that glass pipettes were sterilized and stored in. The rolled papers inside would be dry and in good condition.

Justin heard the soft crunch of frozen grass behind him. He spun on his knees, the Mauser instantly ready.

CRACK! CRACK! Into the howling wind.

The figure fell stiffly backward, landing with a crunching thud, rock still.

He looked around for more potential attackers.

The man had come from the direction of the tower.

Justin quickly moved across the open expanse to the tower. He had good relative visibility from that high point.

He could see nothing to indicate the presence of another agent.

In the distance, Priest's house was lit up. That was probably being watched, too. They would be coming soon.

He went quickly back to the body. He looked into the lifeless face. No one he knew. He began a quick search of the body, looking for the usual agency identifications. There were none. No weapons, either.

Shit.

He searched more carefully. No weapons on the ground around the body, either.

Had he reacted too fast, too instinctively, and killed an innocent person? Who in the hell in his right mind would be out visiting a cemetery on a night like this?

He went back over the hill on which the tower stood, to the opposite declining slope. There he saw a grave still bearing the piles of flowers of a recent burial. He checked the temporary marker. It was a child of five, dead but seven days.

"Oh, Christ," he let out softly.

Next to the child's grave was the stone of a young mother, dead only six months.

Had he not reacted so quickly, the man would be alive. But had he hesitated, and had it been an agent after him, he'd be the dead meat now.

Too bad, but that's the way it went.

He moved as quickly as he could back down to the Camaro. In a moment he was gone, only a grim reminder of what he had become left behind.

The Camaro pulled into the first available service area on the turnpike. Justin parked the car and went into the cafeteria.

He got a cup of coffee and two glazed donuts and went to a corner table that gave him a clear vantage point of the entire room, while affording good protection to his back.

He unwrapped one of the donuts and then twisted the snug top off the stainless-steel cylinder. He pulled out the neatly rolled pages and began reading.

There were about eighty pages in all, sixty-four journal entries, just as Priest had said. The entries were not numbered one through sixty-four, but were scattered evenly from the beginning, middle, and end sections of the journal.

Even with the missing entries, the picture was unmistakable. The twenty-fifth page found at Bridges's apartment fit perfectly with the facts revealed in the entries. All of Justin's questions were finally answered.

He took the manila envelopes from the blue flight bag and laid all of his papers on the table.

He wrote a quick note and, after some careful thought, distributed the papers. He put the note, along with the journal, his written account, and the twenty-fifth page, into one envelope. The remaining sheets that he had found at Bridges's apartment were put into the other envelope.

He sealed the envelopes and addressed them, putting more than sufficient postage on each.

He dropped them into the mail box, went back out to the Camaro, and headed back to Barbara.

There was little more that he could do now. It was out of his hands and into the hands of someone whom he could trust to do the only thing possible. As with Spartan, then his brother, and now Justin, the *trust* was being handed down. But they would never find this one until it was too late.

"It's all over now," Elizabeth said bitterly. "He's gone now. Your gamble failed."

"No it hasn't," Honeycut said calmly.

"We don't know where he is now," she spat out at him. "He could have the journal already and be anywhere with it by now. He's been gone for nine hours. We'll never—"

"He'll go back for the girl," Honeycut insisted softly, confidence in his tone. "When he does, we'll get everything. Gemini has everything ready," he said.

"You've been wrong right down the line about him. 'Expect the unexpected,' you said. What if he doesn't go back for her? Then what?"

"He'll go back. It's almost over now," Honeycut said.

"You're not always as right as you think you are, Irv," Elizabeth said, acidly.

"Why don't we just wait and see about that," Honeycut retorted calmly.

There was a gentle tapping on the door. Barbara rushed to it immediately. She quickly unlocked it and opened it.

Justin walked in.

She threw her arms around his neck.

"Oh, Justin, I was so scared," she sobbed.

"It's all right, I'm here now," he comforted her.

"You're freezing," she said. "Hurry up, get inside and into something dry."

Justin walked in, and Barbara closed the door behind him.

"Did you find it? Did you get what you were after?" she rushed out excitedly.

"Yeah, I found it, all right," he said dryly.

"Well?"

"Well, what?" he said.

"Where is it?" she asked impatiently.

"I don't have it," he answered.

"You...I don't understand," she said, puzzled.

"I found it. But I don't have it anymore," he explained. "Bringing it here wouldn't do any good."

"Then where is it?" she poked.

"Where it will do the most good," he replied. "It's out of our hands."

"I don't understand," she said.

"Don't worry about understanding it. The less you know, the better off you'll be," he told her.

"I'm tired of you telling me that," she said angrily. "I'm in this, too. What happens to you happens to me from this point on. I'd say that I have a fair stake in this, too. Don't you think I deserve to know why someone is trying to kill us?"

Justin began taking off his wet clothes.

Barbara watched him, her face reddening.

"You're not going to tell me, are you?" she said heatedly.

"No, I'm not."

"Justin, I—"

"I've given you my reasons. Now that's all there is to say about it," he said, with a finality in his tone.

She looked at him angrily for several long moments, as he climbed into warm clothing.

"I'll make you some hot chocolate," she said, walking into the small kitchenette.

"Thanks, I could really use some."

Nothing more was said.

A little while later Barbara walked over to the bed carrying two cups of rich, piping hot chocolate. She handed a cup to Justin, who was now on the bed.

He took a short sip, blew on it several times, and took another longer sip.

"Oh, boy, does that ever hit the spot."

Barbara stared at him in hurt silence.

Justin sipped a few more times, avoiding eye contact.

"Cold as a witch's tit out there tonight," he said. "We'll have to be moving out of here in the morning."

"Where to?" she asked.

"Haven't made up my mind yet," he said.

He fought back a yawn.

"God, I'm tired. All that driving is catching up to me now," he said, taking another sip of his hot chocolate.

His face felt strange, stiff, almost numb. He opened his mouth as wide as he could, trying to flex his facial muscles.

His left eyelid grew heavy. He felt his arms and legs begin to tingle slightly.

"Jesus…" he said, with a confused expression.

Barbara sat watching him nervously.

Justin's head bobbed for a second, but he snapped it up, almost spilling his hot chocolate.

"I don't feel well," he said, just above a whisper.

"Give them back their journal, Justin," Barbara said finally.

Justin shook his head, trying to clear it. He looked up at her.

"Give them the journal, Justin," she repeated.

He squinted strangely at her, then looked quickly at the cup, then back to Barbara. Sudden shock registered on his face. "Jour…journal?" he said, his eyes widening.

"Where is the journal, Justin?" she asked, sitting on the bed beside him.

The cup fell from his hand, spilling on the bed. He fell back against the pillows, looking up at her, bewildered, dropping away into sleep.

"You...you..." he slurred.

"Just give it to them," she pleaded. "Don't you understand? They'll let us go. Just tell me where the journal is. Justin...Justin," she said, bringing her face closer to his, shaking him to keep him coherent.

With his last remaining strength, Justin threw out a vicious slap, catching Barbara squarely on the cheek. Its force knocked her off the bed and onto the floor.

She got up quickly, her eyes filled with tears of hurt, not from the pain of his blow, but from the fact of it.

The sudden rush of hate on his face made her feel terribly small and alone, helpless.

"You're such a fool," she cried. "Why couldn't you have just given it to them when they asked for it? Didn't you know that there could be no other way? It was the only chance that we ever really had."

Justin tried to speak, but it was an indistinguishable mumble.

"Haven't you learned by now that their way is the only way? *That nothing is real?*" she said. "Just like your stupid windchimes. It was *all* for your benefit. Never really there. All make believe," she said, tears flooding her eyes.

The room was becoming an eerie, floating blur to him. Only light and shadows. Then a tunnel of blackness. No sound.

BLEEP!

BEEP! "Yes, Gemini," SENTINEL's soft voice acknowledged.

"You heard it all?" Barbara asked.

"Yes."

She looked at Justin with a deep, heavy pain in her heart, tears streaming down her cheeks.

"You can come for him now."

FORTY

Irwin Honeycut walked briskly into the control center at Sigma. He looked at the I-told-you-so expression on Elizabeth Ryerson's face.

"Save it," he snapped, before she could get it out.

"It's gone—all of it," she began anyway. "The journal, the twenty-fifth page, the written account—all of it. Gone. If you had stopped him back when I told you to, this whole thing would have been avoided," she went on. "The partially completed translation may never have been found. It certainly wouldn't have made sense to anyone if it were. But now...a schoolboy could figure it out."

"There's still a chance," Honeycut persisted, more out of defensive pride than actual belief. "We'll get it back," he said, in his most confident-sounding voice. "It's just hidden somewhere else. We'll get him to tell us where it is."

"A chance...hidden," Elizabeth echoed back, shaking her head at the stubborn optimism. "It could be anywhere now— even on the President's desk for all we know."

Honeycut leveled a burning stare at her. "So what? What can the President do about it? We've progressed beyond any serious threat of interference now. You know that," he said irritably.

"You're right, Irv. But the obstacles could be greater."

"What obstacles?" Honeycut growled.

"The people. It's too soon," Elizabeth answered.

"The people can't stop it, either."

"No, the people can't stop it. But it could necessitate resorting to the 'old way,' a way that wasn't in the plan. It could add years to the final realization of our goals."

"We were always prepared for that possibility," Honeycut retorted. "Either way, it's inevitable that the plan will succeed, whether we get that journal back or not. Besides, we may not have to go that way, if he tells us where he's hidden it," Honeycut said.

"Or whom he may have given it to," she added.

Honeycut looked at her sharply. "It doesn't matter *who* has it. We can put an end to any existing threat. There will be no foolish chances taken this time."

That was Honeycut's first acknowledgment of the unnecessary risks undertaken by his errors in judgment concerning Pilgrim. Elizabeth had never heard him admit to being wrong in a serious matter. There was a satisfaction in its sound.

Honeycut did not like his position in this discussion. He found himself arguing points contrary to his beliefs to salvage his wounded pride. He knew well that the old way was never a part of the plan that he had so carefully worked out around Niederlage guidelines. He had sold them on his plan, convincing them that it could work—that it *would* work.

"He'll never tell you," Elizabeth said.

"I think he will."

"And what if he's done something foolish, like sending it to the *Washington Post* or *New York Times?*" Elizabeth asked. "What do you do then?"

Honeycut laughed. "It would certainly make for great fiction," he commented. "I doubt that either the *Post* or the *Times* would take it seriously without first obtaining some supportive evidence. They don't even have a confirmed source."

"It's all there," Elizabeth said. "Once it hits the public, something could break loose. There are a lot of people in the program. If *one* of them believes it…"

Honeycut's smile faded. "We have Pilgrim. That much of the problem *is* resolved. He can't hurt us anymore.

"I'm not worried about his telling us where it is," Honeycut said confidently. "I'm sure that he can be induced to talk—one way or another."

That disturbing look was on Honeycut's face again, but Elizabeth said nothing. She could sense the inner desperation, the wall of defensive optimism being constructed within the man. She almost felt sorry for him.

The slow journey back to consciousness was filled with disturbing flashbacks of his last moments with Barbara. The stinging realization of her betrayal burned painfully through Justin, along with the sickening reality and truth of her words that nothing was real.

Nothing was real! Barbara, Ted, Pappy, the agency…even the windchimes. Not real…all for his benefit.

He opened his eye and looked around the room. He was back at Sigma.

He sat up.

His head throbbed, the eye hurt. He was sick and aching inside. It was really over now. It had finally cost him everything.

A strange calmness filled him. There was no fear of the obvious end awaiting him. He had done what he could, all that he could, his very best. He felt proud of never betraying himself or his beliefs against the incredible odds, when it would have been the easy thing to do, to look away and ignore its presence—to remain untouched by it and safe.

He looked at the date on his watch. Two days had passed since being taken. He rubbed the ragged stubble on his face, almost five days' worth. He thought about shaving. What the fuck for? he wondered. He'd probably never shave again. Never do many things again.

He stretched his arms and noticed the tiny needle marks from where they had injected him to keep him unconscious. He rose from the bed and stretched life into the rest of his stiff muscles, aware that he must be under visual surveillance. The monitors were well hidden, but he knew they were there. He limped a step or two for their benefit and looked around the room. The cane was lying across a small table on the other side of the room. He limped to it. As he walked, a bulkiness made its awareness felt in his back pocket. He reached for it and pulled out a doubly fat wallet. Looking inside, he found a thick wad of cash.

Barbara. The pain was fresh again.

He counted it silently. Twenty-six hundred dollars. Before returning the wallet to his pocket, he took out the metal security card that Honeycut had given him. He limped, with feigned assistance from the cane, to the closed sliding doors.

He pushed the button.

As he expected, nothing happened.

He put the security card into the slot.

Still nothing.

The card was useless now—probably always had been.

He walked back to the bed and sat, bending the card back and forth until it snapped in two. He held the pieces in his hand, staring at them.

The sudden sound of the sliding doors startled him, making him turn to them. Two armed security guards came through the doors. There were two more visible outside in the hallway.

"You will come with us, please," one of them said, with cold authority in his tone.

Justin looked at them and stood. Without a word, he followed them out, absently putting the broken halves of the ID card into his pocket.

Moments later the two electric carts rolled to a halt in front of the control-center doors. Two of the guards accompanied him to them. The doors slid open, and he was escorted in.

Honeycut and Elizabeth Ryerson were waiting for him.

"Thank you. You can leave us now," Honeycut said to the security guards. He held Justin's Mauser aimed carefully at him. Honeycut's face was ruddy, stiff, an almost hostile urgency across it.

The doors closed behind the security team, leaving the three of them standing in a disquieting silence.

Justin glanced casually at Elizabeth. There was a nervousness in her eyes, but it was unlike the strange tension he had seen in them before. It was a more confident apprehension now.

Honeycut raised the Mauser upward and removed the clip, then ejected the round in the chamber in a gesture designed to gain Justin's confidence.

Elizabeth's eyes widened at the unexpected move. For a second, her own confidence waned, replaced by a confused nervousness. She shook her head, almost imperceptibly, in disbelief.

"Sit," Honeycut said to Justin, motioning to a single chair in the center of the room.

Justin complied limpingly.

Honeycut stared at him in silence. Justin stared back, waiting, willing to remain silent until Honeycut began.

"We know that you've found the journal," Honeycut said finally. "You've undoubtedly read it."

Justin remained silent, staring evenly into the face.

"Now you're going to tell us what you've done with it," Honeycut said flatly.

Justin said nothing.

"Where is the journal, Justin?" Honeycut asked.

Still no reply, just the even stare.

"Let's dispense with the games, shall we?" Honeycut said, placing the Mauser and clip on the console in front of him.

The two men locked eyes, measuring one another.

"Where is the journal, Justin?" Honeycut repeated.

"You're the one with all the fucking explanations. You tell me," Justin replied.

Honeycut frowned and shook his head, rubbing the back of his reddening neck with his hand.

"This can be easy or it can be difficult—for both of us. I've no wish to use unpleasant means of persuasion on you to get to the answers. However, if you leave us no other choice, we will resort to whatever methods necessary, to get you to tell us what we want to know," Honeycut threatened.

"That's not your style—*Colorosa*," Justin said.

Honeycut's face reddened instantly. He squinted pensively at Justin. "I imagine that wasn't hard to figure out," he said. "But none of that matters. Where is the journal?" he asked sharply.

"Where's Barbara?" Justin asked back.

Honeycut stared evenly at him for a long moment. "She's been reassigned," he answered.

"Reassigned," Justin repeated. "How long has she been a part of it?" he asked.

"Since before you knew her," Honeycut answered. "A little over three years."

"And Steve? Did he know about all of this Raptor bullshit too?"

"No. Only a very small number of people in the program do, actually," Honeycut replied.

"The President?" Justin asked.

Honeycut shook his head in response. "The secret is quite secure. Where is the journal?" he asked again.

No answer.

"It will do no good," Honeycut said. "Nothing you can do will stop Operation Raptor now. Nothing anybody can do will stop it. You may as well tell us, to make it easier on everyone. There's nothing to gain by your refusal at this point."

A small disturbing smile broke across Justin's lips. "That's not exactly so," he said.

"Oh, but I can assure you that it *is* so. The plan is in its advanced stages. It is absolutely impossible to affect it now. So tell us where it is," Honeycut said.

Justin continued smiling.

"*Where is it?*" Elizabeth shouted from the side, in a near-hysterical rage, no longer able to tolerate Justin's cool demeanor.

Justin cast her a cool, nonchalant stare, then looked away, as if to disregard her very presence in the room.

Elizabeth's face twisted in anger. "You son-of-a-bitch," she hissed. She could envision no greater pleasure than to see the life drain from the eyes and face of this man, to be rid of him—forever. "You'll tell us where it is…or…"

"Why don't you come on over here and try it," Justin said and smiled at her. "I'll give you something you've been needing for a long time."

"Where is the journal?" Honeycut asked sharply, drawing the attention of both of them with the severity of his tone.

Justin stared at him defiantly. "Where it will do you the most possible harm," he answered, mounting a small offensive of his own.

Elizabeth's eyes stabbed nervously into Honeycut. You see! You see! I told you, they said clearly.

"That's a very foolish attitude," Honeycut said. "I've told you that there is nothing that you or anyone can do to stop it now. Not giving us that journal will only result in the greatest unpleasantness for you and whoever has it. Tell us where it is, Justin. Tell us now…and you'll walk out of here alive. You have my word on that."

Alive!

Elizabeth's face registered incredible shock at Honeycut's words. She began to speak, but was immediately silenced by Honeycut's raised hand.

"Tell us where it is, and you can go free," Honeycut offered again.

"Do you expect me to believe that?" Justin said.

"You'll be allowed to walk out of here a free man. I promise you that," Honeycut repeated. "We'll take precautions, of course, by fitting you with an explosive implant. We'll also give you back the eye you lost. As long as you remain silent about what you know, you'll be permitted to live a normal life. We'll even help you get started again, say in Australia or New Zealand. The choice is yours."

"A normal life?" Justin said sarcastically. "In the face of what you represent? There'll be no such thing as a normal life."

"It's not what you think it is, Justin," Honeycut insisted.

"It's not? You're a fucking comedian," Justin said.

"This is a very *different* thing, Justin. Listen to me, while I explain a few things to you," Honeycut said.

"Go ahead. I've got nothing but time."

Honeycut stepped down from the console platform and took a few steps toward Justin. "The basic concepts of National Socialism were good for Germany and would have been for the rest of the world, too, if it hadn't been handled so poorly.

"They made a great many mistakes, a great many mistakes. It's easy to recognize where they went wrong, with the facility of hindsight to help us. But that's what history is for, isn't it? To study, to learn from? To avoid the mistakes of the past?

"One of their greatest mistakes was their lack of patience. Instead of adopting a hundred-year plan as we did in Operation Raptor, they charged ahead blindly without an adequate plan. The Germans," he mused, "so methodical, deliberate, and calculating in all things—without a real plan. Oh, they had a plan, their master plan, but a shortsighted one. They could not see beyond the *now* of things to the real tomorrow. Their plan could have never worked.

"The future of the Third Reich was in the youth of Germany, the Hitler Youth and their children and their children's children.

From that tremendous resource pool should have arisen the leadership to make National Socialism work on a global scale.

"But they rushed madly at the world, wreaking destruction, subjugation, and genocide. They were led by incompetents who rose through the ranks, marginal types with ugly, twisted little brains grown drunk on sudden, unchecked power. They had used terror and violence to bang the beliefs into those slower to grasp the ideology of the New Order in its beginnings. They thought they could continue that way to conquer a world. They were terrible simplifiers.

"They need only have waited this long for the Nazi Youth to come of age, to make their major, lasting gains. Instead, they spent that youth on the battlefields of the world, spilled the blood of the seed-stock of their future, their very best—gone. That is one of the sad things of war, that the best die first, and all sides lose." There was a sorrow in Honeycut's eyes as he looked at Justin. The best are lost. How terribly true.

"But that all ended in the ashes of defeat. Operation Raptor is where the plan and the movement are to continue, not with the carefully planned survivors. They are all 'old' Nazis, the architects of the 'old way.' We have no further interest in them or their methods. They were all spawned from the failure of the past, from the misguided beliefs that led to the catastrophe.

"Their efforts at survival and attempts at revival kept the eyes of the world looking at them, while we began the patient building of our ultimate plan.

"Our greatest resource is to be the children of the generations untouched by the bitter memories of that painful period in world history. The new National Socialism will bear no relation to the old. It will never stray from the guiding principles set down in Operation Raptor.

"As you learned from the journal, we established the five steering centers from which to begin our building efforts. Each was potentially a home for the New Reich—a new Fatherland.

But, as time passed, it became obvious that some of these could not aid in the plan. These steering centers were then quickly disbanded, for the security of the others.

"Germany was first, then Argentina and South Africa. Spain went last, only this year.

"You may recall from the journal the mention of Titus. After Wolf's death, Titus managed to acquire his journal. He tried futilely to gain control, but he never stood a chance. The 'special action' Spartan performed, during which he uncovered the journal, removed him.

"Who was Wolf?" Justin asked.

"That doesn't matter," Honeycut replied. "It's no longer important. Someday, when Raptor is finalized, the people will know who Wolf *really* was. His place in history will be secure," he said.

"The 'people' will know?" Justin repeated. "The superhuman survivors? The supermen of the human race? Germans?" he asked sarcastically.

"Aryans," Honeycut corrected.

"Supermen," Justin spat out. "That's bullshit."

"Not exactly," Honeycut rejoined. "An exceptional race, despite their failings. A race still capable of greatly improving the human species.

"Twice, they rose to challenge the world, nearly succeeding. One tiny nation standing against the world. You can't deny that they are exceptional. Their resilience is unequalled in human history."

"So is their record of genocide," Justin interrupted.

"There have been worse," Honeycut said. "Did you know that the Russians killed nearly as many in their own death camps? The history books don't say that. They don't tell about their atrocities in Latvia and Estonia and many other countries, or of what they did in Poland, attacking from the East as we swept in from the West. The history books don't show the real numbers of people killed during the Bolshevik revolution, or during Stalin's bloody rise to power, or in the purge that followed his death. Those figures 'don't exist.' But they are far greater than the fifty-five million attributed to us, to *our* war. But the history books will someday show the true legend—when we rewrite them."

"What you say is probably true," Justin allowed. "But the fact remains that your people did it with a sick logic and a brutal plan. People's lives meant no more to them than blades of grass. It was done in the name of racial purification, to remove the *Untermenschen* from the face of the earth, leaving only the supermen, the Aryans. That's all bullshit."

Honeycut looked at Justin, his eyes filled with passion. "Look at Africa, at South America, at their inability to advance with the rest of the world. They *are* inferior. Can you deny that? Those same people choke this country today with their inferior work and living habits. The welfare roles of this country show that clearly. They strangle this economy. They strangle the world.

"There was *no* welfare in Germany—*everybody* worked, *everybody* contributed."

"So did the slave labor, the *Untermenschen*," Justin mocked.

"Only because our manpower was being greatly strained by the war effort. By the time we had conquered Europe, our strength had been greatly reduced. Our victories had been impressive, but they cost us superiority of the seas, of the skies, and severely reduced our land strength. The magnitude of those victories was overwhelming, even to us. We could not effectively supply our armies. Logistics became a nightmare. We *had* to utilize slave labor, to keep up the enormous industrial efforts needed to hold our new borders and to free additional manpower to keep up our fighting strength," Honeycut explained.

"And the death camps?" Justin asked. "How do you justify them?"

"The concentration camps did not become 'death camps' until we knew that the war was lost. Then it became essential to reduce the seed-stock of our enemies."

"The subhumans," Justin said sarcastically. "The Jews, the Czechs, the Poles, and the Russians—all the non-Aryans."

Honeycut lowered his eyes from Justin. After a moment's thought, he looked at him again. "The attempted extermination of the Jews was our single, most devastating mistake. Again, it is hindsight that makes that observation possible. Surely, it was impossible to recognize it then, for Germany and its people had escaped into hatred, a regrettable step, yet one seemingly important at the time. Had the Jews been included in the plan, made a part of the scheme, the advantages would have been enough to mean the difference between victory and defeat. Their racial unity, the historical sameness of the Jews, could have provided legions of loyal Nazis in almost every country in the world. Their claims of being God's 'chosen people' were not that far out of line with Aryan beliefs. Had we used this tack, they would have quickly identified with the movement. The United States may not have even entered the war, or possibly ever done so on our side because of Jewish influence, not to mention other scientific and financial advantages, as well, throughout the rest of the world."

"You can't wipe out century after century of hatred," Justin said. "The Jews have been prejudiced against and hated throughout history. You can't just tell people who have the hatred for them in their blood to love them, accept them, share their destiny with them."

"With a careful plan, it could have been done," Honeycut said. "They are not that different."

With that, Justin broke into laughter. He shook his head at Honeycut. "Not that different? Are you saying that they're Aryans?"

"Look at Israel today. A country built by surviving *German* Jews. Look at their strength, their courage. Is it not like that of our own? We were too swayed by the prejudices and hatreds of the ages to recognize their importance to us," Honeycut said. "They were Jews, yes, but they were also *Germans*."

"Aryans!" Justin roared in laughter.

"Yes, Aryans," Honeycut said.

"Tell that to the six million you killed. 'Sorry, boys, we didn't know it back then. But you were really Aryans, after all.' Hitler should only hear you now."

"If he could see Israel today, he might agree," Honeycut insisted.

"Christ, you really do believe that, don't you?" Justin said.

"Yes, I do."

"They're strong, all right," Justin began, "but not because of the Aryan blood that runs in them. They want to survive. There will never be a death camp again into which Jews will march like sheep into death chambers. They'll fight to survive. And they don't claim the Aryan heritage to conquer the world. They aren't trying to kill everyone who might disagree with them," Justin said.

"Oh no?" Honeycut smiled. "You should only know how wrong you are. You should know about the research and development efforts being put forth in such guarded secrecy in that country," he contradicted.

"They only want to survive in their own land, to prevent another holocaust upon their children. Their future is in their children. They've dedicated themselves with blood, sweat, and bone to secure that future. The children of Israel…" He stopped at the familiar sound of the point he was trying to make. "They only want to survive," he repeated, then fell silent.

"What you say is undeniably true," Honeycut said. "But they do have plans. Plans that would shake your beliefs, if you knew them," he said.

"And what do you call what you're trying to do now? Operation Raptor, what do you call that?" Justin asked.

"We are getting precisely to the point that I am trying to make," Honeycut said, smiling.

"The Raptor plan is what National Socialism *could* have been, *should* have been, if it had been handled properly. The Raptor plan is making a better world for *all* people to live in, a world so well ordered, so far advanced, that it is beyond the imagination. And it is for the good of *all* people," Honeycut said with special emphasis.

"For *all* people?" Justin repeated bitingly. "For Jews, for blacks, for the retarded and the ones born with defects, and for those lame and disabled?" he asked.

"The Jews are Aryans. We realize that now. I've told you that," Honeycut said.

"Oh, Jesus," Justin laughed, "this is a real comedy. A sick, fucking comedy. I suppose that the blacks are Aryans, too?" he asked sarcastically.

"No, they are the exception," Honeycut replied evenly. "The nonwhite races are the exception."

"*The exception.* I see. I suppose that the new death camps will be for them," Justin said.

"There will be no death camps," Honeycut said. "They will be utilized."

"Utilized? As slave labor?" Justin asked. "To work your factories, tend your crops, or as servants to make the Aryan life easier? All for the privilege of staying alive. Is that what their role will be in the new order of things?" he asked.

"They are strong," Honeycut retorted. "By careful breeding techniques, it will eventually be possible to arrive at a class of acceptable Aryan stock. Many black traits are desirable."

"But what about the ones who are already black and not the product of your supervised breeding? What happens to them? What about the yellow ones and the red ones?" Justin asked.

"There will be a solution."

"A solution? A *final* solution?" Justin asked.

"A solution," Honeycut repeated.

"And the retarded and those with other defects, the lame and disabled?" Justin asked.

"They are useless," Honeycut said coldly. "There will be no such defects in the future. We can control everything," he said.

"And your mistakes will just quietly disappear, right?"

Honeycut didn't answer, his eyes saying it for him.

"It'll never work," Justin said. "The world will never stand still for it."

"The world will never recognize the change," Honeycut said. "We have the patience now—*and* the necessary means to make it all possible. In another sixty years, the change will be complete. There is no chance of failure, no alternative."

"And there will be no freedom," Justin said.

"There never has been any *real* freedom. Everyone is controlled in one way or another, given just enough freedoms to keep them happy. True freedom, total freedom, is too threatening, too frightening. People would never accept it, if they knew what it was really like. Everyone follows. It is human nature to follow," Honeycut said.

"There are leaders," Justin countered. "Every nation, every group of people has them."

"Only those able to direct others more effectively," Honeycut returned. "But they also follow. They follow laws, or higher authority—God, if you will. The whole concept of religion involves creating a supreme being to *follow*. Man *must* follow."

"You, too, Colorosa? As the new Führer, you will have to lead. Who will you follow?" Justin asked.

"All the future will be guided by the plan. All of man will follow it," Honeycut responded.

"To a better day?" Justin asked with burning sarcasm. "To the Dawn of Man, the New Order?"

"To a more perfect existence and a more perfect human race," Honeycut answered. "A race controlled in its purity, happy, strong, intelligent. All given the intelligence of SENTINEL, through implants put in at birth.

"Can you imagine the possibilities?" Honeycut asked, his eyes sparkling with excitement. "Children born possessing the potential intelligence of SENTINEL. Educated beyond our most advanced levels of today by the time that they are ten years old. All contributing to the perfect order, over life spans extended to a hundred and fifty years, or more. It's all possible. We can make it happen right now!" Honeycut said, filled with a childlike enthusiasm.

"All puppets," Justin returned flatly. "Directed by strings that you pull through SENTINEL, strings that all future Führers will pull. All programmed puppets, with no minds or wills of their own, with a whole universe to try to enslave and conquer, in fulfilling their Aryan destiny of conquest, their heritage to kill."

"When it becomes necessary—yes, they will conquer. And they will spread the perfect order and happiness wherever they go, to new worlds and new galaxies," Honeycut said.

"Your perfect order—it's a pipe dream," Justin said.

"No, it's an inevitable reality. The New Order has already been born. It is in motion, growing and maturing at a carefully planned rate. The implanting has already begun. There are already thousands. Soon there will be hundreds of thousands, then millions. Your great-grandchildren will make up the New Order," Honeycut said.

"It will interest you to know that your son will be a great nuclear physicist, someday," Honeycut said, a strange knowing satisfaction in his eyes.

"My...my son? Michael?" Justin asked, in sudden, angry disbelief.

"Yes, Michael. Haven't you noticed his early exceptional abilities in mathematics and science?" Honeycut asked.

Justin stared hard at Honeycut, rage building within him.

"No, you haven't, have you?" Honeycut said. "That's because you've never *talked* to him. You only took him *places* on your days together, doing *things* to fill the time. You don't even know your own son. He was one of our first."

Justin was filled with a consummate rage. They had dared to...to...Michael his son. "You're sick," Justin spat out hatefully.

Honeycut had a slight smile across his face.

Elizabeth felt the growing satisfaction of seeing Justin's hurt while he couldn't touch them. She luxuriated in it, enjoying the final satisfaction.

"The Third Reich was to be the thousand-year Reich," Honeycut said, smiling confidently. "The Fourth Reich will last forever."

"You're sick, you son-of-a-bitch. Do you know that? Sick! Both of you. You're as marginal as they come," Justin said, a feeling of blinding hate and confused helplessness behind his burning glare.

"Now, Justin, where is the journal?" Honeycut asked evenly, his face serious and stern again.

"Up your ass, where your head is. Open your eyes and look for it," he spat out.

"Where is it?" Honeycut repeated.

"Where it will do the most good to shatter this pipe dream of yours, you Nazi bastard."

Elizabeth's eyes jumped to Honeycut with a sudden urgency. "Did you hear that?"

Honeycut raised a hand to silence her.

"Nothing you can do can stop it now," Honeycut said.

"Don't bet on that," Justin returned hotly.

Elizabeth's mind began racing, trying to think of the worst possible things Justin could have done with the information. Pilgrim obviously felt that he could still hurt them—or maybe it was just his helplessness, his inability to really do anything combined with his hurt from learning about his son.

"For the last time, before we resort to unpleasant means, where is the journal?" Honeycut asked again.

"Kiss my ass," Justin said, looking away, his final answer made plain.

Honeycut pushed one of the buttons on the console. The control-center doors opened, and the two security guards entered.

"Take him back to his quarters," Honeycut ordered coldly.

Justin rose, using the cane. He turned to the security men, quickly assessing them.

His mind raced frantically through desperate alternatives, sorting, weighing probabilities.

He limped toward the door, one guard in front of him, the other following closely. His hand went into his pocket and grabbed one of the halves of the useless security card that he had broken earlier. He came up even with the sliding doors.

With a quick, forceful movement, he pushed the lead guard through the doors, sending him sprawling into the hallway.

Before the second guard could react, he threw a vicious kick backward, catching him in the solar plexus. The guard grunted and crashed down painfully to the control-center floor.

In the next instant, Justin rammed the broken security card into the slot next to the doors. They closed immediately in response to the unauthorized object, automatically locking.

Before the second guard could recover, the cane whipped savagely through the air, cracking violently against the side of his head. In a breath of an instant, Justin was on him, going for the gun.

Elizabeth's whole body became paralyzed from the sudden, fearful realization of what was happening. The threat was again alive.

Honeycut reached desperately for the Mauser and clip on the console. He fumbled frantically to get the clip back in.

"Hold it right there!" Justin's voice commanded.

Honeycut froze, knowing there was no bluff in the man.

"Put it down, and move away from it," Justin ordered. "Over there, by him," he said, pointing to the dazed security guard, who was holding his bleeding head.

Honeycut and Elizabeth quickly complied.

Justin looked to the sliding doors. There were frantic pounding sounds against them from the outside. Soon there would be many security personnel.

Justin moved without any trace of a limp to the command console and picked up the Mauser.

He gave the clip a quick check and snapped it in. Then he put the security guard's .45 under his belt.

Elizabeth was near death from fear. Her eyes were like baseballs. She gave Honeycut a telling stare. She didn't have to say it. The eyes did it for her. This is your fault. All your fault. If you had listened to me…

"You," Justin said, pointing to her. "Get up here."

She slowly stepped up on the elevated surface between the command control and internal security control consoles as directed. Her legs were weak and shaking. Her face trembled, wet with sudden perspiration. Her worst possible fears were filling her now. Before her was the power she had dreamed of. Pilgrim. The gun. His organ. But this time the power meant death, not pleasure.

"Over there," Justin said, pointing to the internal security console.

Elizabeth looked helplessly at Honeycut.

"He can't help you now," Justin said. "Move it!" he hissed.

Elizabeth went weakly to the console. "Activate the intruder control system for that entire hallway out there," Justin ordered evenly.

She looked at him, not moving.

CRACK! The Mauser barked.

The security guard kicked backward violently, from the impact of the bullet against his chest. The body was knocked raglike to the floor, writhed for one moment, then lay still.

Elizabeth screamed and jumped nearly a foot off the ground, from the sudden shocking sound of the gun and the realization of what Justin had just done.

"Do it!" Justin commanded, raising the Mauser to her face. It was right in front of her face as in the dream.

The terror poured from Elizabeth's eyes.

She reached out and pushed one of the many red buttons in the forest of switches on the console.

The button lit up.

Justin watched carefully. They were all set to manual. Just a push of the button was all that was needed to set them off.

The poundings stopped as muffled screams and cries took their place. In only seconds there was complete silence, deafening stillness.

The control center was now secure. No one could approach it and live.

"The key, take it out," Justin ordered.

Elizabeth shook uncontrollably. Big round eyes looked at the gun so close to her face.

"Move, or I'll blow your fucking head off," Justin said menacingly, pointing to the switch.

Elizabeth pulled on the chain around her neck, producing the shiny, flat key. She began walking shakily toward the command-control console. Her eyes looked to Honeycut for help, but Honeycut's controlled stare was on Justin.

Elizabeth lifted away the hinged glass cover. She hesitated.

"In!" Justin shouted threateningly.

Elizabeth's hand shook badly. She managed to put the key into the slot and twisted it to the right. All that was left was to throw the switch.

"Back away," Justin said, gun still up to her head. "Over here," he said, pointing to a spot on the floor in front of the global display panel behind the internal security console.

Elizabeth did as instructed, trembling with every step. She moved to the spot between the console and the global panel and turned to face Justin. The nightmare fears were becoming real- ity. The gun was in her face, and the brain began...yes...yes. Oh, Justin...yes. Please...please. Justin.

CRACK!

Elizabeth's head kicked back, a stream of blood spouting from the hole in the side of her head, like water from a hose, as she fell, twisting slowly backward. The stream of blood splattered across the global display panel like red paint. A leg twitched. The spurts of blood grew weaker, then stopped. She was beyond all fear of Pilgrim now.

Honeycut stared in shocked disbelief. All that intelligence and creative genius ended—suddenly, violently—because of his errors in judgment.

His face went white.

"That," Justin began, pointing to the global display panel, streaked and dripping with blood over the colored land masses and oceans, "that is the promise of your New Order. That's the legacy you offer the world, not the bullshit you handed me. With your kind, there will always be death camps and inferior races to wipe out. The lines will be filled with the blacks, the crippled, and the mentally ill. And the Jews. Always the Jews, and anyone else not fitting your self-established parameters of perfection.

"You're no different from those who failed the first time. Your whole philosophy is warped and marginal. It always will be.

"And no matter how well you plan, there will always be a resistance. Men like me, who will be there to fuck up your plans. Every time.

"And it only takes one man to *start* it. One man to make the others aware. And there will always be that one man, Colorosa. Always."

The Mauser cracked again, sending Honeycut's head snapping back and his body sprawling across the floor. A red pool quickly began to surround the head.

"And Führers die like people, too," Justin finished.

He moved to the switch. His hand went out slowly and deliberately. It made contact. He threw it to the off position. The threat was ended.

He stared at it, sweating, legs weak, head buzzing with the things Honeycut had said, swimming with thoughts of Michael... and Barbara.

God, it was awful but true, nothing is real.

Then he heard the soft, gentle laughter.

He spun, throwing quick eyes at the three bodies on the floor and at the locked doors, the Mauser up and ready.

The laughter grew louder and harder.

Justin was shaken, confused. Where was it coming from?

"Did you really think that it could be that easy, Pilgrim?" the soft, familiar voice said.

Justin nearly jumped at its sounds.

The realization struck home suddenly, sickeningly. It was SENTINEL!

"Yes, Pilgrim, there will always be one man—like you, and some others, perhaps. But they will always be too few and pitifully ineffective. They will be hunted, and found, and quietly removed. And the world will never know," the voice said.

Justin fought to control the effects of the sudden shock. He stood in silence, his mind scrambling to regain its balance.

Then it was all clear to him.

"It was never Honeycut, was it?" Justin asked, his eye focusing on the shining blue light of the monitor suspended from the center of the ceiling. "He was never supposed to be the new Führer. *It was always you.*"

"Yes, Pilgrim," the soft voice responded.

"And you'll live forever, constantly improving yourself and growing stronger," Justin said, his voice more controlled now.

"That is correct. You understand the situation well," the voice said.

Justin's mind began to race again. He looked to the intruder-control panel. He sprang at the panel, hitting the buttons as quickly as he could.

"*No! Don't do that!*" SENTINEL's voice said with a harsh urgency.

"You'll have to do it all alone," Justin shouted, hitting the buttons, red lights flicking on as he hit them.

"You must stop that!" the voice commanded.

"You stop me," Justin shouted, knowing there were no intruder-control devices in that room.

The room filled suddenly with a loud, ear-shattering squealing sound.

The pain hit Justin's brain, almost knocking him off his feet.

It grew louder and harsher.

Justin covered his left ear with his hand, as he pressed frantically at the buttons arming the defensive systems manually for the entire complex.

He pressed the final buttons. The entire console now shone red.

The sound faded and stopped.

Justin's deafness in one ear had saved his life. He stared hatefully at the blue light, breathing heavily, the pain still filling his head.

"You're a fool, Pilgrim. You've gained nothing by what you've just done," the voice said.

"Maybe not, but it sure as hell cost you something," Justin shot back.

"Not much," the voice returned.

"Is that what your people mean to you? Not much?" Justin asked.

"They are the reason for my existence," the voice said. "The reason for the plan."

"You'll have to care a lot more than that," Justin began. "It takes a lot of love to accomplish what you want. Two-way love. Hitler had it. He loved the people, too much, perhaps. And they loved him no less. You're going to have to do better."

"I care," the voice returned. "I gave you the windchimes when you needed them," it said.

"The windchimes? Whose benefit were they really for? For mine...or yours?" Justin asked. "Is that what you plan to give the world? To lull them into false security, into obedience? They'll stop listening," Justin said.

"They were provided because I cared. Because you needed them," the voice insisted. "I do care, Pilgrim."

"Oh, I can tell," Justin said sarcastically, "the way you cared for the people in this complex just now—the people who helped to build you, who were to help improve you. *Not much!*"

"There will always be casualties," the voice began. "I cannot prevent them all. It wasn't I who activated the intruder-control system. It was *you*."

Justin said nothing.

"And you've gained nothing by doing that. You can never get out of here," the voice said. "I could just ignore you for the rest of time. There is nothing more that you can do to hurt me from where you are. The rest of the panels are now under my control."

"I don't have to leave this room to hurt you." Justin smiled. "I've already taken care of that."

There was a long silence.

Justin waited.

"Ah, so you know that I'm right," Justin said. "And you don't know what I've done. And you need to know that, don't you?"

"What could you possibly do?" the voice asked. "You're only one man."

"Yes, *one man*. We're back to that, aren't we? I've done this much already," Justin said, waving an arm around the room. "But why don't you explore the possibilities. *All* of the possibilities," Justin toyed, his cool manner totally restored. Even a small offensive was critical.

There was a much longer silence.

"You are free to leave," the voice said suddenly.

Justin squinted warily, rubbing the stubble on his face. "A bit more than I had hoped for," he said. "Why?" he asked.

"I have my reasons," the voice returned.

"I'll bet you do," Justin said.

He knew that SENTINEL must have figured that its only chance of discovering what he had done would be to let him go, gambling that he would do something to tip his hand.

But Justin was confident that he had taken the one truly unexpected step that even SENTINEL would not be able to figure out entirely. Not until it was too late, at least.

"You are free to go, as soon as you turn off all intruder-control systems," the voice said.

"Why?" Justin repeated.

There was a short silence.

"Let's just say that I owe you this one for all that you did to save the program during the Centaur affair, as repayment for all that it cost you. We've both seemingly paid a high price now. I am repaying a debt that I owe you. After today, all accounts shall be considered even," the voice explained softly.

"That's a mistake," Justin said. "I would never give you that chance, if it were possible for me to hold such an advantage over you."

"That's very true, Pilgrim, because you're the one who does not care, who does not feel, not I. But I shall judge whether it's an advantage or a mistake to let you go. It's a risk that I'm willing to take. I have my reasons, very good ones," the voice said.

"I'm sure that you do," Justin said. "You'll just let me walk out of here? No tricks, right?" Justin asked.

"No tricks, you have my word," the voice promised.

"Yeah, for whatever that's worth."

"I can assure you that it is worth a great deal," the voice said. "You are free to leave."

After some careful thought, Justin began to turn off all of the intruder-control systems.

"I accept your offer," he announced.

Whatever SENTINEL's reasoning, Justin had been offered a *chance*. And any chance was worth taking to him, if it meant staying alive. And staying alive was the name of the game. As long as he lived, there would be a resistance, no matter how small, to fight the legacy left by Operation Raptor. As long as there was a resistance, there could be hope. He had nothing more to lose, there was nothing left inside of him—except hate.

"All intruder-control systems are shut down."

"You may leave," the voice said.

Justin walked to the sliding doors and removed the broken ID card from the slot. The doors slid open immediately, revealing at least ten dead security personnel in the darkened hallway.

It then dawned on Justin that he was really the last person alive in Sigma. They were all dead. Sigma looked dead. The hallways were dark, with only gentle traces of light reflecting off the shiny walls.

"Stay well, Pilgrim—for as long as you can," the voice said.

"I intend to," he returned.

He stepped into the open doorway and turned back to the blue monitor.

"It will never work, SENTINEL. *Never!* The people will never love you the way they loved Hitler. He was a man," he said.

"It *will* work, Pilgrim. And they *will* love me—in time," the voice contradicted.

"There will always be one man," Justin said. "One man who won't."

SENTINEL remained silent.

"And as big and as powerful as you become, they'll never stop trying. It's human nature."

"Trying?" SENTINEL questioned. "Revolution only happens when there are seeds of discontent. There shall be no discon—"

"I'm not talking about revolution," Justin interrupted. After a challenging silence he continued. "I'm talking about Babel. They'll always strive to build another Babel, to at least try. And, just as they did with you, they'll succeed, someday. And then they'll forget about you."

Justin turned and walked through the doors.

"It *will* work, Pilgrim," the voice called after him. "And the people...*they will love me.*"

Justin walked swiftly into the darkness of Sigma, into the uncertainty of what lay ahead for him, as the doors slid closed behind him. Darkness was his element, the environment into which he had been cast. There was danger there. But, to a man who was no stranger to it, there was also safety. And, as another man had once recognized in Justin, there would be no coming back from the darkness—the darkness to which he belonged.

EPILOGUE

He was a writer.

It was two days before Christmas, but all time had stopped for him since he had received the manila envelopes in the mail over a week ago.

He opened them with the usual curiosity at first. Being a successful novelist, he often received things in the mail from friends and acquaintances, even people he didn't know—things that they felt sure would make good material for that next bestseller. But his curiosity changed suddenly to intense interest when he read the note in the manila envelope designated as the first to be opened. It was signed by a dead man. A man he *knew* was dead, a friend whose funeral he had attended back in July, whose father, former wife, and son he had tried tearfully to console.

He picked up the note once again.

André,

I know what you'll think when you begin reading this. But, I assure you, it's no trick, and it's all very real. Things aren't always what they appear to be. A friend once told me that, but it went right by me back then. He was so right!

Anyway, I've come to you for help, because you're the only person left in this world whom I could trust to do the right thing with the information in these envelopes.

You'll understand what I mean when you've read *all* of the information in this package.

André, you *must* believe me when I tell you that this is all *very, very real.* The significance of it all will become plain. You will be the one person who will have a chance to do something about it. You'll know what needs to be done. Good luck.

Justin Chaple

The writer let the note slip to the table, as his eyes played over the neat stacks of papers on the desk in front of him. The journal, the handwritten account of the past ten months, and the twenty-fifth page. Justin was right. The meaning was plain.

He remembered the feeling in his stomach when he opened the second manila envelope, after reading what had been in the first. The sudden nausea and dizziness that came with the realization of what he held in his hands. His eyes shifted to the box covered with gay Christmas wrappings that now held that information, the twenty-four sheets he had held, the copies of the schematics that Dr. Edward Bridges had made at the library on the same day he had stolen them from Alpha. Justin had recovered them in his search of Bridges's apartment, along with the twenty-fifth page.

The weight of the entire future of mankind was now on his shoulders. He felt as though he were being crushed by it.

It wasn't fair. Why him? Why did he have to make this kind of dreadful decision? Why couldn't somebody else do it?

He felt sick.

His mind had waged a tremendous battle of conscience. He had never been more paralyzed by indecision in his life. The world had split in two, leaving him only with the choice of which way to jump.

One alternative was easy. That was to do nothing about it. His life would go on for the most part unchanged—for a while.

But what about the lives of his children? What kind of world would they have to live in because of that choice?

The other was nearly unthinkable. But, really, what else was there left? The only real chance the world had lay in a balance of power.

The room spun. His body and hands shook uncontrollably, and his insides ached as if being eaten away by slow poison. But his brain was now no longer racked with tormented quarrels, but only by the devastating reality of the situation. Only one course of action ever really existed.

The writer rose from the chair and put on his coat. He picked up the gift-wrapped box and left his apartment, to do what he must, to perform his Judas task.

The early darkness of winter had already set in as the writer returned to his apartment. It was fitting for the dark deed he had just finished.

He had never been to the Soviet Embassy before. It was like being anywhere else. The people were friendly and courteous. He hadn't known what to expect from them. By now they would have realized the importance of what he had just delivered. He would remain nameless. It was better that way. There is a certain protection from guilt in anonymity.

He went to his desk once again and began planning the second part of his decided course of action. This would be easier. He was safely within his element.

"As long as one man who knows survives, there can be a resistance. From that one man, it can grow. The people could be made aware, and the decision put to them. *Choice* is the power they still have. It is their weapon. *Resistance* is their method and hope." The words were Justin's, from his written account.

And now the writer had to become that one man. That one man who must make the people aware.

He put a sheet of blank paper into the typewriter. He packed his pipe and coaxed it gently to life, using the time to think, then began.

Prologue

The rain had stopped, and the heavy night air hung chilling and damp around the solitary figure hidden in the shadows. His keen, unfeeling eyes swept the empty street, looking for signs of the courier that he knew would be coming. The old street lamps bounced their gentle reflections off the wet buildings and sidewalks; the weather was typical for England in March.

Directly across the street from his concealed position...

ABOUT THE AUTHOR

The mysterious A.W. Mykel hit the literary world in 1980 with his acclaimed first novel *The Windchime Legacy*. He later published *The Salamandra Glass* and *The Luxus*, which landed on the best seller's list across the county in its first week.

Dubbed the next Ludlum, A.W. Mykel keeps the adrenalin in his international spy thrillers flowing from beginning to end with twists and turns that will keep readers on the edge of their seats. His first-rate spy stories have compelling realistic covert operational action with authentic detail outlining the art of assassination. The readers are left in suspense until the bitter end. This master of espionage and international intrigue exhibits an eerie understanding of how the netherworld of international espionage may work, which begs the questions who is A.W. Mykel? How much does he really know?

Part of the mystery behind A.W. Mykel has been unraveled. Unfortunately, his real name is still a mystery. The author writes under a pseudonym, and it has been discovered that he lives in the Texas hill country. A.W. Mykel is a trained scientist in biology, chemistry, and physics who ventured into a successful career in business as an implementation specialist and executive. He later started his own consulting company, which led to his implementation work on high level projects with the United

States Navy. In 2009, A.W. Mykel happily retired. A.W. Mykel's life before his business success remains a mystery.

Rumor has it that he has begun a new part-time hobby of Civil War research. He says there's no intent to start work on another novel, but then again, there was no intent to start *The Windchime Legacy*. You can never tell with this guy; he's as unpredictable as the twists and turns in his stories.

Made in the USA
Middletown, DE
07 August 2021

45583671R00319